DEFENSELESS

DEFENSELESS

SOMERTON SECURITY, BOOK 1

ELIZABETH DYER

Montlake
Romance

Text copyright © 2017 by Elizabeth Dyer
All rights reserved.

Published by Montlake Romance, Seattle

www.apub.com

Amazon, the Amazon logo, and Montlake Romance are trademarks of Amazon.com, Inc., or its affiliates.

ISBN-13: 9781542048637
ISBN-10: 154204863X

Cover design by Eileen Carey

Printed in the United States of America

For my elementary school librarian, Mrs. Webb, who shared with me her birthday and her love of reading. Thank you.

CHAPTER ONE

If Georgia Bennett were a glass-half-full sort of person, she'd probably find the gently falling snow beautiful. Lying flat on her back, the wind knocked from her chest, she had the perfect view of the fat, wet flakes. She supposed she could add "optimist" and "hopeless romantic" to the list of character traits she didn't possess and didn't want.

"You're about as graceful as a cow on ice, you know that, Bennett?" Her boss's voice oozed amusement, setting fire to cheeks that already stung from the frigid air.

Georgia glowered at Ethan, who appeared above her with a smile. Cursing, she climbed back onto her feet, grabbed the mirror of the car next to her as her legs threatened to go out from under her. Again. She scowled at Ethan's chuckle. People constantly accused Georgia of being cold-blooded—and maybe they were right. Sand, triple-digit heat, and the distinctive cologne of unwashed marines she could handle. Add Humvees and semiautomatic weapons, and she'd consider it a party. But howling wind, biting cold, and snow blowing off the Chesapeake? Oh *hell* no.

Ethan casually stood against his car, beanie low on his brow and a cup of coffee in his gloved hand. He watched, his amusement about as subtle as a middle-aged senator's hair plugs, while Georgia slipped and slid her way around the SUV. Damn East Coast winters. And damn bosses who dragged her out of DC right as a storm was bearing down on the coast. Fresh out of the Marine Corps, she'd planned on getting a tiny apartment in San Diego and enjoying the sun while she figured out what she wanted to do with her life. Why the hell hadn't she stuck to that plan?

"Come on, Bennett. My coffee's getting cold, and I've got somewhere to be." Oh right. Because the jackal striding away as if ice bothered only the pathetic and uncoordinated had offered her a job. A job she liked, and one she was now in serious danger of losing.

Resigned, Georgia adjusted her messenger bag and smothered her attitude. *You can't afford to lose this job*, she reminded herself as she carefully picked her way across the parking lot.

Steel and brick rose in front of her, the upper floors of the fancy loft-style complex disappearing into the undulating gray of the gathering storm. She stepped into the lobby, stomping the snow and slush from her boots on the welcome mat, and looked around. Exposed beams, brickwork, and what looked like reclaimed-wood flooring dominated the space. The finishes screamed high-end. No surprise, given the waterfront location and proximity to downtown, but at least the building had character—an obvious personality it wore proudly in crumbling mortar and the wavy imperfection of single-pane industrial windows. With any luck, her client would fit the building and not the address.

Georgia doubted she had the patience for one more posh DC assignment, no matter how much she wanted to keep her job. Kidnappers, stalkers, and political plots, she could handle. Yappy dogs, shopping trips to Dupont Circle, and the carefully pinned and tucked exteriors of Washington's political housewives made her twitchy. That sort of fabricated perfection was unnatural—creepy, even. So when an environmental activist had approached Congressman Dickinson's wife, criticizing her for the mink draped carefully around her shoulders, Georgia had hesitated. It hadn't helped that every time Mrs. Dickinson deigned to acknowledge Georgia it was with a haughty stare that conveyed in a single dismissive sweep that Georgia, with her blue-collar attire and military bearing, was nothing short of a cumbersome burden to be borne with ill-tempered irritation and poorly feigned manners. The distaste was mutual, and for a split second, Georgia had wanted to see how airborne paint and polished perfection mixed. In hindsight, letting the congressman's wife become a walking Jackson Pollock exhibition probably *wasn't* the way to go. But then again, Georgia prided herself on precision, not tact.

Which, apparently, was the problem. According to her boss, it wasn't enough for Georgia to keep her clients alive and well. Oh no, she also needed them to *like* her. Specifically, she needed *this* client to like her. Ethan had made it very clear that if she couldn't manage to make a personal connection with her next assignment, she'd be looking for a new job. She had to admit that given Mrs. Dickinson's completely overblown reaction—really, it wasn't as if she'd been *shot*—it was a minor miracle Ethan hadn't fired her already. No doubt she had good old-fashioned nepotism to thank for that.

And maybe just a smidge of guilt.

Staring down the barrel of a last-chance assignment, Georgia figured it was probably too much to hope she'd be assigned to a client with a personality. Maybe someone who, like the building they lived in, turned their imperfections into strengths. She'd do her job regardless, but damn, it would be nice to actually respect a client. She used to feel like her job mattered, like the people she worked with made a difference in the world. Like *she* made a difference. But lately it had all become so routine—as hollow and vacant as the carefully crafted smile she'd practiced that morning. People liked others who smiled. The Internet said so.

And okay, maybe Georgia wasn't entirely sure she still liked her job, but she was damn certain she needed it. The last nine months had been a revolving door of uninvited change—she didn't think she had it in her to start a new career as well. What was she even qualified for? She had no college education, and somehow she doubted "excellent marksmanship" and "experience with explosives" rounded out a résumé. Shit, she'd be lucky if she landed a job flipping burgers.

"Good afternoon, Mr. Somerton," called the security guard stationed behind a small desk. "It's nice to see you again."

Interesting that the doorman knew Ethan on sight. Apparently this job had a personal angle he'd neglected to mention.

That should make things much *easier.*

"You, too, Trevor." Ethan turned toward the bank of elevators, then headed for a small cluster of overstuffed seating. "Thanks for coming out on such short notice," he said to Georgia as he gestured to a chair and took a seat.

"You didn't exactly phrase it as a request."

Ethan had called, instructed her where and when to meet him, and hung up. Since she'd been sitting in her studio apartment, practicing "Would you like fries with that?" Georgia hadn't argued.

"Yes, well, you weren't my first call and hardly my first choice. Parker excels at running off the bodyguards I send, and Davis, who Parker at least tolerates, is out of pocket for the next few weeks. Ryan was supposed to be here, but he's stuck in New York due to weather." Ethan grimaced. "Obviously, I'm desperate."

"I'm flattered."

"You should be," Ethan barked. "Right now my desperation and Parker's tendency to be difficult are the only things keeping you employed. I suggest you find a way to play nice with him."

Her brain tripped past her irritation and caught up with the conversation. "What do you mean, 'him'?"

"Parker Livingston. Know the name?" Ethan asked, rolling right over Georgia's surprise.

"Oh God. Not the Jungle Gem guy." She'd pulled Poindexter patrol.

Ethan's grin was downright predatory. He wasn't giving her a second chance; he was giving her enough rope to hang herself.

Practically a pop-culture icon, Jungle Gem was little more than a simple puzzle game that addicted every idiot with a cell phone who dared download it. It was basic and asinine, and it irritated Georgia she'd never made it past level 127. *Wired* had reported that the game had netted Livingston *millions*. To add insult to injury, Livingston's reputation for being difficult to work with preceded him. It was the assignment no one wanted—and no one lasted in.

But none of that explained why the hell Ethan had dragged her out here. She'd never understood why a nerdy app developer with too much time on his hands occasionally needed a bodyguard, let alone why he was considered a VIP client.

Ugh. This assignment was already giving her a headache.

"Why am I here, Ethan? I don't do men."

"Sarah will be thrilled to know she's won the office pool," Ethan replied.

"Very cute." Georgia pulled her gloves off with her teeth. "You know what I mean. I work with our female clientele. It's why you hired me."

"I'm glad we got that cleared up," Ethan snapped. "Because based on the last six months, I was beginning to wonder if you had any idea at all why I hired you." He sighed, placed his elbows on his knees, and leaned forward. "Look, Georgia, I think we both know you're an asset to this firm. There's no question that in terms of technical skill, you're one of my best operatives. Hell, I practically begged you to work here. You have an impeccable background, and obviously, your references were excellent."

Of course they were. As a marine, Georgia had been hand-selected by her commanding officer for close protection detail. It had seemed the perfect assignment. Analytical, precise, and highly motivated, Georgia had fallen effortlessly into the often-invisible role of bodyguard. Still, that wasn't the reference Ethan had based his hiring decisions on, and they both knew it. For Ethan, there'd been one factor and one factor only—Georgia's brother. Ethan and Will had served together, gone through Delta together.

Will had been there when Ethan had ruptured his eardrums in the field.

And Ethan had been there to bear Georgia's brother's flag-draped coffin.

Above anything else, loyalty had landed Georgia her job.

"But you're in the private sector now." Ethan's gaze bored into her, bringing her back from painful memories. "Our business is built on referrals and repeat clients. And in the last six months, not one assignment you've had has requested you a second time." His face turned stern and hard. "Now, I could transfer you to a desk. Have you working in the office as a strategic coordinator—"

Georgia fought a grimace and lost. Ugh. Office work meant cube, cube meant computers, and computers meant sitting in a damn chair all day. How long would it take her to actually miss the socialite crowd? It was a fate she couldn't bear contemplating.

"That face right there tells me exactly how well that would go." Ethan sighed. "I can't afford to lose you. Do you have any idea how in demand female security personnel are?"

"Yeah, I do." Most people assumed the private security sector was all male—and *most* of it was. But the reality was that women could not only do the job but, in some cases, do the job more effectively *because* of their gender. Georgia had interviewed with a half dozen private firms and received offers from four of them. She'd *chosen* Ethan. She liked the guy, liked that he kept his company small and was still interested in building an all-female unit. She'd hoped, given enough time, that Ethan would come to like her, too. At least enough to tell her how Will had died.

If he'd suffered.

If he'd been alone.

There was so much she didn't know. So much the Department of Defense wouldn't say. So much *Ethan* wouldn't tell her. She couldn't accept their scripted statements, their shallow offerings of "We regret to inform you" and "William Bennett died in the service of his country." Will deserved more than hollow words and empty condolences.

All the medals, American flags, and three-round volleys couldn't make up for the one honor Will hadn't received, the only honor that really mattered. His legacy would be lost; no one would remember him. The army had seen to that.

Georgia couldn't, wouldn't, do the same.

She needed answers. Which meant she needed Ethan, regardless of whatever reservations she had about day-to-day life in the private sector.

"Lucky for you," Ethan continued, ignoring the change in Georgia's mood, "I've got a gap in Parker's protection detail, and you're the only person capable of filling in." He withdrew a set of keys from his inside pocket. "Key fob gets you into the building and operates the elevator. The gold key is for Parker's loft—13E. I'd knock first, and loudly. I woke him up ahead of your arrival, but I doubt he's had his coffee yet."

Just waking up? At one p.m.?

"I'm sure I don't want to know, but . . ."

Ethan's grin held a hint of malicious humor, but he didn't make her wait. "He's not exactly housebroken."

"What does that mean?" What the hell was she signing up for? Despite Livingston's difficult reputation around the office, details were thin. She suspected Ethan quashed rumors before they really got started, which only added to the interest and speculation. Still, normally Ethan sent her a dossier: photos, facts, addresses, schedules, and contacts—details about the job. A threat assessment and a biographical profile. So far the only thing she knew was—*what* exactly? That she was babysitting some nerd who "wasn't exactly housebroken."

"Parker's not the usual client. He's a little . . . different. Has his own schedule, his own method of doing things. And as usual, he's adamant he doesn't need private security."

"Then what am I doing here?" Georgia asked as she slipped the key and fob onto her key chain.

"I'm limited as to what I can say here, but since you've got the appropriate background checks in place, I can tell you that even though Parker's wealth comes from app development, the US government considers him a high-value asset. He regularly consults on issues of technology and national security."

National security? "What the hell is a second-rate game developer doing dabbling in national security? Are we in danger of running out of ways to waste time?"

"Judgmental and uninformed." Ethan *tsk*ed. "Maybe it's a good thing I took you off socialite detail; they're starting to rub off."

Georgia let a scowl seize her face. Over her dead body.

"Look." Ethan glanced at the clock on his cell phone. "I know you're used to working with a specific threat or escorting a client to a particular event or function. This assignment is obviously different. Due to the nature of Parker's work"—Ethan glared at the snort she choked back—"his security is carefully monitored."

"Then why doesn't the DoD assign him a detail?" Georgia asked.

"Sometimes they do." He pinned her with a heavy look. "And *sometimes* we aren't all in agreement when it comes to threat assessment. So I'm pulling you and tasking you with a seventy-two-hour assignment. Maybe less if Ryan makes it out of New York. That should give me enough time to follow up on a few things and reevaluate." Ethan rolled his neck, agitation bunching his shoulders and lining his face.

That was it? That was all the information he was going to give her? "I'm not a babysitter, Ethan. And I'm not entirely comfortable with an assignment with no clear threat. Why are you concerned enough to assign a bodyguard when the DoD isn't?" The situation was unusual in the extreme and made Georgia nervous as hell. Withholding facts in their line of work was not only dangerous, it was criminally stupid. Yet Ethan seemed determined to give her as little information as possible.

"It's probably nothing," Ethan admitted. "Parker and I consult on the same government task force."

Translation: Parker and Ethan were part of the same covert, and likely off-book, unit Will had mentioned once or twice. And now something had gotten under Ethan's skin, and it was itching.

"In the last few months, Parker's raised a few concerns that have been largely dismissed or ignored altogether. And though I'd never tell him, there's no question that at any given time Parker's the smartest man in the room. Unfortunately, his intelligence is coupled with a dogged determination to constantly prove he's right and a complete dismissal of military protocol." Ethan sighed and rubbed the bridge of his nose. "I have to look into his concerns, follow up on some rumors."

"What do you need from me?" Georgia asked, though she shouldn't have bothered. She knew Ethan well enough to understand she couldn't pry answers out of him with a crowbar.

"Just give me a few days to clear my doubts. I don't want to worry about the safety of a high-value civilian with Parker's capabilities and clearance." Ethan sighed, some of his tension bleeding out of his frame. It was almost enough to make Georgia regret giving him such a hard time in the first place. Almost. "It should be an easy assignment, but Parker . . . He's brilliant, but the guy doesn't have the sense God gave a lemur sometimes," he muttered, his frustration making the vein at his temple throb. "Given Parker's penchant for pissing people off, you two should get along great."

Wonderful.

"Just make it work for three days. That's all I'm asking."

"How do you propose I do that? You said he's ditched every operative you've assigned him. What makes you think I'll be any more successful?"

The muscle in Ethan's jaw jumped, and his blue eyes pinned Georgia to her seat. "Because I'm motivating you."

Translation: you're fired if you don't make this work. Perfect. An impossible job and a client she knew next to nothing about.

"Look, you know what your problem is?" Ethan leaned forward. "You care. Worse, you *want* to care. But experience has taught you over and over that caring only leads to pain. And it can." Ethan reached for her clasped hands, and Georgia pulled away reflexively. He sighed. "I know the last nine or ten months have been hell. First with Will"—he swallowed hard—"then finishing your tour and deciding not to extend your commitment. Things have been rocky in your personal life for a while now, and I was hoping you'd find some stability here, figure out what you wanted to do." Ethan sat back; his tension and irritation slid from his shoulders on a heavy exhale. "I just don't know how to help you with that anymore."

Shame hit her fast and hard, flooding her system with the angry hiss of nervous wasps. Ethan knew everything, but they'd never talked about it, and if Georgia had her way, they never would. She didn't bring personal drama to work. And that was all this was anymore. Personal drama. Personal history. Buried deep where it couldn't hurt. With just one exception.

"You could tell me how Will died," she forced out, twirling the bezel on her watch. The steady *click-click-click* soothed her. "You know more than you've told me, Ethan. I know you do."

Ethan shook his head. "You also know I can't."

"You mean won't," she said, belligerence as much as frustration fueling her words.

"Fine. Won't. Either way, I need you to stop asking, stop digging. You're drawing attention you might not want. Besides, you know more than anyone that there aren't any answers out there for you. Will's missions were classified—national security isn't something I take lightly, Georgia." Ethan pulled his fingers through his hair on a rough sigh. He was, as always, married to the rules. Unwilling to deviate from protocol, not even for her. "Will was Delta, and you knew what that meant. So did he. You need to find a way to let it go."

Needed to, yes, but Georgia couldn't bring herself to actually do it. Accepting she'd never know how her brother died, what he died for, where he was—it felt too much like abandoning him, something Will had never done to her, even when it had cost him dearly. She could do no less for him.

"Some agents are great because they're cold," Ethan said, seamlessly redirecting their conversation. "Distant and focused, they see the big picture and get the job done. They don't care who they work for or why they're needed. Those are just details. But here's the hard truth . . . You simply aren't one of them."

Ethan held up a hand as Georgia wrestled with the urge to defend herself. She was a lot of things—and her record might not be spotless—but she *was* good at her job.

"I recruited you because you care. You need that personal connection, that flare of respect for the people you're working with. Because you invest. You connect. It's your greatest asset as an operative. But you're holding back, refusing to get to know the people around you. And if you can't learn how to draw a line, how to balance professional distance with genuine care, then you're never going to make it in this business."

Then maybe this wasn't the business for her. Georgia didn't know. What she *did* know was twofold. First, getting too close to a client was a recipe for disaster. And second, she couldn't take losing anyone, or anything, else—not even her job.

A knowing smirk ghosted over Ethan's face. "Consider this an opportunity to get your equilibrium back. Play nice with Parker—I don't care how. He's agreed to work with a security detail on the condition that whomever I choose has 'more brains than balls'—his words, by the way. And as I suspect you have too much of one and none of the other, that leaves you uniquely suited to the job."

Please. The smallest boobs were bigger than the largest balls, which in Georgia's opinion made them the superior measurement of badassery. Not that anyone was asking her.

"I assume you can handle the next three days?" Ethan asked. "No commitments you need to cancel?"

He knew better. Outside of an African violet she kept on her counter, Georgia didn't do relationships. The uncomplicated demands of a sun-loving, water-it-when-you-remember plant was all she wanted.

"No, I got this." Though she still wasn't entirely sure what "this" was, she knew Ethan well enough to know he wasn't going to share any more. Pressing would likely get her another scowl and a muttered, "It's classified." Words she'd heard far too often and couldn't stomach anymore.

Georgia rose and stuffed the keys into her messenger bag. For the first time in forever, she was approaching a job with equal parts interest and dread. She'd be lying if she said she wasn't just a little bit intrigued.

"Give Parker a chance. Who knows, you might actually like the guy."

Maybe, though nerds didn't usually do it for her. Too passive. Too desperate to bang the prom queen. Still, everything Ethan wasn't saying about Parker had certainly caught her interest. Maybe the brain had a big mouth, a high security clearance, and felt like sharing.

"Parker's important to me, Georgia," Ethan said as he stood and walked away. "Make this work."

He left the "or else" to hang unspoken, heavy as the memory of just what could happen when Georgia let herself care.

The persistent buzz of her cell phone interrupted Georgia's ride up to Parker's loft. She couldn't imagine who'd be calling. Ethan had just left, so that ruled out work. She didn't have any family, and the few friends she could claim were still active duty and posted around the world. Fishing her phone out of her bag, Georgia tamped down the realization that somehow, in the last six months, she'd allowed her life to slide into a depressing hole she couldn't seem to climb her way out of. All she had left was her job, and if she didn't pull her head out of her ass, she'd lose that, too.

She supposed she could go back to school, try to survive four years among peers she'd outgrown and couldn't possibly relate to, but the idea held little appeal. Mostly she was sick to death of taking the universe's jabs on the chin. She needed time to figure out what *she* wanted.

Georgia brushed back the curl of anxiety and checked her phone.

Isaac. Because *of course* he'd be calling now. Her ex always had uncanny timing and the inherent ability to say exactly what she was afraid of hearing at the exact moment she was most likely to believe it. She pressed "Decline" and clenched her phone. It was hardly the first time he'd called or texted since their breakup—though he'd certainly been more persistent lately. And because she'd been weak and lonely once—or twice . . . okay, a few times—after her brother's death, she knew exactly how the conversation would go. Isaac would tell her how much he missed her. That he wanted to see her, to apologize for being a jerk.

You were the best thing to ever happen to me, babe. I can't be myself with anyone else, G. They all want something from me. Or her personal favorite: *Will was my friend, too. Please let me take you to dinner.*

She'd already fallen for that line of bullshit and sworn she'd never take another cab ride home with her panties in her purse and her pride in that asshole's bed.

Georgia shoved her phone back into the outside pocket of her bag and prayed that someday the thought of Isaac wouldn't make her so damn homesick. Several years older than she was, Isaac had been a foreign service officer at the embassy in Argentina when Georgia was stationed there as a marine. They'd bonded over kung fu movies, savory street food, and local Malbecs. The fact that Isaac and Will became friends had been the icing on the cake. It was hard, less than two years later, to look back on that time in her life and remember how naive she'd been. How young. How she'd been absolutely certain of her future.

Now, as the elevator dinged on the seventeenth floor, Georgia wasn't sure of anything.

One big, happy family. She'd known better than to buy into that dream. She wouldn't allow herself to forget the lesson again.

Stepping off the elevator, Georgia determined to push the call from her mind. She needed to get her head on straight and focus on the job at hand. She might not be certain of much, not even her chosen career, but she was dead sure she wanted to choose her own path forward. As far as she was concerned, she was done playing defense, done fielding life's volleys. It was time she went on the offense and dealt a few game-changing blows of her own. From this moment on, she was taking charge.

She squared her shoulders, tried on her practiced smile, lifted her fist, and knocked. Then knocked some more. Then pounded on the industrial steel until her fist hurt. What the hell was she supposed to do now? Ethan had clearly advised against just letting herself in, but how long was she expected to stand outside and wait?

Screw it. She fished her keys out of her bag and unlocked the door. If the guy wasn't housebroken, well, she carried a Taser and could fix that quickly enough. It'd get her fired—she could try to spin it in her own mind as the most electric resignation *ever*—but the satisfaction of watching the inconsiderate jerk squirm would be worth it. Probably. Maybe. Okay, so she'd keep the Taser in her bag and stick with the fantasy.

Gripping the welded handle with both hands, Georgia slid open the steel door. She'd expected it to squeal and protest, given its age and condition, but it slid open easily on silent tracks. Which made the appearance of the man standing on the other side, staring blankly at her as if he had no clue how she'd appeared, a little unnerving.

14

Smoothing down her irritation, Georgia reminded herself she *liked* her job. "Mr. Livingston?" He didn't say anything. Didn't blink. Didn't move. "I'm Georgia Bennett. With Somerton Security?" Nothing. Just a vacant stare. Worry crept in, crowding out her irritation. Was the guy hurt? Drugged? "Mr. Livingston, are you all right?"

Georgia inspected him from the top of his shaggy head to the bottom of his bare feet. Ho-ly hell. Her mouth went dry. She'd seen a photo of him in the spread *Wired* had done—a candid shot of a nerd, drawn and pale, hunched over a computer, a No. 2 pencil clutched between his teeth and a gaunt cut to his features. But this guy . . . this guy was . . . was, well, Georgia wasn't quite sure *what* he was. What she did know was that he didn't just punch all the right buttons; he lit 'em up like she'd hit the jackpot on the marquee slot machine in Vegas.

No man had any right to be so drop-dead sexy standing practically comatose in a gray, threadbare T-shirt and a pair of navy-blue Jockeys that left little to the imagination. Add in the sexed-up hair and sheet prints on his cheek, and there was just something warm and soft and utterly disarming about the guy. He was lazy Sunday mornings after sex-against-the-wall Saturday nights.

Whew. Nerds. Who knew?

Focus on the job, Georgia.

"Ethan sent me." Ah, there it was. A flicker of expression across Parker's face, followed closely by a curl of the lip that could sour dairy. He turned and shuffled off, leaving Georgia standing in the doorway. She scrambled in after him. "Hey! You shouldn't leave your door open!" Sexy *and* stupid. A combination sure to kill her interest in three . . . two . . . one . . . Yep, there it went. "Or let a perfect stranger follow you inside."

He glanced over one shoulder as he moved into the open kitchen. "So close it."

Finally, words. Clipped and irritated, but she'd take them. She slid the door shut behind her, then engaged both bolt locks. Dropping her messenger bag next to a coatrack, she followed him, hoping for a few more verbal bread crumbs to lead the way. No such luck. Parker stood at the sink, staring into the basin as if it held the answer to life's mysteries. He scratched the back of his head and yawned as he pulled a mug out of the cabinet and set it under the Keurig. Then he stared. And stared some more, his mouth tightening as if he couldn't understand why the coffee wasn't making itself. Beyond irritated, Georgia snatched the mug, filled it at the tap, then poured the water into the reservoir. She had to open two drawers and a cabinet to find the coffee pods, and she slammed each one closed just to watch Parker jump and glare.

"Sing me the song of my people," Parker muttered as the machine finally hissed and spit, filling his mug with coffee. He grabbed a spoon from the sink, wiped it on the end of his T-shirt, and stirred in one of the pink packets of sweetener that littered the countertop.

Georgia pulled off her wool peacoat, depositing it on a stool, and watched in horrified fascination as, with each gulp of coffee, Parker's slack body straightened and strengthened, slowly filling with an artificial energy that took him from discarded sock monkey to Curious George.

Oh hell. This was the guy she was supposed to get to know? Ethan wasn't just testing her. He was *punishing* her.

Parker looked at her over the rim of his mug and slid an assessing gaze over her as if seeing her for the first time. "So. Who're you again?"

CHAPTER TWO

Parker studied the woman—he was fairly certain she'd introduced herself, but information gathered pre-coffee didn't count—glaring at him from across the kitchen counter. Damn, that full mouth set in stern disapproval was sexy. Huh. That didn't make sense. He took another sip of coffee. Hmm. Nope, still sexy. Usually coffee worked like beer goggles in reverse, rendering whatever, or whomever, he was staring at less interesting or attractive. Wasn't working on the woman in front of him, though. Each sip illuminated something new and interesting. The way her hair, curly and wild, sprung away from her hat as if frustrated at her attempt to contain it. The way she crossed her arms in disapproval, propping up a generous pair of breasts, obvious even under a bulky cable-knit sweater. The way she tilted her chin and stared him down, as if she expected him to say or do something stupid at any moment. The lush curve of her lower lip alone had him contemplating just how stupid he wanted to be.

The answer? *Pretty stupid*, he decided, as he let an impression of her form—wicked delight wrapped up in a fierce femininity that drew him to live dangerously and damn the consequences. As he thought more about it, about her, he decided to amend his answer. He wanted to be *incredibly* stupid.

Damn, if this was a dream, it was a doozy. Coffee and a woman who looked like she'd be feisty as hell in bed. Maybe he'd have himself another cup and move the incredibly stupid portion of his dream back to the bedroom.

"Are you listening to me?" she demanded.

You said stuff?

"Yes, I said stuff!"

Huh. He must have said that out loud. Obviously he needed the aforementioned second cup of mojo. Mmmmm, maybe that should be mo*joe*. He snickered as he set himself to the task of making it.

"I'm Georgia Bennett, with Somerton Security." She huffed out an irritated breath, disturbing the curls around her face. "Ethan sent me."

Oh. Not a dream, then. Bummer.

"What day is it?" Parker asked as he swept his hand over the counter, collecting all the scattered crumbs of sweetener from coffee he didn't remember making. The caffeine was kicking in, and reality was rapidly encroaching. He'd need at least one more cup to deal with it. Hell, it'd probably take a third to tolerate the scowling woman standing in his kitchen. Ethan, the bastard, had no doubt timed her arrival for when Parker would be at his weakest, his most vulnerable. Ethan knew all too well that Parker was basically worthless first thing. Asshole had probably counted on it to ensure his latest guard dog made it through the door.

"The twelfth." Her expression as he brushed the neat little pile of fake sugar into his fresh cup of coffee was nothing short of disgusted. Oh well, waste not, want not.

"No, what *day* is it?"

She looked at him like he was an addict scooping his fix out of a toilet, but she answered. "Thursday."

Interesting. Last he'd checked, it'd been just after 2:00 a.m. on Tuesday. That explained the mess of sweetener packets on the counter and the stack of cereal bowls in the sink. At least he'd finished the last of his coding on his latest program and sent it off to his team. He'd have to check on their progress after he dealt with Ethan's newest pet gorilla. Although that descriptor didn't really suit the woman standing in front of him. Ethan must have finally taken the whole brains-over-balls thing seriously. Parker smiled. Or maybe Ethan just had a twisted sense of humor. Either way, it was time to find out exactly what made Miss

Georgia Bennett tick. It was only fair; if he was meant to put up with her, she should damn well have to put up with him.

"So. Ethan sent you."

"That's what I've been explaining for the last twenty minutes. Think you're awake enough now, or do you need another dose of caffeine?" She snatched her hat off her head and dropped it on top of what he assumed was her coat.

"I should be good for the moment." He walked out from behind the island and into the living room. "You might need a cup, though. You're a little grouchy." He gestured to the Keurig. "Help yourself before you leave."

Oh, if her hair could have curled with indignation the way her eyes lit with fire, she'd have made a picture. "I'm not leaving."

"But you didn't say anything about grouchy, so please, help yourself. There's creamer in the fridge, but I'd smell it first." He scratched his stomach as he moved into the living room. Maybe he should put on some real clothes. Or at least some sweats. Then again, it was his house, so he could dress how he wanted.

"Look, Mr. Livingston—"

Oh yuck, no. That took her from smoldering badass to irritated schoolteacher. "Parker's fine."

"Parker, then."

She sighed but followed him into the living room, *without* coffee.

Shame. Wasn't like he offered to share with just anyone.

"Look, Ethan sent me to do a job. So until that's done, you're going to have to suck it up and work with me."

Oh, he was, was he? "I'm sure I seem harmless enough to you." He took a long sip of his coffee and shot her a look over his glasses. "The intellectually evolved usually do . . . to you Neanderthal types."

"Ne-Neanderthal?"

It was fun winding her up. Almost a shame she couldn't stay.

"But let's get one thing straight. You're in my home. You don't get to dictate my schedule, eating habits, or what color underwear I'm wearing."

Her mouth dropped open as if she were just dying to set him straight. "Yeah, I'm sure you're thinking to yourself, 'God, what an ass.' But before you let the next thought that flits through your brain fly out your mouth, you might want to ask yourself if you really want to irritate an ass with an IQ of 162 who could level your credit report, repossess your car, declare you dead, and hack your phone so it plays the theme from Super Mario Bros. every hour on the hour for the next decade.

"You do *not* attempt to tell me what to do, Coffee-less Woman." He scratched his balls and savored the shocked look on her face almost as much as his next hit of caffeine. "I don't take orders from anyone."

Her eyes narrowed, all the things she wanted to say scrolling across her face like a teleprompter. Finally, she settled on, "Relax, Princess Peach. No one's raiding your castle."

Parker couldn't help it—he snorted coffee out his nose. Laughing through the burn, he wiped at the edge of his mouth with his shirt. So she had a sense of humor *and* a knowledge of vintage video games. He'd have to watch himself, or he might find himself liking this one.

"Ethan sent me to fill in on your rotation until the weather clears."

She didn't look impressed, but her mouth had softened from stern disapproval into something full and pouty and more than a little bit tempting.

"Are you paying attention, Mr. Livingston?"

"Parker," he corrected. "And my ADD diagnosis would say no, I'm not." For once, it was a lie. Normally his thoughts raced a thousand miles an hour in a hundred different directions until something caught his eye—usually a problem or a puzzle to manipulate and solve. No question, the woman standing in front of him, an odd mix of aggression and unguarded softness, was a mystery. Maybe it was the way her freckles peeked out from beneath a thin layer of makeup or the way her cheeks flushed rosy, he wasn't sure. What he was certain of was that despite how Georgia Bennett carried herself—alert, competent, in charge—there was a great deal more swimming just beneath the surface.

"As I was saying, Ethan sent me to fill in temporarily. Seventy-two hours max and I'm out of your hair."

Parker snorted. "And you believed him?" He flopped onto his sofa and grabbed his iPad off the coffee table. He flicked on the television and began channel surfing.

She sighed and sat. "Something like that."

"*Errrrr!* Wrong, but thanks for playing. Please try again." He grinned as an irritated scowl settled over her face.

"What?"

Parker rolled his eyes. "Ethan only assigns me assets who've pissed him off, so regardless of what line of bullshit he fed you, you landed here 'cause you done fucked up." Parker turned his head and smiled. "What did you do? Get frisky in a broom closet?"

"I'm typically assigned to women."

"Oh, so pillow fights and sleepovers—do tell!"

"You're twelve."

"Only at heart." The warmth of her body rolled over him in waves—everything about her was heat and fire. Part of him, no doubt the stupid part that liked puzzles and explosions in equal measure, wanted to know what it would take to set her off. He might not survive it, but damn, he'd die with caffeine in his veins, a smile on his face.

"What's your point, Mr. Livingston?" she snapped.

"Parker." He peered at her out of the corner of his eye, barely restraining a smile. "My point is, I know Ethan, and if he assigned you to me, you screwed up. So spill. What was it?"

"Airborne paint and pretentious politicians," she grunted.

Parker choked down a mouthful of coffee and laughed between wheezes. "Congressman Dickinson's wife? That clip's gone viral on YouTube."

She groaned and sank back into the cushions of the sofa.

"No wonder Ethan saddled you with me."

Georgia tilted her head, staring at him with interest. He could practically hear the cogs turning.

"Question is, why did he saddle me with you?" Georgia asked.

"Is this Groundhog Day? I just explained—"

"Yeah, yeah. Done fucked up, I got it. What I meant was, why *you*? I mean, sure, you've got a rep for being difficult—there's usually a rock-paper-scissors war in the office when your name comes up—but so do a lot of other clients."

He watched her out of the corner of his eye as he turned back to the television, flipping through channels for something to kill time.

The grin that eventually split her face was wicked. "I'm not the only one he's punishing, am I?" She laughed.

"No idea what you're talking about," Parker replied, his eyes glued to his tablet.

"Like hell." Georgia snorted. "What did you do? Build a death ray? Blackmail Ethan into paying ninety-nine cents for five more chances to clear a level?"

"Level 127 stump you, too?" Parker smiled as a flush crawled up her neck. "Don't worry about it. Lots of people get stuck there. Of course, most of them are under the age of ten . . ." Parker lifted an arm to scratch at the back of his neck. The fact Georgia eyed the upward trek of the hem of his T-shirt both surprised and pleased him. "There's a great tutorial by a nine-year-old from South Korea on YouTube."

"I carry a gun."

"And apparently you want to keep your job, otherwise you wouldn't be pouting on my sofa." Parker watched, fascinated by her expression as she wrestled with the smart retort he knew she wanted to launch. "And anyway, in answer to your question, it irritates Ethan when I hack government databases." Ethan just didn't get that Parker needed that information in order to do his job. Those classified field reports, the details behind negative outcomes, were gold in terms of evolving his program.

Georgia lost whatever internal struggle she was waging and dropped her head into her hands. Her sigh was long and had several four-letter words in it.

"Oh relax, it was only barely classified information—most of which I already knew—but every time I do it, Ethan punishes me with a security detail he knows I don't want and definitely don't need—regardless of whatever reasons he gave you." Though maybe Ethan was finally, *finally* looking into Parker's concerns. There were too many inconsistencies, too many ops Parker either hadn't been involved in or had flat-out advised against. If accessing those files without permission had finally motivated Ethan, well, Parker wasn't going to complain.

"I have no idea why you're considered a high-value government asset." Georgia turned to the TV, crossing her arms over her chest. "Or why they don't just toss you in a cell somewhere for safekeeping."

"Because I bring up the group average—without me, no one's solving the *Jeopardy!* questions." He turned off the TV—there was nothing worth watching during the day—and started scrolling through his e-mails for updates from his software development team. "And they don't toss me in jail because I bring the good doughnuts to the staff meetings. You know Fat Al's, few blocks from here? You could make yourself useful and fetch. No jelly filled, 'kay?"

"Look," Georgia said on a huff that ruffled her bangs, "I get it. You don't want me here, and I'd rather babysit a rabid pack of poodles, but that's life. I need my job, so for the next three days you need to not die." She sighed, then muttered, "Though I'm beginning to think you're your own worst enemy."

Ouch. Was he really that bad? So he'd worked for seventy-two hours straight finessing his latest project. Could he be faulted for falling coma-tose into bed after? It was how he worked, and despite Georgia's criticism—which sounded disturbingly like Ethan's—he got the job done. So what if he did it on a nontraditional timetable? Parker took a careful sniff of his armpit. Fabric softener, as far as he could smell. So what was she even complaining about?

"I don't like people in my space." Parker returned to rapidly flicking the buttons on his tablet to keep the urge to explore Georgia at bay. He was naturally tactile, and everything about her was interesting. Would the curl tucked behind her ear spring back if he ran it through his fingers? If he pressed his thumb to the bottom of her lip, would her mouth drop and a sigh escape? There was so much to explore, so much to touch—the temptation was almost too strong to resist. "And I definitely don't like hulking specters who linger in corners and grunt one-word answers as if they're not allowed to feed the animals. I don't need a bodyguard."

"Yes, yes. More brains than balls. Ethan told me." The corner of her lip turned up, amusement and professional distance waging an interesting war on her face. "But it's not your call. It's Ethan's."

Yeah, it was. He'd tried objecting, but that hadn't gone over well in the past. And the few times Parker had actually managed to run off a detail? Well, Ethan had an uncanny knack for sending someone even worse. Someone who pushed him to keep "normal" hours. To sleep at night and work a standard nine-to-five. It was always awful. His anxiety would return, slamming against him as vicious and unexpected as a tsunami. The revolving door of caffeine and Xanax it usually took to maintain any sort of balance drove him to the brink of exhaustion. Parker took a sidelong glance at Georgia. He couldn't quite peg her. She certainly had a personality—one she was quashing for some certainly misguided reason, but it was there. And it was *interesting*.

"Look, you want to stay?" he asked, pulling up his pet project on his iPad. "I'll make you a deal." He stood from the sofa and gestured for her to follow him. "I've been working on a virtual reality simulator for use in training law enforcement and military teams. It's been in production for ages, and the hardware is *amazing*." God, was that the truth. He'd been *dying* to take the tech he'd bankrolled for a spin. And as of this morning, his software development team had cleared the first simulation for testing. He placed his palm against the security access panel to what used to be the loft next to his. The door swung open, and Parker gestured inside with his half-full cup of coffee. "Go ahead, take a look."

Georgia took a few brazen steps into the room. The unknown didn't seem to faze her. Parker watched as she glanced around the empty space. There wasn't much to see. The same synthetic material covered the floor, ceiling, and walls. Even the windows had shades to match. It was a sea of stark, industrial gray. DMV boring, even. Except Parker knew that unlike the DMV, this place was live-action *Call of Duty*. Man, the cyber warfare unit—colleagues and teammates when they weren't abandoning him to Ethan's whims and random protection details—was going to be *pissed*. They'd been angling for time in this room for months now. And instead, some busty brunette with an attitude that damn well shouldn't be sexy was going to get to take the maiden run.

"What is this place?" Georgia asked as she ran a fingertip over the wall, tracing the grooves that connected each embedded laser to the next. The entire room was full of them, each exactly eighteen inches apart.

"My lab." Parker leaned against the open door sipping his coffee while Georgia moved to the only furniture in the room. A small tactical locker stood next to the door, and safety glasses and vests hung from several pegs. "Wanna give it a run?" Parker tapped his personal code into the touch screen on the wall; the file should have been automatically uploaded to his secure network, so all he needed to do was key in the security sequence. The system came on with a low hum. He watched Georgia's face, open curiosity readily displayed, as the ceiling tiles tilted and deployed the grid of lasers. In less than thirty seconds, with little more than a quiet hum of electricity and the motorized whir of tiny gears, what was once a huge, empty space rearranged itself into organized rows of office cubicles. A standard corporate environment, down to the watercooler by the elevator and the halogen light that wouldn't stop flickering, had been Parker's idea. The thought of being trapped in cube hell had always chased his IQ into mediocrity—it was only fair that it should torment everyone else as well.

Georgia stepped forward, running her fingers through the nearly opaque hologram of boring beige wall. "You created all this?"

Astonishment, Parker had expected. Wonder and confusion would have been predictable. But the sheer awe? The way Georgia passed her fingers through the play of light coupled with her face as open hunger took hold and turned her expression fierce? It shouldn't have, but the combination took his breath away.

"Not all of it," he admitted. "The programming is mine, and I helped develop the layout of the grid. I bankrolled the guy who created the synthetic coating on the floors, walls, and ceilings a few years ago. But the simulator? That's all mine." His baby. A chance to send teams into the field better equipped to handle anything and everything. A chance to tilt the ledger of life and death back into Parker's favor. "Bet you thought I only designed mind-numbing apps for attention-challenged adults."

"And yet here you are, a regular Professor X."

Comic-book references from that full, feisty mouth? He was so screwed.

Her gaze turned calculating as she assessed him. "You said something about a deal?"

"I need a guinea pig." Parker grinned. It was almost a shame to break that ego into tiny pieces; he sorta liked the woman. "Let's see how you think on your feet, shall we?" He set his coffee down on top of the tactical rack and pulled out two pairs of headsets and two vests. He handed one of each to her.

Georgia tested the weight of a vest, then slipped it over her head without complaint. "Same weight as standard-issue body armor," she noted. "Intentional, I assume?"

Impressed despite himself, Parker nodded. Observant, this one. He'd worry, but . . . nah. He had no doubt she could bark orders, clear bathrooms, and otherwise make a nuisance of herself. All bodyguards excelled in those areas. But get him through an unfamiliar layout with active shooters on the loose? Please. He'd be lucky if he were shot only once.

She slid on her glasses, then pulled the gun from the front pocket of the vest. She hefted it, testing the weight, then inspected the grip, trigger, and checked the sights. "Beretta M9. But the weight feels a bit off."

Parker scowled. It was a ten-gram difference! How the hell had she noticed? "Yeah, it's the prototype; we're still working on getting the balance right. No bullets, though, just blanks. All the kick, none of the pow. But every time you fire, a pulse is emitted. If it makes contact with one of the simulator's aggressors, you'll see a red ripple spread from the point of contact." Parker took the weapon from her. "Run demo!"

A disgruntled employee in his midtwenties appeared three cubes up and two to the right. Gun in hand, he rose in Georgia's direction. Without hesitation, Parker fired two shots, both to the head. He hadn't always been good with a gun—something Ethan had taken issue with. Parker had spent the better part of a year at the range, practicing until Ethan was satisfied he'd neither shoot himself nor be left defenseless. Parker turned back to Georgia, a smug grin pulling at his lips. "Don't strain yourself. Torso shots'll do the job. But hit a limb and the guy goes down for ten seconds, then reappears in play."

Georgia took the gun from him. "Anyone can be lethal from twenty feet." As Parker fastened his vest at the shoulders, Georgia snagged the gun strapped to the front and tucked it into her waistband. "You won't be needing this."

"Hey!"

"Bodyguard gets the gun; damsel gets the rescue." She gestured between them. "Me bodyguard, you damsel."

"I am not a—"

"All right," she said, completely ignoring him, "give me the rules, Private Ryan."

"Rules are simple. You get me from here to the elevator. Fail and you lose. Die and you lose. Take a shortcut through a wall—"

"And I lose," Georgia said. "Then what?"

"You leave. Sit in the hallway for all I care, but you're done and out of my hair." And he needed her out of his life if he was going to get back to work. Ethan could bitch and moan all he wanted about the definition of *classified*, but something was off. And people were dying because of it.

She scowled. "And if I win?"

"Then not only do you get to hang out with me"—he flashed his most charming grin—"I'll actually cooperate. I won't try to ditch you; I won't intentionally annoy you." He ignored her incredulous huff. "I'll be the model protectee." He crossed his heart with his index finger.

"How many shooters?" she asked, all business.

"Three." Fact was, she was making him a little nervous. If Ethan had sent a dossier ahead of her, Parker hadn't seen it yet. But she wasn't handling herself like some fresh-off-the-bus recruit.

"Piece of cake." She stepped in front of him and glanced over her shoulder. "Stay close, don't wander toward something shiny, and do what I say."

Parker slid in behind her and splayed a hand against her hip. He snuck his fingers up beneath her T-shirt, brushed warm skin, and settled into the sharp groove beneath her hip. And because he was feeling stupid and just a tiny bit worried she might actually be competent, he let his thumb trace the curve of her ass through her jeans. He got as far as the seam on her pocket before she spun, gun leveled at his chest. He slunk back, hands in the air, unrepentant grin on his face. "You said stay close; I didn't want to get lost."

"Let's get something straight, Poindexter," she snarled. "You only said I had to get you to the elevator; you didn't say anything about alive. If you'd prefer that I shoot you, then heft you over my shoulders like the useless sack of potatoes you are, by all means, continue to live dangerously."

Shit, she actually meant it. His grin slid from his face. She could probably do it, too. The only thing worse than losing would be losing like the damsel she'd labeled him. He'd play nice . . . for now. He nodded.

"Good." She turned back toward the room. "Stay behind me."

Well, maybe not too nice. "At least the last thing I see before I die will be the toned perfection of your butt. What is it? Pilates? Tennis? Cruising the mall with the geriatric brigade?"

"Pillow fights in high heels," she said. "Now if you don't mind . . ."

Fighting the laugh that wanted to bubble out of his chest, Parker shouted, "Run sim!"

Game on.

◆ ◆ ◆

"I think they're trying to kill me," Parker whispered against her ear. "What did I ever do to them?" Georgia shot an irritated look over her shoulder. He tried for wide-eyed innocence, missed the mark, and landed somewhere between amused at her expense and genuinely enjoying himself. Did he seriously think she'd fail? Oh, he had better think again.

Because she could—and because, really, what was the worst that could happen?—she turned and gave Parker a solid shove. He stumbled back several feet, straight into the open. The third shooter appeared, and she loosed two rounds, watching in satisfaction as the target disintegrated.

"Hey!" Parker complained. "I don't think you're supposed to use your client as bait."

"Says who?" Georgia grasped Parker by the wrist and hustled him toward the elevator. Part of her had expected the game to end upon dispatching the last shooter, but maybe she had to actually get Parker into the elevator.

"Everyone on the planet?" he grumbled. At least he'd stopped humming the theme to *Mission: Impossible*.

Only twenty feet to the elevator. She considered what she knew of the simulation and, more important, what she knew of Parker. Parker, who was silent and cooperating—more or less—for the first time. Though she hadn't known him long, she was fairly certain in her assessment of him. Smart, sarcastic, and absolutely convinced he had the biggest brain in the room. Which meant he'd leveraged the game in his favor. She'd lay odds there were more than the three active shooters he'd claimed.

Ugh. She was seriously reconsidering the merits of just shooting him and being done with it. Ultimately, he didn't have the power to fire her, or he'd have kicked her ass out already. Which meant that while he could be as "difficult" as he wanted, he couldn't actually get rid of her.

Ethan can, her traitorous brain supplied. Ethan had been clear: make a personal connection or else. And while Parker might be an energetic handful, he wasn't all that difficult. He wasn't demanding or pretentious. He didn't act like Georgia, with her lack of education and blue-collar roots, was beneath him or lucky to be in his employ.

He's different, the part of her brain that lived to torment whispered. *Weren't you just saying you wanted something different?*

Yes, yes. She'd wanted a change. A challenge. Clearly she should have been more descriptive in her wish list. Still, technology that made her swoon and a bed-rumpled geek who looked like he'd majored in seduction and minored in tactile engagement was more interesting than any of her other assignments in the last six months. And, though she'd never admit it, he kept her on her toes, constantly teetering between the impulse to laugh and the desire to maim.

"Oh shit," Parker gasped.

Georgia spun, ready to fire a round or two into the target she was sure was approaching from behind. Nothing.

"Shoe's untied." Parker smiled. "Wouldn't want to trip and break my neck." He glanced at Georgia as he dropped to one knee. "What do you think? Bunny ears or around the rabbit hole?"

Her trigger finger itched.

"You cried wolf a lot as a kid, didn't you?" Georgia inched forward and began mentally cataloging all the ways Parker was going to be a handful, regardless of his promises to cooperate.

"What for?" he asked as he double-knotted his shoelace. "Mom was an addict who invited the wolves inside. After she was gone, there were other things to cry about." Georgia snapped her gaze back to Parker's profile. Was he serious? He'd launched that emotional hand grenade as casually as a flower girl threw petals. Was it a tactic to keep her off balance? Emotional manipulation? She didn't think so. There was something inherently honest about Parker. It was in the way he absentmindedly pushed his glasses up his nose. In the way he'd gasped out a "Nice shot" before he could stop himself. He was all cocksure arrogance wrapped up in subtle, playful charm, but there was no pretense. No persona crafted for the sole purpose of convincing the world he was more than the sum of his parts.

Dammit, it made him attractive. Worse, it made her *like* him.

Just shove him in the elevator, and move on already.

The elevator. Right. She strode forward, her gun at her side. "Let's go, Parker." She jabbed at the elevator call button, though really she was just pushing her thumb against the wall.

"Easy, killer. Those panels run a couple thousand a square foot."

Georgia glanced over her shoulder as the elevator pinged. Parker's smug grin as the doors whooshed open only confirmed her suspicions. Without looking, she pulled up her gun and fired two shots into the fourth suspect. She let the corner of her mouth turn up as Parker's jaw dropped open in shock.

"That . . ." He stared at her for a long, uncomfortable moment. "That was . . ."

She'd seen that look before. The look that said, *You're a woman; you aren't supposed to be good at this.* She hadn't expected it now any more than she'd expected it when she'd leaped between a knife-wielding mugger and Isaac, a man she'd loved beyond reason, a man she'd been willing to die for. She'd thought the fifteen stitches beneath her rib cage had hurt, but Isaac's admission that he wasn't sure he could stand beside a woman who could stand in front of him had devastated her.

"That," Parker said, a bold, determined look settling over his face as he stepped into her space, pressing her back against the wall, "was probably the hottest damn thing I've ever seen."

As her mouth dropped open in surprise, Parker was there, shocking her into silence as his lips settled over hers and stole her breath.

Parker had done a lot of stupid things in his life, but he hadn't enjoyed a single one of them nearly as much as he enjoyed kissing the hell out of Georgia Bennett. When he'd challenged her to prove her skills, he'd expected her to fail—and fail miserably—within the first five minutes. Yet Georgia had stormed in, taken control, and marched across the digital landscape, wreaking havoc and mounting a body count like it was easy. Now Parker was facing down the sudden realization that the bossy, smart-mouthed bodyguard just flat-out did it for him. And, to make matters worse, now she worked for him. Well, technically he supposed she worked for Ethan, which was worse, but whatever. He had to *cooperate*. Something he rarely did, at least not on purpose.

As they moved back through his lab in a frenzy of searching kisses and discarded equipment, Parker couldn't find it in himself to care. Georgia kissed the way she did everything else—like she was absolutely certain there was no one in the world who was her equal. And as Parker slid his fingers beneath her sweater, dipping and sliding along the groove between hip and taut, sexy abs, he was inclined to agree with her.

Nothing to lose, he pulled her back through the doorway to his loft and pressed her against the brick wall with enough force to drive a breathy little moan that aimed straight for his cock. She threw her head back the moment he left her mouth, scraping his two-day stubble across the underside of her jaw and toward the sensitive skin beneath her ear. He drew a deep, intoxicating breath. Damn, how he wished it were summer. The scent of her—fresh rain and something darker, edgier—swamped him. Were the weather warm, she'd be pressed against him in a tank top, the dangerously tempting curve of her breasts exposed and on offer. He'd never wished for the damp heat of a Baltimore summer, but God he wanted one now.

He used his teeth and tongue, nipping at her earlobe, then soothing the sting. She froze, as if caught between the urge to challenge him and the desire to see what he'd do next. Sense told him this was a dangerous game—one he was poorly equipped to win. Desire insisted he play anyway. He pulled back to look at her. Her eyes dilated as he lived dangerously and trailed his hands up the outside of her breasts, skimming against curves he wanted to grip with a desperation he'd never experienced. He let his thumbs stroke and circle and allowed his mind to imagine what her skin would taste like. She didn't move, barely breathed. What would it take to break that control? To elicit a reaction?

Was it indecision or surprise that held her still? He dipped a thumb toward a nipple, tracing the edge of lace he couldn't see but could oh so easily imagine. *What will it take, Georgia?* What button did he have to push, what switch did he need to flip, to set her alight? To strip her bare and ignite the desire he saw simmering just beneath the surface? She was holding back, unconsciously restraining the impulse to push, to flip their positions and take what she needed from him. He wanted to be the guy who brought that out in her, the guy who got to be on the receiving end of an unbridled, uninhibited Georgia Bennett.

She leaned in, teasing his mouth with the promise of hers, then pulling away at the barest touch, the whisper of a challenge passing between them. She stared at him, her mouth inches away from delicious contact with his, her eyes sparkling with mischief and . . . confusion?

Her gaze slid over his shoulder, and she stiffened. Playfulness fled as disbelief seized her expression. A slow whir began to filter through the white noise filling Parker's brain.

"Is that . . . ?"

Parker's arms fell away from her as she scrambled to the side.

"Is that a cat riding a Roomba?" Georgia asked, her voice squeaking.

He squeezed his eyes shut and tried to force blood to defy gravity and supply his brain with much-needed oxygen. He tilted his head and sent a glare across the room.

"Yeah." He sighed. "PITA, perfect timing, as usual." The cat, as if lord of his empire, merely blinked as he rode the vacuum cleaner through the living room, calmly assessing Georgia and completely oblivious to the fact that he would, at the earliest opportunity, be donated to a high school biology class.

CHAPTER THREE

Georgia carefully skirted the Roomba-riding hallucination and moved directly to the coffee maker. Obviously she was caffeine deprived. Or drugged. Yeah, maybe she'd been drugged. How else could she explain her completely unplanned trip down the rabbit hole? A rabbit hole that led to tactical interviews, cats that rode home appliances, and nerds who coaxed her toward impulse-laced regret faster than a car salesman with a bargain-priced cherry-red convertible.

"Oh sure, now you want my coffee," Parker mumbled as he followed her into the kitchen, neatly dodging the cat that swiped at his legs as the Roomba whirred past. "Just ignore the animal; I do."

"Moment's over." And man, was it. What the hell had she been thinking? It was one thing to indulge the guy—taking an interest was hardly the worst way to forge a connection with a client—but she'd ended up pressed against the wall, his hands in places that were still hot and tingling. *Stupid, stupid, stupid.* She was chalking it up to a momentary lapse of judgment induced by a lack of caffeine and an overdeveloped competitive streak. "Better yet, it never happened at all."

Parker nudged his cup toward her across the counter. "Promise to be my coffee wench, and I'll never say a word." Georgia rolled her eyes but grabbed his mug. She didn't know much about Parker—yet—but she was certain withholding caffeine should be reserved for emergencies . . . or coercion. She slid a refreshed mug across the island to Parker, who'd climbed up on a chrome bar stool and was openly studying her. She grabbed her own mug, crossed her legs ankle over ankle, and got down to business.

"Ethan is under the impression you need personal security. Why?"

"This again?" A scowl tightened Parker's features, and he extended a hand across the quartz. "He's a drama queen. Pass the pink packets of palatability, would you? Coffee isn't meant to be consumed black."

Georgia palmed a handful but didn't pass them over. "Sure. Just as soon as you answer my question."

Parker dropped a forlorn gaze to his mug, then looked back up at her. "That's blackmail."

"Uh-huh." It was taking longer than she'd like, but with each passing second, the world was righting itself.

"I already told you," Parker huffed. "Ethan likes to saddle me with a babysitter when he finds out I've been hacking classified records."

"So you said. But that doesn't explain how he justifies the man-hours and expense." Georgia twirled the sweetener in her fingers while she sipped at her own cup of coffee. "I'm getting paid, which means someone, probably the government, is getting billed."

Parker rolled his eyes. "What's your point?"

"My point is that while Ethan may well be punishing you for hacking government files, someone is approving the expense reports. Which means, unbelievable as it might seem, someone considers you valuable enough to assign a bodyguard." She waved a dismissive hand in his direction. "So spill."

Parker sighed. "What are the odds you give me the life-affirming pink stuff if I say please?"

Georgia smiled. "Excellent." He perked up, a charming smile reminding her exactly what she found so damn compelling about him. His openness, the way every thought flared across his face as bright as the morning sun. There was something intriguing about him. Something fresh and honest. Too bad she had to kill his joy. "Right after you start answering my questions."

"You're evil."

"Thank you." She shook a packet just to watch him squirm.

35

"I could get up and help myself, you know." He scowled at her.

"But you won't." She rubbed the sweetener with her thumb and forefinger, crinkling the package. "You want to see how far you can push me? How often you can call me coffee wench? How many times I'll let you dodge my questions? Go ahead. It's not *my* coffee getting cold."

His gaze shot from her fingers to her face, his expression fierce. "Two hours and you think you know me. You. Don't."

She stared him down. She'd been joking, more or less. It was abundantly clear, however, that she'd struck a nerve—she just wasn't sure which one. "Hence, our conversation." They glared at each other for a long moment. It felt juvenile, this game they were playing, but it was one she couldn't afford to lose.

"Hence? Who even says that?"

"People who read books without pictures. Stop dodging."

Finally, Parker said, "You realize I'm not supposed to tell you any of this, right?"

Georgia smiled. "Just think how it'll irritate Ethan."

"Good point." Parker leaned across the counter, cupping his hands around the mug. "What do you know about metadata?"

"What does that have to do with my question?"

"Everything. *Hence*," Parker said, dragging out the word, "the explanation."

"Ha-ha."

"So what do you know about it?"

Georgia shrugged but tore open the top of a packet. "How to spell it, so start at the beginning. I'm interested."

Surprise filtered across his face. She wondered what he'd expected. Hadn't any of his other bodyguards asked for a rundown? Admitted where their knowledge had gaps?

"Okay, practical example." Something in Parker settled, clicked into place. It was as if he transitioned from playful flirt to intelligent tech genius the second someone showed the slightest bit of interest. His eager switch struck her as sad. How often had this side of him been ignored? How often had people missed the man behind the personality? A personality she was beginning to think might be a front. Oh, she was certain her impression of Parker as an affable know-it-all was accurate, but she also suspected it was a fallback, a persona he was comfortable with—and one he knew people expected of him. Georgia was beginning to believe there was a lot more to the man in front of her, too.

Ethan's words filtered through her brain. *You want to care.* She brushed away the thought.

"You know about the Edward Snowden fiasco, right?" he asked.

"Sure." Convinced Parker would keep talking now that he'd started, Georgia dumped the sweetener into his coffee. "He's the NSA employee who leaked all those classified documents."

"Right." He absently snatched a spoon that may or may not have been clean off the counter and stirred as he talked. "He released thousands of documents—but the real damage is that he shined a spotlight on an agency that had—more or less—been flying under the radar of most Americans."

Georgia snorted. "A secret intelligence agency that's not so secret anymore. Wonder how many heads rolled over that disaster."

"Yeah. And for the average American, it's not the classified documents causing the uproar. It's the very nature of the agency."

Intrigued, Georgia brought her coffee around the bar and settled onto a stool next to Parker. "What do you mean?"

"Well, the NSA has always said, 'Look, don't worry. We're just gathering data. It's information, not details.' They want you to believe they're no more invasive than commercial marketing practices—a whole other can of worms, by the way. You wouldn't believe what most retailers know about you." Parker moved aside his coffee and drummed his fingers against the counter. "What they're really doing is collecting mountains of metadata."

"Okay, but that doesn't explain what metadata is."

"Right. So metadata is essentially data that inform or explain *other* data."

Georgia resisted the urge to rub her temples. Barely.

"I know, that makes it sound like the Internet is having an existential crisis." Parker smiled. "So you know how the NSA likes to say they aren't listening to your phone calls?"

"Yeah?"

"Well, that's true. Mostly. They aren't *listening* to your calls. It's simply not practical. There isn't enough manpower to sift through all those conversations, and technology isn't evolved enough—yet—to do the work for them. So they needed a more practical solution."

"Metadata."

Parker nodded. "So when the NSA says, 'Hey, we're not listening to your phone calls,' what they really mean is, 'We know who you talked to, and for how long, and who you talked to next, but we don't know what you talked about.'"

"Okay, so that seems pretty basic. What do I care if they know I spent twenty minutes on the phone with Aunt Edna?"

"And that's exactly what they want you to think." His brow creased. "Do you really have an Aunt Edna?"

Georgia shot him a look she hoped translated to, *You're kidding.*

"Right. Off topic. But what if I told you they know that yesterday morning you called your boyfriend, talked for twenty minutes, then called your doctor, talked for another ten, and later that afternoon called your pharmacy after you Googled 'suspicious rash'? They didn't listen to any of these conversations, but do you really think they're as clueless as Aunt Edna?"

"Okay. So metadata isn't as benign as they make it sound." It made sense. If it were harmless, the NSA wouldn't want it in the first place. "Still, that doesn't explain what this has to do with you."

For the first time since she'd met him, Parker looked uncomfortable. Had she been less tuned in to him, she might have missed it. It was subtle, but he'd stopped twitching. Stopped drumming his fingers or toying with his spoon. For a second, two at most, Parker went completely still.

"What if I told you I'd not only found a way to analyze all that data but that I'd found a way to weaponize it?"

Georgia raised an eyebrow. "Explain."

"You know I work as a special contractor for the government. What you don't know is I've been working for the DoD, in one capacity or another, since I was seventeen."

Seventeen? It was hard to picture Parker working within the confines of the government now, let alone at that age. The man was twenty-eight and had a vintage Indian motorcycle in his living room and the first issue of *Iron Man* framed by the entryway.

"When I was about halfway through MIT, the government approached me about consulting on a variety of projects—and leveraging some programs I'd already developed. Before I knew it, I was spending all my free time developing software programs geared toward national defense projects." He propped a foot on his knee, bouncing it up and down as he talked. "Later, I was attached to a classified black-ops team that dealt specifically with cyber warfare. It's how I met Ethan."

His expression grew distant, and for the first time, Georgia recognized a tinge of insecurity, a memory of shy awkwardness Parker wore physically.

"I used my technical expertise to assist teams in the field." He pushed away from the countertop, a tense line creasing his forehead. "At first I thought it was cool—a video game come to life where I was the man with the plan. I mean, intellectually I understood it was life and death, but it wasn't real to me, you know?"

"It never is, not until it's personal." Georgia knew that better than most. Until the bad shit followed you home, took away the people you cared about, all the warnings in the world didn't hold any more power than the bogeyman. "You lost someone?"

"Yeah. I was just sitting there, playing God, so sure I had everything under control. Seconds," he said, staring into his coffee. "That's all it took for everything to go to shit. I watched, safe and secure in a glorified closet a world away as men I knew, men I liked, died."

"It's something you live through but not something you survive. You're never the same." Georgia rolled the heavy watch at her wrist, memories of the army's representatives taking her into her CO's office rising unbidden. She could still remember the shine of their buttons, the close cut of their suits, the way they'd spoken, calm and collected, official and precise—as if their words weren't irrevocably altering the world she'd lived in. It was that moment she remembered most vividly, the one where everything she knew, everything she'd built her life on—rules, orders, predictability—abandoned her forever. Georgia looked up and caught Parker staring at her. It wasn't the pity she'd expected, nor were there questions in his expression. Just a simple tilt of the head, a gentle, unspoken acknowledgment that touched her more than she wanted to admit.

"I decided I had to do more, be better for the teams that relied on me. It was terrifying. I'd never been driven by more than the idle curiosity of what I could do. It took a while, but I leveraged my academic focus—advanced algorithms and predictive analysis—to create a program that could mine through terabytes of data and create a profile for every individual we were tasked with either finding or stopping. Combining metadata with past behaviors, known associates—you name it—all of it is useful when you have a program that can find connections." A tinge of pride slipped into Parker's voice. "My program can do in hours what it would take a team of analysts years to do. Basically, with the right information, I could predict what it would take to prevent—or enable— a certain outcome. Since we implemented this program, our margin of success has grown, and our negative outcomes have been reduced."

Georgia shivered. Everything Parker was saying sounded powerful, wonderful even . . . unless you were the one his program was targeting.

"Anyway, it's my program, and I'm constantly refining it, but without me it doesn't work."

The sheer ego in the statement should have irritated her, but the flat delivery told Georgia that Parker wasn't bragging or exaggerating, simply stating a fact.

"People say I'm smart. It's a casual acknowledgment of fact. To most people, I *am* smart. But to the government? To them, I'm dangerous." He whispered the last, as if he still had a hard time believing it. "Or at least, I have the potential to be. It's why they very rarely deploy me with the team. Why I don't do fieldwork or consult on cases overseas. The DoD prefers to know where I am, and what I'm doing, at all times." Parker appeared torn between the obvious pride he took in his work and the realization that his talent, his abilities, had landed him a dubious place of honor on a government watch list. Professionalism warred with instincts. Georgia hadn't known Parker long enough to be sure one way or the other, but she just couldn't picture this man—this rumpled, sexy, insanely clever man—as dangerous. Well, at least not to anything other than her self-control.

"Intent, not ability, determines how dangerous a man can be." She wasn't sure why she said it, but the way he let go of a breath and dipped his chin told her it had been the right thing to say.

"Or woman."

Georgia smiled. "Or woman."

"So to answer your question, if the DoD thought I'd put up with it, they'd have me under twenty-four-hour surveillance."

"Why don't they?" Georgia asked, taking her mug to the sink and rinsing it.

"Because I'm a huge pain in the ass who likes his privacy?" Parker shrugged. "And besides, it's like you said, the biggest threat to my well-being is me."

"No argument there," Georgia said as she snatched Parker's empty mug out of his hands before he could contemplate another cup of coffee. "If you're such a high-value government asset, why the hell do you need to hack classified documents? Shits and giggles?"

Parker rolled his eyes. "Please. I could do that faster than you could solve beginner-level sudoku."

"Then why do it at all?" Georgia asked, intrigued despite herself.

Parker yawned and scratched at the abs outlined beneath his T-shirt. "Because in order to continue to refine my program, I need to be able to study the negative outcomes and figure out what we missed. You have to understand, they use my program—use *me*—to calculate the risk versus reward of a lot of operations. In so many ways, it's my call that sends someone's brother, husband, wife, son, or daughter into a dangerous situation. It's a responsibility I don't take lightly. When an op goes bad, when family members have the worst day of their lives, I take that seriously."

Parker clenched his fists against the countertop, then flexed and splayed his fingers, blowing out a deep breath. "Negative outcomes matter—maybe more than the positive ones—in terms of refining the program I developed." He looked beyond her, focused on the framed comic book on the wall, a furrow creasing his brow. "I created this program to save lives. I won't stand idly by and shrug when things go bad." He pushed away from the counter and pinned Georgia with a challenging stare. "And I sure as fuck am not going to let someone use my program to justify dangerous operations that should never have been given the green light in the first place."

"And you think someone's doing that? Using your program to deploy assets into situations that would otherwise never be authorized?"

"Not sure. Hence the hacking," he said with a smug little grin. "But you can bet your ass if they are, I'm going to find out about it," Parker said.

"You think that's what Ethan's looking into?"

Surprise flickered across Parker's face. "What do you mean?"

So Ethan hadn't said anything to Parker. Interesting.

"Just that he mentioned you had some concerns he was beginning to share." She shrugged. "Said someone from the DoJ had reached out, shared some 'disturbing rumors.' He wouldn't give me details."

"That sounds like Ethan."

"Yeah, he's not exactly the caring and sharing type."

"If you believe that, you don't know him very well."

Georgia smothered a laugh. "Right. Ethan tells you everything. And hacking classified files is just your weekend hobby."

Parker rolled his eyes. "Not that part. Ethan's terse, by the book, and plays things annoyingly close to the vest. But I've never met anyone who cares as much about the people he works with as Ethan does. There's nothing he wouldn't do to—"

"Except break the rules, right?" Or tell the truth or give Georgia the answers she needed.

Parker's face softened. "Whatever he's not telling you, I'm sure he has his reasons. I'm sure he thinks it's what's best."

There'd been plenty of people in Georgia's life who'd thought they knew what was best for her. All six of her social workers. Isaac. Ethan. The only one who'd ever had the right of it was Will, and he was dead.

"And for what it's worth? Yeah, under the right circumstances, Ethan would break every rule known to man to do the right thing." Parker grinned. "In the meantime, he's got me. And I'm far less concerned with the rules. I take what I need, refine my program, keep an eye on operations I'm not told about. And every so often a certain someone pretends he wasn't aware I was doing it all along, slaps me on the wrist." Parker shrugged and wandered toward the hall, stretching his arms high over his head.

"It's sort of like that kiss we shared. We both know it happened, we both know it's most likely going to happen again, but for some asinine reason we're going to pretend otherwise."

"Strictly a onetime thing," Georgia assured him, some of her irritation falling away as she watched Parker walk out. Those shorts really did leave little to the imagination.

"Well, if you want to have another 'strictly onetime thing,' I'll be in the shower." He waved as he disappeared through a door.

"Not even if you begged," she yelled as he slammed the door behind him. Despite herself, Georgia smiled. She liked the guy, but somehow she doubted an exhaustive roll in the sheets—and she was absolutely certain Parker would be nothing less than thorough—was what Ethan had in mind when he'd told her to "make a connection." And even if she were willing to lob a Parker-shaped grenade at what was left of her career, Georgia couldn't afford the distraction. Because despite Parker's dismissive explanation, Georgia knew Ethan. He didn't do anything without purpose. He'd sent her here for a reason.

There've been some . . . disturbing . . . rumors. Abuses. Corruption. Things I can't—I won't—ignore.

For the first time, Georgia wondered if she really wanted to know just what the hell was going on.

Georgia stood at the huge, multipaned windows that dominated the far wall of Parker's loft. Nearly floor-to-ceiling, they stretched ten feet high and ran the entire length of his living room. Standing a mere foot from the glass, she shivered. While beautiful in the way they subtly warped and waved, the thin panes did little for insulation—or security. She wasn't certain, but the windows didn't appear to have any sort of privacy film, which basically rendered Parker's loft a glorified fishbowl—and a security nightmare. At least the combination of being on the top floor and facing the water presented a logistical challenge to anyone looking to pop off a round or two through the windows. Small mercies, she supposed. Though at the moment, it hardly mattered. What had begun as fat, wet flakes of snow had given way to a driving storm that sliced through the air at an angry angle, as if hell-bent on wiping Baltimore off the map entirely.

The weather trapping them inside wouldn't be nearly so irritating but for the fact that Georgia had opened Parker's refrigerator, determined to put something other than caffeine and sugar into his system once he got out of the shower, and discovered a veritable wasteland of bio-hazards and empty calories. She'd hoped for eggs, maybe a few veggies. Her culinary skills were limited, but an omelet or two was within her power. Ha. Bobby Flay himself couldn't produce something edible from a twelve-pack of Mountain Dew, an old hunk of Parmesan, a week-old pizza, and a sealed casserole dish she wasn't touching for love or money. The freezer had yielded a box of Bagel Bites and two different kinds of vodka. The cabinets had been little better, stocked full of chips, boxed macaroni—which she couldn't even make do with, as Parker didn't have milk or butter—and a half dozen varieties of snack-size candy bars.

She'd thought her fridge screamed single and lonely, but Parker's took it to a whole other level—one reminiscent of her years spent with Will. The scent of warming bite-size pizzas had tossed her back in time, back to when money had been tighter than the trigger on a rebuilt Colt M1911, frozen dinners a delicacy, and paying all the bills in a single month a victory. She'd had so little . . . and been so happy.

But now the memories were edged with sadness, the Bagel Bites were giving her indigestion, the vodka was calling her name—and it was only midafternoon into the first day of a seventy-two-hour shift. At least she'd found a fresh pack of Twizzlers beneath the stack of takeout menus. She'd rolled her eyes when Parker had suggested they order in. As if anyone was delivering in this weather.

Right on cue, her phone buzzed in her pocket.

She withdrew it, hoping it wasn't Isaac.

But just like the last three times she'd checked, it was.

We need to talk.

Talk. Sure. Because Isaac had done so much of that during their relationship. The Isaac Georgia had met in South America—the open, funny, charming guy who was interested in what she thought, what she liked, who she *was*—had disappeared behind a polished veneer of perfection and manners the minute he'd returned to DC and the influence of his family. Suddenly it was time to take his career to the next level—and his future seriously. It wasn't long after that it became clear Georgia had nothing to contribute to either.

Too brash. Too unrefined. Nothing about her fit among the glitz and glam of DC's elite. How many times had Isaac lamented her lack of feminine grace on the way home from a black-tie affair? Or complained about the assertive way she entered conversations with Washington's powerful? Or criticized her inability to choose the proper fork at a $2,500 benefit for world hunger? It had taken Georgia far too long to realize the Isaac she'd met in South America wasn't real. That he was every inch the blue-blooded, Ivy League–educated snob who liked his women beautiful, even-tempered, and deferential.

Except, on rare occasions, in bed. Then he liked Georgia just fine. At least until the sun came up and his senses returned. Then their relationship was, once again, ill-advised.

It had taken a depressingly long time for Georgia to realize that, at the end of the day, she amounted to little more than a walk on the wild side. An exotic distraction. The equivalent of the slutty waitress or flighty coed.

A laughable cliché.

A role that might not have hurt her so badly if she hadn't loved him so much.

Or had the pride to leave him sooner.

Her phone vibrated again.

Call me. Please. It's important.

Not a chance. She shoved her phone into her pocket.

Georgia turned her back to the window and let the cold seep through her clothes. "Do you hear that?" she asked. She swore something was beeping. High-pitched and consistent, at first she'd thought it was a fire alarm, but she'd checked them all and come no closer to pinpointing the noise. Parker, who'd been wrapped up in work at his desk on the other side of the room a few hours ago, ignored her. Again.

Bored out of her mind and praying Isaac would stop texting her already, Georgia shuffled over to the couch and fell into the leather cushion with a huff. She flipped on the television, turned the volume down, and watched as the local weather girl slipped and slid along a sidewalk downtown. Pulling a Twizzler out of the pack in her back pocket drew the other resident menace to the coffee table. PITA seemed determined to follow her around, glaring and generally informing her of his displeasure at her arrival. That, or the cat was demanding she accept her role as his opposable-thumbed servant gracefully. Apparently, bodyguards in the know brought tuna. Georgia's lack of bribe had placed her firmly on the beast's persona non grata list. The little bastard had tripped her—twice.

"You a Hunger Games fan or something?" she asked, tired of the sound of Parker's *click-click-click* against the keyboard. When he didn't respond, she snapped a Twizzler in half and lobbed it across the room at his head. If she took a little too much joy in the way it bounced off his cheek, well, surely no one could fault her.

"What?" he asked irritably, looking up from his computer for the first time in hours.

"I asked if you're a fan of the Hunger Games franchise."

"No." He looked confused for a moment, then picked up the licorice and shoved it in his mouth. "Why?"

"The cat's name. I figured that's where you got it."

Parker snorted out a laugh. "Hell no, those are his initials. You've spent a few hours with him; you going to tell me he's not a total pain in the ass?"

As the cat took a swipe at the Twizzler that Georgia was twirling between her fingers, she figured the fur ball had probably earned his name.

The beep came again, faster this time, if she wasn't mistaken. "You don't hear that?" she asked. "That beep?"

Parker tilted his head, clearly listening for the tone. "Nah. But I've got a lot of tech; something's almost always beeping to let me know it needs an update or a battery is winding down or something. Just tune it out."

Right, because she hadn't been trying to do that for the last thirty minutes.

"Where'd you get the fleabag?" Georgia asked. Ignoring the way the cat's ears went back, she pulled another Twizzler out of her pack, then handed it over when Parker left his desk to join her on the sofa and extended a hand.

"I don't know," he said, sliding his palm along the little bastard's back. "One morning I woke up, and there was this little warm and fuzzy pressed up against my warm and fuzzies."

Georgia smothered her grin. Why was she not surprised?

"I always assumed Ethan left him in my apartment—he was constantly telling me I needed companionship, something to keep me on a schedule of sorts." He shrugged. "No idea what he was thinking; I kill cacti."

"Cats are nocturnal and more or less self-sufficient." And could be creepy as fuck when they stared at you as if they knew all your most embarrassing secrets. "He should have gotten you a dog."

"Yeah, like I could keep a dog alive. PITA here's only lasted 'cause he bites my toes when he's hungry and occasionally scavenges milk out of my cereal bowl." Parker cocked his head and sat up straight, holding out a hand before Georgia could reply. "Oh wait," he said, standing. "I do hear that."

Georgia slunk down in her seat, folding her arms over her chest. Oh sure. An annoying beep he didn't hear. But the vibration of her phone, that he caught?

"That's my phone," she grumbled, ignoring it as it buzzed against her back pocket.

"You gonna answer it?"

"Nope."

"Secret admirer?"

"Hardly."

"Heartbroken ex?"

Georgia grimaced and snapped off the top of a Twizzler between her teeth. "No."

"Liar," Parker said, a Cheshire-cat smile splitting his face.

"Trust me, his heart's intact." He'd never let her get close enough to touch it, let alone break it.

"Then he's a moron."

Georgia glanced up, surprised at the matter-of-fact way Parker said it. Before she could recover, say something witty and snarky and put them back on even footing, a high-pitched beep cut the silence.

"*That,*" Georgia said, twisting away from Parker to track the noise. "Tell me you heard that. It's driving me nuts."

"It sounds sort of like the text alert on my phone," he replied, standing and wandering toward the kitchen. "Where did I leave it?" Parker moved things around, looking behind the coffee maker and in the cabinets. When he pulled open a drawer, the beep sounded again, a lot louder, at the same time he said, "Ha! With the sweetener packets."

Georgia watched as a frown descended, marring the triumphant smile. Something in his expression gave her pause. She set down the Twizzlers and stood from the couch.

"What is it?"

"A text." Parker read it again, almost as if he expected it to change. "I think it's from Ethan."

"You think?" Georgia walked into the kitchen, unable to ignore the way all the color had fled from Parker's face. "What's it say?"

He didn't respond, didn't look up from his phone. A line appeared, bisecting the space between his eyebrows.

"Parker?"

He looked up but didn't reply. Nor did he protest when she palmed the phone out of his hand. He turned, bracing his hands against the counter.

Georgia glanced at the screen and read the message from an unknown number.

01010010 01110101 01101110

"I don't understand what this means." The way a rigid line seized Parker's shoulders, coupled with the way he went completely, utterly still told her she wasn't going to like it. She hadn't known Parker long, but she knew him well enough to know that "still" wasn't a setting he had. Neither was silence. The guy was like electricity, a constant low hum in the background you got used to but missed the second it was switched off. No, something was seriously wrong. "Parker?"

"It's binary code."

Okay . . . "And?"

He turned from the counter and dragged his hands through his hair. "And it's a message—one only members of my unit are supposed to know." He shoved his fists beneath his armpits, as if trying to contain the need to fidget.

"What's the message, Parker?"

He stiffened, his expression a battle of disbelief and fear.

"Run."

CHAPTER FOUR

"What makes you think this is from Ethan?" Georgia demanded. "Parker, who else would know this code?"

He shook his head. "Just members of my unit."

"No one else?"

"No." He wanted to pace but settled for cracking his knuckles.

"It's an unknown number. You're sure this is from Ethan?"

Parker nodded. Only Ethan, or another member of his unit, would know to send that message. "But it's incomplete," he said. "The binary is the authentication, the way we know the message is from one of us. But there's supposed to be more—the name of a safe house or a meeting place. This doesn't make any sense." Ethan didn't do things half-assed. When it came to protocol, the man was worse than anal-retentive. He'd drilled these processes into the entire team until each of them could recite the procedures in his or her sleep. But this, this *wasn't* right. What the fuck was going on?

"We're leaving." Georgia strode out of the kitchen, heading immediately toward her messenger bag. "Now, Parker."

Parker followed along behind her. Something didn't feel right. "This doesn't make any sense," he said, catching up with Georgia. "This isn't like Ethan. He doesn't operate this way. This?" Parker asked, holding up his phone. "This isn't procedure. There's supposed to be more. Instructions. Locations. *Something.*" Parker shoved the phone into his back pocket and pushed his glasses up his nose. "In the event of a threat, SOP is to either go to the location specified or wait for Ethan to provide an escort."

"That may be standard operating procedure, but that's not what's happening, and I'm not taking any chances."

"What makes you so sure this is real?" he asked, pulling Georgia up short.

Georgia spared him a glance as she removed a handgun and holster from her bag. "If Ethan had wanted you to wait, would the message have said to run?"

"No."

Georgia nodded, slipping the shoulder holster on over her sweater and securing her sidearm.

"Maybe he got interrupted; maybe the storm interfered with cell service. I don't know and I don't care," she said as she shrugged her way into her coat. "Ethan is the only person who knows I'm here. He trusts me to get you to a safe location. So until we have reason to believe otherwise, we're going to assume there's a verified threat. We're leaving. Put on a pair of boots and grab a coat." She stared him down when he didn't move. "This isn't up for discussion, Parker. Ethan said go, so we go."

"I just . . ." His thoughts were running in chaotic circles. There was only one reason he could think of that explained why Ethan would deviate from protocol. "Ethan's in trouble; it's the only thing that makes sense." Sweat prickled at the back of his neck. "If his phone is still on, I can ping it, get a location."

"Absolutely not." Georgia started down the hallway toward his bedroom. "You need a coat, gloves, boots. Now. We've got to go before the weather gets any worse."

"We need to think this through; something's not right." Parker followed her into his bedroom, ignoring the way PITA wound through his legs, chattering at him. "That was a group text; I could at least reach out to someone else on the team, see if anyone knows what's going on."

"If they're smart, they've already done as the message instructed. There's no time to talk about this, Parker."

"Then make time!" He grabbed Georgia by the elbow and jerked her to a halt. "I don't do this. I don't make snap decisions, work with partial information. I'm not a field agent!" Experience had taught him, more than once, that when he acted on partial intel, when he was forced to wing it, to make a best guess, things went horribly, tragically wrong. When he didn't have all the facts, when he couldn't see the big picture, people died. He wasn't a trained operator. Had no experience in the real world. He needed to think it through. He needed time. No one on his team could die. Not because of him and not for him. He needed to force everything to make sense. Ethan couldn't mean for them to leave the loft, to head out in the middle of a severe snowstorm. He just couldn't. "I can figure this out."

"Hey." Georgia shrugged out of his grip and grasped his wrist, her palm warm against his skin. "There will be time for that. I'm not asking you to make any decisions. That's my job." She shook him gently until he met her gaze. "Right now, it doesn't need to make sense. We aren't in your world; this isn't a tactical operation. There's no room for plans and contingencies. We don't have to know why." The lines around her eyes softened, anger and frustration releasing their hold on her face. "All you need to do is listen to what I tell you. This is my job, Parker, and I'm good at it. I need you to trust me," she said, her grip tightening around his wrist. "Can you do that?"

Georgia watched him, a practiced expression on her face. Patience, it seemed, didn't come naturally to her. But she was trying. For him.

He felt like a moth, pinned to a board but fighting for flight anyway. Could he trust her? Someone he'd known only hours? It was one more thing he didn't understand, couldn't analyze or quantify, but he knew the woman standing next to him, who owned a tactical situation and blackmailed him with coffee, was worth trusting.

"I can do that." He took a deep, fortifying breath, pushing back the questions crowding out his thoughts.

"Just take one thing at a time," Georgia coached him. "Boots, sweater, coat. Go."

Parker nodded, sat on the edge of his bed, slipped on a thick pair of wool socks, and shoved his feet into his boots.

Georgia stood by the door, watching him the entire time. As he settled into the simple task of pulling a thermal on over his T-shirt, and then a hooded sweatshirt over that, his thoughts started to slow and reorganize themselves into something that felt familiar. If he was going to do this, he was going to do it right. "We need to grab my laptop before we go."

"We'll power off our phones before we leave, but otherwise we're not taking any electronics."

"I at least need to remove the hard drive. There's too much sensitive information on there. If this—whatever it is—is legitimate, that's what's most valuable. I won't leave it here for anyone to find."

Georgia considered him before saying, "Okay. We'll grab it. You can remove the hard drive in the car, and we'll ditch the rest."

"Fine." PITA jumped up on the bed, rubbing against his thigh. "Shit, what am I supposed to do with him?"

"Unless he's a secret government experiment I don't know about, he stays."

Parker opened his mouth, but Georgia cut him off. "He's got a full bowl of kibble, cable TV, and heated air. He stays."

"I was just going to say I could drop him off at my neighbor's. She watches him when I'm traveling," he grumbled as he snatched his black peacoat off the chair by the door.

"He'll be fine, Parker." She stood to the side, motioning to the door. "Let's get going. The sooner we're out of here, the sooner we can figure out what the hell is going on."

He stepped out of his room, shouldering his backpack and reassuring himself he was doing the right thing.

"Move!" Georgia shouted, slamming him into the wall as a muted *pop pop*, not unlike the sound of a car backfiring on the street below, filled the loft.

Driven to his knees, Parker barely registered the sound of the mirror at the end of the hall behind him shattering.

"Stay down!"

Before he could think to gain his feet, Georgia was pushing ahead of him, charging the gunman with an angry yell.

Heart hammering, Georgia didn't spare a second to think. She shouldered Parker to the side, using her body to block him. In the span of a heartbeat, she assessed the situation. Scant feet separated her from the masked gunman—she'd be dead before she could unholster her weapon. With no room to maneuver, Georgia did what she did best and threw herself headlong into the fight, shouting instructions at Parker and ignoring the way the skin along her ribs sang with fire.

Keeping her center of gravity low, she dropped her shoulder and plowed her way into the man blocking the hallway. Hitting him with all the momentum she'd managed to generate in the tiny space, she caught him by surprise and smashed him into the wall. Before he could recover from the hit, Georgia grabbed for his gun hand, slammed it into the wall, and drove a knee into the bastard's balls. He doubled over with a wheeze, his grip loosening for a fraction of a second. Taking advantage, Georgia knocked the gun from his hand and kicked it down the hall and back toward Parker, whom she could see standing stock-still in her peripheral vision.

"Parker, go!" A blow to her ribs caught her by surprise, forcing the air from her lungs and setting her side on fire. Shit. Either she'd just clipped him, or her attacker had balls of steel. Lucky her. In the space of a breath, he was up, his arms around her waist and driving her into the wall behind her. Black spots danced behind her eyes as she fought for air. Hands gripped her neck, squeezing until taking a breath was next to impossible.

She stopped fighting, shoved her hands up between his arms, and drove her thumbs into the fleshy part of his eyes and digging in until he swore. His choices were easy—she was nice like that—let go or go blind. Personally, she'd just as soon drive her thumbs straight through to his brain, but apparently the bastard liked being able to see. He took two stuttering steps back, then grabbed one of her wrists, pulled her toward him, and drove her face-first into the wall. She managed to turn her head just enough to avoid breaking her nose but not enough to evade taking the brunt of the blow against the ridge of her eyebrow.

Son of a bitch.

A knee connected with her ribs, once, twice. Brutal. Unforgiving. Designed for maximum pain and complete incapacitation. The fourth strike drove the breath from her lungs, her exhalation raw and hot—like choking on seawater. The fifth tore her pride to shreds and drove her to her knees.

"Bitch," he spat as he straightened and turned toward Parker.

Parker. Charming, quirky, doomed-to-drive-her-crazy Parker. The son of a bitch would *kill* him.

Get up, Georgia. Move.

She struggled to her knees, choking on her despair, on her fear that this time she'd be made to *watch* as someone in her life died. Well, fuck that. Determination flooded her, washing away the fatigue, the pain, and leaving behind the shiny patina of the certainty that Parker would. Not. Die. Not on her watch—not while there was something, anything, she could do about it. She lunged, catching the man around his knees and pulling him to the floor with her. He'd thought her weak. Beaten. *Yeah,* she thought as she grasped the back of his ski mask and slammed his face into the stained concrete, *that was your first mistake.* His second was assuming that just because he'd put her on the floor, she'd stay there.

She pushed herself to her knees, trying to move back, to gain enough room to finally draw her sidearm. Before she could take a half step, he pushed to his hands and knees, twisted, and laid a vicious backhand against her cheek, splitting her lip in the process. Driven to her ass, he was on her in seconds, pushing her to the floor and scrabbling for her holster, trying to work the tricky clasp she'd spent hours and hours learning to work until it was effortless. Second nature.

Twisting, Georgia got a boot-clad foot on his hip and pushed, twisting him off-center and knocking him off-balance. As he fell forward, she used all her energy and drove her head up, clipping his chin so hard she heard the snap of his jaw. He reeled, his blue eyes stark and striking in the otherwise sea of black. Her victory was short-lived. She'd landed a blow, but he'd come away with her gun.

She crab-walked backward on hands and knees, breath coming in short, ragged gasps, blood trickling down her chin.

She was out of space. Out of moves. Out of time.

She stared down the barrel of her own semiautomatic, unwilling and unable to believe she was about to be murdered by her own weapon. It was downright pathetic and completely unworthy of the marine she'd been, not to mention the woman she was.

Still, she couldn't repress the flinch that escaped her when two shots sounded in the hallway.

Braced for pain, surprise seized her instead as the man above her crumpled, falling forward and pinning her legs to the floor.

Georgia looked up into Parker's wide-eyed stare. His arm trembled as he stared at the guy he'd just shot, a look of stunned disbelief stealing across his face.

Georgia scrambled out from beneath the weight of her assailant, snatched up her gun, and stood. Carefully, she used her boot to push the gunman to his back. His eyes, blue and hard as polar ice, were open and vacant. She went to a knee and, with a trembling hand, checked for a pulse.

Nothing. She heaved out a sigh. Thank God it was over.

"Georgia?" The sound of her name, unsure and shaky, had her pushing to her feet and turning toward Parker. She used the back of a sleeve to wipe the blood from her chin.

"It's okay." She glanced up at him, caught the way he couldn't stop staring at the dead man on the floor, the way the arm holding the gun at his side trembled, and immediately made her way over to him. "Let me have this," she coaxed as she laced her fingers through his and slid the gun from his slack grip.

"Is he . . . ?" He swallowed audibly, leaning against the wall. He visibly collected himself, forced his body to go stiff and still. "Did I kill him?"

"Yes." There wasn't time for soft deliveries or careful truths. She needed Parker's head in the game.

Parker twisted his neck, his gaze landing on the prone body. "I've never . . ." He swallowed and dropped his head, his skin going sheet white. "I thought it would be different. Harder."

Georgia dropped a hand on his shoulder, doing her best to ignore the way tiny tremors met her fingers. "Hey."

Parker looked away from the man he'd killed but didn't meet her gaze. "I've made decisions, hard ones. Ones that have led to death, some planned, some not," he admitted on a whisper. "I guess I always thought this would be the same. It should be the same. I still own the responsibility." He looked at her, his blue eyes a warm reminder as they searched her face that he was still alive.

Heaven help her, she intended to keep him that way. "It shouldn't be that different. Pull of a trigger, stroke of a key. The end result is the same."

He swallowed hard and looked away. "It shouldn't be different."

"But it is." She slid her hand across his shoulder and let it come to rest against the warm skin of his neck, delighted in the way goose bumps rose and his eyes dilated at her touch. For a moment, she allowed herself the solace of enjoying the steady, slightly elevated beat of his heart. Let the pulse beneath her fingers remind her of what was important. He was alive—they both were—and that was all that mattered. "I can feel your thoughts racing," she said, lightly stroking her fingertips along his neck, following the corded muscle down until she could stroke a thumb back and forth across his collarbone. "If you chase them, looking for answers, looking for sense in this . . . they'll drive you in circles until you second-guess everything that just happened. Until you convince yourself you could have, should have, done something more. Something different." She clenched his shoulder. "You did exactly what you had to do. Nothing more and nothing less."

"He's dead, Georgia." He focused on her, admitting out loud what she knew was tearing him up.

"Yes," she agreed. "And if you focus on that, if you let the thought take root and grow, it will consume you until it becomes the poisonous voice in your head, the one that whispers you didn't do enough, you weren't fast enough or good enough. That you are wrong and guilty and bad."

"How am I supposed to stop that? He's dead because of *me*." He shuddered.

"Because whenever that happens, you're going to look at me." She dragged her hand down across his shoulder and over his biceps. "You're going to look at me, and you're going to remind that vicious internal voice that the important thing isn't that you killed him . . . It's that you *saved* me." Georgia dropped her hand and stepped back. "That's what you focus on, because that's what you did. We didn't start this fight, Parker. We didn't break into his house and threaten his life. All we did—all *you* did—was defend yourself and save my life. That's it, that's all that's important. Okay?"

He stared at her for a long moment, then shook off the fear, the shock, and straightened. "Okay."

"We need to get out of here." Georgia set the assassin's weapon next to his body and began searching his pockets.

"What are you doing?"

"Looking for ID." She came up empty. She hadn't really expected anything—whoever the guy was, he hadn't been hired off the street. He'd worked her over like a pro—he was trained, probably military, which frankly scared the shit out of her. "Grab my phone out of my bag—I dropped it by the door—then go get your laptop. We're walking out of here in sixty seconds."

For once, he didn't argue or question. He just moved. Retrieving her phone, he handed it to her, then disappeared down the hall to grab his computer.

Georgia took a deep, steadying breath, then pulled the ski mask up and off the guy's face. She wasn't sure what she'd expected. He was just so normal, so forgettable. Military buzz cut. Cleft in his chin. Small scar bisecting his eyebrow. If she'd passed him on the street or met him at a bar, she'd have dismissed him. She'd expected something . . . more, though what exactly, she couldn't say. Raising her phone, Georgia took a half dozen quick photos. She didn't know who the guy was, but with any luck she and Parker would connect with Ethan in the next twenty-four hours. Maybe he'd have more intel on him—at the least, Ethan should be able to run the photos through a facial-recognition program. One thing was for sure: someone wanted Parker dead.

"Jesus."

Georgia glanced up as Parker reappeared, beanie on his head and backpack slung across his shoulder. Any color he'd regained fled his face.

"What?" This wasn't the shock of stripping away the mask and revealing the person. This was something deeper. Something far more personal. "Parker, what is it?" A curdle of dread formed in the pit of her stomach as Parker stared transfixed at the dead man in the middle of his hallway.

"I *know* him."

"What do you mean you *know* him?" Georgia shot to her feet and took two quick steps around the body.

Parker had to crane his neck to glance around her, to make certain the stress, the sheer impossibility of the last half an hour wasn't sending him down an acid trip from hell. No, he knew that face. Gordon Fletcher. How many times had Parker seen him at the office? How many times had he swaggered into tech ops, demanding this or dictating that, his smug smile accentuating the cleft in his chin and turning him into the oh-so-familiar frat-boy douche some men never grew out of? Alive or dead, Parker would know the man on his floor anywhere.

"That's Gordon Fletcher. I work—worked—with him."

"Shit."

Yeah, that about summed it up for him, too. It had all seemed so surreal. Ethan's text. Georgia's urgency. The dead guy in the hallway. Too much like a bad dream after a thirty-six-hour coding binge. Everything had felt so disjointed. Fictional. Parker was the guy who analyzed, planned, and executed—and all from the relative safety of an off-book government facility in Virginia. Now, a familiar face had accomplished what Ethan, Georgia, adrenaline, and the sick realization he'd killed someone had not. Parker's thoughts slid into perfect, organized alignment.

"Gordon was competent and a bit of an asshole—"

"A bit?" Georgia choked on a strangled laugh that tinged on the side of hysterical. Given the way she cut off the sound, straightened her spine, and settled into herself, she must have heard it, too.

"Point is, he's not the type to go freelance. Too many variables, too much risk. He liked the easy missions, the guaranteed paydays." He turned and strode down the hallway, pulling off a glove and shoving it in his pocket. "The only reason he's dead on my floor is because someone I know, someone I work with, sent him to kill me."

"You're sure?"

Parker nodded. Nothing about this had made any sense—until now. He didn't have all the details, but this one thing he *knew*. He'd run every single person who worked in and around the cyber warfare unit through his predictive analysis program. He knew Gordon, what he was capable of, what motivated him. "I'm sure."

He entered a security code into a panel on the wall and opened the hall closet across from the kitchen. Placing his palm along the built-in scanner, he waited for the beep, then logged into his personal security system. Glancing over his shoulder, he said, "How certain are you that Ethan is the only person who knows you're here?"

"Not as certain as I'd like to be. But like I said, I was a last-minute assignment, and Ethan plays things pretty close to the vest on a normal day." She shrugged. "Given how the last thirty minutes have played out, I'd say he had a pretty damn good reason to be concerned. Why?"

"Because right now you're about the only advantage I have." He entered in a series of commands, then confirmed his instructions. "I'm erasing the footage from the last twenty-four hours," he said as he slammed the door shut. "The longer we can keep whoever is trying to kill me in the dark about who you are, the better." He slid his phone out of the inside pocket of his peacoat. "Power off your phone and anything else electronic you've got on you."

Georgia did as he asked but stepped in front of him when he reached for the front door. "Me first."

He didn't argue.

She unholstered her gun and slowly slid the industrial door open wide enough for her to scan the hallway. "All clear, but let's take the stairs."

"Agreed." He followed her to the end of the hall, then through a door that led to an emergency staircase. The first frigid bite of cold in the unregulated space clenched the muscles along his spine.

"Does this let out in the garage?" Georgia asked as she descended the stairs, her gun at her side as she carefully scanned each floor below.

"Yeah, but we'll need to take your car. Mine's got in-dash nav and a tracking system the DoD insisted on."

Georgia swore as they reached the fourth floor. "I didn't bring my car. I took the train, then an Uber." She shrugged at his groan. "I don't really like driving in the city, especially to and from DC."

"Well, we can't risk my car, and even if we wanted to, we aren't going to find an Uber in this weather."

"So what does that leave?" she asked as they reached the ground floor. "We could go to my apartment, but we can't really be sure that no one knows I'm with you. Once they do, it's the first place they'll look. We could try one of Somerton Security's safe houses; there are several in the DC metro."

"Risky. Ethan's message didn't follow protocol, didn't tell us where to go. We don't know if he's been compromised or not, and if, by extension, Somerton Security has been compromised, too."

"Okay." Georgia turned toward him, gun at her side, and visibly fought a shiver. "But if we can't risk using our phones, then how do we make contact with Ethan? The safe houses will have some basics. Cash, heat, and, most importantly, a burner phone Ethan should have contact information for. We need to get somewhere safe, but then we've got to figure out what the hell is going on. The longer we're in the dark, the more danger we're in."

"Yeah, but assuming Ethan is free to reach out—" Parker swallowed. Ethan was his lifeline, his safety net for shit like this. If he couldn't make contact . . . No. Parker pushed the thoughts away. He couldn't deal with them—not yet. Maybe not ever. "Assuming Ethan can reach out, I don't think he'll use the phone. Our team has other procedures in place." He tugged at the brim of his hat, then stuffed his fists in his armpits. Fuck, it was cold, which meant outside was going to be bone-breakingly bitter. "The few times I've traveled overseas for ops, we've always had an established protocol. In the event a member of the team gets separated, or if we all have to scatter, there's a half dozen or so message boards we're supposed to monitor. Instructions for meet up or extract are supposed to come within twenty-four hours. That's how Ethan will make contact. Until then, I think we should stay away from anything expected or routine."

Parker watched as the struggle between the sense of his logic and the pull of her training played out across Georgia's expression.

"You're sure someone in the DoD is behind this?" she asked, though certainty drew the planes of her face tight.

"Yes." It was the only damn thing he was certain about.

"Okay. No safe house. How much cash do you have on you?"

"Couple hundred, maybe. You?"

She shook her head. "Don't carry cash."

He opened his mouth, then snapped it shut. It really wasn't the time to lecture her on how easy it was to hack a credit card or bank account.

She palmed the watch at her wrist, twisting it in a nervous habit he was coming to recognize as something she did when weighing a decision. "It'll be enough for a night or two at a cheap motel—but not more. If Ethan hasn't made contact in twenty-four hours, we're going to have to figure something else out." She crossed her arms, a wince creasing her forehead. That cold was going to be hell on the bruises blooming beneath the delicate skin of her face—and that was only the damage he could see.

He resisted the urge to run a thumb along the welt above her eye. She'd taken a beating. For him.

He shook himself out of his distraction. "MARC is still running. We can take that into DC, then transfer to the Metro and find somewhere to stay for the night."

"What makes you think the rail's still up?"

"I get mobile alerts on my phone. I'd have seen a notice it was down when I powered it off." He tried to crack his knuckles through the thick fabric of his gloves, then gave up. "But who knows how long that'll last. We should get moving."

Georgia leaned into the heavy outer door, pushing against the bitter wind. She scanned the open area behind his building, then pulled her head back inside. "You're sure about this?"

Yes. No. Mostly. Indecision seeped in with the bitter cold, freezing his nerve and raising doubts. This wasn't his area of expertise. He didn't know what the best option was. *But you know what the worst options are; sometimes that's good enough.*

"Yeah. We give Ethan twenty-four hours to make contact. Lay low until then."

"Then let's go." She pushed her way through the door and out into the open. Parker followed, the wind catching the door and slamming it shut behind him. As the wind kicked through his layers like a knife through his ribs, he prayed to God this wasn't the one time the universe decided to prove him wrong.

CHAPTER FIVE

"Let me help," Parker said, reaching for the key to the motel room.

Georgia jerked away, ignoring the way every nerve ending in her body screamed to life simultaneously. The damn door was stuck, not technologically complex.

"I got it." She turned the knob and threw her shoulder into the door—God, she took stupid and stubborn to new heights when she was tired—and stifled a gasp as she stumbled into the room, Parker close at her heels. Flipping the switch by the door, Georgia swallowed down a lump of disappointment as a single overhead bulb flickered to life.

"Well, this is cozy." A hint of a grin slid through Parker's voice.

When they'd selected the Starlite Inn, Georgia had adjusted her expectations from clean and comfortable to safe and secure. When the toothless clerk behind the bulletproof glass had smiled and asked if she'd need the room for an hour or an overnight, she'd repressed a shudder and readjusted her expectations from safe and secure to warm and undisclosed. She allowed her expectations to slip another notch or two as the radiator gurgled a dirge from the far wall. If she caught a tepid shower, a few hours of sleep, and avoided bedbugs, she'd score the night as a win and be grateful.

"Can I take that?" Parker reached toward the messenger bag still slung across her shoulder, his movements and expression careful.

"It's fine." I'm *fine*, she thought, letting her bag slide from her shoulder to crash to the floor. *So stop asking.* Leaving it where it lay, she dumped the convenience-store bag on the table and contemplated sinking into one of the two burnt-orange chairs flanking the small table in the corner of the room. Of course, odds were if she gave in to the urge to drop into the scratchy fabric calling her name, she'd never get back up. "Lock the dead bolt and set the chain."

Georgia rooted through the contents of the bag spread across the scarred wooden surface. Cheetos, beef jerky, a few bottles of water, a couple of candy bars, and the makings of a basic first aid kit. She repressed the urge to sneer. She'd passed starving hours ago and now clung to the cliff face of too-exhausted-to-give-a-damn by her fingernails. Had it really only been earlier that afternoon Ethan had called her to Baltimore? In less than eight hours, she'd gone on the run, been shot at, beaten to hell, dropped in a bad part of town in the middle of a blizzard, and called a bitch. She was cranky, dammit, and who could blame her?

And through it all, Parker had remained quiet, almost as if he were in a state of suspended animation, going where she told him, doing as she asked. No complaints. Little commentary. A model client. And so completely fabricated and unnatural that Georgia found herself struggling with the urge to snap him out of it. Violently. Creatively. She didn't care. At first she'd blamed good old-fashioned shock for Parker's docile obedience and lack of ongoing chatter. That maybe he just needed a bit of time, a little quiet to sort through everything. Or a strong cup of coffee. Either way, who could blame him? He'd shot a man—a man he apparently knew—and fled his home. But as the afternoon had worn on, as they'd changed trains and directions, losing themselves in DC and scavenging what they could from the only open store they could find, it had become abundantly clear Parker was coddling her.

As if he didn't believe she could take care of herself. As if he believed her *weak*.

She wasn't. Hadn't been in years. Had vowed she never would be again. One of the few lessons from her youth she hadn't needed to learn more than once. Weakness was exploited. Every time.

And Parker's coddling was a constant condemnation, a relentless reminder that but for his interference, Georgia would be dead. That when it came down to it, she'd needed the rescue.

"You okay?" Parker asked quietly as he sank onto the edge of the single—because of course there weren't any doubles available—queen-size bed.

She didn't turn toward him, the weight of his gaze slow and heavy with misplaced concern across her back. "Fine." She rolled her shoulders, wishing she could cast off Parker's worry as easily as she loosened the cold's grip on her muscles. She sighed. She just didn't have it in her to let Parker continue to fuss over her. To treat her as if she were fragile or broken or in need of protecting.

She wasn't.

And she resented that once again, doing her job had irrevocably changed the way a man saw her.

Only hours earlier, she'd reveled in the attention of a guy who, despite his genetic predisposition for chest-pounding and the general belief that he Tarzan she Jane, had found her—a marine better at marksmanship than makeup—attractive, not in spite of, but because of, her competence.

All blown to hell with a single hallway brawl. Parker's regard shouldn't matter—she'd spent a good portion of the last several hours trying to convince herself that it didn't—but the bottom line was that the only thing that hurt worse than her battered body was her bruised ego.

And really, she should have been prepared for the blow. Isaac's egotistical response to her saving his life had been annoying. Hurtful when he'd allowed it to come between them and ultimately used as one of the many reasons he ended their relationship. But Parker's careful handling, the way he treated her as if she were one stress point away from fracture—it rankled just as badly. She wasn't fragile, didn't need a soft touch or a constant reminder of how close she'd come to failure. How close she'd come to death.

God, but this job had screwed with her head.

What she needed was a hot shower, a handful of ibuprofen, and a soft mattress. Judging from the lumpy bedspread, she figured she might have to settle for two out of three. Palming a Snickers out of the pile of processed food, she weighed her options.

Knowing sleep wouldn't come easily, if at all, she put the candy bar in the pocket of her coat, lest she kill Parker for eating the only thing she considered edible; scooped the medical supplies back into the bag; and made for the bathroom. "I'm going to get cleaned up. Don't leave the room."

She closed the door on Parker's cloying concern. Slowly, as if the entire world were desperate to stand on her last remaining nerve, the door swung open. She pushed it shut on a sigh, waiting for the *click* of the catch. Satisfied she had at least some sort of barrier between her and the outside world, Georgia set to straightening herself out. First she'd deal with her ribs. If she had any energy left over, she could consider tackling her attitude.

Running the tap, she grabbed a hand towel and dumped it in the sink. She shrugged out of her coat, hanging it on the hook on the back of the door, and slowly pulled at the edges of her sweater. Every muscle was sore and stiff, but raising her arms above her head was sheer agony. As she slid the ruined sweater over her head, tears, unbidden and unwelcome, stung her eyes. Easy part done, she let the fabric drop to the linoleum and braced her hands against the cold porcelain of the sink.

Breathe, Georgia. Just breathe.

She watched water run into the basin, steam rising in hypnotic curls, and tried to focus through the pain. How the hell was she going to get her Henley off, let alone separate it from her skin? From the moment she'd felt the bullet graze her side, she'd dreaded this. The wound itself wouldn't be deep—she hadn't lost enough blood to impact more than her mood—but it would be raw and ragged. She'd managed to apply pressure without Parker's notice, but damn, her side burned and throbbed as if she'd stuck a Portuguese man-of-war against her skin rather than the sterile pads she'd fished out of the tiny first aid kit she kept in her bag. Over the last few hours, the pain had dulled to a low, angry throb—so long as she didn't move. Delicately, she ran her fingertips along the edge of her shirt, biting back a grimace. Yep, dried to her skin. *Awesome.*

"Holy shit, Georgia!"

Parker's startled exclamation had her tilting her head just far enough to see him out of the corner of her eye. Damn door must have swung open again after she hung up her coat.

"Get out," she grunted, turning from him to conceal the wound. He didn't need to see it. Didn't need to wonder if she was compromised, if she could still take care of them.

"You're bleeding." His voice went up an octave, and worry speared his brow as he strode into the bathroom, crowding them into a space not nearly big enough for one.

Georgia rolled her eyes. "I *was* bleeding. Now I'm standing here talking about it." She waved a hand toward the door. "I'll be out in a minute. Go do . . . whatever it is you do. Put the new SIM cards we bought in the phones."

"I already did."

"Then take apart the TV, design a rocket ship on a napkin, I don't care. Just . . . go."

She felt like a bug beneath a microscope, ready for dissection and discussion. Nothing good ever came from that kind of scrutiny.

In a move that should not have shocked her, Parker didn't leave. "You're bitchy when you're hurt and tired—hungry, too, I bet."

His lips quirked in a way that shouldn't charm her.

"Good thing we got you that Snickers."

"Which I'd love to eat, so if you could just . . ." She made another shooing motion with her hands. "I'll be done in a few minutes, and you can take a shower or whatever."

"Yeah, sure you will." He pulled his hoodie over his head, his T-shirt riding up with the movement and exposing a line of abdomen that promptly broke out in goose bumps. Tossing his sweatshirt through the door, he approached her. "Let me help."

Over her dead body. She went to take a step back, caught her knees on the toilet, and went down hard. Thankfully the universe's depraved sense of humor seemed to have cut her a break—the lid was down. Before she could stand, Parker was there, taking a knee and crowding her in.

"I'm fine. I'm just going to soak it a bit, then the rest should be easy," she protested, hiding the wound with the palm of her hand.

Parker regarded her for a long moment, studying her as if she were an interesting puzzle he couldn't quite put together.

"Tell you what," he said. "You raise your arms above your head, and I'll go back out there and disassemble the alarm clock."

"I said television."

"Yes, but I might want to watch cartoons later." He grinned. "Come on, Georgia, arms above your head and I'm out of your hair. Shouldn't be too hard. Most people do it every morning. So . . ." He placed his hands on her knees, the warmth of his skin slicing through her damp denim and warming her. "Wakey wakey, eggs and bakey."

She released a long sigh that might have, if she hadn't been so damn tired, aspired to be a laugh. She could raise her arms . . . if she absolutely had to. But they both knew it would be unnecessary agony. Despite every instinct that told her to take care of herself, to treat her own injuries, and to conceal anything that could be used against her, something in the way Parker squeezed her knee, in the way he teased instead of coaxed, put her at ease. As he stared at her, the bold blue of his eyes warm and steady, she let herself fall into his hands.

"Okay, then." He twisted, rose, and pulled the hand towel out of the sink. Turning off the water and wringing out the cloth, he said, "You'll be happy to know that while most of this place is a bargain-basement dump, the water heater is a total champ."

"Great. Dibs on first shower."

Parker knelt in front of her, fingering the edge of her shirt. "Maybe we can share."

As her mouth dropped open, a sharp retort on the tip of her tongue, he pressed the warm weight of the towel to her side, stealing any reply she might have made. Jerk.

"Just going to hold this here a second or two, let the water soak your shirt. In the meantime, feel free to join me in anticipating our shared shower shenanigans."

"Never gonna happen," Georgia said, breathing through the fresh wave of agony.

"Aw, now where's your imagination?" He pulled the towel away from her side, tossing it back into the sink behind him. "Give it a try." Gently, he pulled at the cotton around her wound, working the edges with a delicate patience she'd never have attributed to him. "Just think. It's steamy, and everything's wet. And why, yes, Georgia, water is rolling down my *eight*-pack."

"Now you're just delusional." She snorted. "The only eight-pack you've ever had was in your fridge."

"Sure about that, are you?" He grinned, mischief seizing his mouth and making his eyes sparkle. She wondered if she'd ever get used to the way he was all boyish playfulness one minute, then 100 percent focused intent the next. Charming. Devastating. Mischievous. Compelling. It was a well-choreographed dance, effortless and entirely unique to Parker. And damn but it made her want him to drop the towel and put his hands on her skin, his mouth on her lips.

So very dangerous, this man who knelt before her. She wondered if he even knew.

"All right, let's give this a shot." Slowly, and with nimble fingers that barely grazed her skin, he rolled up her shirt, coaxing and tugging the few pieces that stubbornly refused to loosen their hold. Finally, with far less pain than she'd envisioned, he helped her slide each arm out of the sleeves, lifted the shirt over her head, and discarded it.

"Oh, Georgia." The soft exhale of his sympathy tickled the newly exposed skin of her breasts. A flush of embarrassment crawled across her skin. She'd never planned to be half-naked with Parker—if she had, she certainly would have opted for more than the simple gray jersey of her T-shirt bra. She supposed it was fair, though, for Parker to see her this way. Stripped down, there was nothing flirty or feminine, sexy or seductive about her. Functional, yes. Boring, absolutely. Traits she was comfortable with and usually wore easily. But for Parker . . .

Inexplicably, when Parker looked at her, she wanted to be more. Alluring. Sexy. Can't-keep-his-hands-off tempting. Would she ever feel like she was enough? Would lessons learned in foster care, in Isaac's company, ever let her go? She pulled her arms up, fighting the urge to cover her chest. Parker caught her wrists.

"Shh." He brought her hands down to her lap. "Why didn't you say anything?"

Parker, she realized, was entirely focused on the gash at her side and the livid bruises blooming across her torso. Gentle fingers skated the edge of one the size of a grapefruit, eliciting a shiver.

"There wasn't time. And really," she said, her embarrassment easing, "nothing could have been done. I'll clean and bandage the gash, but the bruises will have to heal the old-fashioned way."

"You need stitches," he said, his voice hoarse. Shaking, he stood, wetting a fresh washcloth from the sink.

"Nah." She tried on a smile, hoping to cut the odd tension filling the room like a heavy cloud of steam. He was angry, but for the life of her she couldn't figure out why. "Nothing a Band-Aid or two can't fix." She smiled as he turned. "But if you want to kiss it and make it all better, go ahead."

"It's not funny, Georgia."

Well, no, it wasn't. But she could see he was winding himself into a first-rate fit, and over what? She'd had worse. "It's just a graze, Parker. A bit of antibiotic ointment, and I'll be fine." Provided she touched absolutely *nothing* in this roach motel, anyway.

"Just a graze?" He rounded on her, resuming his position between her legs. "He shot you, Georgia. *Shot* you." Agony destroyed his face as he set himself about the task of cleaning up her side. "He came for me, but he hurt *you*."

"Hey," she said, laying a palm against his forearm. She tried not to let the way his muscles, bunched and twitching with tension, distract her. "I'm okay. It's my *job* to get between you and the bullets." She stroked a finger along a ridge of muscle and up toward his elbow. "It could have been a lot worse, Parker. We got off easy."

"I don't consider this," he said, carefully dabbing at the cut, "getting off easy. It should have been me."

Georgia pulled away. Of course it should have been him. God forbid his fragile male pride suffer the indignity of being saved by a woman.

"Your ego will recover. And if it helps, remind yourself a woman didn't save you; your paid bodyguard did." She tried to stand, only to have Parker slap a hand on her shoulder and shove her back down.

"You think that's what this is?" he asked, anger lending a frenzied, jerking motion to his movements as he reached for the alcohol and sterile gauze. "Some antiquated antifeminist bullshit? You think my self-esteem is so low that I can't admit when a woman can kick my ass—or that I'm such a self-important prick I can't admit when she's saved it?"

Well, yeah.

"God, you're a stubborn creature." He sighed, letting the righteous indignation he wore so well slip away. "I'm mad because if I'd listened to you, if I hadn't been so busy thinking things through, analyzing every angle, you might not have been shot at all."

That was what was bothering him? Guilt? Concern? For *her*?

"It's all I've been able to think about this afternoon. That if I'd listened, if I'd moved when you told me to, if we'd left, you wouldn't be hurting and a man wouldn't be dead." He put a warm hand, still a little damp from the towel, against her cheek. Brushing aside a lock of hair, he said, "I'm *so* sorry."

Easily, as if the movement were natural to her, as if she could remember the last time someone had showed such concern for her, Georgia let her forehead come to rest against his. Breathing in the scent of warm laundry and sunny afternoons, she opened her eyes and stared into his. "It's okay, Parker. We're okay. You couldn't have known, and there's no guaranteeing how things *might* have played out."

He clenched his eyes shut, then leaned away, the muscles in his neck corded and bunched as if it were the most difficult thing he'd ever done. "Just . . . just let me take care of you, all right?"

At a loss, Georgia fought every instinct, every lesson that reminded her this was a bad idea. That allowing someone else to see her wounded, to see her weak, only led to trouble. She let herself nod, ignoring the way a shallow dip of her chin managed to send her stomach on a plunge worthy of the world's tallest roller coaster.

"This is probably going to sting a little," he said, soaking the gauze with alcohol. Carefully, his face pinched with regret, he pressed the pad to her side.

Biting back a moan, Georgia sank her fingers into Parker's shoulder, holding on and riding the burn as best she could, reminding herself to breathe. Finally, he pulled away the gauze, satisfied the wound was clean.

Cool, gentle air caressed her side, bathing the cut and shocking her far more thoroughly than the burn of alcohol. Gently, Parker dabbed ointment over the cut, blowing cool air to dull the sting the entire time.

A whimper tore from her throat even as her eyes stung. She'd taken cuffs to the head, endured the vicious posturing of group homes, weathered the brutal days following Will's death—all without any show of emotion. Tears, like dreams, were for the privacy of a bedroom and the silence of a pillow. But Parker's gentle fingers and quiet concern for her comfort utterly undid her.

He glanced up, his eyes going soft and sad behind his glasses. "Oh, honey, hasn't anyone ever taken care of you?"

Yes, she thought as emotion clogged her throat. Yes, there was a time when there'd been someone to kiss every scrape, to soothe every fear. And that was the problem. Remembering her parents, her mother's grace and gentle touch, her father's booming laugh and protective grip—it hurt. Hurt so much she did her level best to push away those memories, because the good memories, the ones of family, and certainty, and acceptance hurt so much more than the bad ones. Knowing she'd been loved—first by her parents, and then, in his own awkward, brotherly way, by Will, only reminded her of everything she'd lost.

Everything she'd never have again.

Parker didn't say anything, though his expression changed to something . . . odd. Something determined and stubborn as he taped a fresh square of gauze over the cut and stood, offering her a hand. "Probably best not to get it wet tonight."

"Probably," Georgia croaked around the unnamed emotion blocking her throat.

"I'll get you some ibuprofen and one of the bottles of water," he said, and for the first time she watched as he stepped back and took in the whole of her, his eyes lingering not on the bruises but on the rise and fall of her breasts. With effort, he pulled his eyes to her face. "I'll just . . . I'll just go get those for you."

As he turned, spontaneity and good old-fashioned want—God, did she *want*—had her reaching out, catching his hand.

He stopped, the effort it took to keep perfectly still bunching his shoulders.

"Thank you," she whispered.

Slowly, he stepped back, pivoting to face her. Scant inches separated them, exaggerating the difference in their height. Georgia tilted her head back, forcing herself to steady, to wait for his next move. Ages passed as she stood out in the open, exposed and vulnerable, her every breath loud in her ears.

Slowly, Parker brought a hand to her face, trailed the pad of a thumb across the goose egg on her brow.

On a breathy moan, part agony, part defeat, he laid his mouth to hers.

Why had he thought, for even a moment, he could touch her and not have her? From the second he'd laid hands on her, felt her tremble with hurt and confusion, he'd known he didn't have the strength to keep his distance. That he needed to have her beneath him, moaning and trembling for far more pleasurable purposes. Ignoring all the reasons it was a bad idea, he gave in to the temptation that had ridden him since she'd first stepped into his kitchen and tunneled his fingers through her hair. Her curls, wild and ravaged by winter, snared him, welcoming him into their depths and refusing to let go.

Wouldn't have it any other way.

He palmed the back of her skull, scraping his fingernails against her scalp as he tilted her head and used his mouth to open hers. He wanted to delve and dive, swoop and conquer, to plunder every inch of her until she felt him everywhere. Instead, he wrangled what restraint he had and kept his explorations tentative, his mouth a tease, as he backed her through the doorway, leading her from the harsh fluorescence of the bathroom and into the softer, warmer glow of the room beyond.

Immediately, options flooded his consciousness, a thousand scenarios flashing by in an instant, an infinite number of fantasies presenting themselves for his attention and inspection.

Too easily he could see Georgia splayed across the bed, naked and trembling. Bent over the table, wanton and waiting. So many options. So many possibilities. Every single one guaranteed to blow his mind. There'd be time, he told himself, scraping his stubble along Georgia's jaw, tilting her head until he could pull an unadorned earlobe into his mouth. Time to conquer. Time to claim and be claimed. Time enough to savor every gasp and elicit every response.

But not yet. What he wanted now was to seduce. To explore and map, with teeth, with tongue, with nimble fingers, until he rendered Georgia mute with desire, wet with want. Open to him in a way he doubted she shared with many. And then, with her trembling and needy, shameless and impatient, he wanted to *devastate* her. To snare the control he so admired and wipe it away until nothing stood between them. To take Georgia apart, bit by sexy bit, until all the pieces of her were spread before him. Then, he'd be ready. Then, he would claim.

He backed her against the wall, mindful of her injuries as he slid his fingers from her hair with a groan, then dragged them across the skin of her exposed shoulder. He followed with warm, open-mouthed kisses and backtracked when a spot made her shiver or goose bumps sprang across freshly heated flesh. When he reached the strap of her bra, he paused, let his fingers slide down her arm, then skate, light as air, across the arc of her breast. Palming the weight of her, he nipped at the strap, teeth scraping against flesh and cotton as her heart leaped against his palm.

Slowly, he pulled away enough to watch her face, to brush the hair from her cheek. Her irises, an ultrathin halo of brown, delighted him. The flush crawling across her neck and down her breasts called to him. He trailed a single finger along the soft skin above the cup of her bra, following the curve until his index finger came to rest against the clasp at the front.

"Parker." Half moan, half ragged gasp. All plea for more, more, *more*.

Smiling, he slipped his finger beneath the catch and pulled, the tiny *pop* of sound a brazen statement of things to come.

"I . . ." He pressed his thumb against the plump flesh of her lower lip, surprised and delighted when her tongue came out to meet it, and let his gaze fall. Her breasts, generous handfuls of smooth, pale skin, swayed with every indrawn breath. Slowly, because some moments were meant to be savored, imprinted to memory to last a lifetime, he brought his hand up, trailing the tips of his fingers along the underside of her before letting the fullness of her flesh sink into his palm. She sucked in a sharp breath, capturing her lower lip between her teeth.

He watched as the peak of her nipple, dusky pink and budding with interest, tightened for him. So sensitive, so responsive to even the softest touch. The memory of her shock as he'd blown across her cut seized him. He suspected she knew rough and tumble, fast and thorough. It was a language she spoke fluently and one he knew he wanted to have endless conversations in. But he didn't think she knew *this*. He blew across her nipple, reveled in the startled gasp and the suddenly firm peak. No, tenderness—a light, barely there touch, those she didn't know.

But she would. With him, she *would*.

"Parker." Her body went rigid against his, her back arching to his touch. "Parker, please."

Unable to resist such a pretty demand, he closed his mouth around her, flicking his tongue against the arousal he found and sucked a scream from her throat. Satisfied but not nearly done, he turned his attention to the other one and let his fingers trail down ribs, noting the dips and grooves that made her jump and writhe, cataloging the information away for later, until finally he found the waist of her jeans.

With impatient hands, he undid the button and tugged down the zipper. Her fingers slid into the hair at the nape of his neck, holding his mouth against her chest. He slid his hands up her back, letting the full weight of his palms pull her away from the wall until he could strip her of her bra. As the material slid off one arm, then the other, he trailed his mouth from peak to valley, taking a moment to breathe in the warm, rich scent of her before he continued lower, sliding his tongue across rigid lines of muscles, then taking a knee and dipping his tongue into the pool of her belly button.

"You don't . . . you don't have to," she panted as he slid her jeans down her thighs, pulling his stubbled chin across the ultrasensitive skin above her briefs.

"The hell I don't," he replied, nipping at the curve of her hip as he tugged off her boots. In the blink of an eye, only a thin slice of cotton concealed her from him. He cupped her in his hand, holding her against his palm as she tried to undulate her hips, to grind the core of her against him, every aborted move imploring him for more. Kissing the inside of her thigh, he pulled the material down and away, exposing the very heart of her.

Trembling, she turned her head to the side, as if unable to watch as he breathed her in. As if ashamed of her own want, her own need.

If it took a lifetime, he'd wipe away those thoughts, replace them with the confidence to demand what any man should be desperate to give. Sliding a hand up the back of her leg, he nipped at the inside of her thigh, following the sting with the scrape of his beard. She trembled, her weight sliding against the wall, her fingers grasping his arms. He gripped the back of her knee and hoisted her leg over his shoulder, exposing her to his every whim.

She froze, then tried to pull away, her breathing coming in sharp, jagged gasps. He ran a thumb up her seam and over the rich, wet curls he found there. He took a second to indulge in what was quickly becoming his favorite game and blew across the nub of her clit, delighting in the shudder that traveled all the way down her leg.

"Oh God." Her voice was tight and strained, thick with the desire for something he suspected she'd never had or asked for.

Time, then, to change that.

He smiled, letting her feel the curve of his lips against her throbbing flesh. With teeth and tongue, he set himself to exploring every inch—revisiting the spots that made her gasp and moan—then drank in his victory as she shouted and came.

Tears stung Georgia's eyes, a result of staring too long into the overhead light in the center of the room, she was sure. Panting, she let her head fall, and all at once, as if they'd only been waiting for permission, her muscles loosened and her body slipped precariously down the wall. Even as she thought her feet might go out from under her—and that she might not give a damn if they did—Parker was there, hoisting her until she wrapped both legs around his waist. As he strode toward the bed, she trailed her fingers along the sides of his face, tilting his head until she could press her mouth to his, let her lips convey her praise, her surprise, her gratitude. Never had sex been so revelatory. So powerful. In precious few minutes that had stretched like lifetimes, Parker had taught her what it was to yearn. And what it was to be satisfied.

As he dropped her on the edge of the bed, watching as gravity played with her breasts, she understood he wasn't finished. Not by a long shot.

Thank. God.

She slid back across the thin bedspread until she could recline on her elbows and appreciate the view. Too satiated to be self-conscious, she dragged her gaze down Parker's lean frame. "I'm feeling a bit under-dressed here, Parker."

"I don't mind." He quirked his mouth, his eyes sparkling with mischief as he let his gaze roam and linger in equal measure. His scrutiny was as visceral and physical as his hands, as thorough and talented as his tongue. A part of her wanted to squirm beneath his regard, certain in the knowledge she couldn't possibly be his type. Too many hard angles, too few womanly curves. She'd long ago given up possessing a body that turned men's heads and instead focused on possessing a physique that saved men's lives. Rarely had it bothered her with other partners, and though she wondered what Parker thought, if he found her wanting, she couldn't quite bring herself to care. Something she had him to thank for, no doubt.

"Yes, well, I do." She waved a hand in his direction. "It seems only fair. I've shown you mine . . ." She let the Cheshire-cat grin she'd been holding back curl her lips.

"All right," Parker said, gripping the hem of his T-shirt and pulling it over his head. When he stood before her, miles and miles of smooth, golden skin stretched upon a swimmer's frame, Georgia fought the urge to lick her lips.

"Now, let's see," he said, placing his hands on his hips and smiling down at her. "I believe I said something about an eight-pack."

Yes. Yes, he had. Something she'd chalked up to sheer bravado at the time. And though he couldn't claim to have the tight, packed-on muscles of some men, what he lacked in bulk he more than made up for in definition.

He trailed a finger in a serpentine pattern across his torso. "Two, four, six . . ." He paused, a smug grin curling his mouth as he popped the button on his jeans and tugged his waistband lower. "Eight. Who do you appreciate?" His grin transformed from playful boy next door, to sexy, to mischievous imp in the blink of an eye. "Parker." He canted his hips to the left, knocking his jeans down a notch. "Parker." Another cant, this time to the right. "Parkkkkeeerrrrrr." He dragged out the word, shimmying his hips back and forth until his pants fell around his ankles.

Delighted and incredulous that this man not only had the promised eight-pack but a charming, self-assured sense of humor to match, Georgia laughed. "You certainly don't suffer in the self-confidence department, do you?"

"Nope," he said, stepping out of his jeans and briefs, then crawling up the bed to meet her. "No self-esteem issues here." He laid his mouth against the hollow of her throat, licked a strip of skin as if he'd forgotten the taste of her, then blew a raspberry into her neck. When she jerked away on a chuckle that came dangerously close to being a giggle, he pulled her back, kissing her face as he skated deft fingers across all the grooves that made her jump and laugh.

"You know," she said between heaving breaths, "most men don't like it when women laugh at them in bed."

"Laughter should never be scorned or squandered," he said, settling over her, dragging the hard length of him in slow strokes over her abdomen. "There's far too little to go around, so you should seize it where you can."

"Even in bed?" Georgia asked, trailing fingers along the arm he had braced near her head.

"Especially in bed." He dropped a teasing kiss to the tip of her nose. "Even the best things in life can be made sweeter with a bit of fun. And sex? That's right up there with fresh coffee, warm doughnuts, and conquering level 127."

"Wait. Wait." She pushed him away, fought against the groan of disappointment as the heat of his body left hers. "Just where does sex rank on that list?"

He shrugged. "Somewhere between a third cup of coffee and level 128."

Oh, she was going to remove something important.

"Of course," he said on a slow slide that nudged his length against the throbbing, wet heat of her, "sex with you hasn't been fully assessed and ranked yet."

A sneaky hand slipped between her thighs, magic fingers parting her folds and sliding home with ease. Unbidden, her eyelids fell, and her hips rolled as a twist of his wrist brought his thumb to her throbbing clit. That fast, he brought her to the edge, his relentless momentum enough to have her wishing for the fast, hard fall, but not enough to send her over. Damn him.

Well, two could certainly play at that game.

Locking a leg behind his knee, she rolled her hips, using her body weight and Parker's surprise to flip their positions until *she* straddled *him*. She ignored the way her side pulled and complained—this was too important, too worth it, too once-in-a-lifetime amazing to let even a gunshot wound steal the smallest bit of the experience. She wanted to torment and tease to her heart's delight, so she dragged her seam across the length of him as she raked her nails across his chest.

Eyes that had held nothing but smug laughter a moment ago now blew wide with shock and lust.

"Time to level up." She grinned at the way he groaned beneath her, his fists clenching the sheets.

"I don't have . . ." He breathed deep and gripped her hip as if he'd come apart if she canted her hips just one more time. "I didn't think to bring anything."

Oh. Right. So caught up in the moment, in the push/pull of the game they were playing, condoms hadn't even occurred to her. It should have been sobering, the realization she was so far gone that her own safety, let alone his, hadn't even occurred to her. Usually she was hyper-vigilant, made sure her evenings were always planned for. Yet here she was, sitting astride a man who so thoroughly undid her that protection had never even entered her mind.

Insanity? Or something far more insidious? Something like trust.

Parker ran a trembling hand up her back. "We don't have to, Georgia."

Though he didn't say it, she understood what he was saying. *We don't have to have sex. You don't have to reciprocate.* And he meant it. She knew he did. If she rolled away from him now, which logic and instinct and a whole host of experience told her she should do, he'd say and do nothing to stop her.

Maybe that was why she found it so damn hard to do so.

"I'm covered, and I've never messed around without a condom. Ever," she quietly admitted.

"I'm clean, too." He caught the tip of her nipple with the pad of his index finger.

"Okay."

"Yeah?" he asked, his gaze meeting hers.

She nodded and leaned down to seal her mouth to his. She didn't know or care why, but she trusted Parker. Trusted he wouldn't put her at risk. Trusted that he wouldn't lie. Not about something so important. And dammit, just for once, she wanted to embrace the best of someone else and run with it.

As Parker's mouth opened beneath hers, his tongue darting out to welcome her, she shifted her hips and slid over him in one smooth motion. Georgia pulled back just enough to watch, rapt with fascination, as her torment played upon Parker's face.

A slow slide down brought a curse to his lips.

A teasing clench of muscles blew his pupils until only the thinnest band of blue remained.

A playful twist of her hips and she tore through what was left of his control. Without any of his previous caution and mindless of her injury, he reversed their positions, shocking her as he pushed her flat on her back, his thrusts hard and measured and without a doubt designed to drive her mad.

Lifting her legs, she wrapped her ankles around his back and used her heels to urge him on as she rode out wave after scorching wave of bliss. How was it that movement so harsh, so primal, could be so skilled and deliberate? It was as if every single inch of Parker were pressed against her in just the right way. No learning curve. No room for error. Parker loved her as if he'd been doing it his entire life.

Georgia couldn't fathom how she'd lived before the experience. Parker slid across her body, the heavy length of him filling her, ensuring no part of her, on any level, remained untouched. The scrape of his chest teased across nipples, hard and desperate for more than the tempting touch of his skin. Fingers gripped her hips, pulling her in closer, harder, deeper, until she wasn't sure how long she could last, how much she could take, only knowing she wanted more, more, more.

Finally, as his mouth captured hers for a too-brief kiss, Georgia felt the ground fall out from beneath her as her orgasm crested the edge of her control, drowning her to all but the most basic of sensations.

The heartbeat in her ears, her chest, her core.

The scrape and burn of stubble across her cheek and jaw.

The uttered promises, threats, and pleas against her ear.

The final possessive thrusts before heat and Parker and intimate dominion marked her in a way she'd never allowed.

Slowly, Parker withdrew, but he pulled her with him as he rolled to his back, tucking her to his side and notching her head beneath his chin.

Gentle fingers danced along her arm, skating across skin and raising tiny shivers along sensitized nerves.

"Definitely, *definitely* ranks higher than level 128."

Georgia smiled against the warm breadth of his chest. She'd need an hour, maybe two, then she'd see what she could do about replacing coffee as the number-one need in Parker's life.

A repetitive *plink, plink, zing* woke Georgia from a dreamless sleep. Stretching her legs until her toes curled, she breathed deep, then rolled to her side, bringing the thin motel sheet with her.

"I know you are *not* playing Jungle Gem after the best sex of your life."

Parker's face, backlit in the bluish glow of his smartphone, split into a wide grin.

"Best sex of my life? Pretty confident about that, are you?"

Bracing herself against her elbow, Georgia dropped her chin against her palm and walked her free fingers up Parker's cotton-clad thigh. It wasn't lost on her that for a long moment, as her fingers trailed up past the waistband of his underwear, he didn't breathe. "Oh yeah."

Parker dropped his phone to the nightstand, then leaned over her, catching a strand of hair with his thumb and forefinger. "You know damn well no one could hold a candle to you."

"Sweet words from the man caught fondling his phone in the middle of the night."

Parker rolled to his side, propping himself up on an elbow to mirror her pose. This close, even in the scant light sliding past the curtains, Georgia could see every detail of his face. Commit to memory the glint of stubble, the curve of his lower lip.

"Ethan made contact."

Stunned, Georgia took a moment to catch up. "What?"

"Yeah. He's set a meet for tomorrow—well, later today, I guess." Parker grinned. "I've been testing new levels of the app—everyone with the CWU has a test version on their phones. It's encrypted and still in beta—and it has a messaging feature we use to trade insults, smack talk, and the very rare game-related feedback. I'd hoped Ethan would remember we'd once joked it would make an excellent covert communication tool."

"And he did," Georgia said.

"He did." Parker nodded. "He wouldn't say much, not over a device, but he has answers."

Georgia rolled to her back and stared up at the ceiling. "Good." It *was* good news, she told herself. Great, even. She hated being in the dark, let alone in the dark and on the run, but . . . But she'd allowed herself to fall into a lull, a sexy, surprising, laughter-filled lull, with Parker. For a few precious hours, the outside world had ceased to exist. In this shitty motel, with threadbare sheets and too little heat, Georgia had allowed everything to fade away, allowed herself the rare luxury of true indulgence. She and Parker had created their own private, wonderful snow globe. The minute they met with Ethan, hell, the minute they set out, their glass bubble would shatter.

Swallowing around her disappointment and refusing the temptation to dwell on just what that meant, Georgia said, "That's great. If Ethan has answers, he'll have a path forward." Which, she had to admit, was a relief. Because as much as she wanted to fall into Parker, exist only in the tiny winter holiday they'd created for themselves, she didn't want to be responsible for his safety—not now that there was more than professional responsibility binding them together.

"Ready to get rid of me already?"

Yes.

No.

"You have no idea," she responded with a grin.

Truth was, there wasn't a clean answer to that. Did she want to stay wrapped up in Parker, enjoying his tactile attention and the easy chemistry between them? Revel in the way he looked at her, touched her, drew her so completely out of her reservations she forgot to be anything less than genuine with him? Hell yes. But that wasn't practical. They couldn't just pretend the last twelve hours hadn't happened. That there wasn't a dead guy in Parker's loft. That someone didn't want Parker eliminated.

So for the foreseeable future, Parker's safety had to be the priority. Which complicated things. Protecting a client in the moment was one thing—stepping in front of the knife, taking the bullet or the punch— all of those were easy, ingrained split-second decisions. But keeping someone alive while on the run with no idea who wanted them dead or how they'd earned the death warrant in the first place? No. No, that she wasn't equipped to handle. Especially not now that she'd come to know Parker. Know the kindness of his heart or the depth of his touch. Taking a bullet would be easy, but keeping him alive, constantly wondering if she would be smart enough, fast enough, strong enough? No.

"Your heart's racing," Parker said, sliding his warm palm against the soft skin at her breast. "It's because of me, isn't it?" he asked, his mouth transforming into something cocky she both wanted to punch and plunder.

Shoving the tumultuous thoughts aside, Georgia pushed his hand away. "Don't flatter yourself."

Undeterred, Parker drew his fingers down her torso, sliding between her breasts and dipping across her belly button. "Think of something else I can flatter?"

As his fingers dipped low, sliding into her as easily as if he'd done it a thousand times, Georgia decided she could stand the smug grin on his face—for a little while, at least—and live in the moment.

Regrets, reliable as the morning sun, would be there when she woke.

CHAPTER SIX

Georgia shot a dirty look at the guy in line next to her when he bumped into her again. Decked out head to toe in Redskins gear and clearly a six-pack or two of cheap beer into his day, he wouldn't stop shouting, "Cowboys suck!" into the crowd of fans lined up to get into FedExField.

"Yeah, yeah, Cowboys suck," she grumbled under her breath. "Though they at least have a state-of-the-art stadium with a *roof*."

"Not a sports fan?" Parker asked as they shuffled toward security.

"I like sports just fine," she said, scanning the faces surrounding them. "I don't like frat-boy wannabes, public intoxication, freezing weather, or capacity crowds." While all true, it was the eighty thousand fans streaming into the stadium that had her teeth on edge. Sure, there was safety in numbers, and such a crowded venue would make it almost impossible to stand out, but there were also far too many unknowns. Too many ways to approach, unseen until far too late. The sooner they got in, found Ethan, and got out, the sooner Georgia could relax.

"And why are you so chipper, anyway? It's freezing, and you don't strike me as the type of guy who enjoys sports played by the men who probably shoved you into lockers as a kid."

"You know, considering I had to put up with the swill that gas station referred to as coffee, I'm the one who should be cranky," Parker said, nudging her with his elbow. Finally at the front of the line, Georgia handed over their tickets—Ethan had left them in her name at Will Call—and shuffled through the metal detectors. "And yes," Parker continued, "I'm a fan."

"You're serious?" Georgia asked as the crowd thinned, people streaming in different directions.

"Hell yeah, sports are awesome."

Sports are awesome? Was he kidding?

"You look a little disappointed," Parker said as they headed up a ramp toward the second tier of the stadium.

"Just didn't take you for the ball-scratching, chest-beating, ass-slapping sort of guy."

Parker laughed as Georgia scrutinized the crowd, glaring when anyone pressed too close. How the hell was she supposed to perform threat assessment in this sort of environment?

"Well, I've never been the chest-pounding type, but when they itch, I scratch. And while I'm not typically inclined to smack someone's ass for a job well done, I can think of a few exceptions." His palm landed against her jean-covered butt and lingered as he leaned toward her. "*Nice* job last night."

She glared at him. She'd been trying not to think about *that* all morning. "Hand. Off. Ass."

Parker shrugged, a grin tilting his mouth. "You liked it last night."

Georgia scowled. "I will hurt you."

"Pretty sure *I* liked it last night." His eyes went from sparkle to smolder in a heartbeat.

Georgia grabbed him by the arm and dragged him up the ramp, fighting the warm flush that tried to crawl across her body, igniting memories she had no business reliving in public. Or ever again. It really wasn't fair. Since the moment she'd opened her eyes, Parker's heat surrounding her, she'd been aware of him in all the wrong ways. This, Georgia realized, was one of the reasons why it was so damn dangerous to sleep with a client. One night of blistering-hot sex and all her tactical awareness, all her carefully honed training, had fallen away until the only thing her body registered was Parker's proximity. His heat. His laugh. His smell. Parker filled her senses to the point everything else felt distant, unimportant, and trivial. Which made her nervous as hell.

Worse yet, for a split second, as Parker had frowned at the crappy selection of gas-station coffee, mumbling about enhanced interrogation techniques and cruel and unusual punishment, she'd been amused.

One night of unprotected sex and Georgia had gone and caught feelings. She should have known better.

Emerging onto the second level, Georgia pulled Parker around a curve and past dozens of concession lines—the scents of grilled meat, garlic fries, and stale popcorn creating a cornerstone of the ballpark experience. The sooner she got Parker to Ethan, the better.

"So, Mr. Sports Are Awesome, you a Redskins fan? Because you didn't strike me as the type to celebrate mediocrity, but hey, whatever does it for you." Georgia shrugged, hoping like hell a little mindless chitchat would keep her thoughts in the here and now and out of the bedroom.

Parker blinked. "Yeah, the Redskins are mediocre, but that also means consistent, and consistency is key."

"To what? Subpar ticket sales?" Georgia laughed.

"Oh yeah, no. I'm not *that* kind of fan," Parker said, as if the very idea he'd be so common as to follow a particular player insulted him.

"What kind?"

"You know, the jersey-wearing, high-fiving, trash-talking kind."

Georgia rolled her eyes. "I'm *so* relieved."

"I just like all the statistics. Football, despite what the die-hards will tell you, is just a numbers game."

Oh God, not a fan at all. A nerd.

"Am I about to be bored out of my mind?" Georgia asked as she ignored the siren song of bratwurst and onions.

"Bored? Are you kidding? Sports analysis was one of the first subjects I tackled—pun intended—when I was developing my predictive analysis program."

"If the next words out of your mouth include 'fantasy football league,' I'm going to need a beer." A really big one.

"Relax, I'm not allowed to play."

"Not allowed?" she asked as their section finally came into view.

"Yeah, banned from all three of the major sites for *life*." So proud. And this coming from the man who'd created one of the most sophisticated computer programs in the world. "Top-earning member three years running."

"Enough to keep you in coffee and candy for decades, I'm sure."

"Fifty-eight million over three years."

Georgia missed a step as she descended toward their seats. Was he kidding?

"Stick with me, babe," he said, his voice rife with self-satisfaction. "There's more here than just puzzles, programs, and pelvic perfection."

As her brain was still tripping over the words *fifty-eight million*, she had no response to that. Later, she decided, she'd find a way to bring Parker's ego down to mere mortal levels.

Or maybe not. Turning down the row to their seats, Georgia spotted Ethan, beanie low on his brow, phone in his hand. He glanced up as they approached, the lines around his mouth loosening a fraction.

"Georgia." He nodded, sliding his gaze over first her, then Parker, his worried frown easing but not disappearing entirely.

On a slow sigh, tension Georgia hadn't been aware of slid from her shoulders. She wasn't used to doubt plaguing her or insecurity dogging every step she took. It had been too easy to put aside the worry, the very real threat against Parker while they'd been tucked away in a motel room. But as she'd suspected, reality had been there to slap her in the face, bitter as the cold wind. Finally laying eyes on Ethan, knowing answers were coming, no matter how dire, helped calm her nerves. Besides, Georgia was a lot of things, but too proud to acknowledge the expertise of someone more skilled than herself wasn't one of them. Ethan would know what was going on, and he'd have a plan, she was sure of it.

"What?" Georgia shouted, the roar of the crowd accompanying kick-off drowning out Ethan's words.

"I said, you're late!" he shouted. "I expected you a half hour before game time."

"Getting here wasn't exactly easy." She'd insisted on the Metro, which took forever and dropped off nearly a mile from the stadium. God forbid ownership lose out on prime parking fees.

Ethan stood. "Let's head to the main concourse, meet up with the rest of the team."

Parker sighed and rose from the seat he'd just dropped into, shuffling out toward the center aisle.

"You two all right?" Ethan asked as they made their way, single file, back up the stairs they'd just descended.

"Yeah," Parker said, the energy he'd carried with him since they'd woken, tangled and sweaty, leaving him in a rush. "We're good."

Ethan clasped the back of his neck, squeezing gently. "You sure?"

Parker nodded, shrugged out of Ethan's grip, but didn't say anything. Their dynamic was . . . interesting. And not at all what Georgia had expected. Ethan had told her Parker was important to him, and she'd assumed their relationship was built on mutual, professional respect, but this was different. Ethan treated Parker more like a kid brother who needed looking after, which, frankly, annoyed the crap out of her. Parker was many things, but incompetent wasn't one of them. He may not be the skilled operator Ethan was, but he was far from helpless. She wondered if Ethan had any idea what Parker was capable of when push came to shove.

A shiver had her stuffing her hands into her pockets as they made the climb. She certainly knew *exactly* what Parker was capable of when backed into a corner. His actions had saved her life yesterday. A debt she hoped he'd never need her to repay.

They emerged into a thinned-out concourse. There were still plenty of people milling about, standing in lines, and watching the game on monitors, but far fewer than there'd been even ten minutes prior.

"This way," Ethan said, motioning them toward the right. They rounded a bend; then Ethan led them toward a small cluster of tabletops between one of the ramps leading down to seats and some concession stands. Four men stood huddled around a single table, cups of coffee steaming between gloved hands. Though she couldn't claim to be on a first-name basis with any of them, Georgia recognized a couple of faces. Truth was, this could have been the first time she'd seen any of them, and it wouldn't have mattered. Georgia had spent too much time in the military, spent too many years around men like her brother and Ethan not to recognize warriors when she saw them. Though they varied widely in features and build, could even pass for average and unremarkable in the heavy winter clothing they wore, the tell was in the way they stood, feet apart, weight shifted ever so slightly forward, their limbs loose and ready. Relaxed but alert.

As they approached, a gust of wind cut through Georgia's coat, slicing to the bone and informing her in the bluntest way possible why these particular tables had been abandoned by the crowds. Perched between a stadium opening and a gap in the structure that overlooked the parking lot, the wind barreled through the engineered tunnel, making already-frigid temperatures damn near unbearable.

"Finally," one of the men in the middle grumbled. "My balls fell off half an hour ago, Ethan."

"Like you had any balls to begin with, Ortiz," snorted the tall redhead standing at the right end of the group. His face split into a wide grin when he spotted Parker. "What's up, Peanut?"

Georgia watched, fascinated, as the tips of Parker's ears turned red.

"Peanut?" she wondered aloud, then let her gaze drop to his waistband before slowly making the climb back up to his face. Her lips twitched; she couldn't help it. He scowled.

"What, you thought I didn't notice you take that Snickers bar last night? Figured you got one over on me, huh?" Parker asked, stuffing his hands in his pockets and bumping her with his hip. "I have a minor allergy."

Georgia rolled her eyes. Of course nothing caffeine or sugar related got past Parker. She should have known he'd let her take the Snickers.

"Minor!" Ortiz barked out a laugh. "Gave the guy one tiny protein bar, ten minutes later we're shoving epinephrine in his ass and carting him off to the hospital. Looked like he'd stuck his head in a wasp's nest, the poor bastard." He clapped Parker on the back. "I'm Miguel, by the way," he said, holding a hand out for Georgia. "This is Liam," he said, nodding to the redhead. "Jones," he said, pointing to the tall brunet standing next to him. "And Ryan." Georgia greeted each of them. Liam and Ryan were both familiar; she'd seen them more than once around the Somerton Security headquarters. Ryan, who she recalled had been Ethan's first choice of bodyguard for Parker, had apparently managed to make his way back from New York after all. Was she about to be replaced?

Did she want to be?

Yes, she thought on a rough sigh. Just for once, she wanted to take the easy way out. To let someone else step in, take over. And it would probably be for the best, since the longer she stood near Parker, soaked in his heat, breathed in his scent, the harder it would be to leave him behind. And she should—leave him behind. Before things got any more complicated, any more dangerous—to her life and to her heart.

Parker's face, ashen and stunned as his killing shot echoed down the hall, seared through her brain. No. No, she didn't want to see him hurt or scared, not ever again. The mere memory was potent enough to have her reaching for him, yearning to slip her hand in his and squeeze, just to remind them both he was still there.

She fought the urge and won, though not before her own needs reminded her just how dangerous Parker could be. And how much she needed to step away before one night's mistake became something much, much worse.

Ethan cleared his throat, and all laughter and taunts evaporated faster than spit on desert rock. "I'm glad you're all here. I wasn't sure you'd get the message—or get out in time," he said, nodding toward Parker and Georgia.

Parker ducked his head, dragging his index finger along the cuticle at his thumb, scratching until he caught a ragged edge.

Had he not told Ethan what had happened? Georgia sighed. She'd just assumed Parker had filled him in the night before.

"We didn't," she said when Parker didn't speak up.

Ethan's gaze snapped to hers. "What?"

"We didn't get your message in time."

Everyone went preternaturally still. The roar of the crowd faded to a distant hum.

"We're okay," Georgia began, because frankly, that was most important, and judging from the way Ethan struggled to tear his gaze away from Parker, it was what he needed to hear. "We got your message," she said slowly, drawing Ethan's scrutiny away from Parker. "But we were on our way out when we ran into trouble."

The muscle at Ethan's jaw flexed before he managed, "What kind of trouble?"

"A hit," Georgia confirmed for him. "Definitely a pro. He let himself into the loft, but we didn't stick around to figure out how. He caught us in the narrow hallway between kitchen and bedroom. Good thing, too—if he'd had the room to maneuver properly, we'd both be dead."

"Jesus Christ," Ortiz swore.

"But you're both okay?" Ethan asked. "No injuries?"

Georgia watched as he struggled with the urge to turn back to Parker. To assess him again. So he was aware of the overprotective streak. Interesting. Better question was, did he know how his concern affected Parker? Because from what Georgia had observed in the last five minutes, every time Ethan clucked like a mother hen, Parker deflated a bit more. Grew quiet and still, two things it had taken Georgia less than twenty-four hours to figure out he did when he was off-kilter or insecure.

"We're fine."

For the first time, Parker startled, and then snapped back into the conversation with a scowl. "I'm fine. She was shot."

Georgia rolled her eyes. Drama queen. "Minor graze. No stitches, and definitely nothing to worry about." She shrugged off Parker's concern. Her side was tender and a little stiff, but the rest of her felt like deliciously stretched taffy. "Can't say the same for the other guy . . . What was his name?" she asked, hoping to draw Parker more thoroughly into the conversation, to get that mouth moving and brain firing. She wasn't one for incessant chatter, but Parker's silence was just weird. She hated the very idea he might feel out of his depth, might doubt his own experience and abilities. Bottom line, when it mattered, Parker had made the tough call. He didn't deserve to feel incapable or weak.

"Gordon Fletcher," he tonelessly offered.

In Georgia's experience, facts had the capacity to detonate like bombs, wreaking havoc and destroying terrain that only moments ago felt familiar. She watched as the knowledge that someone these guys knew, someone they worked with and trusted, had tried to kill one of their own.

"Fuck," Liam mumbled. "Fletcher's an ass, but . . ."

"He's dead?" Ethan asked.

Georgia jerked her chin once.

"Then I'm sorry," Ethan said. "I never intended to put you in such a position, Georgia. I didn't know until far too late—"

"Wait, wait." She held up a hand. "First, I'm trained, and I knew the score before I accepted the job. I may not have liked it, but I knew details were thin. And second," she said, glancing toward Parker, who stopped pulling against the cuticle on his thumb long enough to glance up at her, understanding dawning across his face, "I think you've misunderstood. I didn't kill Fletcher." She pinned Ethan with a hard stare. He should know Parker better than this. If left to her, he *would*. "Parker did."

Oh shit, she'd said it.

Parker shifted, resisting the urge to take a step away from the table. In the back of his mind, Parker had known Ethan would find out, that he'd need to know every detail of what had happened in the last twenty-four hours. Given everything the men standing around him had done, everything Parker had done from behind a keyboard, the truth—*I killed a man*—shouldn't have been a big deal. Every single person at the table knew what it was to choose life over death, to make the hard choice. And every single one of them would have done the same thing. Ethan would have done the same thing.

Pull the trigger, save a life.

No apologies. No hesitations.

He'd just never expected to be the blunt instrument. To hold the gun or take the shot.

The remembered scent of gunpowder burned Parker's nostrils. Gordon's face, slack and devoid of emotion, swam to the front of his mind.

You're going to look at me, and you're going to remind that kernel of doubt that the important thing isn't that you killed him . . . It's that you saved *me.* Georgia's voice, clear and strong, pushed away the mental debris.

It was the truth he'd held on to for the last twenty-four hours and the truth he repeated to himself as he met Ethan's gaze. He wasn't sure what he'd expected to find there. Disappointment? Anger? Disbelief? Whatever the case, he hadn't expected Ethan's quiet regard, a calculated look that told Parker he was reassessing everything he knew about him, everything he'd believed up to this point.

As if life had picked him up and relentlessly shaken him like a bottle of Mountain Dew, anxiety fizzed at the edges of everything, disturbing his thoughts and setting the inside of his skin tingling. This, he realized on a sigh, was what he'd been afraid of. That Ethan would look at him and see someone he no longer knew, someone he couldn't classify. Parker had learned, time and time again, that most people didn't understand him, not really. Not unless they could peg him, place him in a clearly labeled box they knew how to deal with.

Meal ticket.

Hapless nerd.

Tech genius.

To Ethan, Parker had gone from annoying know-it-all to protected little brother. A relationship that had begun with discord—Ethan had been adamant he didn't want some snot-nosed twenty-two-year-old geek on the team—changed to genuine respect, though it had been bought at a steep price. If not for the fact that Parker had saved Ethan's life, they might never have arrived at the relationship they now had. And while Parker could do with a bit less hovering and a little more faith, he wouldn't trade Ethan's regard for anything. More than anyone, Ethan had accepted Parker for who and what he was, made an effort to get to know him. In return, Parker had made every effort to rein in his crazy, to temper his sometimes manic tendencies and work within the ordered world Ethan understood most. It was a relationship built on a few universal truths. Ethan was the brawn—capable, agile, and a force to be reckoned with in the field— Parker was the brain, scary smart, handy to know, but ultimately not the guy most people chose in an emergency. He lacked the natural confidence, the cocksure athleticism it took to be a true operator.

It was a reality Parker wasn't comfortable with—he'd never liked the idea he was the weak link in any situation—but one he'd made his peace with. Better to acknowledge his shortcomings and play to his strengths than jeopardize Ethan's regard. He'd driven away enough people over the years; he had no intention of doing the same to Ethan—or anyone else on the team.

Probably best just to minimize the confrontation with Fletcher. Maybe if he dismissed it, Ethan would, too. "Guess all those lessons at the range finally paid off." He forced a smile to his face. "And unlike Ginger Snaps's prediction, I didn't shoot off a foot."

"Pretty sure I said ass," Liam mumbled, scratching at the red stubble along one cheek.

Parker stood under the weight of Ethan's stare, waiting for him to say something. Anything.

"How did you know Fletcher had been sent to kill Parker?" Ryan asked Ethan, pulling his attention away.

He shook his head. "I didn't. At least, I didn't know about Fletcher specifically. Only that there was an immediate threat in play."

"But how?" Georgia spoke up. "When we talked at Parker's loft, you didn't seem especially concerned. You even downplayed the situation."

Georgia shuffled closer as Ethan turned back to Parker. "I had no idea what I'd be walking into—or that things were at such a crucial tipping point."

For the first time, Parker could clearly read the emotion on Ethan's face. Guilt.

"If I had, I'd never have left you exposed," Ethan said.

"You didn't," Parker said. "Georgia was there. She saved my life, got me out."

"We saved each other," she said, clenching his forearm.

"Right, sorry," Ethan said.

Georgia shook her head, brushing aside the apology.

"For months now, Parker's been pestering me about anomalies within the CWU, operations that had occurred outside the scope of his recommendations or outside of his knowledge entirely."

"What sort of anomalies?" Ryan asked.

"Parker?" Ethan said, motioning for Parker to jump in. "Probably best if you explain this part."

Like a snake gearing up for an attack, dread curled in Parker's stomach. Shit. Parker had hoped Ethan was finally following up, finally taking Parker's concerns seriously. But now, given the timing of Ethan's investigation and Fletcher's attempted assassination . . . no way was this anything other than an inside job. Someone within the US government, with nearly unlimited resources and no oversight, was trying to kill him.

Fan-fucking-tastic.

"I'm supposed to have access to all operational files for anything we run a predictive analysis on. Hell, I even sit in on the majority of the threat-assessment meetings and go/no-go decisions. Problem is, a few months ago I started running across encrypted files in our database. At first I didn't think much of it; my security clearance is high, but I'm not privy to everything." Thank God for that. If he'd learned anything, it was that governments operated in shades of gray, that nothing was ever black or white, and that sometimes the cost of one life just didn't factor into the bigger picture. As far as Parker was concerned, he was interested only in information and outcomes that pertained directly to his tech. And his ability to make it better.

"At first, I'd run across an encrypted file every few months, rare enough that it was easy to dismiss. Until I found a file I recognized by name. One of the major players in the cocaine scene in South America had begun targeting an oil company. Stealing shipments, kidnapping employees. We'd considered sending in a team to take out the leader but ultimately decided against it. There were too many variables. Too many risks. Predictive analysis showed only a forty-five percent chance of success, less than twenty percent in terms of maintaining long-term stability in the region. I wasn't okay sending one of our teams into a situation like that, risking lives on a mission that unstable. At the go/no-go meeting, we decided to reassess in six months."

"But I'm guessing that didn't happen," Ortiz said, the line of his shoulders rigid.

Parker shook his head. "When I asked about it, I got the runaround. A lot of *It's classifieds* and *Don't worry about its.*"

"So you snuck a peek," Liam said, palming his cup of coffee in slow circles against the table. They all knew him well enough to know that "classified" was basically like a dog's invisible fence line. Stepping over it carried consequences, but if Parker was curious enough, he wouldn't notice or care.

"Yeah. Someone authorized the op, though the file didn't specify who." Parker sighed and shifted from foot to foot. "Thankfully, that op didn't carry any negative outcomes."

"Negative outcomes?" Georgia asked.

"Significant loss of life or assets," Ethan explained.

"At first, I brushed it off," Parker continued. "But the longer I tried to dismiss it, the more it niggled at the back of my mind. It didn't fit." He cut a rueful smile. "You all know how much that sort of thing irritates me."

"Understatement," Ryan muttered.

"So you started looking," Liam stated.

"Yeah." Parker shrugged. "Honestly, I wasn't even sure what I expected to find. Maybe just that ops we'd passed on were being authorized by someone higher up? I honestly wasn't all that concerned with the obvious questions."

"Then why bother looking in the first place?" Georgia asked.

Interestingly, she didn't sound impatient or irritated—most people were when Parker skipped over or ignored the obvious. They tended to assume he was either too stupid to ask the question or just too lost in his own world to care. Typically it was the latter, which drove people nuts. But apparently that didn't apply to Miss Bennett. Once again, Parker suspected Georgia understood him in ways most didn't—and adjusted her expectations accordingly.

"Because I'm supposed to have access to all outcomes—no exceptions," Parker explained. "I take all that data, the positive and the negative, and work with a team of analysts to filter it into quantifiable information we then use to modify my program." Parker shifted from foot to foot, resisting the urge to stuff his hands in his pockets and hunch his shoulders. "One of the hardest parts of this job is knowing that my program, while it often saves lives, occasionally costs them as well."

"Parker," Ethan warned, "we've talked about this."

"Yeah, yeah, we have," Parker snapped. "Repeatedly. But that doesn't change anything. It doesn't change the fact that tech I built and recommendations I make deploy teams into dangerous situations. It doesn't change the fact," he continued, his voice dropping to a low, rough whisper, "that sometimes I make decisions *knowing* that odds are I'm sending men, good men, into situations where they're likely to be seriously injured or killed. Or that I do so knowing that the long-term outcome, the big picture, justifies the cost. It's my tech making those decisions, justifying those actions. At the end of the day, it's on *me*."

"The hell it is," Ethan argued. "You're not the only person with a voice in this; you're not the only one making decisions or recommendations. This guilt you carry, this sense of responsibility. It's not healthy, Parker—"

"I disagree." Georgia cut Ethan a warning look, and to Parker's surprise, Ethan snapped his mouth shut. "Everything Parker said is true. And he damn well should carry the consequences of his actions, his decisions, with him."

Ethan opened his mouth, but Georgia cut him off with a sweep of her hand. Turning to Parker, she said, "We're all responsible for the choices we make and for the consequences of our decisions. You *should* care about every individual who is put in harm's way. You *should* own the reality that their lives, their fates, are in your hands, for better or for worse—even if you know that risking their lives is the right thing to do. It should matter, Parker. It should be hard. The day you forget that, the day it becomes easy—that's the day you've gone too far." She swept her angry gaze back to Ethan. "It should never become routine to tell someone their loved one died. That there was nothing you could do. That they should move on."

"You think that's how I felt about Will? That it was easy for me to tell you he died?" Ethan ground out, hurt and anger waging a war across his face.

Georgia snapped her mouth shut, though the tension between them remained. Both of them angry but neither speaking.

Parker couldn't parse out all the information flowing through his head, or be certain how it all related back to Georgia. Questions for another time, he knew, but the reminder he didn't know her that well—that *Ethan* knew her better—grated on his nerves.

Georgia turned back to him. "I'm not suggesting it's your fault when things go wrong, Parker," she said quietly. "Everyone has to own their choices—the men you send out, they put themselves in your hands, and in the hands of the government as a whole, in the first place. They know the risks. But caring about what happens to them, *remembering* them, that's important, too."

Parker placed a hand on her shoulder and squeezed, heedless of the stares the rest of the team gave him. "You're right," he said. "Which is why I'm supposed to have access to every outcome, positive or negative. Because while I can't create perfection and I can't make guarantees, I can keep making the program better. I can make sure every single life counts, if not in the moment, then in the future." He sighed and turned back to the group. "So yeah, I hacked some files. Started flagging operations I either didn't know about at all or operations I thought we'd scrapped."

"How many were there?" Liam asked.

"Not many, not at first," Parker admitted. "But over the last eighteen months, I've found thirty-six. Enough to make me wonder what was going on. Enough to mention it to Ethan."

"Right," Ethan said, taking over. "At first, I wrote it off. It's not that uncommon, you know? You operate off book or in a special capacity long enough, you start to realize that compartmentalization is rampant. One department may deem a risk unnecessary, while another decides to move forward. We may decide to pass on an op, but someone higher up may have more insight to cost/benefit than they're prepared to disclose."

"So what changed your mind?"

Ethan grew quiet, as if weighing exactly what he wanted to say. "A contact at the Department of Justice reached out. There've been some disturbing allegations against the CWU. One in particular he wanted me to look into."

"What allegation?" Liam asked.

Ethan grew stiff and still. "I'd rather not repeat it—not until I have confirmation one way or the other."

"But why?" Georgia asked. "Don't you think we have a right to know what the hell is going on?"

"You have a right to the truth, but right now, I don't know what that is." Ethan shook his head when Georgia opened her mouth to argue. "I won't empower a rumor by spreading it. I won't hurt someone with false information."

"Okay, so based on a tip, you went snooping. For what?"

"Files. Specifically the ones Parker had previously singled out." He cut Parker an irritated glance. "You're annoyingly persistent but rarely wrong. I figured best-case scenario I'd take a look, find something to convince the DoJ nothing was amiss, and at the same time convince you to stop risking criminal charges for hacking a DoD server."

"And worst-case scenario?" Ortiz asked.

"If there was a worst-case scenario, then I damn well wanted to know about it. This is our unit—if someone's working against us, I want to know about it. And in any case, I have a higher security clearance, so I figured that diminished the risks of any serious trouble." Ethan sighed. "Obviously, a miscalculation on my part."

"Yeah, well thank God you hover more than Marty McFly," Parker said. "If you hadn't sent Georgia, I'd be dead. No question."

"Okay, but why?" Ryan asked. "What the fuck was in those files?"

"I can only speculate. After I logged in to the server and started opening documents, things went to shit pretty damn fast." Ethan shook his head. "But based on what I saw? I think someone's been using Parker's program to engage in private for-profit operations."

War profiteering? Off his program? The one he'd designed to decrease risks and save lives? Parker pulled at the scarf wrapped around his neck. *How dare they? How the fuck dare they!*

"A mercenary?" Liam asked.

"Or a group," Ethan continued.

"How can you be sure?" Georgia asked.

"I can't," Ethan said. "Not yet. But all the files I accessed had one thing in common—they all centered around private businesses with massive corporate profits at play. Oil, big pharma, things like that. Companies that would either benefit or suffer in the event of unchecked instability in the region."

And that was only the tip of it. Political instability was only one facet of what his program could combat. The possibilities were limitless—and so many of them were negative. This program was the best of him, a project he'd begun in school and perfected at the DoD. He'd only ever considered everything it could do to help, all the lives it could *save*.

Power corrupts. He'd just never thought it applied to him.

"Companies with deep pockets, you mean." Ortiz scowled, as if the idea itself tasted bitter.

Ethan nodded. "But I can't prove it. Not yet, anyway."

"That doesn't explain why someone's trying to kill Parker."

"Isn't it obvious?" Georgia said. "If anyone could prove Ethan's theory true, it's Parker. He knows more about his program than anyone else, and worse, he's been party to the go/no-go discussions. He'd be integral to proving wrongdoing."

"Right," Ethan said. "But it's not just Parker at risk here. The moment I used my credentials to log in to the system and started accessing these files, a flag went up."

"Meaning what, exactly?" Liam asked.

"Meaning the minute I accessed more than one of those 'hidden' files, a command activated. Parker's program ran a full threat analysis on every single one of us."

No. No, no, no, no. The freezing wind ceased to matter as everything in Parker flushed hot and furious. If the program had been activated, it wouldn't just run a threat assessment. It would go far, far deeper than that.

"As of right now, the program's sole focus is the systematic takedown and destruction of our entire team."

Fuck. Parker struggled to breathe against the vise compressing his chest.

"What about your contact at the DoJ? Any help from that quarter?" Liam asked.

Ethan shook his head. "Until we have proof of what's going on, I don't trust anyone outside this group."

Parker choked on the hysterical laugh that tried to bubble up as an old movie reference—one of his favorites—crossed his mind. *Shall we play a game?*

No. No, he didn't want to play. Not this game. Not against a supercomputer with all his intellect and none of his weaknesses.

"So what the hell do we do now?" Ortiz asked as Parker struggled against the urge to fall apart. To say fuck it all to hell and back, that there was nothing they *could* do.

Ethan pulled a thumb drive out of his pocket. "Now we stay alive long enough to prove it."

◆ ◆ ◆

"How many did you get?" Parker asked, starting at the tiny drive Ethan held.

Georgia still wasn't certain she knew exactly what was going on, but she understood enough to know she was way out of her depth.

"At least fifty, maybe more," Ethan said, passing the memory stick off to Parker. "I didn't have a lot of time once I realized what was happening, but I copied what I could."

"So what do we do now?" Ryan asked, running a hand over his shorn stubble.

"Now we split up and go dark. Priority one has to be looking through these files," Ethan said.

Was he kidding? Priority one needed to be figuring out how to keep the US *government* from killing them all.

"For what?" Ortiz demanded, the tight frown marring his face convincing Georgia she wasn't the only one considering their priorities.

"Right now it seems like there's a lot of speculation and not much else. So what the hell are we supposed to do while Poindexter's evil twin hunts us down?" Ortiz asked.

"We can't stay together," Parker said. "It's too dangerous. The program has too many statistics on how the CWU behave as a unit, how we operate in the field. Our best bet is to split up." He sighed, shoving the drive into his pocket. "I'll need some time to go through all this."

"How much time?" Georgia asked, wondering if the pit of uncertainty was to be her new normal. She'd signed up for seventy-two hours, for a simple protection detail. A detail that should be over. Ethan was here. Ryan was back. Parker had ample protection. Technically, he didn't need her anymore. Which rendered her what? An unnecessary third wheel? A distraction? She wasn't part of this, of them. She had no role within the CWU. She could go home.

Should go home.

Why wasn't she rushing for the exit?

"I won't know the answer to that until I crack the files. I'll have to search these the old-fashioned way, which could take a while."

"Yeah, but what are you even looking for, Parker?" Liam asked.

"Proof," Ethan said. "If we can't prove misuse of assets and war profiteering, we're screwed. Right now we've got to assume anyone outside our team could be implicated, and I'm sorry to say that includes a whole lot of highly influential and very powerful people. It won't be enough to confirm our suspicions. If we want to live to see spring, we've not only got to verify our theory, we've got to prove it."

"So what now?" Georgia asked. Where was she supposed to go? She didn't have any family left. And she'd be damned if she'd risk any of the few friends she had. Worse, she had a grand total of $300 in her bank account. DC rent was pricey, and outfitting her apartment had wiped out her savings. And even though payday was less than a week away, it hardly mattered. Direct deposit left a paper trail and ensured she'd have the money, just not be able to access it.

"For now, we split up," Ethan said. "Keep our communication to a minimum."

"The app should still be secure," Parker said. "It's on a private server, no government affiliations. Not even my program can access it."

"Okay," Ethan said, stepping back from the table. "So we go our separate ways. Does everyone have somewhere they can go? Access to funds and supplies?"

Of course they do, Georgia thought as everyone nodded. Every man here was part of a specialized task force. It would have been weird if they weren't ready to move at the drop of a hat. Unfortunately, she couldn't say the same. This was nothing she'd signed up for, nothing she was equipped to handle. What the hell was she going to do?

"Georgia," Ethan said, interrupting her spiraling thoughts, "you've got a choice here."

Oh goody. By the tone of his voice, behind door number one was pain and dismemberment, and behind door number two was waterboarding and bamboo shoots.

"There's a good chance you're not implicated in any of this. No one knows I sent you to stay with Parker, and as far as the files at Somerton Security are concerned, you were given the standard number of days off post-assignment. You can call in tomorrow morning for a new job, and Sarah will get you set up. I can't tell you that it's entirely without risk, but in all likelihood, you can step right back into your life as if this little blip with Parker never happened."

Relief hit first, fast and hard, taking her breath in a heavy rush. Home. She could go home. For the first time, her tiny apartment might actually feel worthy of the name.

But next to her, Parker went suddenly stiff. She glanced at him, but he kept his gaze fixed on Ethan, refusing to look at her. Guilt rushed in, bringing indecision and reluctance. Which, really, told her everything she should need to know. There was no legitimate reason she should stay. Parker had the protection he needed. Professionally, Georgia was redundant. Which meant any reason she could possibly think of to stay was entirely personal, entirely unprofessional, and a complete dismissal of every instinct she had.

"You said choice," she said, turning away from Parker and back to Ethan.

"You can come with Parker and me—but if you do that, there's no going back. Any hope you have of resuming normal life fades with every second you take to decide—if you come with us, you're stuck until this gets resolved."

He didn't need to say "One way or the other"; Georgia heard it loud and clear. No matter what she chose, there was considerable risk involved—probably more than they even realized. Certainly, the easier decision would be to go home, call Sarah first thing in the morning, and get back to work. She wasn't Parker, not by a long shot, but she could fabricate a decent enough paper trail to convince someone she'd been home, avoiding the inclement weather, for most of the weekend.

Or . . .

Or she could stay with Parker and . . . And what, exactly? Keep him alive? He had Ethan for that. Hold his hand? He hardly needed it. So, what then? No question the sex had been great. Phenomenal, even, but she wasn't accustomed to making important life-and-death decisions based on the whim of her vagina. Not to mention she was pretty damn certain sex—no matter how amazing—wasn't what Ethan had in mind when he'd said to make a connection.

It made sense to go home. To put everything behind her. If Sarah assigned her someone new, she'd get the second chance Parker was meant to be, avoid the dreaded stench of french fries, and maybe, just maybe, live to see the New Year.

Only problem was, she didn't *want* to go. She wasn't ready to turn her back on the growing connection she had with Parker. With him, in some incredibly convoluted way, things were easy. Sure, he was an overcaffeinated nerd with an IQ too high for his own good and a body determined to distract her, but he was also honest. He slipped right past her bullshit filter and settled in, warm and steady, next to her. Even better, he didn't seem phased by her. Not intimidated or irritated—he truly didn't seem to wish she were more feminine, less abrasive. He didn't care that she could save his life or kick his ass. Walking away from Parker would mean walking away from the first person who genuinely liked her—a familiar comfort she hadn't felt since Will died.

And that right there told her everything she needed to know. If she stayed, it wouldn't be because Parker needed her. It wouldn't be because she thought she could help Ethan or felt an obligation to see things through. She'd stay because she wanted to. Because she was weak and desperate and lonely and, for a moment, Parker had filled that void in her life.

But how long would that feeling last? Days? Weeks? Or just the amount of time it took to remove the threat against Parker's life?

How long would it take before Parker didn't need her anymore? Before he walked away and she had to figure out how to go back to her empty apartment and her hearty African violet and figure out how to be alone. Again.

"I'm in the way here," she said around the lump in her throat. "I should go." The moment the words left her mouth, she wanted to call them back. Where she'd expected relief or approval, instead Ethan looked . . . surprised. Like he'd thought she'd stay. And Parker . . . Georgia could barely stand the split-second glance she cast in his direction. In the thirty-six hours she'd known him, Georgia had seen just about every emotion cross Parker's face.

Caffeine-deprived irritability. Focused intent. Playful regard. Stunned horror. But never had she seen him resigned. Never had she seen what it looked like when he'd expected more of someone who'd disappointed him.

That his disappointment had the power to shame her so completely, so thoroughly, only reminded her of everything she risked if she didn't go. She'd given this man far too much power already; she couldn't afford to give him any more. Georgia sighed, her chest tight. Just once she wanted her life to be fair. Wanted to roll the dice on another person and believe that, just once, that path wouldn't inevitably lead to hurt and heartache.

"You're sure?" Ethan asked.

"Yeah." She nodded. She had to be. Parker was safe. She needed to ensure the same for herself.

"All right," Ethan said as he studied them. "Everyone should head out separately. Use different exits; don't go at the same time. Parker and I will wait for the game to end, slip out with the crowds."

Ethan turned to Georgia. "You good with finding your own way back to DC?"

"Yeah. I can take the Metro back into the city, walk from there." It wasn't like she was in any sort of rush to get home.

"Time frames for check-in?" Liam asked.

"Let's say once every twenty-four. We can reassess as needed," Ethan said.

"You got it." Ortiz clapped Parker on the shoulder. "You keep your head down, let us know what you need."

Parker nodded but didn't say anything as, one by one, Ryan, Liam, Jones, and Ortiz all wandered away, Parker tracking each of them until they disappeared into the crowd.

Finally, after long minutes had passed, Georgia made herself step away from the table. Made herself look at Parker as she said, "Be careful." She nodded at Ethan, then forced herself to turn, to walk away before she lingered too long, before she couldn't make herself go.

As she turned down one of the ramps leading to the lower concourse, Georgia cast one last look at Parker. She caught his expression. Stumbled. Stopped before she could think better of it.

How many times had Georgia worn that same look? The one that said, "Please don't go" and "I'm alone again" and "Everyone leaves." And worse, so much worse, the look that said, "I know they always will."

It shouldn't have caught her off guard, seeing *that* look. She'd worn it often enough. When she and Will had buried their parents. When she'd climbed into the social worker's car and driven away from her grandmother's tidy trailer. When Will had aged out. When he'd enlisted. Every single time he'd deployed. When Isaac had told her in the bluntest way possible there was no future. Not with *her*.

When she'd stood there, quiet and compliant as the notification officer told her Will was gone, knowing deep down she'd almost expected that last blow, that final piece of proof she would always, always be left behind. Left alone.

She'd thought herself finally, blessedly immune to the pain.

Right up until the moment she put that same expression on someone else's face.

On *Parker's* face.

She couldn't do it, she realized. Couldn't leave. And it wasn't fucking *fair*, she thought as she turned, took that first halting step back. She knew damn well she couldn't trust Parker not to leave her. Not to hurt *her*.

But if it came to it, if she couldn't find a way to hold herself apart, to keep herself safe, she'd weather the pain. Again. Learn to live with it. Again.

But she'd be damned if she put that look on someone else's face.

She strode back, her spine straight, her heart in her throat.

When Ethan turned, looked at her as if he was only half-surprised to see her there, she forced herself to say, "More brains than balls, right?" and ignore the grin that split Parker's face.

Georgia leaned against the cinder-block wall between the two restrooms and let the cold seep through her layers and into her skin. With any luck it would numb the tickle of panic pushing along her frayed nerves that pulsed and ebbed in waves she couldn't control or predict. Acting against her own self-interest—she shook her head. She'd made the decision, so now she had to get on with living with it.

"Drown Parker in a toilet?" she asked when Ethan settled against the wall next to her.

"Tempted, but no." He shoved his hands into his pockets, scanning the crowds beginning to filter out of the stands and into the concourse. Two minutes left in a game with a point differential it would take time travel and eight Hail Marys to overcome, and it seemed a lot of fans had given up and were heading out. "Parker said, and I quote, 'You may be my boss, but my dick is a rebellious little shit and refuses to cooperate with you standing there ready to critique the strength and color of my stream. Go the fuck away.'"

Georgia took a sip of her coffee, concealing her grin. Yeah, that sounded about right.

"So, want to tell me what led to your association with 'the rebellious little shit'?"

Georgia choked, coffee scorching her sinuses and threatening to come out her nose.

"What?" She gaped at him. She'd be lying if she said she hadn't expected Ethan to pick up on the vibe between Parker and her, but she certainly hadn't expected him to be so damn direct about it.

"Let's agree not to lie to each other, okay?" Ethan said, turning so he faced her. "We have neither the time for, nor the luxury of, hiding things." He stared her down, as if his disapproval had some weight she'd actually recognize.

Fine, if he wanted to play it that way. "We had a rough day, considered ice cream but, given the weather, opted for sex against the wall." She shrugged, willing her blush to stay under the collar of her sweater. She smiled around a sip of coffee when Ethan swore.

"Jesus, Georgia."

"Oh, I'm sorry. Too honest? It's a bit hard to see the line of propriety when my boss is questioning me about my sex life."

"Don't pretend I've offended your delicate sensibilities; we both know you don't have any."

"Then don't pretend you give a damn about who Parker sleeps with." Georgia rolled her eyes. "Just say what's on your mind, Ethan."

"Fine. I'm worried you're too close to this." He sighed. "You were leaving. Already halfway out the door. But one look back, and what? You just changed your mind?"

"Pretty much." What else could she say? At best he wouldn't understand her reasons for staying, but at worst he'd think them a liability. And maybe they were. Georgia wasn't sure, but she'd made a decision she couldn't take back. It was done, regardless of what Ethan thought.

"Right. And I suppose your feelings for Parker had nothing to do with it."

"Oh yes, one night of hot sex and I'm making tactical decisions with my vagina." It was so, so much worse than that. "What really bugs you, Ethan? That I stayed? Or that I surprised you?"

"I gave you the choice, didn't I?"

"Why? If you were so damn certain I'd leave, why give me the choice at all?"

Stony silence met her question, as if Ethan hadn't thought about the implications of his own actions or questions.

"Your assignment, your call."

Georgia rolled her eyes. How many times had she heard that in the office? How many times had Ethan used it as a way of giving his operatives more autonomy, more input on cases? It was a thin excuse, and he knew it.

"I think I'm entitled to a few reservations. I assigned you to Parker twenty-four hours ago. Hardly enough time to get close."

"Oh, so sorry. I must have heard you wrong when you told me to *form an attachment*."

"You know damn well I didn't mean like *that*," he said on a harsh whisper.

"Guess you should have been more specific," Georgia replied, bringing the cup of coffee to her mouth to stem the tide of everything she wanted to say. She sighed. Technically, Ethan wasn't out of line. He may have been clumsy in his approach, but he wasn't wrong. Georgia knew damn well there were rules against sleeping with clients. "Look, we had a rough day. By the time we got to the motel, all the residual fear, tension, and adrenaline had to go somewhere. It didn't mean anything." The words carried the metallic tang of a lie—or a truth she just didn't want to believe.

"That's what I'm afraid of." Ethan sighed, then glanced toward the bathroom. Turning back to her, he said, "The situation you faced yesterday was extreme, and you're hardly the first pair to succumb to the moment. But Parker's different. Sensitive. What was a convenient release for you may well have been more to him."

"And you're concerned that my staying is going to encourage his attachment," Georgia said, neatly ignoring the fact that Ethan was treading dangerously close to calling her a slut. He got a pass, but only because he thought he was protecting Parker.

"Yes."

"You're a sanctimonious bastard, you know that?" She'd let Ethan question her morals but not Parker's intelligence.

"I'm just worried about him, Georgia. Parker's not like us."

What? Not jaded? Not used to being hurt? She'd noticed, thanks. And look where it had gotten her.

"You don't know him half so well as you think you do, Ethan. No," she said when he opened his mouth to argue. "The truth is, the only person too close to this situation is *you*." Georgia reined in her temper, struggling to stem the tide of choice observations she desperately wanted to make. There just wasn't time. Parker had emerged from the bathroom and was headed toward them. "Parker is capable of a hell of a lot more than you think he is. He saved my life yesterday. Most would have hesitated, would have frozen. He didn't."

She spared Parker a smile as he approached, hoping he wouldn't read the tension snapping like static between Ethan and her. "He did what had to be done and held it together long enough for us to get somewhere safe. You coddle him, and worse, you undermine his faith in himself." She shifted her focus back to Ethan, pinning him with a hard look. "Before you spend any significant time worrying I might hurt Parker's *feelings*, you ought to take a moment to consider the damage you've done to his confidence. Parker *trusts* you, Ethan. So much so that when you act like he isn't capable of defending himself, he actually believes it." Georgia pushed past Ethan before he could say anything and went straight to Parker. "What, did you get distracted by all the chrome handles? Fascinated watching the water swirl down the bowl?"

"Nah. I have this weird ritual where I actually wash my hands. They were out of paper towels, though. See?" he said, sliding a palm against the back of her neck.

She elbowed him in the ribs, suppressing the shudder the cool of his hand against the warmth of her neck elicited. "You are disgusting."

"What? It's just water." He shrugged, a more relaxed grin creeping across his face, as if he'd just been waiting for equilibrium to be restored, for them to move forward as though Georgia had never thought of leaving. And that was fine—a good working relationship, a casual trust, those could be assets. But nothing too personal, she reminded herself as she, Parker, and Ethan slid into the exiting crowd, following the ramp down and toward one of the open gates.

"How'd you get here, Ethan?" Georgia asked as they reached an intersection. "We came in on the train . . ." God, she didn't want to make the trek back to the station. If anything, it had gotten colder and grayer since they'd arrived. She hated being frozen to the point of numbness. Dreaded the tingling burn of returning sensation to her extremities. But she'd much rather endure the experience from the warmth of a car.

"I've got a clean car in lot D; we'll head that way. Change vehicles when we get to town and go from there."

"Sounds like a plan," Parker said, taking a right and heading toward the parking lots beginning to clog with exiting vehicles.

Ethan saw his approach a fraction of a second before Georgia did. Intercepted the gun the guy pulled out of an oversize Redskins coat. The gunman was a little shorter, but with the twenty or thirty pounds of muscle he had on Ethan, the struggle over the gun erupted into a brawl in seconds.

"Ethan!" Parker yelled.

"Get Parker and go!" Ethan grunted, still struggling with the gunman. Around them, people were backing up, starting to yell and point.

"Gun!" someone screamed.

"That guy's armed!"

Georgia grabbed Parker by the sleeve, tried to haul him toward a break in the crowd.

"No!" He pulled away, heading back toward Ethan, who finally got in a clean hit, disarming the gunman and laying him out on the sidewalk with a vicious blow to the head.

"We need to go," Ethan said, tucking the gun into his jacket and grabbing Parker by the elbow. "Now."

"Hey man, nice job!"

"Where are you going?"

"Did someone call the police?"

Morbid curiosity had the crowd surging around them, pushing in until Georgia couldn't take a step without brushing against a stranger's shoulder.

"Stay with me." She tucked in tight next to Parker, grabbing a fistful of his back pocket. The last thing they needed was to get separated.

Ethan stepped in front of them, using the breadth of his shoulders to push his way through the crowd, and picked up his pace toward the parking lot.

A muzzle flashed, the muted but distinctive sound of a suppressor filling the air. Three shots caught Ethan in the torso, picked him up off his feet, and threw him a few steps back into Parker and Georgia. Ethan hesitated a second, then through what Georgia could only assume was a potent mix of training and sheer stubborn determination, flung his failing body at the attacker.

"No!" Parker screamed.

Barely keeping her feet, Georgia linked her arm through Parker's elbow and swung him around, dragging him into the terrified and panicked crowd. In seconds it swallowed them, concealing them from the shooter . . . and he from them.

They were blind.

Sirens wailed in the background, and the crackle of radios came to life as the crowd surged and fled, chaos raining down upon the stadium.

"Georgia, stop!" Parker shouted. "We can't leave him!" He tried to pull away from her, but the force of the panicking crowd, thousands strong, kept him moving forward. As the throng of innocent civilians shielded their escape, herding them away from danger and a gravely injured Ethan, Georgia allowed grim gratitude to slide through her. Without the cover of a panicked mob, they'd have been shot in the back by now. Without the stampede of terrified people, she probably wouldn't have the strength to muscle Parker away from Ethan.

Ethan. She pushed away the thought. Nothing she could do for him now but hope and pray he'd survive long enough for authorities to arrive, for someone to help him.

Georgia's priority had to be Parker.

She shoved him forward, daring a glance behind her. Pandemonium. Chaos. People running and screaming and crying. But no shooter, at least not as far as she could see.

"Georgia, stop!"

"No." The crowd was beginning to thin as people veered off in different directions, toward different parking lots and exit points. Too soon they'd be exposed. The people in front of them parted, a couple of taxis idling at the curb. She yanked open the door and muscled Parker into one.

"Morgan Boulevard station," Georgia demanded, wedging in next to Parker. The driver, as if immune to the chaos around them, just nodded and pointed his car into the crowds, honking and cursing at people to get out of his way.

"We can't just leave him," Parker said, though the fight had gone out of him, reality descending like lead in the back of the cab. "We can't just leave him," he repeated.

"We can't help him, Parker. We have to hope . . ." The word turned to ash in her mouth, choking her with the futility of such a thing. "He needs medical care, far more than we could give him," she whispered, mindful of the driver who was still laying on his horn and honking like a native New Yorker.

"They shot him. They shot Ethan."

"I know."

Parker clenched his eyes shut, breathing deep, his breath fogging the window. When he opened his eyes again, he looked at her, calm and resigned. He brought his hand up to her cheek, brushing gently against her skin. His fingers barely trembled when he pulled them away, wiping the blood against his jeans. "What do we do now?"

"Nothing's changed," she said, forcing herself to believe it, even though she knew everything had. "We go. We figure out what's on that drive. We stop whoever's doing this."

And they'd have to do it, she realized, without any of Ethan's knowledge, resources, or connections.

They were on their own.

CHAPTER SEVEN

Parker and Georgia rode the Metro back into DC, silence yawning between them from the moment they grabbed two empty seats near a central door. Somehow, the loud chatter of the crowded train—word of the shooting was spreading quickly, even to those who hadn't been present when it happened—made the thin and brittle stretch of quiet between Georgia and him all the more pronounced. Parker wrestled with the urge to ask what they were doing, where they were going. She'd said in the cab that nothing had changed, that their goal was still the same. He didn't think she believed that any more than he did, but every time he glanced at her, ready to demand a plan, a path forward, he saw the face of a woman wrestling with those very questions.

For the first time, it occurred to Parker that perhaps Georgia felt Ethan's absence every bit as strongly as he did—maybe even more. As she sat there, twirling the bezel on the watch, she had to know that now everything was up to her. She had to decide where to go and what to do—choices Parker was certain Ethan had already made, possibilities he'd meticulously planned for, now rested squarely on Georgia's shoulders. And while Parker understood his program, knew in a very technical sense how to live off grid, he had no idea how to actually put that knowledge into practice.

So he kept his mouth shut. The least he could do was give her a bit of time to acclimate.

It was hardly a fair trade. A few minutes of silence in exchange for the rest of her life. Tension buzzed at the base of his skull like angry wasps, the beginnings of anxiety threading through him. Ethan. Georgia. Not to mention his own life. All hanging by the thinnest of threads—and all because Parker insisted on proving time and time again he was too smart for his own good.

How many people had already died needlessly because of his program? How many more would share in that outcome?

Even if they came out of this, even if he and Georgia managed to not only figure out who wanted him dead and why, but also prove it, nothing would be the same. Ethan was either dead or dying, and all because of his technology.

A technology he no longer had faith in. A program he was no longer sure should even exist.

In a matter of hours, everything Parker had believed about himself, about the world and his contribution to it, had been destroyed.

He pushed away the thoughts before they consumed him.

There were at least a few things he could do in the meantime. Pulling his phone from his pocket, Parker launched his web browser and searched for headlines surrounding the shooting at FedExField, desperate for any mention of Ethan, terrified he'd find only a vague reference to a single fatality. Five minutes of scrolling and scanning yielded little. Reports were still evolving, details thin and contradictory. One outlet mentioned a man taken to the hospital with "severe injuries" while another mentioned a "mass shooting." The only thing clear was that no one really knew what had happened or why. At least not yet.

Did the rest of the team know? They'd left hours before the end of the game, going their separate ways per Ethan's instructions. Shit. They may not even realize an attack had occurred, let alone that Ethan had been shot.

Closing the web browser, Parker opened his test version of Jungle Gem, the familiar opening tones soothing his nerves. Thumbing over to the messaging board, he began typing out the details of what had happened.

"What are you doing?" Georgia asked.

"Updating the rest of the team." Though "update" might be over-stating things. Even though he'd been there, standing behind Ethan as the shots had caught him in the chest, Parker knew little more than anyone else. He closed his eyes, desperate to recall details. Had Ethan taken all three dead center? Had any hit his shoulder? Grazed his arm? With startling clarity, Parker realized he knew basically nothing. Couldn't recall anything beyond the simplest sensory details. The roar of the crowd. The smell of the powder. Ethan's surprised grunt. Remembered terror flooded him, catching his breath at the bottom of his lungs and pulling it to his stomach until breathing became a struggle. Random details, lots of information. But nothing useful. Nothing relevant. The story of his life.

"No," Georgia whispered, pulling his phone away from him. "It's too dangerous to make contact right now."

"What? Why?"

Georgia leaned toward him, her voice a harsh whisper. "Think about it, Parker. Three people among tens of thousands. That was a coordinated hit. How did the shooters find us? Know which gate to be at? How did they even know we were at the stadium to begin with?"

"What are you suggesting?" A stupid question, of course. He knew damn well what she was suggesting, what she was worried about. But he couldn't, wouldn't, believe it.

"Look, I get it. This is your team; you know these guys. Trust them. But that's the problem. You're too close to this." She sat back against her seat, letting her head fall against the Plexiglas window.

"No. No way." He knew those men down to their most basic, ingrained traits. Lethal? Yes. No question. But traitors? To their country or to those they called brothers? Not a chance. "You don't know them, Georgia. But I do, and I trust them. They need to know what happened. If Ethan made it to the hospital . . ." He couldn't bear to contemplate the alternative. He just couldn't. "Ethan's at risk. Someone needs to be there to protect him while he's down."

Georgia studied him for a long moment, reluctance pulling her brows together. "Send it to the wrong man and we're more than risking Ethan's life."

"I trust these people. Worked with them, lived with them day in and day out for years. They wouldn't do this."

"But someone did," Georgia snapped. "Someone you know. Someone you work with. That's the reality, Parker. Someone close to you wants you dead. How can you be so certain it's not one of them? Especially given the nature of the ambush—no one should have been able to find us there."

Parker shook his head. There had to be another explanation.

"It's my program," he said. "It must have profiled Ethan, churned out the most likely scenarios. Once it established FedExField as a possibility, the rest would be easy."

Georgia stopped turning the bezel on her watch, focusing entirely on him. "Explain."

"The basics are pretty straightforward. The program is designed to look for patterns, look for connections."

"Like an analyst," Georgia said as the train rocked around a curved track of rail.

"Exactly. Except the program doesn't have human limitations. It doesn't sleep; it doesn't eat. There's no human error. If there's a connection to be made, no matter how thin, the program will tag it, then add it to a dedicated database tasked solely with the operation at hand."

"Our elimination."

"Yeah." Parker nodded.

"So basically, there's a supercomputer spending every second of the day trying to predict our next move, trying to kill us."

Never, in all the hours Parker had spent developing this technology, had he thought it would be used against him. Used to hunt down and kill his friends. His family. Because that's what this team was. And now it was on him to put a stop to it.

"The program doesn't actually sit on a supercomputer, thank God. All we need is my program running a trillion FLOPS a second."

"What?"

"Never mind, not important." Parker waved her off. She didn't need the technicalities, he reminded himself. Just the cold, hard truth. "But basically, yes. The program is trying to predict the most expedient way to kill us." Expedient but not subtle. Parameters could have been geared toward discretion and efficiency, but a hit at a crowded stadium hardly qualified as restrained. Which meant whoever wanted him dead wanted him buried *yesterday* and was willing to take enormous risks to achieve it. Voicing his thoughts, Parker said, "Ballsy, coming after us at a crowded game."

"Yeah, that had occurred to me, too. In a matter of hours, they've escalated from a quiet hit they could have staged as a home invasion to a massive public spectacle. There were literally thousands of witnesses—authorities may even have the shooter Ethan took down in custody. Why take such a risk?"

"It's got to be the thumb drive. It's the only thing that's changed in the last twenty-four hours." Parker patted the zippered pocket on his coat, reassuring himself it was still there. More than ever, he was certain the proof they needed was in those off-book operations. He just had to find it.

"But that still doesn't explain how they knew we'd be at the stadium, let alone which exit we'd use."

"Okay." Parker angled his body toward her, glancing around them as people filed on and off the train, letting a blast of icy air into the car. "Back to the analyst example. Typically, in intelligence a team of analysts is tasked with research, with digging through all kinds of information and flagging and categorizing it. Then, once there's enough information, they start cross-checking, drawing connections and making assumptions. But what it could take a team of dozens months if not years to do, my program can do in a matter of minutes. Worse, it's a government-controlled asset. It has access to every database you can think of—every branch of the military, the FBI, the CIA, the NSA, and probably a whole host of other databases that local, regional, and international law-enforcement agencies use in everyday business. There are no boundaries, no borders, this program can't cross."

Deus ex machina. An accomplishment he used to be proud of. He'd been so caught up in what he could do, he'd never stopped to think about what he *should* do.

"Great," Georgia said, tapping her fingertips against the plastic seat. "That sounds awesome."

"It gets worse," Parker admitted.

"Of course it does."

"Normally, the program is hindered by the fact that we have incomplete or insufficient intel. Fleshing out the details of emerging third-world threats can be almost impossible at times. Only recently has terrorism and other types of organized crime taken to social media, left a paper trail. Tracking back more than a year or two for most persons of interest often isn't feasible. Sometimes even confirming date of birth is a challenge. So the program has to compensate, make an educated guess based off race, gender, nationality, family ties—a whole host of information. But that's not an issue here."

Georgia dropped her head into her hands, her fingers gripping her curls. "Of course not. You're all government employees—high-value assets, no less. The DoD probably has dossiers a mile thick on all of you."

"Yeah," Parker said on a sigh. "And the program knows how we function as a team. How each member reacts under pressure, how we work in the field. My best guess? The program went searching for the team, filtering through all of Ethan's known associates. Ethan told me he pulled strings with a trusted client to get last-minute seats to the game today. Seats held under your name at the box office. Seats for every single member of our team."

"But I'm not part of the team," Georgia said. "I'd skew the number of seats the program expected to find, and up until yesterday, I wasn't affiliated with any of you."

"No. But you're an employee of Somerton Security—Ethan's company—and the connections don't have to be perfect, just close. One additional ticket wouldn't be enough to throw off the program." Parker rubbed his palms together, balancing his elbows on his knees. "From there, it would have been a piece of cake to predict Ethan's actions. His training, as good as it is, worked against him. Made him predictable. Waiting for the end of the game to leave, slipping out with the crowd, heading toward one of the closest parking lots . . . for the program, all too easy to predict."

A twisted sense of pride slid through Parker. He'd never really believed his work, his legacy, would be so damn successful. "No one betrayed us, Georgia. My program is just that good."

"Are you as certain of your own judgment? Are you willing to stack everything you know about these people against everything your program does?" She shot him a hard look. "Are you willing to risk your life—and mine—on the assumption they would never betray you?"

"Yes." The answer came so fast it left him breathless. The truth was, he shouldn't be so certain. He knew better than anyone that the face you showed the world was a tiny fraction of the entire person. He couldn't claim to know everything about Jones or Ortiz. Ryan or Liam. But he trusted them. Partly because he'd always, even in the beginning, felt safe with them, which when he thought about it, really came back to Ethan's leadership.

Ethan. Even if Parker didn't know the men he worked with, trust them, like them . . . he knew and trusted Ethan. And his judgment.

"Yes," he repeated.

"Okay." Georgia sighed, obviously willing to defer to him on this but not happy about it. "I'd like to know how Ethan's doing as well, and I'd feel better if someone was watching out for him. So if you're sure, go ahead and reach out." She placed her hand on his, halting the message he wanted to type out. "No details about us, Parker. I mean it. Nothing."

"Okay," Parker agreed, typing out a fast note on the game's messaging center. Once done, he slipped his phone into his jacket pocket and sat back. If he'd expected to feel even the slightest hint of relief, he'd have been disappointed. Now there was just one more thing to wait for.

"So it knows our moves before we even make them," Georgia said after a long silence, her tone cautious, as if she were wrestling with a puzzle that could fight back. "The program, I mean."

"No," Parker said, the first thread of hope winding through him. "It knows Ethan, me, the team. But it doesn't know *you*." Parker tried for a smile. "Beyond the most basic information, the program doesn't know *anything* about you. And as you don't strike me as the type to Instagram every meal you eat . . ."

"I don't even have Facebook," Georgia admitted.

"No social media at all? No adorable cat named Mittens? No tiny Yorkie named Sasquatch you feel compelled to subject to the world?"

Georgia shook her head. "I don't like cats, and a Yorkie's just a high-priced, overfluffed rat for rich people."

"Ouch." He chuckled, then slid his hand into hers. Squeezed. "You might be the only one who stands any chance at beating my program." He took a deep breath. He was straying dangerously close to a "Help me, Obi-Wan Kenobi, you're my only hope" moment, which yet again cast him in the roll of the damsel. Still, if he had to put his life entirely in someone's hands, he couldn't think of anyone he'd trust more than Georgia. Which meant he had to be all in. He had to put his faith in her, had to let her make the decisions from here on out. Model client, as promised. He'd never have guessed just how important that bet would become. Or that he'd be so damn grateful she'd passed his test.

"What do we do first?"

◆ ◆ ◆

What do we do first? Words she'd spent the last hour wrestling with. Words that took on a whole new meaning in light of Parker's explanation. How the hell was she going to keep them alive? This was nothing she'd ever trained for, nothing she'd ever even considered. Funny, how basic training and private protection details didn't prepare a girl for homicidal computers with a God complex. Ethan *really* should have read her in from the beginning. Now, no matter what she did, she'd always be catching up to the situation. Always a step too slow. Which could be deadly.

"I guess this is an obvious question, but is there any way to shut down the program?" He'd probably have mentioned such a thing by now, but a girl could hope.

"Yeah, one." He picked at his cuticles.

"But?" Because, oh, there was a *but*. She could see it all over his face.

"But it's not a magic bullet—the program has already run, already produced dozens of potential outcomes."

"As that thing is trying to *kill* us, I'm going to need you to walk me through your thought process."

Parker's smile was grim. "The program sits on a highly secured government server—something I'm not supposed to have access to outside of either my government-issued laptop and security key or when I'm physically present at the office. With decent Internet access, I can probably work around that part, but it's harder on an out-of-the-box computer. The problem is, it'll take some time—"

"How much time?" she asked.

"At least an hour—an eternity in terms of exposure. And even if I'm careful, even if I do everything right, it's going to expose us to scrutiny."

"What kind of scrutiny?"

"Our IP address, for one. Possibly our physical location as well. You have to understand, hacking isn't easy, and more, it takes a lot of time. To even have a shot at doing this completely undetected, I'd need to spend days prepping, then hours upon hours actually executing it. It would take all my time and attention."

"Which means you wouldn't have the resources to go through the files Ethan gave us."

"Right. It's probably going to take both of us to do that as it is, if only because we have no idea what we're looking for."

"Needle in a haystack." Awesome.

"If we're lucky," Parker said. "Shutting down the program would consume all our time and energy but ultimately wouldn't put us any closer to the answers we need."

Georgia rubbed at the bridge of her nose. "So we let it hunt us down? Wouldn't it be better to disable it and run, buy us some breathing room?"

"Maybe. But the program has already performed an analysis. You have to understand, the program will cycle every time it's provided with new intel, but at this point, that's going to be pretty damn minimal. It already knows everything there is to know about me, about Ethan and the rest of the team. Those predictions are made. There might be variations, but if we don't give it much to work with, not much will change. We can't unring that bell." Parker laced his fingers together, bracing his forearms on his knees. "The only new intel for the program to work with is you."

Shit.

"And you don't think it'll find much?"

Parker shrugged. "Based on what you told me? No, I don't think it'll have a lot to work with. But even if that weren't the case, I can guarantee they're already working on identifying you. Even if I wasn't worried about getting caught, by the time I get to a computer and disable the program, odds are it will already have factored you in."

The weight of everything Parker said settled, heavy and immovable, on her shoulders. How was she supposed to work like this?

"All right, what if we throw caution to the wind and say screw flying under the radar? How fast could you take down the program?"

Parker grew quiet and still for a long moment, as if a brute-force Hail Mary tactic had never occurred to him. "Assuming my credentials haven't been pulled? I could log in and take down the program, but the minute I do, our location is burned, and we've tipped what might be the only hand we have to play. No one knows I can kill this thing, but the minute I do, they'll be alerted."

That felt less like having an extra card up their sleeve and more like pressing a self-destruct button. And if Ethan was right, and this was all about the money, disabling the program was going to make whoever was behind this desperate.

And desperate people were dangerous.

So, what then? She fought back the hysteria, the absolute conviction that she was so far out of her element she couldn't possibly hope to compete. She needed to breathe. To think. If she looked at their situation as a whole, let herself focus on everything she didn't understand and couldn't solve, fear and sheer panic would breed hopelessness. Enough people were trying to kill them. Georgia had no intention of defeating herself.

One decision at a time.

Start with a goal and work backward from there to create the steps for dealing with it. *I can do this. I can do this.*

"Let's say we risk it and remove your program from the playing field—is there anyone who could get it back up and running?" she asked.

Parker shook his head. "Not likely. If I trigger my fail-safe, it's going to pull down huge sections of digital infrastructure, which I'd have to rebuild."

"And there's no one on your team who could do that? No one at the DoD who could re-create what you destroy?"

"Over time—months, weeks if they hired outside help, maybe. But overnight? No way." The train car shifted, barreling around a curve and pressing her closer to Parker, who asked, "Why, what are you thinking?"

"That we have something else to gain from disabling the program."

Parker turned his head to stare at her, his brow creasing with confusion.

"Right now, someone is making a fortune off your work, and they want you out of the way."

"Thanks for the reminder. I'd almost forgotten about my impending death." His tone was wry, but Georgia laced her fingers around his forearm anyway.

"I may not have all the insight your tech does, but I do know one thing: people driven by power, money, stature—they will do *anything* to keep what they have."

"Meaning?" Parker asked.

"Meaning that priority one is keeping you alive—and the best way to do that, for right now at least, is to make you more valuable alive than dead. If you're the only person who can bring your program back online . . ."

"Then the objective changes from kill to capture."

Georgia felt a tremor roll through Parker.

"Not sure I like that idea much better."

"I know," Georgia said, squeezing his forearm once before letting go. "But *if* something happened, it would buy me time to find you. This plan also increases the odds that you survive any encounters from here on out."

"Doesn't do anything for *your* odds," Parker said, his words heavy with fear and regret.

Georgia tried to smile. It wasn't just her. The only person this would benefit was Parker. Everyone else remained expendable. "One problem at a time, all right? I'm still the bodyguard; you're still the damsel."

"Ha-ha," Parker muttered, then heaved out a breath and thankfully didn't argue. "Okay, let's say we go with your plan. Then what?"

"Then the priority becomes getting somewhere safe. Somewhere entirely off grid." Which meant anywhere she and Parker had ever been was out of the question. She should probably strike anything that felt familiar or comfortable. Which left what, exactly? Places dangerous, terrifying, or both? As if her subconscious sensed her vulnerability, one possibility came to mind. Discreet, they could pay in cash, no one would ask questions . . . The smell of lingering cigarette smoke, decades old and stale, flooded her nose. No. Not there. Not unless it was the only option.

She pulled her thoughts away from worn, nubby carpeting and long, cold nights.

Regardless, lodging wasn't the first problem they needed to solve. Falling off the grid meant functioning without the burden of a paper trail, and that meant they needed cash. A lot of it.

Her nerves settled under the blanket of a decision.

"How much money do you have on you?" Georgia asked, studying the Metro stops on the map above her.

"About seventy bucks—we spent a good portion of what I had last night."

Yeah, but there hadn't been much choice. She'd put off worrying about it because Parker had seemed so certain Ethan would make contact. When he had, she'd dismissed the concern almost entirely. Stupid, though her worry wouldn't have changed anything. But seventy dollars . . . barely enough for a decent dinner for two, let alone enough to get them good and lost. And since she didn't carry cash at all, their options were limited.

Time to get creative—or just acknowledge they were desperate.

Georgia twisted the bezel on her watch, the weight heavy against her wrist. For once the steady *click-click-click* provided more hurt than comfort, a reminder time was ticking and her options were few. She shoved her hands into her coat pockets. So many things she'd sworn she'd never do were lining up before her, as if they'd always been there, just waiting for the day the universe decided to slap her back down. She wasn't ready to take the hit. Not yet.

"Let me see your watch." Parker was a tech genius with millions; he had to have something on him worth pawning.

He held out his wrist, shoving back his sleeve. A hysterical laugh bubbled up her throat.

"A Swatch? Seriously?"

"What?" Parker asked, brushing his sleeve back down. "It's vintage. Worth a hundred and fifty bucks on eBay."

"It's Spider-Man." Which didn't surprise her at all. In any other scenario, she'd have found it oddly charming. And so very true to form. Nothing pretentious about Parker, though in the moment she wished to God there was. "Anything else we could pawn? Designer wallet? Other jewelry?"

Parker looked at her as if she'd grown a second head. "My wallet is from Target. I don't wear jewelry, and I'm guessing my watch didn't impress. So no." He shrugged. "Anything we could pawn for cash is back at my loft."

Great.

"Forget it, sorry I even asked." She shook her head. It was on her, then. Her heart twisted, but she pushed aside the feelings. With no other choices, she couldn't afford to be sentimental. Hell, she should have gotten rid of the thing months ago. Losing something you weren't attached to in the first place didn't hurt.

"All right," she said, shrugging off her darkening mood and focusing on what she actually had any control over. "Before we do anything else, we've got to get our hands on some cash. ATMs are out of the question, so we're going to have to get creative. There's a pawnshop walking distance from DuPont Circle. We'll get off there and walk."

"What are we going to pawn?"

Just say it. Quick. Clean. A knife between the ribs and as close to painless as she'd be allowed. "My watch. It's a vintage Rolex Submariner. Worth several thousand, easy, even at a pawnshop." And completely irreplaceable. Georgia smothered the flash of grief that threatened to drown her.

"You don't have to do that," Parker said, reaching for her, sympathy lacing every word.

Georgia pulled away. "Unless you've got something valuable on you I don't know about or another way to get a lot of cash fast, yeah, I do."

He sat back in his seat, quiet for a long moment as he ran through possibilities. "The only thing I can think of would be trying to get to one of the Somerton Security safe houses. I know Ethan usually has them well stocked. But . . ."

"But that's too predictable."

"Yeah."

A thought occurred to her. One she hadn't yet considered. "Couldn't that work to our advantage? If it's that obvious, isn't it possible the program would take into consideration that you'd know it was risky?"

Parker shook his head. "It'll factor that in. But it'd still consider those safe houses likely outcomes. If we can't come up with an alternative, then our options narrow considerably. It's too risky."

"Any other ideas?"

"No." Frustration and regret mingled on his face.

For a split second, Georgia found it all too easy to resent him. This was his fault. The situation, their limited choices—and what was he being asked to sacrifice to secure their safety? What was he being forced to give up?

Nothing. As usual, *she* was on the losing end.

It wasn't fair.

But then, life never was.

Suck it up, Buttercup. An expression her father had been fond of and one he'd said often, even when she'd been a little girl, too young to really understand the truth of the words.

"Right." She shook off the memory, wishing it had bolstered her resolve more than it had. "So we go to the pawnshop, then find another place to crash. I'm guessing your program has access to facial-recognition software?"

"Yeah," Parker said cautiously. "What are you thinking?"

"That all the DC Metros have plenty of security cameras. How long do you think it'll be before your program is scanning feeds for our faces?"

Parker grimaced.

"Yeah, that's what I thought. Once we leave DuPont station—and we need to be ultracareful when we do—no more trains. Which means we need transportation."

"We can't risk my car."

"No. And I don't think we can risk mine, either. Not if you think your program has flagged me as Ethan's employee."

"I'm sure it has."

"Then we need to consider all my assets off-limits, too."

"Then what? We can't exactly walk onto a lot and buy a new car."

"No," Georgia agreed, thinking through their options. "And we'll need to be conservative with our cash. Pull up Craigslist," she said, nodding toward his phone. "Search for a late-model Toyota or Honda. Something reliable and common. Private sellers only. The last thing we need to do is try to talk our way out of registering the car with the dealership. We'll have to settle for something high mileage, but make sure the ad says it runs. Fifteen hundred dollars or less, if you can manage it."

"Okay," Parker said, tapping the screen on his phone. "Then what?"

Then . . . then the hard part. "We'll arrange a meet to look at the car, preferably within walking distance of a big-box store that sells computers and has Internet access. I'll buy the car, you'll take down your program—we'll need to scout for security cameras, try to find a route that lets us meet up without getting caught on surveillance—and then, God willing, we disappear."

"That easy, huh?"

"It's gonna have to be." The whole idea was risky and in no way Georgia's first choice. But it was her best choice, so she'd find a way to make it work.

"Then we hole up and let you work on the thumb drive Ethan gave you." Somewhere they could pay in cash, where people wouldn't ask too many questions. Somewhere they could start digging through those files. Their options were depressingly limited. Did they stay in the DC area? Head back to Baltimore? What was most predictable, most obvious? Georgia shook her head. A motel that took cash without requiring a credit card to secure the room would eat up funds quickly.

"How long do you think you'll need to go through those files?"

"I can't know. Not until I look at them. Ethan said he grabbed fifty or so files, but each file could be like a Russian doll. I have no way of knowing how much information is in here—or what I'm looking for."

"Days?" Georgia pressed.

"Maybe." Parker shook his head, dropping his gaze to the floor. "Weeks, even. I just don't know for sure."

So she had to plan long-term. Even if she got a fair price for the watch—a long shot, as she had to settle for pawning it—the money wouldn't last forever. And a car was going to put a dent in their funds. Even if they were lucky and found somewhere that could pass for decent for less than fifty a night . . . The math just didn't work in their favor. Not to mention staying anywhere typically rented by the hour for more than a night or two was likely to draw suspicion.

So, a monthly, in-cash, no-questions-asked rental.

Running from what was fast becoming the most obvious option was beginning to wear Georgia down.

Suck it up, Buttercup.

"Ever been to Pittsburgh?" she asked, staring out the window as DC slipped past them in a blur of white and gray.

"No."

"Me neither." Though it hardly mattered. For what she had in mind, any big city would do.

"Would that make it more or less likely to ping your program?"

"Less, probably. If neither of us has any personal attachments there, it becomes a really big haystack. And anyway, the program has a decent database on human psychology to use as a filter and help assign values to each prediction. Most people, when threatened or cornered, go back to what they know. Fall back on something familiar. That's what makes disappearing so damn hard. Everyone's first instinct is to go where they feel the safest."

"So if we did the opposite?"

"What do you mean?"

Shame tried to stick her tongue to the roof of her mouth. "My childhood was . . . tumultuous, to say the least. I spent some time in foster care." She glanced up, trying to gauge Parker's reaction. It wasn't a period of life she'd had any control over, not something she'd chosen for herself. Yet it seemed like every time she admitted that, every time she trusted someone with it, he or she looked at her differently. As if the person expected something . . . less . . . of her. Parker stared back, his expression still but engaged. As if the information had slid right past him and he was still entirely focused on where she was going with the conversation. "Unfortunately, most of the foster-care system is reliant on people who need the government stipend. Which means most kids grow up in low-income, high-crime areas. Areas where rentals are easier to come by."

"Okay, but we shouldn't revisit anywhere you've been. Anywhere that's familiar or comfortable."

"Which is why I think this is our best solution." If she understood Parker's program correctly, and she thought she did, they needed to be unpredictable. And what better way to do that than to return to a life she'd sworn to never revisit? "At this point, your program is probably digging through my past, piecing together my backstory. There won't be much. My parents died when I was seven. My grandmother when I was ten. Aside from my birth certificate, school and medical records, there will be little to discover. Not up until my twelfth birthday." She pushed down the well of anger, pain, and resentment that threatened to drown her. "That was the year Will and I went into foster care. From that point on, there will be sealed juvenile records."

"Yeah, the program will find those." He didn't ask *what* the program would find, though she could tell by the way he fidgeted that he really wanted to.

The nubby scrape of ancient shag carpet. The acrid stench of urine. Fear. Desperation. All as real as if she'd lived them yesterday.

"I rolled through seven foster homes before I left the system permanently." A blessing she'd been afforded at fifteen only because Will, her beautiful, selfless brother, her personal white knight, had put his entire life on hold to take custody of her. "But by far, the worst placements were the ones in trailer parks." The ghostly tap dance of a roach crawling across her bare leg sent a shiver down her spine. "I'd never go back to one, not willingly. If your program is as thorough as you say it is, it'll come to the same conclusion."

Parker looked unconvinced. "But if you've been there before . . . it's like I said, people always fall back on what's familiar, even if it's been years, decades. They call old friends, return to old neighborhoods."

"Not me." No, she'd spent her entire life running. Never had she returned to her childhood home in Charlotte. Not once had she even had the urge to visit her grandmother's old place in South Florida. She'd never visited her parents' graves or even so much as driven past Arlington Cemetery. She didn't lay a wreath at Christmas or send flowers for anniversaries. She moved forward. Away from the hurt, away from the pain. Away from all the memories, good and bad, that only served to remind her of what she no longer had.

No. If Parker's program was as thorough as he claimed, it'd dig through her juvenile file, through every social-service report, and come to the conclusion that she'd rather die than go back to a trailer park. Which, of course, meant that was the one place she had to go.

"It's our best bet. We can find a trailer park with rentals on the Internet. Most will take cash up front and rent from month to month."

"And you're absolutely certain the program won't track us to one?"

He wanted to ask for details, for proof of her theory; it was all over his face. Though he wasn't a man who took anything at face value or made any decision, no matter how small, without all the facts at his disposal, Parker wasn't pressing her. If she weren't so desperately tired, she'd thank him for it.

"I'm sure." And even if the program did consider it a possibility, what then? There were hundreds upon hundreds of trailer parks in major cities along the East Coast. With no digital footprint and neighbors who were likely to be wary of law enforcement anyway . . .

It was the best she could come up with. There wasn't a perfect option, no safe place for her and Parker. Not anymore. Their best bet was to find a decent car, take the long way to Pittsburgh, avoiding tolls and cameras, then find a place they could disappear into. Just two more people life had kicked to the bottom.

Parker nodded once, then turned back to his phone.

A few minutes passed in silence before he said, "Here's a 1996 Toyota Corolla. One owner. Good condition. A hundred and forty-two thousand miles."

"Asking price?"

"Sixteen hundred."

"Make the call when we're on street level," Georgia said, standing as the train squealed into the station. She leaned close to Parker as they exited. "Keep your head down, and let's stay with the crowd as much as possible."

Wordlessly, they exited the station, emerging onto the street into the bitter DC cold. Georgia took a moment to orient herself, then headed north, toward a pawnshop she knew. Next to her, Parker dialed the owner of the car, surprising her when he slipped into accented but passable Spanish. As they walked, Georgia tried to tune out the heavy weight of her watch and the burden of the responsibility she now found squarely on her shoulders.

Turning her chin up, facing the wind head-on, Georgia forced herself forward.

One step at a time, she reminded herself.

If only she didn't know where those steps were leading her.

A place that had nearly destroyed her.

A place she'd sworn never to return to.

And maybe the only place that could save them.

Who said you couldn't go home?

◆ ◆ ◆

Nearly twenty-four hours later, Georgia pulled into the crushed-gravel driveway of Shady Pines RV Park as the sun dipped beyond the horizon, casting the bare branches of the trees and just about everything else in a depressing wash of gray. Leaning over the steering wheel, she glanced up through the windshield and confirmed the lot number. Four brass plates screwed into the siding of the 1970s Skyline told her they were in the right place . . . Well, almost—102A, while old and in need of some minor updates around the exterior, was in remarkably good shape; 102B, however . . .

Well, the second trailer wasn't nearly so welcoming, but as it was about to be home for the foreseeable future, Georgia did her best not to dwell on it.

Carefully, so as not to wake Parker, Georgia climbed out of their ancient Corolla. She left the engine running and the heat on low, hoping Parker wouldn't wake yet. Their luck had finally begun to turn over the last twenty-four hours. It had taken three calls and one missed connection until Georgia and Parker found a model that fit their needs and budget. When they'd met the owner—a sweet nurse in her late twenties named Amelia—at a Target parking lot three blocks from a Best Buy, Georgia had been shocked to find the car in exceptionally good condition. Newer tires. Consistent and documented engine maintenance. An immaculate interior. It was more than she'd dared hope for on the limited budget her watch had afforded them. When Amelia had exchanged the keys for cash and broken into sobs, Georgia had promised she'd take good care of her car.

One nerve-racking hour later, she'd pulled onto the highway, Parker in the passenger seat, his program off-line for the foreseeable future.

Exhausted and stressed, there was just one last hill for her to climb. Trudging up the wood steps that were in need of a fresh coat of paint, Georgia knocked against the weathered storm door of 102A. While she waited, her shoulders hunched against the cold, she glanced back at Parker. Still sleeping, thank goodness. She needed a few minutes alone, a bit of time to adjust, before she dragged him with her into reality.

"What do you want?" a voice burdened with a two-pack-a-day habit asked from behind the door.

"I'm looking for Betty. I'm picking up the keys for 102B," Georgia said. "We talked on the phone this morning."

The interior door cracked open, a weathered face appearing beyond the glass of the storm door. An older woman, cigarette dangling from lips smudged with lipstick the same shade of coral as the trim around her home, stepped forward, eyeing Georgia suspiciously. "I'm Betty. You said you'd pay cash up front; that's five seventy-five and includes utilities."

"Right." Georgia shivered on the porch, wishing the woman would just get on with it.

"Then let's see the cash."

Sighing, Georgia pulled an envelope from her pocket—she'd separated out the correct amount earlier that afternoon—and pried it open so the woman could see.

Nodding, Betty said, "Wait there." She disappeared back inside, cursing and mumbling as *Entertainment Tonight* loudly broadcast the details of the latest Hollywood divorce. "Here," she said, reappearing with a set of keys in her hand. She shoved open the storm door, forcing Georgia back a step, and motioned for the cash with her free hand. Georgia handed over the envelope. Betty took it, pulled the bills out, and shoved the envelope under her armpit. Licking her thumb, she flicked through the bills, then nodded. She hesitated before handing the keys over, eyeing Georgia up and down then glancing over her shoulder to the car idling in her driveway. "I don't want no trouble—no drugs or loud music. No people comin' and goin' at all hours, you hear me?"

"Yes, ma'am." When Betty still hesitated to hand over the keys, Georgia elaborated. "My mama's over at Presbyterian Hospital, cancer. We just need someplace to stay until she's on her feet. The damn retirement home I help pay for won't let us stay there—"

Betty shoved the keys at her, then slammed the door closed on an "I'll pray for her."

Good to know not much had changed in the years since she'd been in a park. Fastest way to get rid of someone was to tell your sob story; God knew those were as common as fleas, roaches, and feral cats around

143

here. No one cared, and no one wanted to hear it. Turning, Georgia strode down the steps, bypassing the car and heading toward 102B. For a long moment, she stood at the bottom of the three porch steps, the paint faded and peeling. She took a deep breath, let the cold sear her lungs and the fresh air remind her of where she was—and where she wasn't. If finding a place to stay hadn't been so damn difficult, she'd have passed on the 1971 Skyline single-wide in front of her. Too many bad memories, too many things she didn't want to relive. But it wasn't identical, she reminded herself as she climbed the steps, brushing snow from a banister that swayed precariously beneath her palm. Paint the color of oatmeal and dark-brown shutters graced the siding, not the white and green she remembered from that foster-home placement long ago.

Gripping the handle of the screen door, Georgia pressed the button, then had to shimmy it back and forth to get the catch to release. She pulled it open, bracing it with her shoulder as she slid the key into the dead bolt on the door. Grabbing the doorknob, she took a deep breath. No more stalling; she needed to get over her irrational fear and go inside. Twisting the doorknob, Georgia startled as the storm door disappeared from her shoulder.

"Jesus, Parker. You scared the crap out of me."

"Sorry." He smiled sleepily down at her.

"Did you turn off the car?" The last thing they needed was for someone to drive off in it. Wasn't like they could risk reporting it stolen.

He held up the keys and gave her a look that clearly said, *What do you take me for, a moron?*

"And I grabbed our stuff out of the trunk, too. Surprised you didn't hear me slam the lid." He nodded toward the trailer. "We should get inside."

Something in the careful way Parker said it set off alarms.

"What is it?" Georgia asked, reaching for a few of the plastic bags hanging from Parker's arms and casting a careful glance over her shoulder. Well after dark and cold as fuck outside, the trailer park was blessedly quiet. No people. No cars coming or going. Maybe she was just tired and overreacting.

"I checked my phone for news related to the shooting. I've been named a person of interest. The profile *Wired* magazine did—and the photo they took—is making the rounds."

Of course it was. When they'd managed to quietly slip out of DC, she'd let herself hope things would get easier. She should have known better. Whoever wanted Parker dead was getting desperate.

And her job was getting harder.

"Yeah." Georgia swallowed down her irritation and the constant fear that hummed just beneath the surface of her skin, turned the knob, and bumped the door open with her hip when the frame refused to release it. The three-pronged assault on her senses hit with merciless proficiency. Peeling wood paneling greeted the eye as worn-thin shag carpeting hissed a greeting beneath the soles of her shoes. And the smell . . .

"Oh my God, what *is* that?" Parker asked as he followed her inside, dumping their bags next to the front door that led directly into a sitting room that hadn't seen a change in furniture or decor since the seventies.

"The heater."

"Is it always going to do that?" Parker asked. "I mean, I'm grateful the heat's on, but geez . . ."

"It should get better. The landlady probably turned it on just before we arrived. Dust tends to accumulate on the coils when they haven't been used in a long time. Turn on the heat and it all burns off, which is what you smell."

"It's like . . ." He sniffed, then grimaced.

"Burned hair."

"Yeah."

Scooping a few bags off the floor, Georgia strode across the living room, heading for the kitchen tucked into the corner. More wood paneling. A dented stainless-steel sink. An ancient refrigerator doing an admirable impression of the ghost in the attic. Depositing the bags on the counter, Georgia pulled open a cabinet—no evidence of rodents, thank God—and started piling things away.

"Holy flux capacitor, Batman, I think we landed in 1974," Parker said, awe painting his tone as he plucked at the laminate peeling away from a cabinet door. "On the upside, I've always wondered if I'm cut out for living in one of those tiny homes you read about online. This'll be a little bit like that."

No. No it *wouldn't* be like that, Georgia thought as she slammed a cabinet shut and jerked open the refrigerator. Those homes were new. With modern amenities. Most of them were green. They didn't creak like a backwoods shack every time the wind blew. They didn't have water rings the size of inner tubes on the ceiling. They didn't smell like someone was roasting a dead cat or have closets men locked little girls in when they were bad.

All at once, Georgia couldn't breathe. Couldn't think. She had to get out. Sleep in the car, on the porch. She'd freeze to death, but anything was better than being in here for one more second.

"Georgia?"

She shoved past Parker, ignoring his concern and his outstretched hand. Broke into a run as she neared the door, slamming through to the outside so hard she missed the top step, tumbled down the next two, and landed on her knees in the half-melted snow. Slush coated her jeans, soaking into the denim as she knelt and fought for breath. She'd hoped the fresh, cold air would help drive away the nausea. Instead, the moment frigid air met overheated, sweat-slicked skin, her nausea doubled down, and acid surged up her throat. Tears burned her eyes as she knelt on the frozen ground and puked what little she'd managed to eat for lunch.

Finally, when the heaving stopped and Georgia could suck in great lungfuls of cold air without choking on a sob, she leaned back onto her heels and, brushing the tears from her face, stood. Tilting her head back, she let the back of her skull fall against her shoulders. Above her, an inky black sky stretched in every direction, a few stars broadcasting through the haze of city light. Though the nausea had passed, she felt it there, crouched in the back of her mind like a lion in the dark, ready to pounce and devour the moment she least expected. She needed to calm the hell down. Fast. She couldn't go back into the trailer like this. Parker needed to believe she had everything under control, that she could protect him long enough for him to get the job done.

Truth was, as the day had slid by along endless stretches of highway, Georgia had settled into her present situation. Adjusted to the fact she'd be working in less than ideal circumstances.

Which meant her little breakdown of a moment ago was entirely personal. And entirely unprofessional.

"Here." Parker appeared beside her, handing her an open vita-minwater. "It's not very cold, but it'll help rinse the taste out of your mouth."

So he'd seen her lose it. She expected the knowledge that he'd watched as she'd completely fallen apart to somehow make her feel worse, but instead she found she was far too exhausted to care.

"Thanks." Her fingers trembled, the traitorous little jerks, as she reached for the drink. "Go inside. Crack a few windows. Place won't warm as quickly, but it'll help with the smell." And give her a bit of time to pull herself together. With any luck, Parker would assume the smell had turned her stomach inside out, rather than . . .

Than what? Distant memories that should have only the power she gave them? A child's sense of desperation and anguish she should have long ago outgrown? God, she needed therapy. Or better yet, vodka.

Definitely vodka.

Too bad alcohol wasn't in the budget. Hardly fair, as she'd agreed Parker needed coffee—even if it were the crappy kind that came in a canister.

She swished a bit of water through her mouth, then spit it out. She repeated the process until her mouth held only the vague sense of something fruity. Slowly, she sipped, waiting to see if her stomach would raise a protest.

"Breathing better?" Parker asked, reappearing at her side.

"You shouldn't be out here, Parker." Neither of them should, but it wasn't her face littering the news outlets. She just needed a minute to get her head on straight.

Parker turned, trod up the steps, killed the tiny porch light, and reappeared at her side. "How often do you have them?"

Georgia crossed her arms, balancing her drink in the crook of one elbow. "What do you mean?"

"Panic attacks," he clarified.

Georgia straightened, shooting him an angry glare. "I didn't panic." She hadn't. She'd just needed a minute to process—a minute he'd denied her when he hadn't stayed asleep in the car.

"Sorry, I never liked the term. Never really liked 'anxiety attack,' either. Made me feel like it was something I should be able to turn off. Something I could control."

Anxiety attack? No. No way. Georgia shook her head. "I'm fine."

Parker stared at her for a long moment, a tiny vertical line appearing between his brows. "First one, huh?"

Georgia walked away, heading back up the steps and opening the door. The smell assaulted her, weaker but still there. Her stomach rolled, and an angry buzz of energy slid through her like a whirling, dancing, diving group of birds hell-bent on ripping her open.

Nope. She definitely needed a little more air. Too tired to keep standing and too wet to give a damn, Georgia brushed off the clumps of slush along the top step and sat, letting the cold seep through her wet jeans and numb her. With the porch light off, it was dark enough to risk a few minutes of fresh air. No streetlights for the poor. As long as they stayed on the steps, in the deeper shadows cast by the small porch overhang, they'd be invisible.

"Try taking deep breaths, then longer exhales. It sounds trite to 'just breathe,' but that always helped me." Parker sat next to her, heedless of the wet and cold. He bumped her with his shoulder, the tilt of a grin curling one side of his mouth. "Welcome to the club. There's no secret handshake, but the little blue pills don't suck."

Georgia snorted out a laugh. "I'll be taking Viagra in this club, will I?"

Parker laughed. "I was thinking more along the lines of Xanax, but sure."

Georgia rested her elbows against her knees, rolling the bottle she held between her palms. "Sorry," she said quietly.

Parker turned his head to look at her. "Don't be. Frankly, I'm a little relieved." He palmed the back of his neck, rubbing as if he were self-conscious. "I haven't had an episode yet . . . A little strange, actually." He dropped his hand, staring across the lot at the trailers lined up like regimented tombstones. "My anxiety is pretty well under control—way better than it used to be—but little sleep, tons of change, and epic amounts of stress are triggers on their own." He sighed. "I think that after Ethan, I sort of shut down a bit. Let you tell me what to do and handle the rest. Then as soon as we hit the road, I dove into the files Ethan gave us. It let me have something to focus on. Avoiding things I don't want to think about is practically my superpower," Parker said, toeing a rusty nail straining away from the board beneath his feet. "So I'm sorry. I checked out on you, didn't even really think about how much stress you're under. I know you didn't sign up for this," Parker admitted on a whisper.

Well, hell. He looked miserable, as if the weight of the situation had finally caught up to him. To both of them, she supposed, though in rather different ways. Regardless, she couldn't let him shoulder guilt that wasn't his.

"It's not that," she assured him. "I mean, don't get me wrong. This"—she waved a hand at the hulking tin can behind her—"isn't going to be easy. It's one thing to take on a long-term client. To be with him day in and day out. But he isn't usually under *constant* threat. I'm a little out of my depth here."

"You got us this far, Georgia. You'll take us the rest of the way." The way he said it, as if, obviously, she would get them through whatever lay ahead, humbled her. She wished she were a tenth as certain of their future. Or her ability to protect him.

But that wasn't really what was bothering her. "It's this place," she said, kicking at the rickety handrail next to her. "You ever feel like something's cursed? Like no matter what you do or how far you've come, this one place, this one thing, has the power to screw it all up?"

"Yeah. I do."

"I hate it here. I hate that *I* brought us here." She took Parker's advice, drawing in a long, shaky breath, then letting it go on a drawn-out sigh. As her breath danced away from her in a cloud of steam, Georgia turned to Parker. "I hate that even after all these years, this place still has the power to wreck me."

She stared at him for a long moment, though what she was searching for, she couldn't quite say. Something familiar, maybe. Disinterest. Pity. Or maybe something as bold and refreshing as Parker himself. Something like understanding.

"Will you tell me why?" Not a demand. Not a morbid quest for personal details he could judge her with. Just . . . an invitation to share.

For the first time in her life, she found she wanted to.

"I went into the foster-care system for the first time when I was ten years old. Six months later, my foster father, drunk as usual, locked me in a closet before he beat my foster mother to death, then shot himself in the head. The police found me forty-eight hours later."

CHAPTER EIGHT

Parker braced his forearms on his legs and laced his fingers together. He ached to reach for her. To take one of her cold hands between his and rub away the chill. Metaphorical or physical, he didn't care. He just wanted to make it better for her. Knowing that he couldn't wrecked him. Only the knowledge that she wouldn't appreciate tenderness, wouldn't want gentle sympathy, held him still and let her talk.

"In so many ways, that home was the worst placement. Too much change, way too fast. And without my brother. That was the hardest part."

"You were close?" Parker asked when she paused, reaching for her wrist and the watch that was no longer there.

"Very." She laughed, the sound stretched and brittle. "Well, not when we were kids, I guess. Will was four years older, and I worshipped him, which basically meant wherever he was and whatever he was doing, I wanted to be right there in the thick of it." She glanced at Parker, her mouth twitching with remembered amusement. "He used to call me a tick. 'Mom,'" she imitated, her voice going high and nasal, "'I need a match, there's a life-sucking parasite attached to my side.'" She shook her head.

"What an ass." Parker laughed.

"Yeah, well, I used to call him a weasel—no one was better at getting into or out of trouble." She chuckled. "He never forgave me. The name stuck, followed him all the way through Special Forces."

What was it with spec ops guys and awful nicknames? Mouse. Snake. Weasel . . . Peanut.

"It's so hard to picture you trailing behind anyone," he said.

"Will was the only exception. And if my hero worship annoyed him, my desire to prove I was just as good or better at everything he did drove him *nuts*." She tapped her chin, finger sliding along a thin white scar. "This one I got when I bet him I could get the swing at the playground higher and then jump farther at the peak than he could. Four stitches. My mother was furious." She shot him a smug look, the memory of the challenge lightening her expression. "He told me a month later that it didn't count because I didn't stick the landing." She shook her head.

"Let me guess. You stuck the landing."

"Hell no. My mother took one look at my blood-covered clothes and declared that I was obviously *not* her daughter and should be returned to the hospital posthaste." The corners of her eyes crinkled. "My father just shook his head and grabbed his keys to take me to the ER. Said that being on a first-name basis with the on-call doctor was a Bennett family tradition . . . though seven times in six months might have been pushing it."

"They sound amazing," Parker said, not bothering to hide the potent jealousy that flooded him, momentarily smothering his sympathy. What wouldn't he have done for a family like that? For even one moment in an emergency room with an exasperated mother and oddly proud father? He pushed away the envy and reminded himself that while Georgia had wonderful memories of her childhood, of her family, it was probably those memories that had made her adolescence so much worse. Hard, Parker knew, to miss what you'd never really had. "How old were you?"

"Seven."

"And when they died?" he asked.

"The same year," she said, her energy draining as bad memories eclipsed the good.

"And that's when you went into foster care?" Parker asked.

"No. Actually, Will and I went to live with our grandmother—my father's mother. My mother's parents had her late in life. I never knew them. But Gran we grew up around. That was the first time I lived in a trailer park, actually."

"Yeah?" Parker had assumed her only experience had been with the foster family who'd locked her away.

"Yeah. Though it never felt that way. Gram had a double-wide, a manufactured home, she called it. Three bedrooms, two baths. Small, compared to what we were used to, but nice. Clean. Most of the neighbors were older snowbirds, so the place was quiet and well kept. And we were close to the beach, which was great."

"How long were you there?"

Georgia shrugged, toying with a loose strand of hair. "Almost eighteen months. Enough time to get comfortable, to think things were leveling out and getting better. It was an especially hard time for Will. He was thirteen, had left all his childhood friends behind and had to start over. That's when we got close."

Parker waited, letting Georgia get comfortable in the silence between them, process the memories he could read on her face but that she wasn't ready to share. He hoped they were good ones.

"But then things changed again. Gram tripped—on a lawn ornament, of all things—and broke her hip." Georgia turned to him. "Did you know the mortality rate in the year following a hip fracture is greatly increased?"

Parker shook his head. He'd never known his father at all, and his mother's extended family had been long estranged by the time he came along, for reasons he'd only learned when he was nearly an adult himself.

"Yeah, neither did we." She stood, brushing the snow from her ass, and stretched. Ready to run but nowhere to go.

Parker knew the feeling. Understood the desire to just go, leave everything behind you, and start fresh. He also knew the minute you thought you'd run far enough, hard enough, or long enough, you'd turn a blind corner and be right back where you started.

"That's when social services stepped in."

"And they separated you," Parker said, imagining a ten-year-old Georgia, who'd lost far too much already, being taken from her brother. Had she cried? Or just stood there, unsurprised at how life could be so endlessly cruel? Both options tore at him, and both evolved his understanding of the woman she was.

"They separated us," she agreed. "Then . . ." Her shoulders hitched as she stood, the yellow blur of the cheap porch light casting a sickly glow. "You have to understand," she said, turning to him, "so many foster families take kids in solely for the check the government cuts them every month. Cheryl and Wallace, they needed the money having kids around brought in."

"That money was for you, Georgia. For your care, your benefit."

She smiled at him, her eyes watery. "It doesn't really work that way, though."

"Doesn't make it okay." God, the knowledge *burned*. The first priority of all parents should be the child in their care, the child they'd promised to protect. It was something he hadn't always understood or believed—he had his own dysfunctional family to make excuses for, after all—but Ethan had drilled it into his head until it stuck. *You are not the parent. You are not meant to take care of her. Sacrifice everything for her.* It was a truth Parker had embraced, one he repeated to himself every time he spoke with his mother. Every time he denied her request for money. Every time he hung up on a screaming, crying rant. But he also knew that severing some ties was almost impossible. That excuses and explanations were second nature. Sometimes it was just easier to believe that things hadn't been that bad.

"No," Georgia said. "And when Wallace drank, things got worse. A lot worse." His brow furrowed as she stared at him. "You know something weird? I never remember him hitting Cheryl. He'd grab her by the arm. Throw things—probably why it was always paper plates and Solo cups. But never, not once, did I see him hit her."

Abuse was sneaky like that, though. Could make someone believe it was tolerable, could make someone grateful it wasn't worse. Until the day the switch flipped and all hell broke loose.

"I still don't really know what changed. The dialogue that night was the same. 'You're a cheating bitch. You're a drunk asshole.'" She sighed and shivered. "It just started earlier that night. They were already going at it when I got home from school. I'd wanted to just take my dinner to my room, but it was one of Cheryl's rules." She rolled her eyes. "Family dinner at the table. No exceptions." She walked back to him, plopping down in the spot she'd vacated. "I still can't eat peanut butter and jelly sandwiches."

"Nutella is clearly the only way to go." He bumped her with his shoulder, loosening a grin as he did.

"Clearly," she said, amusement releasing some of the tension in her expression. "It's weird. Those forty-eight hours seem so fluid now. I'm sure they must have felt eternal when it was happening, but I don't remember them that way."

"Compartmentalization."

"Probably." She picked a piece of lint off her coat. "But some things are crystal clear, just waiting for something to remind me. I keep my nails short because I tore them to shreds trying to pry open the door. I hate New York in the summer because the humid, fetid stink reminds me of that hot Florida summer. I don't go to concerts or sporting events because I screamed myself raw hoping someone would hear me." She pulled her arms around her, shivering hard. "No one ever did."

He couldn't help it; he slung an arm around her and pulled her into him, dropping a kiss to the top of her head. Jesus.

"And after?"

"After, I just sort of . . . checked out. Let things float by me. I didn't say a word, not for three months. Every counselor, social worker, and doctor said the same thing. 'It's the trauma, the stress, the loss on top of loss.' Blah blah blah."

"You don't think so?" It would have been understandable. A long op, too much time in the office, a bad outcome—all had the power to send Parker running for his loft, locking down his security system and pretending the rest of the world didn't exist.

"Hell no." Georgia scoffed. "I was *pissed*."

Her mouth curled, pride and stubborn satisfaction transforming her into the woman he knew.

"I made up my mind that I was *done* until I saw Will. It took time, but once they put us together, things changed. Said we had to be placed together for my health and well-being." She shook her head. "Morons."

Parker chuckled. "Things get better after that?"

"Yes and no."

Georgia leaned into him, letting Parker scoot her farther into his side and share his warmth.

"Foster care is a little like fighting a war on all fronts. You don't fit in at school. You're always fighting for resources. Food. Clothing. Whatever. There's never enough. But at least Will and I dealt with it together. Looked out for each other. I helped him with English. He taught me how to throw a punch." She shifted toward him. "You have to understand, most placements aren't violent or abusive. They're just . . ." She shook her head and sighed. "They're just not *interested*. Each kid is a check in the bank, a pair of hands to help around the house. Usually? Usually you're just flat-out ignored. Without Will, it was like I was invisible. Like I didn't exist anymore."

Her hand went to her wrist, fingers looking for a watch she'd sold to protect them. To provide for them. As Parker now suspected just what it meant to her, he couldn't suppress a flinch every time she repeated the gesture. He hurt *for* her.

"But yeah, while we were together, things were good. Or close enough."

"While?"

"Will aged out of the system four years before I did. Our placement at the time threw him out the moment he turned eighteen. No more government stipends. So Will crashed with friends, graduated high school—thankfully he had a May birthday—and then he enlisted."

"And left you behind." He couldn't help the resentment in his voice or prevent the sudden intense dislike for a man he'd never met. It was clear Georgia had *worshipped* her brother. How could he just leave her? Especially knowing what it would be like. A thought struck, the answer to the question he hadn't dared ask so damn obvious.

"And that's why you came back," he said, voicing his realization. "At the stadium, I mean. You looked over your shoulder, saw me standing there, and you couldn't go through with it. Couldn't leave me behind."

Georgia swallowed. "You looked . . ."

Sad. Scared. Devastated. He'd tried to stand there, convince himself he was better off with Ethan, that Georgia was doing the right thing. But then, he'd never been particularly good at the whole poker-face thing.

"Well, let's just say I recognized the look. I didn't want to be responsible for making you feel that way. For making you feel like I'd given up on you, or that it was easy to go, or whatever." She flicked her fingers, dismissing her decision as if it'd been easy. As if it hadn't cost her anything. As if it might not cost her *everything*.

"You didn't want to hurt me the way your brother hurt you," he said, anger lacing his tone.

"Don't say it like that. It's not like we had a lot of options. He deserved a life. A shot at something for himself. And anyway, we thought I'd be fine."

"Thought?"

"I did all right for about a year. We checked in regularly, stayed close. But then he was deployed, and I was bounced into a group home. If I'd thought other foster homes made me feel invisible, they had nothing on the group home. Between Will being so far away and the come-and-go nature of the home . . . depression came fast. My grades slipped. I lost the few friends I'd made. I felt invisible, so it was easy to act that way."

He couldn't imagine it. For him, everything about Georgia stood out. She radiated energy, drew him in. No question, he was attracted to her, but it wasn't all physical. If it were, he'd have lost interest the moment they'd hooked up. But with Georgia, every hour he spent with her was one more hour that seemed to exist solely to prove to him how badly he wanted to spend the next hour with her, too.

"Anyway, when I withdrew from him, started dodging calls and stopped answering e-mails, he petitioned for emergency leave and came home." She reached for her wrist, but this time when her fingers encountered bare skin, she left them there. "He'd been hand-selected for spec ops—one of the youngest ever. But he walked away from it to come home and raise *me*."

The way she said it, all incredulous, shocked awe, tore at Parker. To him, Will simply did the right thing. Loyalty. Family. Words Parker hadn't understood in his youth were sacrosanct now. All because of Ethan.

Ethan, who could be dead or alive. In a hospital or in the ground. With a medical team or with someone much, much worse. He shook away the thoughts.

"The army let him go?"

Georgia nodded. "Only this time, luck seemed to run our way. They worked with us, got Will assigned stateside. And again, things got better. I graduated early, joined up, too. And Will got his career back on track . . ." Her voice dipped, trailing off again. "I almost wish he hadn't. Maybe if he hadn't followed through, hadn't made it to Delta, he'd still be here."

"How did he die?"

"I don't know," Georgia ground out, anguish creasing her forehead. "Ethan won't tell me, but I'm sure he knows what happened." She surged to her feet again. "I get it, you know? I get that Ethan *shouldn't* tell me.

That technically he can't. Will and I both knew the risks and rules of special ops. But not knowing . . . it just feels like, like . . ."

"Like you're quitting on him. Like if you don't know what it was all for, that it doesn't count. That *he* doesn't count. That he's invisible again."

"Yes," she whispered on a broken sob, jerking her head up and down. "Yes. I've asked *everyone*. Gone through every process, every petition. But no one gets why I have to know. Why I can't just let it go."

"You haven't asked me," Parker said, leaning in until he could bump his head against hers.

She jerked back, shocked surprise adding a nice flush of color to cheeks that had been too pale. "What?"

Parker smiled gently. "Rebel government hacker, remember?" He used his thumb to brush away a strand of hair clinging to her cheek. "It really never occurred to you to ask, did it?"

She shrugged, her eyes watery but her face clear. "Guess after all that 'I can ruin your credit, repossess your car, and declare you dead' stuff, it should have."

"Um, yeah." The next words were harder, scarier to say. He needed Georgia on his side; he didn't want her to look at him differently. But she'd saved his life and trusted him with some of the most intimate details of hers. He could do no less. "But in this case, I don't need to hack any files."

"What?" Georgia's head snapped up so fast she nearly clipped his chin.

"I thought you already knew," Parker said, swallowing down his hesitation. "Will and Ethan served together, were friends. Did it really never occur to you that we approached him about working with the CWU?"

Georgia's mouth dropped open in surprise. "I didn't know anything about the CWU until I met you. I mean, I knew that Ethan was still involved in special ops and that he had the sort of clearance that could get me the answers I wanted, but . . ."

"But nothing else."

"No," she said, her breath puffing out of her in a tiny cloud. "But if Will was working for the CWU when he died . . ." She paused, her face falling as the reality of what Parker was really telling her descended. He braced himself for the accusation, for the tears and the blame. *If Will was working for the CWU when he died, then* you *had a hand in it.* Your *program chose him. Sent him. Killed him.* She wouldn't be wrong, Parker knew. The very idea that he couldn't save everyone, that he had a firm hand in sending men into dangerous situations, had kept him up more than a few nights. But to have the devastated proof of his decisions, his failures, sitting next to him? It gutted him. So he braced for her scorn and told himself it was no more than he'd deserve.

Instead, Georgia simply said, "Then there's a file, right? Even if it's a negative outcome? You . . . you would have made sure that it—that *he*—mattered in the end. Even if it just improved your program for someone else?"

"Yeah." Parker nodded. "There's a file. I pulled it off the server about a week ago. That was the info grab that landed me with you, actually," Parker said, scratching the back of his neck.

"Oh." Georgia grew quiet for a moment, as if processing everything he'd just told her. "So then you didn't send Will . . ."

Parker shook his head, resolving to be completely honest. Even if it changed things between them. "Not exactly. I didn't know that the operation was a go. I thought it had been scrapped."

"Can you tell me about it?" she asked quietly.

"How much do you want to know?"

She looked at him for a long time, her gaze steady, her face devoid of emotion. He wondered if she'd ever thought this far ahead. If she'd ever really expected to find her answers.

"Everything you remember, everything you can tell me."

Georgia fought off a shiver, though she'd grown numb to the cold. She'd waited for this moment, hoped for it, begged for it . . . and to some extent never believed it would ever actually happen. Now, faced with the answers she'd wanted for so long, she felt only a sad sense of duty to listen, to know.

She only hoped it would be enough to finally, finally let her move forward. To put Will to rest and remember her brother for the remarkable man he was—and allow herself to live as the woman he would have wanted her to be.

"At any given time, the CWU is tracking and assessing dozens of evolving situations around the world." Parker shifted on the warped steps leading up to the trailer, dragging the toe of his Chuck Taylor across the boards. "Even with the benefit of the program, with the edge the assessments give us, we don't have the manpower, the physical resources to be everywhere, to do everything."

"So you had to prioritize," Georgia offered, hoping even a little input from her would make this feel more like a conversation and less like a confession.

"Yeah. A very small percentage of situations we evaluated was given the green light for operational involvement." Parker laced his fingers together, cracked his knuckles. "It was . . . frustrating. To have all this information, to know people were suffering, dying, and that we had the ability to make a difference—we passed on so many operations due to funding, or lack of resources in the region, or just because we didn't have anything to gain from becoming involved." Parker shoved a hand through his hair on a rough sigh. "Doing the right thing never mattered, not really." He glanced up at her, helplessness written across his face. "It kills me, knowing everything we could do and just how often we didn't because there just wasn't anything in it for us."

Georgia nodded. She'd never really stopped to consider the personal cost for the people who made or influenced decisions. Some, she knew, were good at compartmentalizing, at seeing the bigger picture. But for someone like Parker, who so obviously wore his heart on his sleeve, the burden would be so much heavier. He'd remember every person he couldn't help—and every person who died in connection with one of his operations. Somehow it made listening to everything he'd said, everything she knew he still had to say, easier.

"Nearly a year ago, I began work on gathering intelligence so we could run an assessment. South American cartels are nothing new, but there was one growing rapidly in several countries. The Vega cartel has fingers in every illegal pie you can think of—weapons, drugs, money laundering—you name it; they've done it. But it was their rapid expansion into human trafficking that brought them to our attention." Parker scrubbed his hands over his face. "In particular they'd become scarily adept at abducting and ransoming foreign executives. The kidnappings were . . . violent. More than a few went bad when governments or corporations didn't pay up." Parker shook his head. "It took months—but I was finally able to put together a solid profile and locate what we thought was the cartel's primary compound.

"But the logistics were a nightmare," he said, tipping his head back to stare at the cloudless night sky. "Hundreds of miles from any major city, an assault would have been . . . impractical."

"Why not use a drone? Wipe the compound off the map entirely?"

"We considered it, but our intel suggested the cartel was holding five or six high-value assets on location. Two were children of foreign dignitaries." Parker shook his head. "Blowing the compound off the map wasn't an option. Which left us two options. Wait for a better opportunity or send in a ground team."

"You sent in a ground team."

Parker looked at her, guilt tightening his face until all trace of the boyish charm he wore so easily disappeared. "I advocated for it," he admitted. "The kidnappings were escalating, growing a lot more violent. But there was also the human-trafficking side to consider. So many people, so many *kids*. Sold without a second thought."

When he grew quiet, Georgia laid a hand on his forearm.

"Anyway, I advocated for a ground assault." He looked up at her, his expression apologetic. "I thought the risks were worth it."

"But . . . ?" she asked.

"But no one agreed. Truth is, there just wasn't anything in it for us—humanitarian concerns just aren't enough to convince the US government to get involved."

"So what changed?" Georgia asked. Because something had. Otherwise Will would still be here.

"I honestly don't know," he admitted with a shrug. "The file only detailed what happened; there wasn't anything in there to indicate why."

A few days ago, it wouldn't have bothered her. She'd spent ten years of her life taking orders, learning not to question, not to wonder. Compartmentalization. She used to be good at it. But now, knowing Will might have died so someone else could line his pockets? That was something she wouldn't overlook.

Parker took the hand she'd placed on his forearm, linked their fingers together. Instinct to withdraw warred with the desire to stay. Comfort, sympathy, care. In so many ways those were so much more intimate, so much more dangerous than sex.

"Will was part of a twelve-man team that went in to extract the hostages and raze the compound." Parker sighed, his words tumbling from him in a rush. "But from what I read, the compound was heavily guarded. Far more men on-site than the original assessment had indicated." His shoulders slumped, guilt and questions and frustration writing lines across his forehead. "I don't know if that's something I missed or if things had just changed that much in the intervening months."

"I need to know . . ." She'd never really understood why she had to know how her brother had died. Dead was dead, right? But the void in the last days of his life bothered her; the lack of information made it feel as if Will had just been wiped clean off the board, almost as if he'd never existed in the first place.

"Will was part of the team involved in setting the explosives," Parker said slowly. "He and his partner took heavy fire—his partner was shot twice, and Will got pinned down defending him. From what I read, Will's options were stay and be killed or leave his wounded friend behind."

"He stayed." She said it out loud so she could taste the words, know their truth. Because of course Will had stayed, Georgia thought, struggling with the emotions trying to strangle her. Will would never leave someone behind like that. It wasn't in him, wasn't who he was. Except that he had, hadn't he? In choosing to stay, he'd also chosen to leave *her*. Permanently.

"He stayed," Parker agreed. "Waited for the all clear, then detonated the explosives."

"He was killed in the blast," she said, anger, grief, and something like pride tumbling around until she wasn't at all sure how to feel. "I'd always assumed something like that had happened." She glanced at Parker. "Closed casket," she said, watching as understanding dawned. "Just sort of added to the sense I never got to say goodbye, you know?"

He nodded, and for a long time, he didn't say anything.

"I don't know if it helps, but those kids? They went home because of your brother. So did four adults—one of whom had been missing for almost eighteen months." Carefully, as though he wondered if his touch would be welcome, Parker pressed his leg to hers. Leaned in until his warmth bled through the cold.

"It helps," she said, more for lack of any other reply. Of course it helped. Will had always been larger than life in Georgia's eyes. Her touchstone, her home. It was an absence she'd felt so keenly in the first months, a loss that had pushed her to the brink. Even in her darkest moments as a child, she'd had the surety and safety of her big brother. Of knowing Will was there—it hadn't mattered if he'd been in the room next to hers or thousands of miles away. Will's unconditional love, his complete trust and devotion—it had been her home.

She'd tried so hard—maybe too hard—to have that with Isaac. Oh, she'd loved him, she was certain of that. But it had been . . . thin. Two-dimensional. Born of a desperation she hadn't recognized at the time, and one that saddened her in hindsight. She'd never considered herself the sort of woman to *need* a man in her life. The realization should have scared her—she'd always thought herself so damn self-aware. The idea that there was this needy, clingy desperation within her, that she'd all but thrown herself at a man who didn't want her, should scare the crap out of her.

But the truth was, her feelings for Isaac *paled* in comparison to the way she felt about Parker. And that terrified her.

"Thanks for telling me." Georgia turned so she could study him. Parker was so . . . so unlike anything she'd ever expected or wanted. There was a softness about him, a gentle heart he took no care to protect. Maybe it was that openness, that vulnerability she was only beginning to understand might actually be strength, that drew her to him in a way she didn't understand—and couldn't bring herself to resist. No matter how much it scared her.

"Does knowing help?" he asked, staring up at her as she stood and brushed cold slush and fallen leaves from her pants.

It was a good question. One she wasn't sure how to answer. Having the details didn't lessen the pain of the reality, didn't change the fact that she'd never see her brother again. Never hear him laugh or yell at him for stealing the last of her beer. In every way that mattered, Will was still gone from her life.

Except . . .

Except that wasn't *entirely* true.

Georgia still had her memories of him, and now, finally, she had that last missing piece. The part of the story that confirmed what she'd long believed—Will had died in the same way he'd lived. He'd put others first, always had. And in that, Georgia was able to take some comfort.

"Yeah," she said, realizing she meant it, "it helps." She extended a hand, pulled Parker to his feet, running a hand down his arm, squeezing his fingers before pulling away. "I know it probably doesn't make sense, but I feel better knowing."

"I get it," he said, his face an odd mix of shadows cast by the pale glow of the porch light. "And I promise you, I'm going to figure out what changed." His expression grew hard, his voice tight and controlled. "If two men died so someone else could get rich, I promise you, they are not going to get away with it."

All at once his strength fled and his face crumpled. "I'd do anything to bring him back to you. I'm so sor—"

She couldn't stand it—the pain, the guilt, the absolute knowledge that when Parker said "anything," he *meant* it. There was no price he wouldn't pay to bring Will back. For *her.* So she swallowed her fear, went up on her toes, and pressed her mouth to his.

◆ ◆ ◆

If Parker were a better man, he'd step back, chalk up Georgia's gentle press of lips to the emotions of the moment.

Instead, he hauled her close, slanting his mouth until hers opened and their combined heat chased away the chill.

Parker kicked the door shut as he followed Georgia into the trailer, his mouth still sealed against hers. Hands dove beneath his jacket, pulling his shirt from his pants. He danced away from the icy skate of her fingers across his abs. Her mouth quirked into a grin when he arched and gasped—one part desperate to avoid her torment, one part eager for more. Panting, Parker took a step back, fighting for breath and trying to calm his racing heart. "We should . . . We should . . ." He exhaled and forced his lust-laden muscles to uncoil. "We should probably close those windows I cracked."

"What?" Georgia asked, licking swollen lips and running a hand through her hair.

"The smell's gone, more or less. And I'm about ready to give my left nut to be warm." He walked into the living room, going to the small window he'd opened a few inches before following Georgia outside.

"Parker." Her tone said stop. Turn around. Drown in everything we both want so badly.

Instead, he moved toward the kitchenette and the little window above the sink he'd opened.

"Parker." Desperation this time. A need he understood but didn't want to take advantage of. For Georgia, he didn't just want to be a better man. He wanted to be the only man she'd ever need. The one she told her secrets to, the one she let comfort her, challenge her. The one she let hold her—against a wall or against his chest. Both, if he had his way. And that meant he had to be stronger than the bone-deep urge pressing him to take her, strip her, inspect her while she stood before him cold and pale and shivering with want. Everything from his mouth to points south tightened, bracing him to leap, pounce, tackle, and take. God, but he wanted to. Between them, it would be so easy to chase away all the fear, loneliness, and uncertainty with something fast and hard and exhausting.

But Parker wanted more. Releasing the pressure, taking the edge off—they'd never be enough. Not where Georgia was concerned. Not ever again. He had a piece of her now, a bit that belonged to no one else, a part she'd never shared. Until now. Until him. It made him possessive as hell. And lent him control he'd never known before.

But when she called his name again in a tiny whisper that puffed across the back of his neck, raising his hair and stoking his desire, he turned and braced himself to resist. He wanted more than she could give, and he had no right to ask for anything else. Not tonight. Not when she'd already given so much. "We should . . ."

"Just . . ." She shook her head. Whatever she'd seen on his face bolstered her confidence and chased away the insecurity he'd heard in her voice. Her full pink lips twitched. "Just shut up." She stepped into him, nimble fingers working the buttons of his coat.

He grabbed her hands as she moved to slide the wool from his shoulders. "I . . . We've had a rough day," he mumbled, forcing himself to ignore the way her hands warmed in his and reminding himself not to imagine how they'd feel against cool skin. "A harder night. I don't want . . ." He shook his head, searching for words to explain but not offend.

"Livingston—"

He shivered. His last name should have been off-putting. Should have felt stern and bossy and all wrong falling from her lips.

"I bared my soul to you tonight. The least you can do is drop your pants."

He barked out a laugh. Only Georgia.

"Oh yeah? I should just drop trou and take it?"

He stepped back as she moved toward him.

"Might make you feel better."

"I feel fine." Or he would if he ignored the way his jeans grew tighter by the second.

"Might make me feel better." She grinned and pressed herself against him, tilting her chin up, part request, part challenge.

He stepped away, right into the sink. She pinned him there, hands braced on either side of him as she gripped the stainless-steel basin. She brushed her hips against his, swaying just enough to tease at his control.

"Tell me you don't want me, Parker."

"I want you," he admitted roughly, allowing himself the pleasure of pulling her hair from the ponytail she'd captured it in. "Too much. Way too much." Every time he touched her, he worried he'd never be able to stop. That she'd become as natural and necessary as breathing. More integral than coffee. "I just don't want to take advantage. Don't want you to regret—"

"I'm not ever going to regret this, Parker." The way she said it, as if the idea were so alien, so outlandish, she couldn't even contemplate it . . .

"I'm not asking for commitment—I'm not even asking for tomorrow. Neither of us should be making promises." She sighed and took a half step back. "Everything is . . . heightened. This situation, it's forced us together, amplified everything. Maybe it will last and maybe it won't.

But right now?" She curled her fingers into the waistband of his jeans, pulling him closer. "I don't fucking *care*."

On a sigh, Parker gave in to the desire to touch. He drew the pad of a thumb along the curve of her cheek. Watched as her eyes fluttered shut.

To taste. He dipped his head, letting his mouth brush against the corner of hers before he settled over warm, soft lips that immediately opened, inviting him to savor, delve, explore.

To feel. He trailed his hands along her back until he found her denim-covered ass. He slid his hands into the back pockets of her jeans and pulled her toward him, massaging her cheeks as she thrust her hips against his. A tease. A promise. A dance he wanted to end only to start over again and again.

Releasing the sink, Georgia went to work on pushing the coat from his shoulders, then began flicking open the top several buttons on the cotton Henley he wore. "Up," she demanded, motioning for him to raise his arms as she tugged at the hem of his shirt. In seconds she had him bare, taking the Henley and undershirt in one smooth pull over his head.

Parker had been scrutinized his entire life. Studied. Judged. And always, always, he found the weight of a stare uncomfortable and restrictive. But when Georgia stepped back to blatantly take in his chest, when she let a finger trail across his abs, when that finger dipped and danced and trembled just a bit as it came to rest against the button of his jeans? Power, exhilaration, anticipation. And the life-changing realization that he didn't believe he'd ever feel like less than the best version of himself under Georgia's stare.

"Seriously," she said. "Where did these come from? You mainline sugar, drown in caffeine, and you don't strike me as the gym-rat type. So spill." She smiled up at him, her mouth the worst sort of tease. "Zumba? Water aerobics? Chasing squirrels in the park?"

"Yoga."

"Yoga?" she repeated, her tone skeptical.

"*Hot* yoga." He ground his hips against hers. "Wanna practice a few moves? A little downward dog, perhaps?"

"You want that?" she asked, pulling his jeans and underwear down around his ankles. "Want me on my knees, ass in the air, panting for it? Begging for it?"

He swallowed, clenching his eyes shut as she circled thumb and forefinger around the very tip of him. Not fair. "Y-yes."

She waited until he opened his eyes and met her gaze. "I can do that. If"—her grin turned wicked—"you beat me to the bedroom." Lightning quick, she turned and dashed for the door, her laugh ringing out, loud and clear, as Parker tripped over his own feet, still tangled in the loose fabric of his jeans and briefs, before finally shoving out of his shoes and kicking off the remainder of his clothes as he gave chase. He caught her in the hallway, her hand on the doorknob to what he assumed was the bedroom. They slammed across the threshold together, his chest to her back, his momentum carrying them straight to the bed. He drew up short, staying on his feet as she fell, catching herself on the mattress in front of her. Parker stepped back, hand searching for the switch along the wall. Warm yellow light bathed the room. Oak covered everything. The paneling, the bed, the headboard, and the built-in shelves on either side of a huge mirror. Even the floor was done in a linoleum to match. Well, at least it wasn't shag carpeting. As fascinating as the room was—it felt like entering a long-buried time capsule—Parker couldn't focus on anything beyond Georgia. Stretched out against a garishly floral comforter, she faced him, ankles crossed, weight propped up on her elbows.

"Beat you."

"Pretty sure it was a tie."

"Which is just another way of saying you didn't win," she shot back.

"Neither did you. Not to mention, you cheated."

"Which is just another way of saying I was smarter." She swung her legs back and forth, a sly grin curling her lips.

Parker nudged her feet apart with his legs, slipping into the space her open knees created. He watched, transfixed, as she flicked open one button after another on her shirt, revealing just enough cleavage to send his mind reeling with images of what it would be like to bury himself between them, to thrust and slide and come as she held them up for him.

"Do I get a consolation prize?" he asked, desperate for her to flick open another button, to take the fantasy one step closer to reality.

She leaned forward until her breath ghosted over him, eliciting a shiver, a groan, an unbearable desire to have her mouth on him. By sheer force of will, he didn't move. Just stood above her, looking down as she peered up at him, her mouth inches from where he wanted it most. Never had he found himself in such a position, fully nude while his partner sat before him, still dressed from head to toe, teasing him with images and fantasies of all the things they weren't doing.

"I'm no one's consolation prize," she said, then slid her mouth over him, watching him as she did. She licked, tasted, dragged just the tip of her teeth across sensitive skin. Never staying in one place, never increasing the pressure, the pleasure . . . No, she didn't play fair at *all*.

"Georgia."

She drew back. "And you thought I'd be the one to beg," she whispered, her full, wet lips mocking him. She knew he would, too. Beg. Plead. Promise damn near anything within his power to give and a few other things besides. All to have one more moment of her mouth.

She slid a hand up the back of his thigh, using the blunt tips of her fingernails to bring him closer. When he trembled, she smiled and took him into her mouth, wrenching a strangled gasp from his throat. He raised his hands, then dropped them to his sides, unsure what to do or where to touch. Never had sex been so one-sided for him or so entirely focused on his pleasure. Georgia dipped her head, pulling him further toward the edge, then grabbed his hands, drawing them up until her hair slipped through his fingers. Her hands slid up his forearms, then around to his back, her message clear and her trust implicit. Everything in Parker screamed at him to fist the hair beneath his fingers, angle her face the way he wanted, and plunder her mouth until she'd tasted every part of him. To snap his hips, driving himself closer and closer to the edge of oblivion. He wanted that and more. Endless hours and countless orgasms as he stood above a fully clothed Georgia and played out every delicious thought his imagination could come up with.

Instead, he cupped the back of her neck, reveling in the way her silk-soft hair slid between his fingers, and in strong, languid strokes, pumped his hips. Watching in rapt fascination as she took him, her eyes closed, her cheeks flushed, her mouth a warm, wet haven he never wanted to leave. He scratched against the base of her skull, encouraging her to tip back, to take and give even more. Her moan rippled through him, forcing him to his toes as he tried desperately to forestall the orgasm that wanted to tear through him, stealing the experience in one red-hot moment he was certain would kill him. But no, he wanted something hotter, tighter, wetter. He wanted her, naked and spread beneath him, trembling with every plunge, begging with every clenched finger and curled toe. Though he barely believed himself capable, Parker stepped back and out of reach.

Georgia opened heavy, lust-laden eyes. He groaned. At some point she'd opened her own jeans, dipped a hand beneath the waistband to seek her own pleasure.

Someday, Parker assured himself, they'd replay this moment, and he'd let her finish them both.

"I want to be inside you. I want to touch you. I want to feel you as you come apart when I do."

◆　◆　◆

It took Georgia a few moments to force enough blood to her brain to process Parker's words. A little stunned, she leaned back and considered him. She'd fully expected him to take the control she'd given him, to use her mouth ruthlessly as he sought his own release. She hadn't expected to enjoy it, though. Not really. In her experience, oral always ended in a landslide of pleasure for one person—and if she were lucky, a trickle of arousal for her. But with Parker . . . Well, as usual with Parker, he didn't bother to exceed her expectations, he blew right through them as if they were utterly beneath him. In the moment he'd stood before her, naked and trembling at the barest breath across sensitive flesh, Georgia's expectations had collapsed in a cloud of heated arousal.

Parker had stood there, utterly at her mercy. Undemanding. Just ready to drown in whatever Georgia would give him. She'd never had that before with a lover. Everything had always been rush, take, conquer, then do it all again. Not that she was complaining; she'd gotten what she needed from those encounters. But Parker . . . Whether he intended to or not, he forced her to acknowledge what she'd always suspected—that there was more to sex than a quick, dirty tumble designed exclusively for maximum reward in the shortest amount of time. And more, that such a thing might be in the cards for *her*. With Parker, Georgia found she wasn't as focused on the outcome—though she knew from experience just how good it could be. Instead, as cliché as it sounded, she found herself looking forward to the journey as much as the destination. And even more surprising, she trusted Parker to ensure the experience was memorable for both of them.

"What did you have in mind?" she asked, watching as he dropped to his knees in front of her. Bringing his mouth in line with hers, he kissed her.

"Well, much as I like the idea of pulling your jeans down around your knees and taking you as you writhe, trapped in your own clothes, I think I'd rather have you naked."

"Yeah?" Georgia asked, surprised at how the idea of Parker stripping her only as much as absolutely necessary turned her on. Next time. God, a stupid part of her hoped there'd always be a next time.

"Yeah." He unbuttoned the rest of her shirt and slid it off her shoulders. A warm palm settled on her neck, fingers brushing against her pulse. Georgia bit her lip when that hand trailed over her chest, palming her breast, then down to the top of her jeans. Parker let his fingers dip inside the waistband and pull until the zipper slid the rest of the way open.

Under coaxing hands, Georgia braced her feet against the floor and raised her hips, allowing Parker to slide her jeans down her legs. Given the desperation she'd heard in his voice, the tension that hardened every line of his body, she'd expected him to hurry. To rip away the denim, taking the soft cotton briefs with them.

Instead, he slid only the jeans down her legs as she leaned back on elbows to watch. Pressing a kiss to her navel, he trailed his mouth south as he unlaced her boots. A scrape of teeth against the top of her underwear as he pulled off one boot. A teasing brush of nose against her center as he pulled off the other. An open-mouthed kiss to the inside of one thigh as he slid off a sock. A matching one as he removed the other before finally, finally sliding her pants away.

Georgia lay there in nothing but matching gray underwear as Parker knelt between her legs and drank in the sight of her. Any other time, with any other man, Georgia might have been embarrassed. She wasn't dressed for this, her bra and briefs too plain, too boring. Too functional. But as Parker knelt there, palms skimming up the tops of her thighs, thumbs darting in to nudge at the only barrier between them, Georgia didn't care. All the leather, lace, and demi cups in the world couldn't have made her feel more attractive or more powerful than the sight of Parker on his knees between her legs, staring up at her as if he couldn't decide where to begin, as if he couldn't believe she was there, stretched out beneath him and ready for the taking. No one had ever looked at her that way. Awed. Reverent. Humbled.

With Parker's expression fixed firmly in her mind, Georgia turned to her stomach and went up on hands and knees. Any reservations she had about the position, one she didn't particularly enjoy and had too often found demeaning, vanished when she caught Parker's reflection in the huge mirror before her.

Stunned admiration graced his face. Had him stepping forward and lifting a hand, reaching for her as if to prove her existence. A shiver tore through her when gentle fingers slid against one cheek, then spread until a full palm cupped her ass.

"Yeah?" he asked, licking his lips.

Georgia arched her back, pushing her ass against his hips, letting them sway against him. "Yeah," she moaned, shocked at how just the feel of him pressed against her lit up every nerve ending until each heartbeat throbbed from the center of her. She shivered, rocking back and forth, brushing the very tip of her hardened nipples against the rough fabric of the bedspread. "Parker." She couldn't stop her undulating movements. Couldn't process anything beyond the way his fingers gripped her hips, pulling her ass against him until every inch of him slid against her as rough fabric teased at sensitive nipples. God, she could come like this. On display, ass in the air, and without a single touch to tip her over the edge. Could, but didn't want to. "Parker, *please*."

He glanced in the mirror, caught her agonized expression. Slowly, he came back to himself, a smile spreading across his face. "Please what?" he asked, firmly dragging fingers over cotton, hard enough to dip between her cheeks, sliding against skin no one had ever touched before until finally, finally, toying with the soaked scrap of fabric covering her. He let his fingers dip, and nudge, and play . . . but only against the cotton of her briefs, never beneath it. Always teasing her with what might be, reminding her of what he could give. Georgia shook her head. Greedy bastard. He knew now, the power he held over her. The things he could demand from her. The things she'd willingly, if not readily, give.

"Please what?" he asked again, using a finger to push against the bundle of nerves that had her choking on a desperate sob.

"Please . . ." She rocked against him, shifting her hips, trying to grab the orgasm she knew lay just beyond her reach. When he used his fingernails to scrape back and forth against sensitive flesh, Georgia broke. "Please, *please* fuck me."

A predatory grin slid across his face as he removed his hands. Georgia dropped her head, a desperate sigh escaping as she rocked her hips against

nothing but air. Why? She'd done as he demanded, so why would he . . .
Fingers grasped the elastic of her underwear and slowly dragged them over
her ass and down her thighs. She choked on her relief. Gasped when he
blew cold air against her overheated flesh. She lifted a knee, ready to lose
the only garment standing in their way. A hand stopped her, pressing her
leg back against the mattress.

"Leave it. I like them there. Holding you in place, open and ready."

Georgia shivered. A pretty illusion they both knew wasn't real. But as
she shifted, her briefs preventing her from widening her legs, the cotton
sliding against her skin with every movement, a new sort of arousal wound
through her. One that had her wondering what else she might enjoy. What
else she might explore with Parker. Before the thought could run away
with her, Parker slid his fingers between her folds, exposing her to him in
the most intimate way she could imagine. One finger slid up, brushing
against a bundle of nerves that had her crying out, straining forward and
pushing back, her body confused about what it wanted most. Parker held
her still and open, one finger circling and pressing and rubbing as he slid
into her in one smooth, strong stroke.

Grabbing her hips, Parker held her still as he began a long, slow dance
of thrust and withdraw; all the while his finger circled and scraped, ensuring she was wet and ready and desperate for whatever he gave her. How
he had such control, she had no idea. He slid a hand across her hip and
up the length of her spine, stopping just long enough to flick open the
clasp of her bra before continuing up until he curled a fist in her hair and
pulled her head up.

"Take it off," he said, studying her in the mirror.

Georgia complied, sliding her bra from one arm, then the next.

"Open your eyes." He removed his finger when she didn't immediately
comply, drawing a strangled groan from her lips. Slowly, she opened her
eyes, staring as he took her from behind.

"Watch," he commanded. He snapped his hips forward, the momentum rocking her back and forth. She did as he said and stared, lips parted

and mouth dry as he set a brutal pace, his hips connecting with her ass, her breasts bouncing and swaying with each thrust. Sweat slicked across his chest, glistened on cut abs she didn't think she'd ever tire of tracing. His fingers returned, rubbing and rolling and pinching until Georgia was a breathless heap of wanton need she didn't know how to quench.

Finally, as her vision began to fuzz at the edges and her body began to protest the ongoing assault of sensation, Parker's movements grew jerky and less coordinated until finally, finally, he was throbbing inside her, spilling on a shout of pure pleasure that seized her muscles and dragged her over the edge right along with him until everything was gray and soft and distant, and the only thing she could feel was a heartbeat—his, hers, she couldn't tell—reverberating through her.

She collapsed to the bed, Parker following until he sprawled across her, breathing heavily. He rolled to his side, slipping from her as he did. Pulling her close, he brushed aside her hair and laid his lips against the bare skin of her shoulder, eliciting a tiny, tired shiver. When he opened his mouth, licking and sucking and nipping at the skin he'd exposed, Georgia sighed.

"I think you staked your claim, Parker."

He sucked hard, pulling blood to the surface, leaving a mark that would linger for days.

"This'll last longer," he said, drawing a finger across the newly sensitized skin. "You'll see it in the mirror, feel it rub against your clothes, and remember what you let me do. What you *wanted* me to do."

"Bit smug, are you?"

"Yes." He nodded into her shoulder. "And I'll see it and want to do it all over again. I'll get hard as I stare at you, watch you squirm as you grow wet and ready. I won't even need to touch you; the memory will be enough."

As heat pooled between her legs, Parker pulled the comforter over them and tucked her into his chest.

The memory, Georgia realized as she went limp and languid in his arms, could never, ever be enough. Not where Parker was concerned.

Damn him.

CHAPTER NINE

Parker thrust his thumb and forefinger beneath the rim of his glasses and rubbed at tired, burning eyes. Any sane man would be in bed, wrapped up in the naked perfection he'd left for the cold light of a laptop. For once, sleep should have come easily. He'd felt it, hovering just beyond his grasp, heavy and waiting. An hour had passed, then two, Georgia dropping into a deep, restful sleep. For a long time, Parker had been content to lie there, to let the luxurious heat of her seep into his bones until he was loose and languid and quiet. The quiet, he now realized, was the problem. It had allowed thoughts to circulate, surfacing one by one, like bubbles from a deep dive, popping to the surface and bursting across the front of his brain. Sleep, no matter how tempting or needed, wasn't his to achieve. Not until he answered the questions bouncing around his brain.

Will. Why did it feel like everything came back to him?

Probably because in one way or another, everything *did* come back to Will.

Georgia's brother. Ethan's teammate. More than once he'd worked with the CWU. And then, finally, there'd been the off-book mission that had gotten him killed. Was it coincidence that the Vega operation had been one of a dozen files Parker had hacked just a week ago?

The part of Parker that ran on data—numbers, patterns, statistics—balked at the idea. Coincidence ranked right up there with medical miracles, winning lottery numbers, and perfect Pac-Man scores. They happened, but only rarely.

And never to him.

The suspicion, growing like an itchy weed Parker couldn't ignore, had finally driven him from bed—and a soft, sleeping Georgia—to dig through files.

God, how he wished he hadn't.

He rubbed the heels of his palms against his eyes, wishing he could so easily wipe his memory. A part of him wanted to delete the open file in front of him, close the computer, and pad back down the hall to slip beneath the covers. Parker wished he were the sort of man who forgot things, or at least the sort of man who could willfully ignore them. For once in his life he wholeheartedly believed ignorance could be bliss.

Instead, he forced himself to study the frozen image before him. To stare into oh-so-familiar blue eyes. Hands trembling, he pulled a pair of earbuds from a pocket on his backpack and plugged them into the computer. For a long moment, his finger hovered over the track pad, his gaze glued to the screen and the tiny "Play" icon on the video file. One click, that's all it would take, and *everything* would change.

If he didn't know what it contained, if he didn't know how it ended—in life, in death, in something worse, something in between and agonizing—then he wouldn't have to decide what the hell to do about it. Wouldn't have to hurt the woman sleeping down the hall. Again. Only this would be so much worse, because Parker knew the moment he watched this file, the moment he told her about it, he'd be taking away every ounce of closure he'd given Georgia.

Nothing good could come of this.

But Parker was at least part of the reason William Bennett stared back at him, hands bound behind his back, his face shockingly thin—the pallor of sickness, injury, and abuse obvious even beneath a months-old beard, as a man stood behind him, the sharpened edge of a machete resting against Will's shoulder.

The front page of the *Wall Street Journal*, dated just four weeks ago, sat against Will's stomach.

Steeling himself, Parker hit "Play."

"Diga su nombre," a disembodied voice demanded. When Will didn't respond, the demand for his name came again, this time accompanied by a violent cuff to the side of his head with the flat side of the machete. Will slumped in his restraints, blood sliding down the side of his face from where the blade had connected with his scalp. Righting himself, he stared stoically into the camera—silent, defiant, his jaw set in a way Parker was all too familiar with.

"Diga su nombre," the voice repeated. *"Diga su nombre, o voy a quitar una oreja."*

The speaker stepped forward, out of the background. Using his free hand, he grabbed a fistful of Will's hair and jerked his head to the side, sliding the blade up to the top of Will's right ear.

"Cinco."

Will didn't move. Didn't blink.

"Quatro."

The muscles at his neck bunched and corded.

"Tres."

Parker clenched his fists, even as Will sat there. Quiet. Determined.

"Dos."

He didn't move. Didn't jerk or struggle. Just leveled a stare to the right of the camera and set his jaw.

"Hazlo."

Will fought an agonized scream with clenched teeth and locked muscles as three rough, ragged strokes separated the top of his ear from the rest of his head.

Breathing heavily, Parker forced himself to sit there, to watch and wait and fight down the rush of nausea that wanted to send him running for the sink. He swallowed it down. Determined to be present, to endure. Parker wouldn't look away. Wouldn't shrink from the violence, from the agony and desolation carved in the lines etched across Will's face.

He'd be here; even if it was too little, too late, he'd be here.

It was the least he could do.

As Will slumped in his restraints, a man stepped into view, coming to a stop at Will's left. Parker recognized Hernan Vega immediately. How many hours had he spent studying the head of the Vega cartel? How much time had he spent wading through the filth this man left in his wake? The kidnappings, the trafficking, the brutal hits against competitors and usurpers alike?

"You make this hard on yourself," he said in heavily accented English as he stared at Will. "You will tell me what I want to know." He placed a hand on Will's shoulder, tightening his grip when Will tried to jerk away. "Who sent you?" Vega asked.

Will shook his head, his gaze trained on the dirt beneath his feet.

"You have another ear. Fingers. Toes. Would it not be better to give me what I want?"

"Can't," Will mumbled, his lip turning red with blood he'd drawn fighting a scream. "Don't know."

"Then we begin again. And I ask again." Vega patted his shoulder and walked away. "But you will tell me. One way or another."

The screen went black.

Shit.

Shit. Shit. Shit.

What the fuck was Parker supposed to do with this? What was he supposed to tell Georgia?

He dropped his head into his hands, fingers pulling at his hair.

He couldn't tell her. Not now. Not knowing how she'd twisted herself into knots over the mere *idea* she'd abandoned her brother's memory. That somehow she'd left him behind.

How the fuck was he supposed to tell the woman down the hall that she'd done exactly that? That they all had? It wouldn't matter that she hadn't known.

This would destroy her.

And for what?

Would telling her change anything? This video was weeks old, and there'd been no mention of names. No indication of who was behind everything.

And Will . . . Will could be dead of injury or infection or worse. Even if he was alive, what could they do about it? Right now, Parker couldn't even guarantee their own safety, let alone do anything to assist a man half a world away.

His hands shook as he stared at the screen.

Could he stand next to her, sleep beside her, knowing it was all a lie? The man she'd buried had been some nameless, faceless stranger. Her brother might be alive even now—alive and trapped in a hell he couldn't hope to escape alone. Even if she didn't know, even if she never found out, the knowledge would dog Parker. Remind him every time he touched her, kissed her, held her, that he was quietly hurting her.

That he didn't deserve her.

He shuddered hard. Trapped. Snared in a prison of his own making.

"Hey," Georgia said, her voice thick with sleep that hadn't fully released its hold. "What are you doing up?" she asked, padding down the hall, her footfalls silenced by thick socks.

Tell her.

He looked up, found her in the Henley he'd stripped out of earlier. Too big, the shirt engulfed her, the hem coming to midthigh, the sleeves to just past her fingertips. She hadn't bothered to button it, and every time she breathed, the gap widened, revealing the shadowed valley of her breasts. She shifted, rubbing one leg against the other as she stared at him, sleep-mussed and sexy.

She didn't fight fair.

How could he tell her what he knew would destroy her when she stood there so soft, sexy, and inviting?

He couldn't. Not when he couldn't offer answers or any hope he could fix things.

"Can't sleep," he said, his voice rough with guilt. "You should go back to bed." With a click of a button, he closed the file.

A lazy grin curled her lips. "Warmer with you there." She held out a hand, palm up, fingers curling as if beckoning him toward her.

"Georgia . . ." He could be honest. Rip off the Band-Aid. Deal with the consequences. He could.

Reality began to dawn across her face, tension returning to her frame. "Is something wrong?" she asked, pushing away from the wall and coming to stand in front of him. "Is it Ethan?" Wakefulness seized her as she stared down at him. "Is Ethan . . . ?"

"No." Relieved to have something positive to discuss, he filled her in. "Ortiz got in touch. Turns out, Ethan was wearing a vest."

"You're kidding," Georgia said, pulling out one of the ancient chrome-and-vinyl chairs and joining him.

Parker shook his head, grateful for Ethan's tendency to be vastly overprepared. "Shocked me, too. But I guess once he realized what was going on, he took every available precaution, and thank God for that. Even with the vest, he broke four ribs and punctured a lung. One of the bullets tore through his shoulder."

"High-velocity rounds?"

"Probably," Parker admitted. "He had to have emergency surgery, and he'll have a long recovery ahead."

"But he's safe? Ortiz is with him?" Georgia reached for Parker's hand, lacing their fingers together.

"Yeah. Ortiz put a call in to Somerton Security; Ethan's got around-the-clock protection. As soon as possible, Ortiz will get him quietly transferred to a private facility under an assumed name."

"I'm surprised Ethan isn't fighting with the hospital staff as it is."

Parker grinned. "Apparently, he's heavily sedated."

"Ah." She pulled her chair closer, leaning into him, her body still warm and loose with the powerful combination of good sex and hard sleep.

He dropped a hand to her knee, toyed with the hem of the shirt she wore. Looking at her, touching her, his eyes burned and watered.

"Ethan's going to be okay, Parker," she said, misinterpreting the source of his emotions.

"I know." She was right, of course. Assuming Parker could get them out of this mess, Ethan would recover. Things would get back to normal. Parker just couldn't say the same for Georgia or himself.

Or Will.

Parker had no idea how, after just a few days, Georgia had managed to make it feel as if she'd always been there. Imagining his day without her snark, her scent, her touch . . . he hated the very idea of it.

"Can I ask you something?" She pressed her thigh against his, trailing her fingers along his arm.

"Sure."

"You and Ethan seem . . . close, I guess."

"We've worked together a long time." He skimmed his fingers in a never-ending figure eight against the inside of her knee.

"It's more than that, though. Ethan's professionalism slips when he's around you. For him, you're personal. Why is that?" she asked.

"Why?" Parker said on a grin. "Jealous? Worried Ethan just can't quit me?"

She shoved away his fingers. "I was thinking more bromance, less illicit love affair, but sure—"

Parker pulled her back, swinging her around until her legs draped over his lap, and his fingers had access to miles and miles of soft skin. "Ethan and I didn't always get along. In fact, I'm pretty sure Ethan hated me on sight."

"A lot's changed."

"Yeah, it has. But it didn't come easy or cheap. When I was first assigned to the CWU, Ethan pitched a fit. I had next to no tactical experience, had never been in the field . . . Looking back on it, I get why Ethan was less than thrilled to be stuck with me."

"Bet you didn't feel that way at the time."

"Nope." Parker smiled. "I was pissed. I knew I could contribute on a technical level, knew I was one of the only people qualified to run point with my program. But Ethan saw me as a liability, plain and simple. Treated me that way, too."

"What changed?" Georgia asked.

Parker slid a palm up her thigh, running his rough hand against smooth skin and enjoying the casual way she allowed him to touch and explore, as if she understood tactile distraction was an inherent part of the way he thought.

"My work ethic, for one. I was the first one there, last one to leave. Never unprepared for briefings or late on reports. Ethan's a lot of things, stubborn to a fault for sure, but he respects people who show up for the job." He slid a sly look her way, dipping his fingers toward the inside of her thigh. "Something I think you know."

"Yeah. He's a workhorse and expects the same from those around him." The skin beneath his fingertips pebbled.

"Yeah. So that helped. It took more than six months, but he went from openly hostile to grudgingly tolerant."

Georgia rolled her eyes. "What a revolution."

"Yeah." Parker laughed. "He's not the easiest to impress."

"So what changed?"

"An op gone bad." Parker lifted a hand, trailed a fingertip along the groove of Georgia's collarbone. "We got intel about a tech bomb being sold on the black market—a device strong enough to take down every modern electrical appliance in Manhattan."

Georgia shivered against him.

"Ethan and the team had orders to destroy the bomb and eliminate the buyer and seller, but things went to shit. Jones had to be medevaced out. Long story short, they destroyed the device, but all hell broke loose. Ethan got separated from the team, and ultimately the chopper had to leave without him."

Georgia swore. "That must have been hell."

"Mostly for Jones, I think. Ethan sort of took it all in stride. When he made the call, ordered the team to leave, he sounded stone-cold calm."

"Think anything ever gets under Ethan's skin?"

"A few things." Family, for one. Loyalty. The need to protect those he cared about. Something he and Georgia shared.

"Someday, some woman is going to come along and turn him inside out. I can never decide if I want to be there to witness it or be well out of the blast radius."

"That view might be best from a distance and through high-powered field lenses." Georgia grinned. "I've known Ethan long enough to know there's no wilting flower in his future."

"I'll bring the popcorn if you bring the Twizzlers," Parker said, a shared future so real and vibrant and perfect it hurt.

"Deal." Georgia brushed a strand of hair away from her face. "Finish your story."

Parker sat back, letting his fingers trail over her bare calves, unwilling to let go even for a second. "By the time we could get additional air support, it was too late. While we'd neutralized the device, we hadn't taken out either buyer or seller. Things went to shit pretty fast after they started turning on each other, calling in reinforcements. It was a tactical nightmare. A lot more ground support and high-tech weaponry in the region than we thought."

"No way you were going to get a chopper back in without risking the crew."

Parker nodded. "Yeah. It didn't take us long to reach that conclusion. Orders were for Ethan to find cover and wait it out."

"That didn't happen?"

"No." For a moment, helplessness surged, echoing through him and reminding him of the impotent fear that had swamped him at the time. Like now, he'd struggled with whether or not he was good enough, smart enough, to win. More than once the fear had gotten the better of him. "No, things got progressively worse. On entry we'd breached the compound's security, left a gaping hole in the wall. It didn't take long for locals to start warring over what was left, the violence attracting more and more attention. Ethan couldn't stay there. Either they'd stumble across him accidentally or he'd succumb to the elements trying to wait them out."

"Must have been hell, watching it all play out on a monitor."

"Thirty-six hours in, I'd had enough. I borrowed a satellite in the region—"

"B-borrowed?" Georgia sputtered. "From who?"

"Not important," Parker said, waving her off. "Point is, I had eyes on Ethan, the region, and a way to get him out of there. Sixty-four hours and forty-three miles later, Ethan made it to the rendezvous point."

Georgia let out a low whistle. "That's a lot of ground in a very short time frame."

"Yeah. Neither one of us slept much. But we got to know each other—kind of had to; it was as if we were the last two people on Earth." Parker rubbed at the back of his neck. "Ethan was on fumes by the time he set out, so the only thing he asked was that I talk to him, keep him moving." Parker barked out a laugh. "Chitchat died inside an hour."

"Something that extreme . . . it pulls people together sometimes," Georgia said, tugging the sleeves of his Henley down over her fingertips.

Or tears them apart, Parker thought, his fingers pausing in their never-ending loop against her legs. He pushed away the thought. What he and Georgia had, it wasn't the same. It wasn't born of desperation and fear and survival. Not at first anyway. Their chemistry had surged from the moment Parker had enough caffeine in his system to take a good, hard look at her. What they had was more than the sum of their circumstances, and he refused to believe otherwise.

Which would make the hurt that much worse when she discovered everything he wasn't saying. When she turned her fury, her hatred, her grief, on him.

"By the time Ethan got home, things were just . . . different," Parker said, pulling his thoughts away from things he couldn't change and instead remembering the immense wave of pride that had flowed through him when the elevator doors had slid open and Ethan had stepped out. He'd expected a handshake, maybe a clap on the shoulder. Instead, Ethan had stepped up to him and, in the middle of the clapping and congratulations, pulled Parker into a hug and whispered thanks against his ear. That moment was seared in Parker's memory forever. To know without doubt or question that for once he'd been everything someone needed him to be . . . Even now it was a powerful feeling.

"After that, I expected things to settle, to go back to the way they'd been before."

"They didn't?" Georgia asked, sliding her leg back when he ran a finger up her arch—a reaction he stored away for later.

"At work, yeah, more or less. Ethan trusted me in ways he hadn't, was more inclined to listen if I had any input beyond program analysis. And because he wore his faith in me so openly, everyone else started to pay closer attention to me as well." It had been overwhelming, the sudden attention, the immediate rise in responsibility. It wasn't that Parker had been slacking or that he hadn't understood the consequences of his job. In theory, he'd always known what was at stake, and in practice the point had been driven home in the days he'd spent helping Ethan navigate a potentially deadly situation. But the pressure of knowing that men and women were now looking to Parker to pull off the impossible, to keep them safe . . . It had been overwhelming—and Ethan had noticed. "He got . . . protective, for lack of a better word. All of a sudden he was keeping an eye on the hours I put in, making sure I ate, slept, took time off."

"Does it bug you that Ethan thinks you need taking care of?" Georgia asked quietly.

For a long moment, Parker distracted himself by sliding his fingers along her legs, eliciting shivers and trembles, watching as Georgia responded to him on the most basic level.

When he didn't answer, Georgia said, "You're different around Ethan. Deferential. Kind of . . ."

"Intimidated?"

"Sort of, yeah."

"I think I'm just comfortable with our dynamic. Did you know Ethan had a brother?"

Georgia withdrew her legs, sat up, and leaned forward. "No, I didn't."

"Yeah. Younger. Ethan told me a little about him. They were as competitive as they were close. Always outdoing each other, always watching out for each other. I think when Ethan's brother died, he lost that sense of closeness. That feeling that someone out there had his back, no questions asked."

"Until you stepped in, commandeered a satellite, and helped him walk out of hell."

"Yeah." He studied her reaction, hoping the turn in their conversation wouldn't throw her into thoughts of Will. He didn't want to watch painful memories grip her face, steal her focus. He didn't want her to hurt at all.

If only it were as simple as hijacking another satellite.

"You know how you look back on your life, and there's a handful of moments you can point at and say, 'That changed everything'?" he asked, steering the conversation forward.

"You know I do," Georgia whispered, pulling her legs to her chest.

"Those few days, holed up in the office, chugging Red Bull so I could stay on the line with Ethan—they changed the course of my life. Ethan changed the course of my life. Because while he needed someone he could both protect and rely on, I needed someone in my corner. Someone who, at the end of the day, was on *my* side. No questions asked. I was so lonely, Georgia," he croaked. "You have no idea."

"Yeah," she said reluctantly. "I think I do." She leaned forward, placed a hand against his shoulder, and rubbed her thumb against the base of his throat. Just like that, he could breathe again. Every touch, every gesture she bestowed on him, made it that much more impossible to tell her the truth. To throw a chasm between them he'd never be able to bridge.

"Until Ethan, I didn't know what it meant to have a friend like that. A brother who would take me out for a beer after a long day. Someone who had my back no matter what I needed. I didn't grow up like that, never had it. And for a long time, I didn't even really know enough to want it. To miss it. Not until Ethan forced his way into my life."

"You mentioned once that your mother . . ." He watched as Georgia searched for the right words, as if any such thing existed. "That she maybe didn't protect you as she should have."

"My mom . . . She did the best she could." Everything in him wanted to withdraw, to change the subject. He wasn't even sure how the conversation had taken this turn.

"You don't have to tell me, Parker."

Didn't he? After everything she'd told him and everything he already wasn't telling her? Didn't he owe her the same vulnerability, the same honesty?

As if reading his mind, she said, "I told you about my childhood because, well—" She ran a shaky hand through her hair. "I told you because I didn't want to carry it alone anymore, and because I trusted that you wouldn't use it against me, that you wouldn't think less of me." She leaned forward, gripping his forearms. "It was the right decision for me, and I'm glad I told you. That doesn't mean it's the right call for you, and you definitely don't owe me anything, okay?"

She was right, of course. He didn't have to tell her anything. Didn't owe her the sordid personal details he'd never willingly shared with anyone—even Ethan only knew because he'd bulldozed his way into Parker's personal life. But as Georgia sat next to him, bathed in the gray shadows his computer screen created in the dark, everything about her read warm, and soft, and intimate. And intimacy, Parker had come to realize, was something to be shared.

"My mom, she wasn't a bad parent," he said, starting with the truth he so often had to remind himself. "She wanted so desperately to be good for me, to make my life something incredible. But it almost felt like that quest, that desire, ate her alive. Tormented her until she'd swing wildly between emotions. She was so determined to be the best at everything that every failure, no matter how small, was cataclysmic." He wrapped his fingers around Georgia's forearm and pulled until she rose and came to him. "I wouldn't understand until years later that she had schizoaffective disorder—a main course of schizophrenia and a second helping of bipolar depression. I couldn't know she would devolve to the point I barely even recognized her. Or that she self-medicated with drugs through the majority of my childhood."

Hands cupped the side of his face, lifting his chin as Georgia settled over his lap, one leg on either side of his chair, and placed a light kiss against his lips.

"I can see how that would be incredibly lonely for a child."

"It didn't help that my IQ separated me from most of my peer group. Or that I never knew my father. But I lucked out—a counselor at school got me tested, had me placed in advanced programs. By fifteen I was applying to universities and so desperate to be away from home it hurt. At that point I'd seen two different dealers beat my mother unconscious." He grasped Georgia's hand, placed her fingers against the crescent-shaped scar an inch into his hairline. "One hit me with a beer bottle when I tried to intervene."

She brushed a kiss against the ridged flesh, a simple, gentle gesture that nearly undid him.

He didn't deserve the comfort she freely gave him. Not when he knew her brother suffered alone.

"I hated her so much," he croaked, burying his face against her chest. "Hated her for something she didn't understand and couldn't control."

Strong arms pulled him close, holding him as he confessed to hating his mother. Who did that? Who hated someone sick? Someone desperate and just as lonely as he'd been?

"You were a kid, Parker. No one could blame you for feeling that way."

"Things got better when I went to school," he said, pulling away so he could look at her. "I was still lonely—a fifteen-year-old, no matter how smart, does not belong on a college campus, let alone in the dorms. But for the first time, things were stable. For a while, my mom even saw a doctor and was properly medicated. We got to know each other a little bit. I know she wanted more, wanted us to be closer, but I . . ."

"Couldn't risk it," Georgia said. "It's not a hard lesson to learn. People will disappoint you. Betray you. Hurt you." She looked down at him, her eyes dilated in the darkness until only the blacks of her irises were visible. "Expecting the worst of people, wondering when, not if, they'll leave . . . it's a hard habit to break."

A punch of guilt stabbed him in the ribs.

"It took a long time, but things got better. We saw each other regularly." It hadn't lasted, of course. A reality that no longer brought him anger, only a resigned sadness he could never quite shake. "The sad truth is most people diagnosed with schizoaffective disorder don't stay on their medications. Those moments, however long they last, are like living in the eye of the storm. Eventually, things are going to turn dark and ugly again."

"What happened?"

Parker shrugged. "I don't have all the details. But not long after I started working with the CWU, things changed. We went longer and longer between visits, until eventually I lost all contact with my mother. I couldn't find her. Turned out she'd lost her job, been evicted. She disappeared entirely."

"That must have driven you crazy."

"Yeah. By then I was old enough to understand what was happening—and determined not to abandon her again."

"Hey," Georgia said, running a finger along the rough stubble of his jaw. "You didn't abandon her the first time. You didn't know, and even if you had, you were too young to do anything about it."

Parker tucked a piece of hair behind her ear. "Regardless, I couldn't do it again. Run off, start a new life, pretend she didn't exist. I drove myself into the ground trying to find her." He slid a hand down over her shoulder and along her back. "Finally, Ethan noticed. Intervened. He found my mother in some backwater county jail. Got her released. Helped me with the legalities of getting her into a state-of-the-art assisted-living center and back on medication. I didn't ask for the help—at first I didn't even want it. But you know Ethan."

"Stubborn? Almost condescending in his certainty he can take care of things? Yeah, I know him."

Parker smiled. "Thing was, for the first time, I didn't have to go it alone. When I was walking through hell, wondering if there was ever going to be a light at the end of the tunnel, Ethan was there, making sure I got to the other side."

"As you were for him."

"Right."

Georgia sighed. "That certainly explains why you two are so close, but not why you're so deferential to him. It doesn't explain why when you're with him, your confidence withers. Why you seem so unsure of your own capabilities."

"I think it's just easiest sometimes. To play the role assigned to me. To let Ethan take the lead, to be who he expects me to be."

"That's not fair to you, though." The fierceness of her reply broadsided him. "I don't care what Ethan's done for you or how well he knows you. He doesn't get to make you feel less than the capable man you are. No one does." She forced him to look up at her, to hold her gaze. "You don't have to water down who you are just to make it easier for other people to like you, Parker. You don't owe anyone that much; I don't care who they are or what they've done."

He shook his head. "It's not that I think of myself as less or that Ethan undermines my confidence. It's just that at the end of the day, I know who I am. And who I'm not."

She leaned back to look at him. "What do you mean?"

"I mean that I'm attached to a highly trained, incredibly smart, could-kill-you-with-two-fingers-and-a-paper-clip special-operations team." He used the edge of his thumb to rub away Georgia's frown. "Every one of them brings a technical specialty to the table, an area of expertise."

"So do you."

"Yes." He nodded, resisting the urge to lick a stripe up her neck. "But I don't have the field experience. I'm not the guy people want in their corner or the one they call in an emergency." He chuckled. "Well, if the cable goes out, the Wi-Fi goes down, or the printer decides to be a little bitch, then yeah, I'm your guy. But I'm not . . . capable. Physical. I can shoot, but only because Ethan insisted. But in a fight? Hand to hand, life or death? I'm not the winner. I know it, and the team knows it, too." Parker sighed, running his fingers along the shell of his ear. He didn't have to wonder how he'd have reacted in Will's position. He wasn't a warrior. Couldn't hope to maintain his composure, his resolve, under such a threat. "And even though they'd never say so, even though Ethan would never directly imply it, there's always going to be a question about whether or not I'm a liability."

"Liability," she said, as if she couldn't quite believe what he'd just told her.

He shrugged. "I'm not Special Forces. I'm glorified tech support."

"You're a damn drama queen is what you are."

He glanced up, surprise sitting him up straighter—and nearly depositing her on the floor. "What?"

"Come on, Parker. Surely you've thought this through."

"Let's assume I haven't."

"You make it sound like what makes someone special is their physical ability. That's crap."

"I know a joint task-force unit made up of SEALs and Delta guys who'd disagree with you."

"If you believe that, you don't know shit." She used her open palm to thump him against the forehead. "Come on, Parker. Use that big brain of yours. How many guys go into the service every year? And how many of them swear up and down they'll be going Special Forces? And yet, how many are actually recruited, let alone make it through training?"

"I don't know," he said, gripping the backs of her thighs and pulling her close when it felt like she was about to spring up and start pacing.

"It's a tiny number."

"Because the training is so demanding."

"Yeah. But it's not the physical part that defeats candidates." She looked at him like he was an idiot. "They're all fit," she said, smacking the back of her hand against his abs as if to remind him he was, too. "It's the mental struggle that separates those who can from those who can't, Parker. The body can be trained to do just about anything—but the mental willpower to function under extreme conditions, to keep going when it hurts, when you know you're losing, when you're terrified . . ." She shook her head. "That's a decision that's made here"—she flicked his forehead—"and here," she said, pressing her palm against his heart.

He stared at her, looking for the platitude, evidence of the verbal participation trophy she was offering him. Truthfully, he'd never actually thought about what it took to be like Ethan or Ortiz or Jones. He'd always just stopped at the assumption he didn't have what it would take. But now . . .

"Are you really going to sit there and tell me that, when push comes to shove, there's *anything* you couldn't do if you decided you wanted it badly enough?"

He grinned up at her. "I might if it means you'll keep stroking my ego like this . . ."

She rolled her eyes and moved to climb off his lap. He grabbed her by the hips and pulled her toward him until he could slide his tongue against a path of skin along her throat. A sensitive spot he'd discovered earlier. One he wouldn't forget.

A breathy little sound escaped her. She leaned back but settled against his thighs.

"And for the record?" She trailed her hands through his hair. "You're the guy I want at my back."

High praise he didn't deserve and would never be worthy of.

If he lived a thousand years, he'd never understand why the universe had dropped Georgia into his lap—for the life of him, he couldn't fathom what he'd ever done to deserve her. God, he didn't want to lose her. He inhaled, breathing in the fresh, clean scent of her. He just wasn't ready to give her up. Wanted to keep her for as long as life would let him. It was the cruelest of catch-22s. Lie to her and destroy everything building between them. Tell her the truth and watch the agony, the uncertainty; destroy the woman she was.

In the end, it was an easy decision. Parker would never, ever be the reason Georgia lost herself. Even if that meant he'd have to give her up. Even if that meant she'd eventually come to hate him.

But not yet.

She shifted closer, and he let his hands run along the cotton-covered length of her back. Let one palm slide over the taut muscles of her ass until he could cup his fingers against her, rubbing back and forth, encouraging her to rock against his hand. When the shirt she wore rode up and he discovered she wore nothing beneath, he moaned.

He'd tell her everything, but only when he was in a position to do something about it. Only when he could offer her a path forward—and the head of whoever had set this all in motion.

"Feel like maybe you're ready to come back to bed?" she asked.

He nodded as he gripped the hem of her stolen Henley and pulled it up, exposing a wide expanse of soft, pale skin. When she lifted her arms, he pulled it over her head, licking a stripe up the exposed side of one breast as he did. Ditching the shirt, he ran his hands back down her sides, cupping her breasts, scratching at the sensitive skin along her ribs. He watched as she shifted, fought the urge to moan, succumbed to the desire to shift her hips against him.

Slapping the lid of his computer shut, he rose, gripping both globes of Georgia's ass, encouraging her to wrap her legs around his waist. As he headed back toward the bedroom, he slid his fingers along her cleft, finding her soft and warm and wet and ready. In the welcoming heat of her body, oblivion beckoned. If this was a test of his strength, of his character, Parker knew he was doomed to failure.

He didn't know how, but he'd find a way to tell her.

And pray she forgave him for it.

CHAPTER TEN

In her entire career, Georgia had never had a client she wanted to both strangle and seduce in equal measure.

Just another way Parker excelled at setting himself apart. Jerk.

One minute he'd be all soft lips and sleep-mussed hair. Warm. Inviting. Enticing in the worst way. A way that invited Georgia to press herself close, to taste and touch. To tease and torment. To fall into Parker until the rest of the world faded away beneath a haze of languid lust it would be all too easy to get lost in.

But in the next minute? Then she wanted to do far more creative things to the man. Bamboo shoots, water torture, electroshock—all too good for him. Oh no. When Parker fell into his snarly, surly funk, she wanted to do far, far worse. Like force him to walk barefoot over a field of LEGOs. Or hide his coffee.

Better yet, brew a fresh pot and refuse to share.

Yeah, she thought, watching Parker as he stared at his computer, a pad of paper and a half dozen pens at his elbow, the detritus of dead ends and failed scenarios scattered across the linoleum floor, she wanted to hurt him. Or kiss him.

Tough call, really.

And it wasn't like she didn't understand his piss-poor mood. Nearly seventy-two hours had passed since they'd arrived—she'd hoped for answers by now. Judging by the tense set of Parker's shoulders, so had he.

Georgia sighed. If something didn't change, and soon, Parker was going to crack under the pressure. He wasn't eating well; sleeping only in short, restless stretches; and consuming caffeine by the caseload. It wasn't sustainable, but Georgia didn't know how to help him. She'd tried going through some of the files, looking at the notes he'd made, but without any idea of what to look for, she'd basically been useless. A fact Parker had, rather condescendingly, pointed out two hours ago in a fit of frustration.

In any case, the tension and irritation and unending monotony were better than the alternative. For a bodyguard, boredom was always preferable. It meant no one was shooting at them.

Georgia gathered the wreckage of Parker's frustration. Empty energy drinks littered the table, and a half-eaten ramen cup sat at his elbow, no doubt hours cold. Parker needed a break, a fresh perspective, but the last time Georgia had tried to coax him away from his computer, he'd damn near bitten her head off.

Disposing of the trash, Georgia grabbed two cold bottles of water from the fridge and the bag of M&M'S she'd secreted away and joined Parker at the table.

"Here," she said, twisting off the cap and pushing a bottle of water toward him.

Red-rimmed eyes looked up at her from an exhausted face. "Thanks."

He gulped down half the water, then set it aside and tore open the package of M&M'S. Dumping them out on the table, he starting pushing them into piles, organizing them by color. Georgia couldn't help her small smile of amusement. Parker always had to have something to occupy his hands, especially when he was deep in thought.

"Ever try LEGOs?" Georgia asked, sneaking a few M&M'S from the green pile.

"What?" Parker asked, blinking at her as if she'd spoken Greek.

"As a distraction, a way to reorganize your thoughts."

"Oh." Parker glanced down at the neat piles of candy in front of him and shrugged. "I don't even pay attention. Just like to keep my hands busy."

"So I've noticed." She shifted, crossing her legs and ignoring the ghostly sensation of Parker's tactile exploration. As he watched her, heat slid through his expression, then his face fell and he glanced back at the computer. With every passing day, Parker withdrew more and more. Was it merely the stress? Or had something changed the night they'd arrived? It had been . . . intense. Automatically, Georgia's fingers reached for the bruise Parker had sucked to the surface of her skin. She shivered. It was nearly gone now, but not forgotten. Not even a little.

"There's just too much information," Parker said on a sigh. "I need something to work from. Someplace to start."

Shoving insecurities and emotional entanglements aside, Georgia forced herself to tune in and troubleshoot what mattered. "Ethan said he thought this was an elaborate war profiteering scheme," Georgia said, careful to keep her tone neutral. More than once Parker had gotten defensive when she'd tried to play devil's advocate. "No luck running with that?"

"Not really. Based on what I'm looking at, the general idea makes sense." Parker started in on the blue M&M'S.

"How can you tell?" She'd looked at several different files over the last few days, but nothing had stood out to her; nothing had seemed suspicious. They were all standard military reports—nothing to get excited about.

"It's the obvious deduction. All these files have three things in common." He pushed his computer aside and looked at her. "First, all the operations were considered, run through my program, and ultimately rejected as nonviable. The justifications include everything from budgetary issues to too much risk to personnel on the ground, with a hundred reasons in between. But they were all rejected."

"Okay, I'm with you so far." And no closer to having a clue what was going on. She might not be traditionally educated, but Georgia had never felt a step behind her peers. With Parker, he was so far ahead of her he was a speck on the horizon. Funny, but it didn't bring out her competitive side. It just . . . was. Maybe it didn't bother her because it didn't seem to bother him.

"Second," he said, flicking a brown M&M back and forth between thumb and forefinger. "Every single operation eventually got the green light. And every time, the decision was made at the last minute and bypassed the traditional screening process."

"Traditional screening process?" Georgia asked.

"Yeah, typically if we want to reconsider an operation—which happens more often than you'd think—we run the program again and reconvene a go/no-go panel. A lot can change in very little time, but none of these operations were ever reassessed by anyone."

Georgia rolled the bottle of water between her palms. "How often did things go wrong because of that?"

Parker flinched. "There were . . . losses," he admitted. "But mostly, things seemed to go okay. Whether that's because the details hadn't changed much or because whoever is doing this is cherry-picking easier operations, I don't know."

"And the third thing?" Georgia asked.

Parker sighed. "In every single file, there's a third party with *very* deep pockets that stands to lose big if the situation isn't resolved. Ethan was right—those files contain operations that would have benefited companies and organizations across several different sectors." He flicked through the pages on his notepad. "I've seen everything from drug companies to large-scale manufacturing operations . . . but never the same one twice. Nothing to connect them all together."

"Except for your program," Georgia said, sneaking more candy from the red pile. "So then Ethan's conclusion is simply the obvious one. Someone's using your program and the men and women of the US Armed Forces to get rich."

Parker nodded. "No question. Nothing else makes sense."

"So we know why . . ."

"But not who, which in this case is far more important." Parker shoved away from the table, knocking his chair back a few feet. "Maybe, *maybe* if I had my program, I could find a pattern, see whatever it is I'm missing. But on my own, with a shitty computer and my own damn program trying to off me, my hands are tied." He spun, pushing himself into a frenzied pace across the carpet. "Worse, I'm average. Basically useless to everyone."

"Okay, hold up a second," she said, reaching for his sleeve as he passed. He jerked away, crossing his arms against his chest, a bullish expression on his face. "Your program is just an extension of *you*," Georgia said, rising to follow Parker into the living room. "You designed it—" She waved him off when he opened his mouth to argue. "Yeah, yeah. I know. It's infinitely complex, doesn't eat, doesn't sleep, blah blah blah." She stopped a foot in front of him, pinning him to the wall so he couldn't escape her. "But it's still you. Your brain—and yes, maybe it's your brain on steroids, but it is *you*, Parker."

"I can't just re-create it, though. It's the product of years and years of R and D."

"And so are you," Georgia said, bumping her fist against his shoulder. "You weren't born yesterday, Parker. Yeah, sure, the program has evolved over the years. But you have, too. You have the benefit of hundreds of operations, hundreds of outcomes. You've got your own intellect, the benefit of Ethan's training."

"I'm not like them, though. I'm not a skilled operator. I don't work well under pressure—I need data, time. I can't just glance at a situation and make a best guess."

Georgia rolled her eyes. Why Ethan had allowed Parker on a tactical team but never taught him the confidence needed to succeed in that environment, she didn't know. But it damn well stopped now.

"We talked about this, Parker. Everyone's skill set is different. That doesn't make it any less effective or deadly. The whole point of special-ized units is to decrease redundancies and increase specialized skill sets. You may not be an expert marksman or proficient in hand-to-hand combat, but aren't you the guy who said he could erase my entire digital existence? Didn't you stand in your loft, barely caffeinated, and swear it would be *easy?*"

"Yeah." Parker swallowed hard, and Georgia pressed her advantage.

"Don't you get it? The team doesn't *work* without you. They can't fix this; they wouldn't even know where to begin. At the end of the day, the CWU starts and ends with you!" She really wanted to tack "you moron" onto the end of that sentence but didn't want to push her luck. "Your team trusts you to figure this out. Ethan came to you. I trusted *you!*" She took a deep breath, caught off guard by just how much she meant it.

"Past tense?"

"Don't be a moron." She glared at him. "I know you can do this. The answers are there, but if you keep up this cycle of doubt, if you keep convincing yourself that Parker 2.0 is better, faster, stronger . . . then yeah, this is going to end badly."

Parker sighed, bringing his hands up to settle on her hips. Staring down at her, he asked, "So what do you suggest?"

"First, step away from the computer. Staring at it unblinkingly is only going to give you a migraine."

His mouth quirked. "And second?"

"You," she said, curling her fingers into the waistband of his jeans, "need a distraction."

"So far, I like your plan," he said, sliding a hand along the decon-structed collar of her sweatshirt, pulling it to the side to expose her shoulder and trace the mark he'd left there.

"What is it"—Georgia fought hard against a shudder and lost, goose bumps rising across her skin—"with you and leaving a mark?"

"I like knowing it's there. Like knowing if anyone else stumbled upon it, he'd know I'd been here. Left my signature, marked my territory."

"Such a stupid, macho thing to do," she complained with a forced roll of her eyes. Truth was, she liked it. Liked the way it brushed against her clothes, the way her fingers sought it out, almost as a reflex.

"It's a hacker thing, too. Leaving a mark, a signature, so others would know your work . . ." Parker went stock-still, his mouth dropping open in a stunned expression she'd never seen him wear before.

"Parker?" Georgia asked.

"I," he said, looking down at her, "am an idiot."

Excitement propelled Parker straight back to his computer. Finally, finally, he knew what to look for. That it had taken him three days to see what should have been obvious infuriated him. He'd been so torn up about Will, so busy keeping Georgia at arm's length, he hadn't been able to concentrate, to close out everything else and focus exclusively on what mattered. He wasn't sure that had ever happened before.

"I've spent all this time combing through the files, looking for details and connections."

"Yeah?" Georgia flicked her fingers at him in an "oh, do continue" motion.

"I was so busy looking through the data in the files, I never stopped to look at the files themselves." He started pulling them up, one by one. "If Ethan grabbed these straight off the server, I should be able to look at the security logs."

"What?" Georgia asked, pulling her chair in closer to him.

"The government tracks everything. Every file accessed, every person logged on to the server—it all leaves a mark. That way, if any files are ever tampered with, we can see who's had access to them."

"Aren't there ways around that?"

"Sure," he said, fingers flying over the keyboard. "But whoever this asshole is, he's been pretty fucking brazen. He never expected anyone to notice—and why would he? All these operations were closed, their files sealed, the information classified. And I guarantee you, whoever's doing this has the right level of access. So why hide?"

Georgia leaned over to look at the screen. "How long will it take to go through the records?"

"I don't need to," Parker said. "I've scrolled through the history on ten of them while we were talking. Only one name aside from Ethan's is on every single one of them." It was such a fucking cliché, too. Overworked, under-recognized bureaucrat close to retirement and looking to pad his bank account. What a prick. "Charles Brandt."

"Should I know who that is?"

"No," Parker said. "But I do." On some level, Parker had known that there'd be a personal connection, that he'd know the person responsible, but he'd still hoped that no one he knew, no one he worked with and trusted, would be capable of being so selfish. Of risking so many lives.

Of leaving a man behind to rot in a South American hell.

Georgia placed a hand on his shoulder and squeezed.

"He's the director of the DoD's off-book operational forces." And was about as untouchable as anyone Parker could possibly imagine. What a nightmare.

"So who does he report to?" she asked, watching over his shoulder as he opened another file history. Then another. All produced the same result.

Parker turned and looked up at Georgia, the full weight of what they were up against settling around his throat like a noose he'd always known was there but had only just been cinched.

"Not a fucking clue," Parker admitted. "You have to understand, we aren't dealing with traditional chains of command here. The CWU is entirely off book, and oversight is thin at best."

"But you're still a government-controlled entity. There has to be some sort of hierarchy, some sort of reporting structure. The budget alone means other people have to be involved, to be aware of what's happening."

Parker shook his head. He couldn't fault Georgia's logic, but it was all based on traditional military perspective. Neatly ordered. By the book. But none of it applied. CWU was an off-book unit, and operating without oversight was the whole point of being off book. "All our funding gets appropriated in very small amounts from other sources."

"Surely someone must notice, keep track of what money goes where . . ."

Parker laughed. "I'm sorry, were you under the impression our government was actually good at working with a budget?" He shook his head. "More than a trillion dollars was allocated to discretionary spending last year alone. Shifting small amounts, even amounts in the thousands of dollars, would be comically easy to do."

He barked out a laugh that tinged dangerously toward hysterical. "I guess I should be grateful."

"What do you mean?" Georgia asked.

"Charles Brandt may be a greedy bastard, but he's also unimaginative. He's using the program to get rich, to fleece major corporations"— *not to mention cartels*—"of what I can only assume is millions of dollars. Can you imagine if he'd had grander ambitions? In the wrong hands, my program could be used to play the long game—all the world powers on one chessboard. Depose this dictator, empower that one. Remove this head of state, spark a civil war." Parker looked up at her, devastation sucking him under a wave of guilt. "In the wrong hands, my program could destroy nations, kill millions."

In the wrong hands, his program had torn apart a family. And so much worse.

"I never should have designed it."

Georgia leaned forward, lacing her fingers around his wrist, the touch at once welcome and heartbreaking. He didn't deserve her.

"You've spent the last several days looking at all the ways your program has been used for the selfish gain of one—you aren't seeing the whole picture, aren't considering all the good it's accomplished. You have to take it as a whole, Parker. Consider *everything*, weigh all the factors. And there will be time for that. Time to figure out what's next. But right now, we've got to deal with what's in front of us."

She was right; he'd told himself as much every time he'd wanted to crawl into bed next to her, whisper out his confession. One problem at a time.

"So where do we go from here?"

"Proof. This"—Parker waved at his computer—"isn't going to be enough. We need something ironclad. Something undeniable."

"Such as?"

"I'm thinking paper trail. We can already show that Brandt accessed these files; if we can connect him with large-sum payouts from the organizations involved, that should be enough to do it."

"Motive and opportunity." Georgia stared off across the kitchen, drumming her fingers against the table. "And we do that how, exactly?"

"Accessing Brandt's personal computer shouldn't be that hard." Parker grinned; there really was little he enjoyed more than letting himself into a system he wasn't supposed to know existed. "At least not for me."

"Okay, hacker extraordinaire. You adept at tracing complex financial records, too?"

"God no." That sort of analysis was time-consuming and mind-numbing in equal measure. He had neither the patience nor the thought process for digital forensics. "Ethan, on the other hand . . ."

"You're joking," Georgia said after a long, stony silence.

"Bet you thought he was only good at barking orders and pulling triggers."

She shifted, a blush climbing up her neck.

"You're forgetting, Georgia, everyone permanently attached to the CWU has a technical skill set to match their Special Forces training. Ethan's a force to be reckoned with in the field, but he didn't start out that way. He had a full ride on the table from three different Ivy League schools when he graduated high school."

"Awesome. I'm surrounded by geniuses."

"If there's a paper trail, Ethan can produce it," Parker continued.

"Is he up for this? The guy was shot three days ago."

Did it matter? Every day that went by heightened their risk of discovery—and was one more day Will had to hold on . . . if he wasn't dead already.

"He's going to have to be."

Now, more than ever, Parker felt the pressure to end this. For good.

"Ready?" Georgia asked, putting two fresh cups of coffee on the table, then pulling a chair close so they could share the screen. Parker, freshly showered and smelling of soap and timeworn cotton, radiated a casual warmth Georgia wanted to fold herself into. There'd be time for that, she reminded herself. Time to stay up late, sleep in later, and discover the strength of the bond growing between them.

After Parker was safe. After Brandt had paid.

Parker's computer beeped, and as he enlarged the screen, waiting for Ethan to appear, Georgia shrugged off the feeling that everything started now. That one way or another, they were hurtling toward the finish line.

"Can you see me?" Ethan's voice, strained and tired, came through the speakers.

"We can see your T-shirt," Parker said, adjusting his monitor so that he and Georgia sat squarely within the frame.

"I told you to let me tilt up the screen." Ortiz's exasperated voice filtered through the connection. The picture wobbled, slowly rising from Ethan's Columbia T-shirt to the man's face.

"Hey," Parker whispered, then swallowed hard.

Georgia understood why. Ethan's appearance was nothing short of haggard. She'd been prepared for it, knew what to expect—she'd visited more than a few people with serious battlefield injuries, knew the toll massive trauma took on the body. But Parker didn't. Not really. Georgia slipped her hand beneath the table and placed it on Parker's bouncing knee, giving him a reassuring squeeze. There was no way he'd been prepared for how Ethan, who had this way of appearing forever young, fit and indestructible, would look post-gunshot.

Stubble Georgia had never seen covered Ethan's jaw; deep circles carved crescent-shaped grooves beneath his eyes; and new, tense lines bracketed his mouth as if they'd always been there.

Ethan looked *old*.

"You look like crap," Georgia said, stating the obvious to get it out in the open. "So maybe don't get shot again."

"I'll take that under advisement." A crease formed at the edge of Ethan's mouth, though if he was laughing or grimacing, Georgia couldn't tell. "I assume you wouldn't have made contact unless you were somewhere safe and had news. So fill us in," Ethan ordered, his stare intense even through the camera.

"I went through all the files you grabbed. You were right; the only thing that makes sense is private war profiteering. None of those missions were authorized, and there's too many conveniently tied to parties with deep pockets to assume anything else." Parker took a breath. Reached for his coffee, trembled so hard liquid spilled over the rim. "Ethan, it's Charles Brandt."

"You're sure?" Ethan asked, not so much as a flicker of surprise crossing his face. Ortiz, at least, cursed violently off camera.

"Yeah." Parker nodded. "Positive. He's the only one to access every single record. And really, it makes sense. He's got the access, the clearance— no one would think twice if he sent an operational directive down the chain outside of normal channels."

"Okay. So we know who, and we know why. But?" Ethan asked.

"But we still have to prove it," Parker admitted.

"Which means we need to follow the money," Ethan said on a sigh. "That takes time, Parker. And a level of access to Brandt we don't have."

"Actually," Parker said, "we do. I had a few hours to burn before our call, and I got to thinking."

"Danger. Danger," Ortiz chimed in from the background, breaking into an impressive imitation of a siren.

"Yeah, yeah, very funny. Anyway, I realized you'd need access to Brandt's personal files, his digital history. Banking records at the very least. I could hack my way in, but that would take forever and potentially expose us." Parker brushed a hand toward Georgia.

"Not to mention be illegal."

"Seriously?" Georgia choked around a mouthful of coffee. "I think we're way past that."

Ethan grimaced as if it burned the very fabric of his soul to even think about breaking the law.

"Anyway," Parker said, bringing everyone back on track, "it was a long shot, but guess who's a Jungle Gem fan?"

"You're kidding," Georgia said, staring at him openmouthed.

"Nope. And since I'm the app developer, guess what I store on the company servers?"

"Passwords," Ethan answered.

"Bingo."

"How does a password to your silly game help us?" Georgia asked.

"It shouldn't," Parker agreed. "Unless the head of the DoD's black-ops division doesn't bother to read the interdepartmental memo about cybersecurity." Parker let his mouth quirk into a full smile. "Guess who uses the same password for *everything?*"

"You're sure?" Ethan asked, for the first time relaxing back against the pillows propping him up.

"Oh yeah. I took every available precaution, then used the remote log-in portal to access Brandt's computer using his e-mail and password. It worked. I downloaded his browsing history and did some checking. Same password across the board—the cable company, utilities, banking—you name it, you've got access to it."

It couldn't be that easy. Yeah, they were due for a break, had earned it if Georgia's opinion counted for anything, but still . . . it just felt too easy.

"I'll need a list of webs—"

"Already done." Parker pulled up a new window, uploaded the file, and sent it to Ethan. "A link should pop up on your end; just click accept."

"Got it."

Georgia watched the sheer effort it took Ethan to maneuver the track pad. And now they were asking him to spend hours, maybe even days, combing through Brandt's digital history for a smoking gun. He should be blissed out on the happy drugs and focusing on his recovery. Only one of many things Brandt had to answer for.

"You sure you're up to this, Ethan? We could find someone else," Georgia said, immediately regretting it as Ethan straightened and leaned toward the screen.

"Who?" Ethan asked, his voice a harsh accusation. "Forensic accounting is my specialty, no one else on the team is equipped to handle this, and we can't risk bringing anyone else in."

Georgia sat back. Nodded. He was right, after all; there wasn't a choice. And no time to wait for him to recover.

Ethan sat back, sweat breaking out along his brow. "I only wish I had something more specific to look for." He brushed off Ortiz when he offered Ethan a plastic cup with a straw. "I usually have an account number or a transaction ID to start with."

"Actually," Parker said, going suddenly stiff and still, "I think I can help with that."

What? Since when? And why the hell hadn't he told her any of this before the call? Georgia did a slow pan to her left, studying Parker's profile even as the hair at her nape stood up.

The muscle at his jaw twitched, as if he were putting a considerable amount of effort into staring at the screen . . . and avoiding her.

"What is it?" Ethan asked, drawing Georgia's attention back to the screen. Ethan licked his lips, pushing himself up against the pillows, jostling the computer until the view skewed, cutting away half his face. Swearing, he fixed the laptop. "Anything could be useful. Account numbers. Dates. Transaction origins or destinations."

Beside her, Parker stiffened in his seat. "Look for transactions originating out of South America."

Ethan blanched, and for a split second, his eyes shifted to Georgia, then back to Parker.

It was a confirmation she hardly needed. The moment Parker had mentioned South America, Georgia's thoughts had sprung immediately to Will, to the op that had taken his life.

"Then it's confirmed," Ethan said on a weary sigh.

"Yes." Parker shifted in his seat, cast a careful tip of his head toward her.

But why? Did he think her so fragile? Will's death would always feel like a fresh bruise, but she'd learned to live with it, and maybe that process hadn't been seamless or easy, but she was getting there. Once they brought Brandt to justice, she'd learn to live with the why and the how, too.

Still, she was sick to fucking death of being left out of the loop. Of being given the smallest piece of information and being told that was enough. The hell it was. She was part of this now. Her life was on the line as surely as anyone else's. She had the right to know everything. To be treated like a competent adult rather than a child whose parents felt the need to spell out certain words.

"Glad to know my brother's life was worth something, even if it is just proof," she spat as Ethan visibly startled, staring between her and Parker and back again. "Yeah. Parker told me what happened. Guess the cat's out of the bag." When Ethan's mouth dropped open, she steam-rolled right over him. "You can lecture me about the definition of 'classified' later. I think we have more important issues to deal with." She forced a shrug, tried to tamp down on the anger swirling just beneath the surface. "Will's dead; we need to focus on making sure the rest of us don't join him."

Ethan was silent a long moment, the weight of his stare every bit as heavy as if he'd been sitting across the table from her. Finally, he glanced to Parker, a question Georgia couldn't decipher sketched across his face.

Parker shook his head, his mouth set in a firm, tight line.

What weren't they saying?

"Parker?" she asked, her voice a tightly coiled rasp.

"Next steps?" Parker asked.

"Wait—"

"I find proof that Charles is dirty."

"Parker—"

"But then what? Who do we take this to?" Parker asked, completely ignoring her, even as she turned in her chair to stare at him.

"I have a contact in the Justice Dep—"

"Enough!" Georgia roared, slamming her hand down on the table's chipped Formica surface. "I will not be treated as if I'm not here! Whatever conversation you two are having but not saying, it ends now." Georgia shoved to her feet as stunned silence flooded the room. "Parker, look at me."

Slowly, he lifted his chin, his pale blue eyes finally meeting hers.

"Whatever it is, just spit it out."

Gravel crunched beneath tires, silencing Parker before he could say anything. Georgia froze, tilting her head toward the driveway. Betty? Unlikely. She used the gravel drive on the opposite side of the trailer that led to an ancient carport. Whoever it was, they'd pulled in behind the Corolla, blocking them in.

"Georgia?" Ethan asked, his voice low and quiet.

"Shhh." On silent feet, she took three steps toward the door and the curtain-covered window beside it. Georgia waited, her heart pounding so hard it threatened to drown out the sound of an idling car. When the engine died, she reached for the curtain, a thousand innocent explanations—everything from pizza to package delivery—fighting for space in her head. The hiss-spit-crackle of a radio had her freezing in place, too terrified to move, or breathe, or think.

Boots crunched over gravel, heading, blessedly, toward Betty's trailer.

Slowly, Georgia peeled the curtain an inch away from the window and watched as a uniformed sheriff's deputy rapped on Betty's door.

"Georgia?" Parker asked, keeping his voice low. "Is there a problem?"

She held out a hand, gesturing for Parker to stay where he was. God, let this be unrelated to them. They were so *close* to finishing this.

Betty opened the door, a cigarette dangling from her lips and TV remote in hand. Though only yards and thin panels of rusted metal separated them, Georgia still couldn't hear what was being said. It hardly mattered. The minute Betty flicked her cigarette ash over the rail and jerked her head toward their trailer, Georgia knew. She forced herself to wait as the sheriff glanced over his shoulder. To hold absolutely still until he turned around and, in what could be described as only a small mercy, followed Betty inside, closing the door behind him.

Gently, Georgia let the curtain fall shut. "We're going," she said in a whisper that brooked no argument. "Now." Moving fast, she pulled her coat off the hook by the door and slung the bag she'd kept packed and ready over her shoulders.

"What's happening?" Ethan asked even as Parker slowly rose, a stricken expression on his face.

"Sheriff just arrived on scene; he's with the neighbor," Georgia said, grabbing Parker's coat off the back of a kitchen chair and shoving it at Parker. "We're ditching the car and going out the back." Where, she didn't know or care. Priority one had to be getting the hell gone before the authorities descended. There were options. A convenience store. An all-night diner. A superstore. A gas station popular with truckers. All within two miles. She'd planned for this. Considered her options. She'd just prayed she wouldn't have to use any of them.

"Get clear," Ethan said as Parker zipped up his coat and shoved the computer cord into his bag, following the procedure Georgia had made him walk through a half dozen times since they'd arrived.

"We'll make contact when we're somewhere secure."

"Isaac Flores is on standby. He'll arrange transportation."

Only her training, the rehearsal she'd mentally run through every spare second of the last three days, kept her moving, kept her focused on the task at hand rather than wondering just how stupid she was. Because *of course* her ex was Ethan's contact in the Justice Department.

Grasping Parker by the arm, she pulled him down the hall as he snapped his laptop shut and shoved it in his bag. "I go first," she said, reaching for the window she'd greased with cooking oil until it slid open on silent tracks. She ducked her head outside, then pulled herself through, dropping to the ground on silent feet. She peeked around the corner as Parker followed her out to find the sheriff standing by his patrol car, talking into the radio at his shoulder.

"Let's go," she whispered, pulling Parker around in the other direction and back toward the tree line. The sun was dropping fast, darkness already creeping through the trailer park. Thirty minutes from now, slipping out unseen would be easy. It was time they didn't have—two more sheriff's vehicles and a local patrolman were bouncing their way up the pothole-ridden main road. Going unnoticed would be almost impossible, and barren trees provided no cover.

Which left only one option—a contingency she'd considered but prayed they wouldn't need.

"Over here," she said, pulling Parker off course and back toward what had once been a mint-green single-wide. From here, there was no direct line of sight to their trailer or the road, but there was direct access to the tree line. Georgia forced herself to drop to a knee, to focus on what would happen if they were caught, and pry back a loose piece of metal skirting. "We have to wait for nightfall," she said when Parker hesitated. "There's not a choice."

There wasn't, she told herself as Parker dropped to his hands and knees, then army-crawled his way under the single-wide.

I can do this. I can do this.

On a deep breath, Georgia followed him into darkness, carefully pulling the metal sheeting back into place, blocking out what remained of the fading gray light. The scent hit her first—the decaying stench of leaves, dirt, and something else, something she couldn't, wouldn't, put a name to. Bile built in the back of her throat even as sweat pricked up along the nape of her neck and across her forehead. She jerked as the trailer groaned and creaked on cinder-block pillars. She dropped her head in her arms as footsteps fell heavily across the floor less than two feet above her.

Breath caught in her throat, and tears burned at her eyes. A shiver racked her body.

"What can I do?" Parker whispered, his gloved hand coming to rest between her shoulder blades. She shook him off, sinking another inch into wet earth that hadn't fully frozen, her heart and the footsteps above competing to fill her ears.

I'm not there, she thought as the first hot tear burned its way down her cheek. All at once the remembered stench of urine, blood, and rot filled her nose. She gagged, more tears spilling against her will.

Hands grasped her by the shoulders. "Shh," Parker whispered, pulling her in and tucking her face into his neck. "You're not there, Georgia," he said, his breath a warm puff of air against her ear. "You're not alone. Not anymore."

She trembled, then tucked her face into Parker's chest and breathed through a sob. She couldn't afford to lose it now. Couldn't let fear, exhaustion, and ghosts she'd thought she'd buried give them away.

"Shhh." Parker's hand came to the back of her head, his fingers threading through her hair, anchoring her in the moment, reminding her she wasn't alone, that the past couldn't hurt her, not unless she let it.

Notched against Parker as if the world had created him just for her, Georgia forced herself to count the steady beats of his heart, to match her shallow, rapid breathing to the slow and steady rise and fall of his chest. To ignore the way the trailer swayed, to tune out the muted mumble of a too-loud television. To wait. For sunset. For safety.

For answers to questions she'd only begun to ask.

CHAPTER ELEVEN

Georgia sat, stiff and uncomfortable, across from Isaac and resisted the urge to shift or sigh. She hated this goddamn chair. Tufted leather and chrome finishing, it was half sophisticated taste and half modern extravagance—and 100 percent bullshit. For something that came with an awful lot of zeros in the price, it sure sucked at its primary function. Overstuffed to the point it had no cushion, the thing squeaked whenever Georgia so much as breathed—twenty-four times over the last hour, by her count—each and every squeal of leather hit her ears like a tiny *You don't belong here!* broadcast for the entire room.

As if that were even in question.

Forget the fact that she was covered in dirt and grime, Georgia had never felt comfortable in Isaac's Victorian-era townhouse, and she never would, not when she was too damn nervous to touch anything—*Those are antique highballs, Georgia!*—or sit on anything for fear her blue-collar ass would tarnish the surface. Everything in Isaac's immediate orbit screamed wealth and refinement. From the zip code to the furnishings, absolutely everything had been hand-selected and carefully curated to fit a very specific brand Isaac had been groomed to take over. Was it any wonder, with her unrefined manners and lack of social graces, that she'd never felt welcome, let alone at home, in the place?

"This is all very . . . ," Isaac said, drawing Georgia's attention back to him, something she'd been actively avoiding through Parker's explanations and all of Isaac's surprisingly thoughtful questions, "disturbing."

Georgia fought the urge to roll her eyes. *Disturbing.* Was Isaac ever anything but politically correct?

He rose and moved toward the sideboard he kept in his personal office. After one in the morning, Isaac was still in his work suit, looking like he'd stepped out of the pages of *GQ.* Tailored pants with a faint charcoal pinstripe, a matching vest, and a starched white shirt. Only the missing jacket and the rolled sleeves showcasing forearms Georgia used to fantasize about gave away that he was off the clock. Georgia watched out of the corner of her eye as he used a silver pair of antique tongs to fill glasses with ice. Once, not so long ago, watching him do that very thing had turned her on. Something about the restrained, controlled way Isaac moved had drawn her attention. The way he'd looked at her had kept it. Now his practiced manners served only to annoy her. She and Parker had come all the way back into DC, and for what? For Isaac to say it was all so *disturbing?*

"We don't have a lot of time, Isaac. Ethan sent us here for a reason; we need to know what you think."

Parker snapped his head around, a scowl twisting his forehead. Yeah, he didn't like it when she talked to Isaac. He'd made no secret of the fact that he was none too happy with the idea of asking Georgia's ex for any sort of help. Too bad. At this point, Georgia didn't give a damn who they had to negotiate with to get out of this mess. Enough was enough. This had to end.

From the moment she and Parker had slipped, muddy and freezing, into the back of a car Isaac had sent for them, she'd made her peace with the situation, even if Parker hadn't. Isaac was, if nothing else, ambitious as hell. There was no question that exposing a corrupt government official with the sort of power Brandt wielded would be a huge stepping-stone in his career. Parker could sulk all he wanted, but at the end of the day, Isaac would do what was in Isaac's best interest. And right now, that meant he'd help them.

On his terms, as usual.

Perfect cubes of ice clinked against $300 crystal as Isaac set a drink at her elbow.

"Still the way you like it, I assume?" he said with the confidence of a man who believed he'd once known her, possessed her.

"I don't want a scotch. I want to know what you think."

He took his time walking back to the bar, glancing over his shoulder at Parker as he did. "I'm afraid I don't know your drink."

Please don't say Red Bull and vodka. Please don't say Red Bull and vodka.

"Scotch is fine. Macallan?"

"Yes," Isaac said, preparing two more drinks and handing one to Parker. He watched as Parker took a careful sip, then placed the glass on the table next to him. "Not to your liking?" Isaac asked, the hint of a grin at the corner of his mouth.

"It's perfectly adequate," Parker replied, leaning back in his chair. If the creak and groan of leather bothered him, it didn't show.

"A thirty-year scotch and you consider it adequate?"

Parker shrugged. His movements moderated and controlled in a way Georgia was unfamiliar with. "I rarely indulge."

Isaac wore his disbelief across his face, as gaudy and obvious as the diamond pin in his tie. He thought Parker was bluffing, which was just great. Parker had made it clear he didn't like Isaac, and he was just stubborn enough to take the bait—and lose. Isaac had been raised in wealth, afforded every privilege. He'd take the opportunity to humble Parker simply because it presented itself—and because it had taken Isaac all of ten seconds to figure out Georgia was sleeping with him.

"I see. And on the occasions you do?" Challenge issued, Isaac settled back into his chair, comfortable in the knowledge Parker likely didn't have an answer. Or if he did, not one Isaac would consider worthwhile.

"Dalmore. The sixty-four was a memorable evening."

"Dalmore?" Isaac paused, for the first time running a considering gaze over Parker. Dressed in jeans, Chucks, and a slightly wrinkled long-sleeve T-shirt, *casual* would have been a kind description. Still, Isaac studied him as if he'd just appeared on his radar. "Only three of those bottles were ever produced. The last one sold at auction for more than one hundred and fifty thousand dollars."

Parker smiled, his teeth a predatory flash of white in the dark-walled office. "I know."

Isaac tapped the side of his glass with a finger, then propped a leg up on one knee. "You have excellent taste."

Parker glanced at Georgia. "I know."

Sick of the whiskey-laced pissing contest, Georgia leaned forward. "What are we doing here, Isaac? Either you're willing to help us or you're not. Time to make a decision; the longer we're here, the more dangerous this is to all of us—including you."

"Why didn't you come to me sooner?" he asked, a hint of a command lacing his tone. "Surely you must have considered it."

Georgia felt more than saw Parker's gaze fix on her. What did Isaac want to hear? That in a moment of need, when her life was on the line, when she had no other options, she'd thought of him? She hadn't. Why would she? She and Isaac were history, a part of her past she'd wanted to leave behind. And Parker. Just what did he expect her to say? All evening he'd been on edge, as if expecting some grand reunion, some trite declaration of love and devotion. Please. Georgia preferred the trailer park to the townhouse. At least there she knew where she stood.

"I've been a little busy, Isaac, what with the assassins and the shootings and the running for my life." She sneered at him. "You'll have to forgive me if your name didn't pop up under the header of 'trustworthy' or 'good in a crisis.'"

"So what, this is just a last resort?"

Georgia stared at him. "And nothing else." Though easy to say, Georgia was surprised it was also easy to believe. A part of her had wondered if seeing Isaac again would open old wounds, awaken old feelings. Oh, she hadn't worried she'd be stupid enough to fall in love with him again, but she had wondered if she'd fall back into insecurities that had followed her for most of her life. The ones that said she wasn't good enough. Smart enough. Pretty enough. Instead, she wondered how she'd ever lasted so long in his life in the first place.

Isaac stared at her for a long moment, then inclined his head. "I'll give you credit; you two did your homework. Coupled with what Ethan's provided—"

"Which was what, exactly?" Georgia asked. There hadn't been time or energy to press Parker for answers. Everything had happened so damn fast.

"Proof," Isaac said simply. "I hadn't wanted to believe it possible. That someone within the government could do such a thing—"

"There are dozens more files," Parker said, for the first time offering something that was neither a response to a question nor a snarky comment. "And that's only accounting for the files Ethan pulled off the server. There could be more."

"So this could go deeper than Brandt?" Isaac sat back in his chair, steepling his fingers as he considered them.

Parker stiffened. "We don't have any reason to believe this doesn't start and stop with Charles Brandt."

Isaac stared at Parker, twisting his chair back and forth in tiny increments. "From everything you've described—the sheer potential of your program—it sounds like there are plenty of reasons to assume this goes beyond Brandt."

"Such as?" Parker flicked at the cuticle at his thumb as he sat forward.

"Human nature?" Isaac asked, a smug smile gracing his face. "I don't know. Maybe you're naive, or maybe you just lack imagination—"

"Or maybe he's just a decent human being," Georgia snapped, shooting Isaac an irritated glance. "Not everyone puts his ambition first."

"Not everyone," Isaac conceded with a dip of his chin. "But most of us are easily dazzled by what could be, by what we *might* accomplish.

You certainly were," he said, casting a glance at Parker, who for the first time withered under Isaac's scrutiny.

Georgia wanted to reach for him, to lace her fingers in his. She might have if she wasn't half-convinced the gesture would only compound Parker's guilt, convince him he had something to be guilty for.

"Otherwise you might have spent a little more time considering the implications of your software and a little less time considering your own achievements." Isaac sipped at his scotch, then set the glass on the edge of his desk. "I can hardly blame you. Presented with the opportunity to arrange my fortunes, to dictate my fate? I'd be tempted."

Yes. Yes, he would. But Isaac had been born to privilege—he had the right family name, the fashionable address, the expensive degrees. He hardly needed the edge. But if it were there, his for the taking, would he walk away from it? Take the harder, less certain path?

Would she?

Georgia wasn't sure. She, more than anyone, knew there were no guarantees in life. What would she give up for even the chance at leveling the field? What would she have paid to protect Will? What would she do to save Parker? All questions she couldn't answer.

"I suppose for now it doesn't matter. Even if what Ethan sent is just the start of it." Isaac ran an exhausted hand through his honey-blond hair. "I've never had such a slam dunk fall into my lap."

Where Georgia had expected excitement, the thrill of an impending win, she saw only hollow resignation, as if what Brandt had done bothered Isaac on a personal level, rather than simply a pragmatic one.

"I'll need to get a federal judge on the line. Issue an arrest warrant for Brandt," Isaac said, reaching for his mouse and waking his computer. "I've got one in mind who owes me a favor."

"How long will that take?" Parker asked.

"I'm making the call now. With any luck, they'll pick up Brandt tonight." Isaac grabbed his phone, then dialed the number he'd pulled up on his screen. "Give me a second?" he said, rising and walking toward the French doors that led to his balcony. A knot of tension unwound in Georgia's shoulders. The end was finally, blessedly, in sight. No more shitty trailer. No more crappy showers. No more tiny quarters or shared spaces. And soon, no more questions. No more missing pieces.

She'd close the file on this job, bring Brandt to justice, and endure the final briefing where she *would* ensure all her questions were answered. Then she'd give in to the call of the comfort of home, of clean sheets and her own bed. But for all that she wanted to sink into the soft familiarity of her memory-foam mattress, she couldn't help but wonder what it would be like to wake up alone. Make coffee for one. Maybe Parker would come home with her for a day or two, just to get resettled. It wasn't fair to expect he'd stay any longer than that, or even that he'd want to see her again at all. But then, given Parker's possessive behavior over the past hour, maybe that wasn't something she needed to worry about.

Georgia leaned toward him, pitching her voice low. "A hundred and fifty thousand dollars for a bottle of scotch?"

Parker shifted closer, the tips of his ears going pink. "Ethan finally, *finally* invited me to poker with the guys. Told me to bring a bottle of scotch." He shrugged, laughing a little under his breath. "I panicked."

Georgia slouched into her chair. "You panicked?"

"I wanted to be invited back," Parker said, as if that justified everything.

"Were you?"

He scowled. "No. They said my brain cheats. Not my fault they only play with one deck."

Georgia snorted out a laugh. "Was the scotch good at least?"

"Yuck, no." Parker made a face. "Cheap or expensive, they all burn like a bitch on the way down."

Georgia shook her head, her smile so wide for a moment her cheeks hurt. Only Parker.

"Wheels are in motion," Isaac said, striding back into the room and stealing Georgia's good humor. "Judge issued an arrest warrant for

Charles Brandt. FBI are going to go tonight, try to grab him at home before he realizes what's coming."

Georgia breathed a sigh of relief. "Thank you, Isaac."

His face twisted, something like remorse stealing over his features. "Did you really think I wouldn't help, Georgia? Why didn't you come to me? Why didn't you trust me?"

Truthfully? Isaac was a lot of things—self-righteous, arrogant, ambitious—but not corrupt. And not heartless. "Last time I was here . . . we didn't end things on good terms."

"No, we didn't," he agreed. "But Georgia, even if my feelings for you were less than cordial, did you really think I'd turn my back on your brother?"

What did Will have to do with this? Sure, he and Isaac had been friends—part of the reason Georgia had wanted so badly to make things work with him. He'd known Will. Had stories and memories. Things to share and love. But how was any of that relevant now? "What are you talking about?"

"You don't know?" Isaac asked, shock seizing his expression. "Jesus, Georgia. I thought you said you'd been through the files?"

"Isaac . . . ," Parker said, a warning.

"You didn't tell her, did you?" Isaac asked. He didn't wait for Parker to respond. She'd thought it something small. A detail Parker had tried to spare her—after all, he'd told her what no one else had. Isaac turned to her. "Didn't you wonder why I kept calling? Why I wouldn't stop texting?"

"I . . ." She forced a shrug. "You only ever texted when you wanted one thing." She'd just assumed it was the same old bullshit. The offer of sex and nothing else.

Isaac sat back as if she'd slapped him. "Maybe I deserve that," he said, then leveled a look at Parker. "Are you going to tell her?"

A wave of sick nausea crashed over her.

"Parker?" she asked, her voice cracking as she turned to look at him. His face fell, and his mouth dropped open.

"No?" Isaac asked, his voice clipped and mean. "Why don't I show her, then?" He shoved his monitor until it faced her and, with a click of a mouse, destroyed everything.

She watched, horrified, as Will appeared on screen. Broken, bloodied, but so heartbreakingly alive. Studying every detail, she caught the date on the paper, did the math, even as those bastards severed his ear. Tears she thought beyond her, the hurt too deep, the loss too complete for such a simple emotion, tracked down her face.

It took everything she had to look away from a face she'd lost all hope of seeing again.

A thousand questions fought for dominance.

Was he alive?

Who had she buried?

How had this happened?

One, stronger than the rest, rose to the surface.

"Did you *know*?"

Parker didn't say anything, but then he hardly needed to. The truth was written across his face.

"You *knew*." She rose, clenching her hands against her sides. "You knew and said nothing. Even after I told you *everything*."

Something hot and heavy and familiar settled over her, calming her, grounding her. Hurt. Humiliation. Betrayal. She should have seen it coming. Should have known. Nothing good in her life lasted. It either wasn't hers to keep or wasn't real to begin with.

"I want to hear you say it," she ground out.

Parker looked up at her from where he sat, shock giving way to resignation. His face crumpled, a thousand apologies twisting his features. "I knew," he whispered, watching as she placed a shaking hand on Isaac's desk.

When Georgia stared at him, silently demanding all of it, every detail he didn't want to give, Parker finally said, "That first night in the trailer, I found the video file. I didn't know what to say!" His voice, half desperate plea, half apology, did nothing to soothe her rage. "I . . . What could I say? That he *was* alive? That he might be worse than dead? That he'd been *left* behind?" Parker shoved his thumb and forefinger beneath his glasses, rubbing at his eyes. "I couldn't offer any answers, offer any hope. I didn't want to hurt you," he whispered.

Georgia stepped back, wrestled with the urge to run, to scream, to yell until her voice was gone entirely. He'd known. All this time and Parker had known. And said nothing. Sad, stupid little Georgia. Trusting Parker with secrets she'd never shared. Baring herself to a man she hardly knew. Served her right. Only one person in her life had ever put her first, had ever deserved her trust—and he was . . . God, she didn't even know. Dead or alive, Will had been left to suffer. To wonder if anyone was coming, if anyone cared. An ugly, broken noise sobbed out of her.

"You son of a bitch." She launched the words at him, dangerous and destructive as a live grenade. "You did this! You *chose* him! You *left* him." A cold fury raced through her. "It should have been *you*." Regret and agony and all-consuming rage battered her. Even as she said it, she knew how unfair it was. Knew that Parker, stupid, foolish Parker, had only wanted to spare her the pain, the uncertainty. But it just didn't matter. It was too late. The world had changed *again*, and she couldn't undo the damage caused by careless words.

The power in Isaac's townhouse cut out, and something solid crashed through the window, throwing glass and light and noise in every direction. On instinct, Georgia threw herself to the ground.

And lost the ability to take it all back.

Georgia pushed herself to her hands and knees, her ears ringing, completely blind to the room. She lurched sideways, catching herself on the edge of Isaac's desk, and groped for Parker.

"Parker?" If she whispered or screamed, she couldn't tell. All that mattered was finding Parker. Doing her job and making sure he lived. He had to live.

He was her best shot at finding Will. Of bringing him home.

She slid forward, staying low to the ground and keeping as much of her body in contact with the floor as possible. The entire room felt as if it had suddenly been tossed to sea, and nothing was stable—an inner-ear reaction to what she'd quickly realized was a stun grenade. Pushing her palms along the wood floors, she searched for any sign of Parker. Where was he?

Hands scrabbling, she found his foot, followed the length of his leg up the rest of him. Her vision adjusted to the darkness in time to find him sitting on the floor, back pressed to the front of Isaac's solid-oak desk. "You okay?" she yelled, her own voice sounding thin and distant but miles better than the silence of moments ago. She shook her head, reaching for Parker with one hand and unholstering her weapon with the other. The moment her fingers met his chest, she breathed a sigh of relief. He looked shell-shocked, but his chest rose and fell in steady intervals, and his heart *thump-thump-thump*ed against her palm in a fast but steady rhythm.

Thank God.

"Grab Livingston!"

Someone seized Georgia by her hair, wrenching her away from Parker. She kicked on instinct. Legs catching the edge of Isaac's desk, she used the weight of it to brace herself. She shoved with every ounce of strength she had, forcing her assailant back. Off balance, whoever grabbed her stumbled back, caught his legs against one of the chairs flanking Isaac's desk, and they both went over. Working with the momentum, Georgia let the fall carry her, let her attacker take the brunt of the blow, then leaned into a roll that set her free of his grasp. Rising, she had her gun up in a second, firing at the man climbing through the window. Three bullets caught him in the chest. He pitched backward on a curse, falling out of the window he'd just climbed through.

She'd caught a break, but it wouldn't last. Men in full tactical gear had breached the bay window facing the back of Isaac's home. No way they weren't wearing vests.

One down at the window, another at her feet, a third man struggled with Isaac on the other side of the room. Seemed her ex had brushed up on some self-defense in their time apart. He was holding his own.

For now.

Moving fast and using the distraction Isaac provided, Georgia searched the room for Parker. He rushed toward her, glass and debris cracking beneath his shoes.

She grabbed his wrist, pulling him behind her, and kept her gun trained ahead. She backed up, pushing Parker with her hip toward the door as the man who'd grabbed her rose. On his first step forward, Georgia pulled the trigger, launching two rounds into his vest and a third in his thigh. He went down on a scream, clutching his leg and abandoning his weapon. She scooped his gun off the floor and prayed he stayed down. She'd take the head shot if it came to it, but odds were these men didn't know or care why they'd been sent. They were just following orders.

Which made things a hell of a lot more difficult.

Between the downed power and the privacy Isaac's newly constructed garage provided, no one would have any idea what was happening until it was far too late to help.

They were on their own, Georgia handicapped by nonlethal force.

This wasn't a fight they could win.

"Door. Go." Running their only option, Georgia kept her back to Parker's front, shielding him as they moved backward through the office and toward the exit. "Check the hallway, and if it's clear, run," she ordered, pushing the gun she'd retrieved into Parker's hand when he paused, back to the wall next to the partially open door.

"I can't."

"You can. You will. I've seen you shoot. Remember what I told you. Focus on keeping you alive, me alive, and pull the trigger. You owe me that much." She shoved him again. "Take it and move."

Parker ducked his head around the door, then stepped carefully into the hallway. "It's clear."

"Then go." Georgia stepped back, glancing over her shoulder. "Run. Straight out the front door. They want you alive. You see anyone coming after you, aim, fire, and scream your damn head off. Wake the neighborhood, then keep on going."

"Wait, you aren't coming with me?" Parker asked, his expression unsure but ready for a fight.

No time. They had no time for this.

Georgia shook her head and shoved Parker toward the stairs. "I can't leave Isaac. We planned for this. You know what to do." She'd forced Parker to run through exit strategies on the drive back from Pittsburgh, but it had never truly occurred to her she wouldn't be with him. But she couldn't leave Isaac to fend for himself, not when every blow, every grunt, every curse echoed through the room. He was fading fast. "Go. I'll meet you."

Before he could say anything, she slammed the door shut and whirled to face the room. How many rounds had she fired? What did that leave her with? Didn't matter. Isaac went down under a vicious uppercut and didn't get back up.

Georgia fired two rounds, sending one bullet into the ribs of Isaac's attacker—even with the vest it would hurt like a bitch—and aiming the second for the fleshy part of his shoulder where she knew vest coverage was spotty. The force of the blows had him staggering back into the built-in bookcases, but he kept his feet. Two more to the vest? Or aim for something unprotected? Would he even care if the situation were reversed?

Before she could make a call, someone grabbed her by the ankle, jerking her to the ground. She hit the floor hard, glass embedding in flesh, her head bouncing off the wood so violently she saw stars. She flailed as a body settled over her, pinning her to the floor. A huge hand grabbed her wrist, slamming it down by her head, then slipped the plastic of what she assumed were zip ties over her fingers.

If he got the loop on the other wrist, she was screwed.

Bucking her hips, she shot her free hand above her head, as far away from the guy's grasp as she could. He grunted, as if her efforts amused him, then shifted his body weight forward and made a grab for her hand—exposing his balls as he did.

Perfect.

Georgia got a knee up and drove it into his crotch, enjoying the way the bastard grunted, curling in on himself as the pain in his testicles warred with the pain of a bullet hole.

The unmistakable sound of gunshots wrenched her attention to the open window.

Parker.

She twisted, scrabbling for freedom, ignoring the way glass dug into the meaty flesh of her palms, pierced her jeans, and scraped against her thighs and knees. She was nearly free when a hand grabbed the waistband of her jeans and yanked her back. In the blink of an eye, he had her pinned, both arms wrenched behind her back, wrists secured in zip ties. The asshole braced a hand on the center of her back and pushed himself up, forcing the air from her lungs.

"Just grabbed Livingston. Let's go," someone said from the other side of the room, his voice wet and thick. Sounded like a broken nose. She hoped it hurt like hell.

"What about these two?" the guy above her asked, bracing himself against the desk. "Bitch shot me."

"So shoot her. Van's waiting."

Georgia stiffened. Should have shot the bastard when she'd had the chance.

"Orders were just for Livingston," the guy above her said as he limped toward the window. "These two are neutralized. I'm not pulling a trigger without a directive."

"Whatever. Let's go."

Georgia lifted her head, watched as the first guy climbed out the destroyed bay window, disappeared over the edge.

She shoved herself to her knees as her attacker approached the window, bracing his palms against what was left of the casing before swinging his bad leg over the ledge. Georgia pushed herself to her feet. She couldn't let him go. He'd had orders—they'd wanted Parker alive. Odds were the guy knew where they'd take Parker. What they wanted from him.

Before she could think better of it, she charged, slamming into the guy's broad back and sending them both flying through the window. Georgia had four seconds of air time to regret her decision before she bounced off a compact wall of muscle and slammed her head against unforgiving brick.

An engine revved and tires squealed, the van speeding away as Georgia lay on her side, every breath a painful gasp. She stared at the unmoving form next to her. She didn't care what it took or what it cost her.

One way or another, she was bringing *everyone* home.

◆　◆　◆

"Are you out of your mind?" Isaac yelled as he appeared over Georgia, blood streaming from a cut along his hairline. Georgia could do little more than groan. Everything hurt. Isaac pulled her up to a sitting position. "Anything broken?"

Everything? "I don't think so." She winced as the skin along her right side tugged and pulled. Road rash had torn up part of her forearm and scraped away the flesh at her hip. Thank God for winter. If she hadn't been wearing so many layers, the damage would have been a lot worse.

"Get me out of these?" she asked, indicating the zip ties still holding her wrists together.

"Yeah, give me a second," Isaac said, then disappeared through the open back door. Georgia took a moment to sit and breathe through the pain. She was going to be black and blue for weeks, and she was damn straight lucky she hadn't broken or dislocated anything. But even as her T-shirt stuck to the scraped skin on her arm and her jeans dragged against the destroyed flesh at her hip, she stared at the guy laid out next to her and decided the price had been worth it. Getting to Parker, as fast as possible, had to be her priority.

They won't kill him, Georgia reminded herself. *Not yet.*

It didn't take Parker's IQ to figure out why Brandt had suddenly switched tactics. The minute Parker disabled his program, the target on his back quadrupled. Brandt had gambled everything on that program—and, according to Ethan, made an awful lot of money. He wasn't going to give up his cash cow unless he absolutely had to. He needed Parker alive to restore the program's functionality.

Which bought Georgia some time to figure out what to do.

Cold, hard dread formed a fist in her stomach. Every minute Parker withheld the program was a minute longer he lived. But at what cost? Brandt had to feel the noose tightening—taking Parker instead of leaving the country was an enormous risk. Georgia didn't want to imagine what lengths Brandt would go to in order to make it pay off.

Isaac strode out the back door, a pair of scissors in hand, then knelt behind her and released her wrists. "I called it in. Feds are on their way."

Georgia stood, bracing a hand against Isaac's shoulder when the ground shifted uneasily beneath her feet. "Shit," she said, pulling away from him when he tried to grasp her forearms and lead her back toward the house. "You shouldn't have done that."

"Done what?" Isaac asked, anger tightening his face. "Called the authorities? Or helped you up?"

Georgia rolled her eyes. "We don't have time for this." She carefully approached the man on the ground. "Go get my phone. I need to make a call."

"You need to sit down before you fall down."

"I'm fine. But we don't have a lot of time to get answers."

"Let the authorities handle it, Georgia. They'll get to the bottom of this, have Parker released and Brandt arrested."

Georgia shook her head. He didn't get it. And she didn't have the time or energy to argue with him. The minute the cops arrived, Georgia lost all opportunity to be the one asking the questions. Reasonably assured her attacker was still out cold, Georgia knelt and removed a pair of plastic cuffs from his belt, looped them around his wrists, and cinched until his hands were neatly secured behind his back. He groaned when she grasped him under the shoulders and hefted, breathing hard and panting through the pain, until he more or less sat upright.

"I need my phone," she told Isaac, gesturing back toward his office. "It's in my bag by your desk. You'll recognize it; it's the 'ugly' messenger you always hated."

"It wasn't the bag, Georgia," Isaac said quietly.

She waved him off. "Whatever. My phone." She knelt in front of the man she'd secured, watching as dazed eyes blinked open, and his forehead wrinkled in pain. "I need to call Ethan, update him on the situation. So please," she said, putting all the force she could behind the word, "just get my bag."

"Fine." Isaac sighed, striding off toward the house, cursing under his breath as glass, wood, and general debris crunched beneath the bottom of his handmade shoes.

Georgia waited, watching until he disappeared inside. It would take him a minute to find her bag in the wreckage of the office, and though she did need to call Ethan, she needed the uninterrupted time with the man coming around even more.

She had maybe five minutes to get answers before chaos descended and her window closed.

"Hey." She shook the shoulder beneath her hand, getting little more than a grunt and a string of curses in response. "Hey."

He mumbled something she didn't quite catch.

Shit. She needed him coherent *now*.

Fine. Georgia reminded herself the only thing that mattered right now was finding Parker, and she pressed her thumb against the gunshot wound she'd inflicted.

He jerked to full awareness on a strangled shout, reflexively curling in on himself and drawing away from the pain.

"Where'd they take him?" Georgia asked, easing up the pressure a fraction.

Clear blue eyes looked up at her from an all-American, midwestern face. Blondish hair. Square jaw. He looked . . . nice. The lines along his eyes and mouth indicated he smiled a lot. Her hand slipped, and his face relaxed. God, she didn't want to do that again.

"Where did they take him?" she asked again, praying he'd just cooperate. Make things easy for both of them.

"Ugh. Go away."

She squeezed her eyes shut and dug her thumb into his flesh until he squirmed.

"Stop." He jerked, his legs kicking out and his body tensing.

Doesn't matter, she told herself. *Parker does.*

"Just tell me where you were supposed to take Parker."

"Or what?" The guy panted through heavy breaths he forced into laughter. "You'll tickle me some more?"

Georgia winced but didn't let up the pressure. Couldn't.

"Tell me and I'll stop," she said, using the palm of her hand to amplify the pressure even as she dug her thumb more deeply into the wound. "I just want to know where."

"Yeah. No." He trembled beneath her hand, his body spasming and sweat breaking out along his brow. "Not happening."

She narrowed her eyes. "I'll—"

"What? Torture me?" He grated out something that sounded like a laugh. "Honey, you don't have it in you. You can't wait to let go, wash your hands, and pretend this never happened."

"You think I don't have the stones?" Georgia asked, grinding her thumb into muscle. Praying that every curse, every jerk, every grunt of pain she extracted was one less Parker would have to pay.

"Not about balls, sweetheart," he said, jerking his head back and forth. "You bodychecked me out a fucking window with your hands tied behind your back. You got a bigger pair than most. But you don't have the thirst." He looked up at her, focused on her face. "You're desperate but not sadistic."

"Doesn't matter," she said.

"Trust me," he said, his expression slamming into her, pinning her with the absolute conviction of experience, "it matters. Torture? The kind that makes you want to peel off your skin with a paring knife just to escape it? The kind that convinces a man to say anything, everything, just to make it stop?" He shook his head. "You gotta embrace it. Enjoy it. Love every moment, every shudder, every drop of fear." He smiled at her. "You don't have it in you. Lucky me."

"Maybe not," she said, doubling down on the pressure in his leg. The muscles and tendons of his neck snapped tight, bulging in protest. "But you're right. I *am* desperate."

But desperate enough? She couldn't lose anyone else. Couldn't bury anyone else. The grief, the failure, the loneliness, they'd wreck her. There'd be no coming back, not this time. She just wouldn't want to. She was barely hanging on as it was. So what choice did she have?

"Where did Brandt take him?" she asked, doubling down on her resolve.

Finally, a reaction. Startled brown eyes met hers. "Charles Brandt?"

The question was enough to loosen Georgia's grip. "He's the one who gave the order."

The guy shrugged.

Georgia paused. But if that were true, he wouldn't have been so surprised when she said Brandt's name. "Who are you?"

"You mean aside from the guy you're fingering?" he asked, hiding his pain behind cocksure arrogance and a frat-boy sense of humor.

"Besides that," Georgia said, holding her hand against his bullet hole, ready to push if he didn't start talking.

He shrugged. "No one special."

She didn't buy it. Not for a second. He'd snapped to attention the moment she mentioned Brandt's name. But why? Why was he surprised? "I want to know who you are and why you're here. Now." She let her fingers dig into the muscles around his wound.

He flinched, his face going white and ashy even as he tried to keep his tone casual. "I thought you wanted to know where we were taking your friend." He *tsk*ed. "First rule of interrogation, babe, one question at a time."

"Fine," Georgia said, digging her palm against the wound. "Parker first." She ignored the way he writhed and jerked beneath her palm. She was done playing. Done hesitating. She didn't care who this guy was or why he'd been sent. Parker was what mattered. Everything else could wait.

"Jesus, Georgia, stop," Isaac said, grabbing her by the shoulder and pulling her back. "What the hell are you thinking?"

Georgia jerked away. "I need to know where they took Parker." She turned to the man on the ground, but Isaac grabbed her by the shoulder and forced her toward the house. Stepping away, she rounded on him—all her fear, adrenaline, and agony surging to the forefront. "I need answers—not hours or days or weeks from now when the feds sort through all the bullshit and figure out what we've known all along—now!"

"You can't have them. Not like this."

Screw him. Their entire relationship had been one long stream of things Georgia couldn't do, couldn't have, or couldn't be. "You don't get to tell me who I am, Isaac, or what I can and can't do."

"No," he agreed, shaking his head. "But I know you, Georgia—"

"The hell you do."

He ignored her. "I've known you a long time, since before Will died. Before you forgot what it was like to trust other people."

"Fuck you, Isaac." She trusted people. She just trusted the wrong ones.

"You're loyal to a fault, and I didn't see that until too late." He grabbed her by the shoulders, holding her still.

"If you really believe that, then you know why I have to do this," she said.

"And I know what it will cost you. I know the ways it'll eat at you, haunt you, destroy you. The cost is too high."

"Move," she said, trying to step around him as the first sirens echoed in the distance. "Get out of my way, Isaac."

"No." He grabbed her by the wrist, swinging her around until she was back where she'd started. "You'll get your answers—I'll make sure of it. But not like this. Not doing something you'll hate yourself for when all is said and done."

She wanted to take a swing at him. To drive an elbow into his gut until all he could spew was air.

"Why do you even care?" she asked, anger throbbing through every inch of her, pushing her to do something, anything. "They came into your house. Beat the shit out of you. Destroyed your precious office. So why the hell do you care what happens to him?" Georgia asked, pointing at the guy on the grass.

"Henry," he chimed in helpfully.

Georgia glared beyond Isaac. Henry sat in the grass, breathing heavily, with a cocky grin on his face he probably thought was charming.

"Don't do this, Georgia," Isaac said, drawing her attention back. "Brandt's not worth it."

Tears stung the back of her eyes. Not worth it? Maybe not to Isaac. But he didn't know Parker. Didn't know his character, his strength, his laugh. Didn't know all the ways he'd touched her. Couldn't possibly understand how he'd changed her. Even now, drowning under the agony of Parker's lie, knowing it would never, could never, be the same between them, she couldn't let him go. Couldn't stand the idea of him hurt, scared, or alone.

She hated him, even as she cared about him. And no matter what lies he'd told, no matter how thoroughly he'd destroyed her, Georgia couldn't stand the idea of someone hurting him. Torturing him. Breaking him down until she didn't recognize him anymore.

And they would. She knew they would. If Parker didn't believe in his ability to withstand, to hold out—if he didn't embrace the idea that the next several hours would test his mental stamina to the very limits . . .

It would kill him, one way or another.

She couldn't help Will. Not right now, not in this moment. But she could help Parker.

Sirens pulled up outside, wailing from the front of the townhouse. Too late.

"Look, just give it a little time," Isaac said, pressing her phone into her palm as agents filed through the house and out the back door. "We'll get answers. We'll find Parker."

Just wait. That's all she'd ever done. Waited for her parents to come home. Waited to be found. Waited to be enough. Waited for answers.

Well fuck that. She was done waiting.

She dialed Ethan's number. He answered on the first ring. "How'd it go?"

She straightened her shoulders, forced a reply past the heavy weight of the sob lodged in her throat. "They took him."

But they couldn't keep him.

"I'm on my way."

CHAPTER TWELVE

When they'd grabbed him off the street, Parker had known what was coming.

When they'd strapped him down, ankles and wrists bound to the plywood beneath him, he'd prepared himself for the inevitable.

When the black hood slid over his head, obscuring his vision and drawing every sense in close and tight, until all he could hear was the frantic pattern of his own breath, he'd reminded himself that Brandt needed him alive. Needed him cooperative.

Reminded himself that torture, no matter what kind, was meant to break him mentally.

Logic. Reason. Endurance. All things Parker had in spades. All things that should have made the cloying press of the hood, the brutal spray of water, the all-consuming fear of drowning, easier to handle.

Bullshit.

It was all bullshit.

Water hit his face, forcing soaked fabric against his mouth and nose. Like every time before, Parker held his breath and shook his head, thrashing in his bonds until the unforgiving cuffs cut into his exposed and already damaged skin.

When the water stopped, he coughed and sputtered, reaching for the air just beyond the heavy weight of the waterlogged hood. Every breath was thick, wet, labored. A fight to breathe even as the torment relented.

"You're wasting my time, kid," Brandt said, his voice near. Parker could picture him, leaning against the wall, carefully protecting his suit from the water, wiping his glasses on the microfiber cloth he kept in his pocket—something he routinely did when stuck in a meeting or situation he felt was beneath him.

Prick.

Parker gasped, his chest heaving as his sinuses burned.

"Just enable the program, and this is over," Brandt said on a sigh, as if Parker's resistance was little more than an irritant to be dealt with then brushed aside.

Parker shook his head, reminding himself what was at stake.

My tech, my responsibility.

"Go again." The words had barely registered before the water was back, splashing over Parker's face in a steady torment he couldn't escape.

His lungs burned as he struggled and failed not to inhale water.

You're not drowning. You're not drowning.

But he was. Slowly. Agonizingly. Drop by drop, he was drowning, but without the relief of unconsciousness or a last, fatal breath to fill his lungs with water instead of air. Brandt's men were too controlled for that. Too skilled. They'd done this before.

They wouldn't screw up. Wouldn't let Parker die.

Instead, they'd let him dangle between worlds, between life and death, consciousness and unconsciousness. Trapped in the moment where everything was heightened—every sense sharp, insistent, and so painfully vivid. Every nerve screamed he was drowning, even as his rational mind insisted he wasn't, couldn't. There wasn't enough water; he wasn't submerged. It wasn't real.

The harder he fought the idea, the more he tried to rationalize his way through the experience, the worse things got. Logic and intelligence warred with instinct and primal fear.

A break. Blessed air flooded his mouth and nose and lungs as he gasped.

Then water hit his face, its greedy, clawing fingers snatching away his relief and sliding down his nose and over his tongue, jerking his gag reflex to the fore until he thought he'd be sick.

Over and over again, the fear won, until even the rationalization that Brandt wouldn't let things go too far, would never kill him without retrieving the program, only fed the frenzied panic of his thoughts.

The water ceased as blackness fuzzed at the edges of his thoughts, momentarily dulling everything until it all came rushing back in one vivid crush of Technicolor agony.

I'm okay. I'm okay.

He coughed, ignoring the bitter scrape of an already raw throat, and pretended his eyes didn't sting. Or at least if they did, only because of the waterboarding.

"Can't think your way out of this, Parker. Even the best men fail under this technique." Parker tracked the clip of Brandt's shoes as he moved around the room, circling, waiting. Secure in the knowledge Parker would fail. "We both know you aren't the best. Not at this. Not even close."

Parker flinched as a hand came to rest at his shoulder, patting the wet fabric of his T-shirt. Brandt always had been a condescending bastard. But he was right about one thing at least. Parker couldn't think his way out of this. He clenched his fists, forced himself to take deep breaths, exhaling for twice as long as he inhaled, getting much-needed oxygen into his system. The breathing technique had the added benefit of slowing his heart rate and fighting off the encroaching panic—or at least beating it back to semibearable levels. He shuddered as his muscles loosened, his body sagging against his bonds.

How many times had he been here? Trapped in an endless cycle of panic he couldn't escape, couldn't fight, could only endure?

This wasn't the same, of course. This had a physical component Parker had never endured before, adding a layer of pain and terror to the experience he'd never thought to fear. But the basics? The fight-or-flight?

The all-consuming desire to run away from something inside him? Something he could understand but not address, something he could label but not conquer? Yeah, he'd been here before. And through trial and error, he'd learned fighting the panic always, always made it worse. Yoga helped. Running burned off some of the energy. But always, the bottom line was the same—he had to roll with the energy, acknowledge it, and let it have its say before it would begin to ebb. Before it lost its power.

Hadn't he helped Georgia through a similar experience? Hadn't he seen the panic riding her, recognized her urge to run from the building desire to flee, or fight, or hide—anything to escape the sensation of being torn apart from the inside? He had, and he'd helped her through it. Not by distracting her but by having her voice the fear, address the nightmare.

Fighting a sense of powerlessness did so very little to improve the situation. Ethan had taught him that. Told Parker, in a hushed whisper from three thousand miles away, trapped in enemy territory, that one of the worst things you could do when scared was try to talk yourself out of being scared in the first place. That the only real way to conquer fear was to face it, acknowledge it, then decide to move the fuck past it anyway.

"Just give me what I want, Parker, and this all stops."

He wanted to shake his head. Wanted to tell Brandt to go lick an outlet or play in traffic. To fuck off and die. Violently. Creatively. Painfully. Parker didn't really care. Instead, he kept his mouth shut. Afraid if he said anything, even something two syllables and four letters long, he'd open the floodgates and give voice to his cowardice. Beg for everything to just stop. Promise anything to make it so.

Brandt sighed, and the water returned. As his head grew fuzzy and his ears rang, the desire to quit, to make it all just *stop*, stalked him like a hungry hyena—already laughing and ready to pounce at the first sign of weakness.

It took him a long moment to realize the water had disappeared again. For now. But not for long, never for long.

Georgia would come. No matter how angry she was, no matter how badly he'd hurt her, she wouldn't leave him here.

She needed him, even if she hated him.

He just had to last long enough for her to find him.

Voices filtered through the white noise in his head.

"We've been at this for almost five hours. Too much more could kill him."

"I don't care," Brandt said, his voice clipped and irritated, the same tone he used whenever someone brought up budgetary restrictions in one of their operational meetings. "I need the program now. Go again."

"We should wait, try again tomorrow," a voice Parker didn't know argued. "Let the experience sink in. He's strong now, but throw him cold, wet, and exhausted in a cell, and the fear will find him. Dread soon after. He's survived it once . . . some guys do. But few last even half as long in the next round."

"I said do it again," Brandt hissed. "I'm out of time and out of options. I've made promises that I intend to keep."

Promises? Parker wondered. *To who? For what? More of the same privately funded, off-book operations?* Or was there more at stake than he realized?

"And if he vomits? He could aspirate it and drown in his own puke. Is that what you want?"

God, please no. Parker shivered, fought the urge to fight the ties at his wrists, to tear his flesh deeper than it already was. The pain, the fear—those he could deal with. But the humiliation of choking on his own vomit? No.

"I want my goddamn program!" Brandt yelled. "Now do it again."

The suffocating press of water pulled Parker under again, pinning him to the back of the board, helpless, exposed . . . dying.

He couldn't keep doing this. Wasn't trained to resist interrogation. Wasn't cut out for fieldwork. He was tech ops, dammit. A brain. An IQ. An asset at a desk but a hindrance in the field.

From far away, Georgia's voice whispered against his ear. *"Are you really going to sit there and tell me that, when push comes to shove, there's anything you couldn't do if you decided you wanted it badly enough?"*

Air, crisp and cold and powerful, rushed into his lungs. A choice. Deceptively simple and still unrelentingly difficult. Mind over matter. Reason over strength.

Bright lights seared through his vision as the hood was ripped from his head.

"Give me what I want, Parker. Now." Brandt stood over him, anger tightening every line of his face. "There's not going to be a tomorrow, not for you. That choice is out of my hands."

A choice. Simple. Painful. And in the end, with Georgia at the front of his mind, not that hard at all.

My program, my responsibility.

"You're the one calling the shots here," he ground out, his voice tight and rough.

Brandt scoffed, his shadowed form moving closer. "Did you really believe a program with that much potential would go unnoticed? That people wouldn't think bigger than applying that kind of power to a few dozen black ops in bumfuck nations we forgot to care about decades ago?"

Fuck. When Isaac had looked at him across his desk, smug and certain that Parker hadn't thought big enough, dark enough, Parker had hoped he was wrong. Believed what the data had told him—Brandt, and only Brandt, was all over the files. No one else was involved; no one else knew enough to even be tempted.

"Come on, Parker," Brandt continued, his pudgy fingers sinking into the flesh of Parker's shoulder. "This is Washington. The only thing people covet more than money is power. And your program? It levels the playing field in ways most people could never dream of. Do you have any idea what that's worth to the right person?"

"Millions, judging by your bank statements," Parker spat, his mind racing, trying to figure out who, besides Brandt, stood to gain from his program. He shook his head, clenched his fists, and wrestled with the urge to fight the ties at his hands and feet. Too many. Brandt was right. There were hundreds, even thousands, of people in DC alone who stood to gain everything from economic footing to political power. Where would he even start?

"Millions." Brandt chuckled. "Don't be ridiculous. Those were tests. Practice runs. Proof the program worked. No. The real money is in brokerage. Tell me, Parker, what do you think a sixty-five percent market share is worth to the right corporation? What do you think the right family would pay to secure their son the presidency? What do you think a cartel would pay to have their rivals wiped from the face of the Earth?"

"Is that why you sacrificed William Bennett? To get rich? To give an evil organization a leg up?"

"Don't be so naive. World governments buy and sell the lives of soldiers every day for a lot less. Bennett was an unfortunate casualty of the war on drugs."

"So he's dead?" Parker asked, dreading the answer. Would Georgia survive the blow twice? Survive the agonizing hope that her brother was alive, even if that meant he was in hell, even if he wished he were dead, only to discover he died anyway?

"I really don't know." Brandt withdrew his hand. "If there's any mercy, Will Bennett died of infection weeks ago. Unfortunate. Though not as unfortunate as the fact that you involved his sister in this."

Parker's heart stopped.

"I suppose I could find a way to spare her," Brandt said, leaning over to study Parker's face. "I would hate to destroy an entire family." He shrugged and stepped back. "But then that's not my choice to make."

Parker snorted. "You clearly don't know Georgia Bennett."

"I know people," Brandt corrected. "Everyone has a price."

Parker shook his head. Not Georgia. She was many things. Stubborn. Unforgiving. Beautiful. Fragile. And completely uncompromising. "You can't buy everyone."

"I suppose not. But those who can't be bought can be killed. Rather easily, as it turns out."

"Program's dead," Parker said, proud his voice didn't tremble, that his fear and frustration didn't show. "And I won't change that." Not for Brandt. No matter what it cost him.

"No?" Brandt asked, fury darkening his voice. "Gun." He held his hand out behind him, then repeated, "Gun. Now."

Someone out of Parker's line of sight stepped forward. "Brandt..."

"Shut up." Brandt took the gun, cocked it, and pressed it to Parker's temple. "It's not up to me. One way or another, you die."

"Who—" It was all he could think about, all that mattered. Who else was involved?

"It hardly matters," Brandt said as he loosened the knot of his tie, then shifted the gun from Parker's head until it rested at the side of his knee, the barrel digging painfully into the bone. "If you can't be bought, then you'll be broken. I'll start with your joints. A bullet in each knee—excruciating, truly, you have no idea—then move up, hit both shoulders, let the bullet bounce around. If that doesn't work, I'll put one in your gut." Brandt stared at him, all expression bleeding from his face until the only thing left was the stark visage of a man desperate enough to do absolutely anything to get his way. "I'm told it's an incredibly slow, very painful way to die. If you still won't talk, I'll have one of these men start removing things."

Brandt stared steadily down at him. No anger. No reservation. He'd do it and never let the memory of it steal so much as a second of sleep.

"You'll give me the program, Parker. And when you do, I'll let you die."

The absolute certainty Brandt would do it, and that Parker would beg for death before the end, assaulted him—but didn't change his mind.

Brandt didn't understand, couldn't possibly grasp that Parker would rather die than give up his program. Not because it was the right thing to do. Not because hundreds of thousands of innocent lives could be ruined. Not because it was his tech, his work, and his responsibility.

No.

He'd do it for Will, who'd been sacrificed in an operation Parker had designed and Brandt had exploited.

He'd do it for Georgia, who'd lost too many people in her life, who'd survived the thought of losing the only person she truly loved and come out stronger, tougher, and so achingly vulnerable Parker had fallen hopelessly, irrevocably in love.

She'd shared herself with him. Seen him. *Believed* in him.

Made him strong enough to do this much. For her.

"Go fuck yourself."

A gunshot clapped violently through the room.

"Don't move!" Georgia commanded as she followed the path of her shot into the room, ready to pull the trigger again if anyone so much as twitched.

Parker, strapped to a board. Brandt in an unmoving pile next to him. The other two men didn't move, stunned still as Ortiz, Liam, and Ryan filed in behind her, guns up and ready. The minute they had the other two men contained, Georgia rushed to Parker.

Soaked and shivering, he stared up at her from the flat of his back, a crooked grin twisting his lips. "Aren't you supposed to warn him first?" he asked, his lips blue and his voice thin.

"What?" Georgia holstered her gun and pulled a knife from her belt.

"You know," Parker said, a full-body shiver shaking him against the table. "'Stop or I'll shoot.' Or, 'Don't move!'"

"I said that." Georgia slid her knife beneath Parker's palm, careful to catch only the plastic zip tie and not his damaged skin.

"Yeah." Parker wheezed as he flexed his fingers. "*After* you dropped Brandt like a fifty-pound bag of kitty litter."

"You wanted me to *warn* him?" Georgia shook her head. "Ask him nicely not to shoot you in the knee?"

"Well, no." Parker smiled up at her, his eyes glassy and his voice raw. Blood spatter decorated his face like a Rorschach test. "But aren't you supposed to?"

Georgia released an ankle, then moved around the table. "You watch way too much TV," she said as she cut the last tie, grateful the sweat slicking her palms hadn't interfered. Now if she could just get them to stop trembling. "He was prepared to shoot you. Had announced his intention to maim and then kill you. He'd *tortured* you, Parker," she said, hitching her shoulders in a helpless shrug to fight off the urge to fall apart. "And you wanted me to give him a heads-up? A chance to change his mind or use you as a hostage?" She put an arm beneath his shoulders and helped him sit. "I'll pass, thanks," she said as he braced his hands against the board and took deep, long breaths.

Truth was, killing Brandt hadn't felt like a choice. Even before Ortiz had opened the door and Georgia had taken up the point position and breached the room, she'd heard enough. One glance had confirmed everything she needed to know. Parker, helpless. Brandt with a gun to his knee. She'd pulled the trigger, blowing a .40-caliber bullet through the back of Brandt's head without a second thought or a moment's hesitation. She'd trusted her training. Made a decision and acted. Brandt was dead, and Parker was alive. She sure as shit wouldn't apologize for it. The man had tried to kill Parker—not to mention Ethan and herself—more than once. Would have made good on his threats to take Parker apart a piece at a time and never lost a second of sleep over the decision.

To say nothing of what he'd done to Will.

Will . . . Where had her thoughts been of her brother? Brandt was the one person on the planet who'd had any contact with Will's captors.

And she'd killed him. Without hesitation or second thought.

She'd saved Parker, yes, but had doing so condemned her brother?

She shook away the thoughts and fought down the surge of bile.

Oh God. What had she done?

Parker placed his feet on the floor, flinching when cold concrete touched his bare skin. Pushing himself up, he listed dangerously to the left, heading for the floor before she caught him under the armpits. "Easy."

He let his head drop until his forehead touched her breastbone, his hands coming up to grip her forearms as she pushed him back onto the edge of the board. He trembled, his breathing ragged. His voice was a desperate, strangled thing as he whispered, "You came for me." He shook, gripping her arms tighter, pulling her in closer. "Thank you."

Had he thought she wouldn't? Had he believed, even for a moment, that she'd been angry enough to leave him? To let him die? She brought her arms up, letting her hands run through his tangled mop of wet hair. "It's my job, Parker." The words left her lips on a gentle whisper but with the leaden weight of a lie. The way Parker sagged against her suggested he either didn't hear the blatant dishonesty of the statement or just didn't believe it. Intentional or not, she'd hurt him. She just didn't know how to fix it. How to fix them.

Or even if she wanted to.

"He all right?" Liam asked from across the room. Ortiz and Ryan had secured the remaining men, and now Ortiz was on the phone—probably with Ethan, who they'd had to sedate to keep in bed.

"Yeah, Peanut, you all right?" she asked, fighting emotions she couldn't name and didn't understand. She'd always thought death the worst-case scenario. Dreaded another loss, feared what having another person violently ripped from her life would do to her. She'd never imagined arriving in the nick of time could be so much worse. To cross a threshold and wonder if this time she'd be made to watch. If this time she'd be there when her entire world crumbled around her.

It wasn't a reality she wanted to experience again. Ever. If she'd been a second too slow, hesitated just a little . . . Even the thought of failing Parker, of watching him die, tore at her with titanium teeth, vicious and hungry and desperate to devour her whole. It just wasn't a possibility she could live with.

But at what cost? Could she have spared Brandt? Had emotion, rather than training, pulled that trigger?

"Oh God, Peanut's going to stick, isn't it?" Parker said on a groan. He pulled his head back until he could look at her. "I'm okay."

No. No, he wasn't. Using her thumb, Georgia gently brushed away blood and grime as she stared down at him. Wide, dilated eyes stared back at her, drinking her in as if Parker still couldn't quite believe she was there.

"Hey," Liam said, appearing next to her as authorities began to file in. Damn, Ethan was fast. "Why don't I take a look?"

Parker coughed but shook his head. "I'm good. Just tired and cold." He made to stand up again, but Liam pushed him back down.

"Yeah. Last I checked, I was the medic and you were the kid with the keyboard." Liam took Parker's wrist, checking his pulse. "How about we stick to those roles for a bit longer?"

Georgia tried to step aside, give him room to work, but Parker's grip tightened until the bones of her wrist rubbed together.

Parker sighed and visibly slumped. "Fine. I'm too damn tired to argue with you."

"Well, yeah," Ortiz said, appearing beside Parker, a hand going to his shoulder. "I thought we agreed, no solo fieldwork for you?"

"Buddy system's for kindergarten and night swims," Parker mumbled, a half-hearted grin stretching his mouth.

"We should really get you to the hospital and checked out," he said, inspecting the torn flesh at Parker's wrists. "No stitches, but we definitely need to get this cleaned up."

"Can't you just do a field dressing?" Parker asked. "I want to go home."

"Humor me." Liam accepted a blanket from the paramedics who entered the room, but he waved off the stretcher they were wheeling in. Smart. Parker looked ready to put up one hell of a fight. Dropping the fabric across Parker's shoulders, then patting his back as Parker pulled it tighter around him, Liam said, "From the look of things, Brandt came at you pretty hard and over a long period of time."

Parker nodded quietly. "Hours, I think. I lost track of time."

"Hours?" Ryan asked, his voice taking on a dangerous edge. "That fucker went at you for *hours*?"

Jesus. Georgia repressed a shudder. She'd never had the displeasure of being waterboarded. But as former special ops, Liam, Ryan, and Ortiz most certainly would have as part of SERE training. But hours? Of agony and panic and desperation?

"Yeah. Felt like fucking ages, though." Parker shuddered, water dripping from his hair and sliding down his neck. "Brandt didn't really waste any time."

"Shit, Parker, don't you get it?" Ortiz asked. "Typical interrogations usually last twenty minutes—a half an hour at most. Some advanced SERE training might go for longer, but not like this." Ortiz shook his head. "Fuck, I barely made it through one round of this shit, and that was in training."

"What's the difference?" Parker asked, exhaustion starting to creep into his voice and steal across his shoulders until they slumped beneath the weight of it.

"The difference," Ryan said, "is that in SERE training you *know* they aren't going to kill you. You *know* it's going to stop. Maybe not when you want it to, and yeah, it doesn't make the moment any easier. But you still know what day you're heading home. You just have to last."

"How the hell are you still holding it together?" Ortiz asked, watching Parker with the expression of someone taking a long, hard second look at a man he thought he knew.

Parker glanced up, surprise and confusion flooding across his face. "Lack of alternative appealing options?"

"Did you lose consciousness?" Liam asked, gently bringing Parker's attention back to him. He picked up Parker's hands, inspecting his fingertips. Still a bluish-purple in color and trembling.

"I don't think so," Parker said hesitantly. "Things got . . . distant a few times. Fuzzy. But I don't think it ever got past that."

"Yeah. You're going to the hospital," Liam said. "No arguments, Parker. You should never have been subjected to that for so damn long. I want you monitored for secondary drowning and treated for early-stage hypothermia." When Parker opened his mouth to object, Liam cut him off. "Twelve hours, Parker. That's all I'm asking. Then you can go home and sleep for a week."

"Please," Georgia said when Parker looked unsure. "Let them take care of you."

Parker reached for Georgia's hand, squeezed her fingers. "Hey. I'm okay. You found me, and it's over."

Georgia tried to ignore the fact that Parker, who'd just been tortured, wanted to make sure *she* was okay.

Damn him.

Clutching the blanket tighter, Parker sighed. "Fine. I'll go."

Georgia slid in next to him, hovering as Parker stood on shaky legs and took his first unsteady steps out of the room. Shit, he was barefoot, in wet jeans and a soaked shirt. He'd freeze to death before they got to the car. She should have thought of that. Brought him his things. And where were his glasses? Could he even see well enough to walk? She should have planned better. Anticipated . . . everything.

This time, when the panic swelled, threatening to send her to her knees, she recognized it for what it was. She beat it back. Barely. There'd be time to process everything. To feel all of it. The relief, the anger, the worry, and the sadness. There'd be questions, many without answers, and decisions. So many decisions. But she just couldn't deal with it all right now. It was too much.

"How did you find me, by the way?" Parker asked as they made their way down a poorly lit hallway, then up a set of stairs, before finally emerging into a parking garage.

"I wounded one of the men at Isaac's townhome—he eventually provided the coordinates," Georgia explained, wincing at the memory of what she'd done to try to extract that information in the first place. Not that it had mattered. In the end, Ethan had arrived, pale and exhausted but determined to work things out. As usual, he had. "Turns out the State Department has been looking into Charles Brandt for some time now. Had even managed to place a few people close to him—including Henry."

"Who?" Parker asked.

"One of the guys who led the assault on Isaac's townhome—undercover for one of the alphabet agencies, apparently. Would have been nice if he'd *said as much* before I started digging around in his bullet hole."

"What?" Parker choked.

Georgia waved him off. "He wouldn't say where Brandt had taken you until Ethan got involved. Some bullshit about clearance. Anyway, we're still working out who knew what, if this was just a case of following orders or if some of these guys were being paid off."

"It's not over, Georgia. Brandt wasn't in this alone."

"I know," she whispered, placing the palm of her hand against his back, letting the heat of him soak into her skin and loosen her muscles. "Henry implied as much. Ethan's working that angle—he'll get the answers eventually."

"Am I safe?" he asked, his voice quiet and small, as if the question was both necessary and terrifying.

"Ethan seems to think so." In that, it really did appear Brandt had acted alone. And now that he'd been caught, his under-the-table deals brought to light, anyone working with him wouldn't risk exposure. Parker, it seemed, had gone from one of the most hunted men on the planet to one of the safest.

She only wished she could say the same for Will.

"What do you think?" Parker asked, trailing his fingers along her hip.

"I think there's time to deal with all of this later," she said, resisting the urge to wrap her fingers around his wrist, to count the steady beat of his heart and remind herself he was okay. "Until then, someone will be there." Ethan would make sure, which would give her the space to catch her breath.

She'd spent so much time pacing Isaac's kitchen, waiting for answers, imagining the worst. Anticipating the moment someone showed up, their face calm and void of expression as they explained nothing could be done. That Parker was gone. It had been its own sort of hell, standing around, desperate to do something, anything, yet knowing the only thing she could do was wait on the actions of others and hope and pray and bargain that she wouldn't have to attend one more funeral.

"You're coming with me, right?" Parker asked, refusing to release Georgia's hand as he slid into the back seat of a waiting SUV. "To the hospital."

She wanted to say no. Wanted to go home, take a hot shower, and drown herself in a Jack and Coke until the last few days were nothing but a distant, fuzzy blur. It wasn't that she wanted to forget, not really, but she missed the numbness, the disconnected way she'd been floating through life. It was bland and boring, but it also didn't hurt so damn much. But looking at Parker, at the naked desperation on his face, she just couldn't do it. She slid into the back seat with him, repressing a flinch as Liam slammed the door shut behind her. "Sure."

"And you'll stay?" Parker asked, his voice quiet and vulnerable. "I—there's so much I need to say. I have to explain why I didn't—I promise, I *promise* I'll bring him home." Georgia pressed her fingers to his mouth and shook her head. She couldn't listen to him make that promise, no matter how well intentioned. Right now, no one could guarantee anything, least of all Parker. And worse, if she let him have his say, let him convince her of all the things he could and would do, let him teach her to hope—she'd do something stupid. Something she'd only live to regret. She needed to wait until the fear, the cloying need to assure herself he was fine, left her. Until she built up the defenses Parker had swept aside as if they'd never existed at all. Until she was strong again.

"I'll stay."

For now.

CHAPTER THIRTEEN

Seventy-Two Hours Later

"I said I'm coming," Georgia yelled in response to the insistent knock at her door. She shot a glance at the boneyard of take-out containers strewn across her kitchen counter and littering the coffee table, then shrugged. She hadn't invited anyone over, and there was no one she wanted to see, so her unannounced visitor could deal with the mess. In any case, it was probably Ethan, and until he was willing to talk about the only thing that mattered—finding Will and bringing him home—she saw no reason to continue to be cooperative or to accept his platitudes of "It's going to take time" and "I've already got people working on it." He could deal with the mess.

She shoved her fingers through the wild tangle of curls—she hadn't bothered to dry her hair—then swung open the door on an irritated huff. "What do you wan—"

Isaac.

What. The. Hell.

"Hey," he said, a bunch of peonies resting on top of a pastry box.

"Hey." She stared at him, trying to make sense of the man before her. Dressed in jeans and a chunky sweater pulled over a collared shirt, he was the most casual she'd ever seen him. "Your khakis at the dry cleaner or something?"

He flashed his thousand-dollar smile. "Or something." He glanced behind her, though to his credit, his lip didn't curl at the mess plainly visible. "Going to invite me in?"

"I'm not really in the mood." The last thing she wanted right now was company. There'd been a steady stream of calls and e-mails and texts, none of which she gave a damn about. While sitting around with her thumb up her ass was driving her crazy, the only thing that sounded worse was killing time in any sort of social situation. And anyway, what was Isaac—or this parallel-universe version of him—even doing here?

"What do you want, Isaac?" she asked on a tired sigh. She hadn't slept for shit in days, and she didn't have the energy for . . . well, for whatever this was.

"I want to talk." He dropped the practiced grin, his face softening into something honest and relaxed, something Georgia wasn't sure she'd ever seen from him before. "Please, Georgia. There are things that need to be said."

Eyeing the pastry box, Georgia asked, "That from Baked and Wired?"

Isaac nodded. "I was worried the flowers wouldn't get me through the door."

They certainly wouldn't have. What was she going to do with a bunch of flowers? She didn't own a vase, could only imagine Isaac's face when she stuffed them into one of the many plastic cups lining her shelves.

"You've *never* bought me flowers, Isaac." God forbid he act the boyfriend in even the most casual ways. She couldn't fathom why he'd bought them now.

"Just one of the things I need to apologize for."

"You are going to *apologize*?" What sort of screwed-up world had she woken up in? "This I have to hear." Then she could kick him out. She turned to head back into the house, letting him catch the door before it swung shut in his face. He followed her into the kitchen, setting the flowers and the bakery box on a clear span of countertop. That was when she noticed the huge envelope tucked up under an armpit. That, he set next to him. Large and puffy, it was one of those eight-and-a-half-by-eleven mailing envelopes lined with Bubble Wrap. It was completely blank but for the messy scrawl of her name across the middle. She'd recognize the handwriting anywhere.

"I called," Isaac said, hovering between the living room and kitchen. "A couple of times."

Him and everyone else. Ethan. One of the secretaries from Somerton Security. Even Ortiz.

Everyone except Parker. Which was good, she reminded herself. They needed the distance, and she needed the perspective. She just hadn't expected to miss him so much. To hate the smell of freshly brewed coffee because there was no one there to snake her mug. To roll over in the middle of the night and wake to only cold, empty space where she'd anticipated a warm, welcoming body. To be so angry she couldn't think straight one minute and so lonely in the next that she hated herself for the weakness. For missing him. For wanting him.

"I've been busy."

"You look good," Isaac said, casually flicking some containers that had once held last night's kung pao chicken out of the way.

Georgia shot him a disbelieving look as she filled the kettle with water to make tea. "You're kidding, right?" She had on no makeup, her hair looked like she'd started licking wall outlets for fun, and her sweatshirt-and-yoga-pants ensemble missed cute and landed squarely between mental-ward escapee and sentient pile of laundry. Personal hygiene just hadn't been a priority. Not while she'd sat through four separate debriefings before she finally started telling everyone to fuck off. Not while she waited for Ethan to get his shit together, to stop asking how she was doing, for fuck's sake, and start talking about what the hell they were doing to find Will. All of which had rendered her a far cry from the polished visage Isaac preferred. While the water heated on the stove, Georgia grabbed a trash bag and began clearing out the wreckage of the last few days. Something in here *smelled*.

"No, I mean it," Isaac said, making himself at home in her kitchen. "Dessert plates?" he asked.

Georgia rolled her eyes. "Small or large, that's all I've got, and they're in the cabinet above the dishwasher."

"Right." He retrieved the plates, then searched until he found utensils and thankfully didn't comment on the fact that she didn't have anything dedicated to the consumption of pastries. "I think I got your favorites." Isaac turned the box around, a hopeful look on his face.

Georgia stared into the box, stunned speechless. Never, in all the time he'd known her, had Isaac expressed an interest in what she wanted, what she preferred. "What the hell is going on, Isaac? Why are you here?"

Isaac slid onto a bar stool. Running his thumb along the edge of the envelope Georgia was doing her best to ignore, he looked at her. "I'm trying to apologize."

"For what?" For breaking her heart? For treating her like a convenience who was good enough to screw but not good enough to date?

"For so many things, but mostly for being the sort of self-important dick who'd drive away someone like you."

Gobsmacked, Georgia couldn't think of a single thing to say.

"You made me happy, Georgia. And to be honest, it scared the crap out of me." He shook his head, pulled one of the shortbread bars from the box, and placed it on a plate. "I didn't know how to reconcile you with the rest of my life."

"Not for lack of trying," Georgia grunted, pulling her own bar out of the box.

Isaac grimaced. "Yeah. I spent so much time trying to make you fit into my life, trying to make you right for my life, I didn't stop to think about what it all meant. That maybe, if you were what was working for me, it was my life that had to change. I get that now."

Georgia shook her head slowly as the kettle began to wail. Retrieving a clean mug and bag of Earl Grey, Georgia turned her back on Isaac and set herself to making her tea. What did Isaac want from her? Forgiveness? He could have it. She didn't have the energy to be angry with him anymore. A second chance, though? Part of her wanted to. It would be easy to sink into the familiarity between them. If Isaac was genuine in his realizations—and she thought he was; he simply wasn't the type to lie or admit mistakes otherwise—then a future with him was possible.

Possible but not passionate. For all that she'd loved him once, Georgia understood now how shallow, how easy, how unfulfilling that love had been. Isaac wasn't a man she could share silence with, a man she could be herself with. A man who could be her equal and be okay with that.

She'd rather be alone.

Had it really been only a week ago that the prospect had filled her with a sad sort of resignation? How was it possible for things to change so quickly and so completely?

She blamed the damn near-death experiences.

"You know that ship has sailed, right?"

Isaac nodded, then took an oh-so-proper bite of his dessert. He chewed slowly, swallowed, then said, "I do."

"Then why are you here?" she asked, grabbing a carton of milk from her fridge. She took a sniff, thought better of it, and put it back.

"Because you could have left me behind, could have left my townhouse with Parker and never looked back, but you didn't."

Georgia stilled. "You needed help."

"I did," he agreed. "I got my ass handed to me."

"I couldn't just leave you there. Not like that." Though part of her still expected him to hate her for it. To bristle at the fact she'd saved his life *again*.

"And so I owe you," he said, no hint of grimace or resentment. "But more important, I'm here because there was a time when we were friends, and I'd like for us to get there again."

"Why?" Georgia asked. It wasn't like him to settle for a relationship that didn't pay dividends on his investment of time and attention. Georgia had nothing she could offer him—no political ties, no valuable insight he couldn't get on his own.

"Because Will is my friend, and when he finds out how I've treated you, he's liable to knock my teeth down my throat."

Georgia swallowed hard. Is. When. All present and future tense. God, she wished for Isaac's certainty. Wished that she didn't find it easier to believe the bad than the good. Wished hoping didn't hurt so damn much.

"I'm perfectly capable of defending myself, thanks." Though he would have been—would *be*—happy to get between her and the rest of the world, Will had always made a point to ensure Georgia could stand on her own.

"And that's why I'm here," Isaac said, his voice turning soft and guarded. "There was a time you were one of my very best friends, and I hope someday we can gain some of that back. But what I have to say can't wait for that to happen."

"What are you talking about?" Georgia asked, dropping her tea bag into the sink with a wet *plop*.

"You're screwing up, Georgie."

"Don't call me that," Georgia said, pinning him with a glare. *She* was screwing up? Seriously? "This is some apology, Isaac."

"I've made my apology. Now I'm going to be who I should have been since Will . . . in Will's absence—your friend." He placed his fork on his plate and stared her down. "You're screwing up, and I'm about the only person who knows you well enough to say so. I only hope you're willing to put aside our past and hear me out." When she didn't say anything, he took a deep breath and continued. "Where's Parker, Georgia?"

Her hand trembled as she brought her mug to her mouth. "Don't know. Don't care." She took a long gulp, rinsing the bitter lie from her mouth.

"The hell you don't." Isaac held up a hand, forestalling the smart remark she wanted to let fly. "You forget just how long I've known you. So don't lie to me, and definitely stop lying to yourself. You care so much you're terrified." Isaac stared her down, his moss-green eyes unwavering, the smile lines beside his mouth relaxed grooves that barely marked his face. "You're in love with him."

Georgia shook her head but couldn't force the words past her suddenly tight throat.

"Yes. You are. And it's got you so twisted up inside you're about to make the worst mistake of your life."

"He *lied* to me. He knew how close Will and I—" She swallowed hard around the word *are.* Present tense. Why was it so damn hard to hold on to the hope? When had that become scarier than the alternative? "He knew. I told him *everything.* I gave him *everything.*"

"So what?" Isaac said. "You shared part of yourself—good for you. But what, you thought that was it? You'd just blurt out the worst parts of your life, share a few fears and insecurities, and boom: relationship?"

Isaac actually had the audacity to laugh at her.

"Life's not that easy, Georgia. Relationships take work—"

"How would you know?" she snapped.

The vein at Isaac's temple, the one that always throbbed when she said or did something to deliberately infuriate him, pulsed. "I fucked up. I apologized. That's done."

Of course it was, because the great Isaac Flores said so. At least he'd returned to form and someone she recognized.

"This is about you and your persistent expectation that people are going to hurt you, fail you, betray you."

"Because they do!" Anger, frustration, and a loneliness she'd always hoped to outgrow tore at her. "Parker lied to me about the only thing that's ever mattered!"

"Bullshit," Isaac roared. "Parker *spared* you. He knew what the knowledge would do to you. That it would eat at you. That you'd let it consume you." Casting a judgmental glance around her apartment, Isaac said, "And from the looks of things, he was right."

"Get out."

He grabbed her wrist as she went to stand. "I'm not done yet."

Her mouth dropped open in shock.

"Parker lied because he didn't want to hurt you. Maybe he shouldn't have. Maybe it was a mistake. But what would it have changed? You couldn't have done anything but worry. Telling you would have only hurt you." Isaac scowled. "The only thing that man cared about was you."

Georgia tried to pull away. "How would you know?"

"Because," Isaac said, releasing her hand, "he did what I could never have done."

"Yeah," Georgia said, rubbing the bare skin of her wrist. "What's that?"

"He called *me*."

The quiet admission hit her with the force of a sucker punch. Unexpected. Powerful. Parker had called *Isaac*? They'd spent all of an hour together and engaged in some ego-driven pissing contest. There was no love lost there. No mutual respect between them.

"Yeah. Surprised the hell out of me, too." Isaac shook his head. "I wanted to hang up on the bastard. He had what I wanted—your attention."

"You had that once, too," Georgia offered quietly.

"No, not like this. I saw you in that office, Georgia. Saw the way you looked at him, the way you reached for him, even when you weren't aware of it." Isaac smiled sadly. "And when you realized what he'd done—I thought I'd seen all your expressions. Seen the depth of your passion, your loyalty. Turns out I'd only seen the barest glimmer of the surface."

Had she worn her feelings so plainly? Had she been so obvious? It certainly hadn't felt that way. Everything had happened so fast—like a tsunami that rushed in, dragged her under, and spit her back out in a totally unfamiliar landscape. Nothing felt the same. She wondered if it ever would.

"And so, what, you felt sorry for the guy?" she asked.

"No," Isaac admitted with a frustrated grunt. "But he was worried about you. So worried, in fact, that when you stopped responding to Ethan's texts or e-mails, Parker broke down and called me. Begged me to check on you."

But that didn't make any sense. Parker hadn't reached out. Hadn't called or texted.

"And so out of the goodness of your heart, here you are?"

"Hardly." Isaac snorted. "I hung up, figured good riddance, he was out of your life."

"But?"

"But that's when it hit me." He stood from his stool. "I was prepared to ignore his request, just to spite a man I considered competition. But you deserve better than that. You deserve a man who puts your needs first, who cares more about you than he does his own ego. A man who'd call someone he hates just to make sure you're all right." Isaac ran a hand through his perfectly cut hair. "It's something I'm going to have to work on."

"Well, you're here. You can see I'm fine," she said, waving a hand over herself.

"I can see you're self-destructing."

Frustrated, Georgia snatched the pastry box off the counter and stalked into the living room, collapsing on the couch on a heavy sigh. "Aside from the fact that I may very well eat this entire box of baked crack, I am not self-destructing."

"That you don't see it doesn't make it any less true." Isaac joined her in the living room, hitching up his jeans as if they were custom-made pants before he sat on the coffee table in front of her. "So I'll make this fast, then leave you to it."

"Oh, please do," she said, snatching something liberally coated with chocolate from the box.

"You're pissed as hell, and you're taking it out on the people around you."

"He lied to me, Isaac—"

"I'm not talking about Parker." When she didn't say anything, he sighed. "Will, Georgia. You're furious with your brother for abandoning you, and you can't even see it. And until you find a way to deal with it, to move past it, you're not going to be happy."

What. The. Fuck.

"Will did *not* abandon me," she yelled, dumping the pastry box to the floor as she surged to her feet. "He *loves* me."

"Just not enough to come home."

"Go fuck yourself." Tears burned at her eyes, and she slapped away the hands that reached for her.

"You've never forgiven him for not coming home, Georgia. It's why you kept looking for answers, looking for reasons. You needed proof he died for a reason—something, anything, that could justify the fact that he left you behind."

She shook her head, fighting the sob that tried to claw its way up her throat. "He isn't dead."

"But for months you thought he was. People leave. That's what life's taught you. They leave. Even people like Will, who are supposed to always, always put you first."

Tears, fat and wet, leaked from her eyes and rolled down her cheeks. She brushed them away in a jerky, angry motion. Yeah. People left. So what? Knowing that didn't make her self-destructive; it made her smart. Kept her expectations in check. Kept her from shattering into such tiny pieces she'd never be able to pull herself back together.

"You put so much faith in Will that when he failed you"—he shook his head when she tried to speak—"he did, Georgia. By his choice or not, he left you. And if Will, the standard by which all others are to be measured, could fuck up, what hope do any of the rest of us have?"

That wasn't fair . . . Was it? Because yeah, Will had always been larger than life to her, always perfect in her eyes, but so what? He'd earned that regard from her.

"And now here you are," Isaac continued, "so in love you can't see straight. But for the first time ever, you have the opportunity to leave *first*. You aren't mad at Parker, not really. But it feels safer, smarter, easier to push him away before he has a chance to leave."

Georgia stared down at Isaac, who hadn't moved from his spot on the coffee table, not even to brush the crumbs from his shoes.

"Don't do it, Georgie," Isaac whispered. "You, more than anyone I know, deserve to be happy."

"This doesn't feel like happiness," she croaked, the truth tearing her to pieces.

Isaac stood, pulling her into his arms. "Because it's a leap of faith, and you know just how far down the drop is—and how much it hurts when you hit the bottom." He kissed the top of her head. "It's scary as hell, but the best things usually are."

"I don't know if I'm strong enough." What Isaac wanted, what he was suggesting, was so much more than a leap of faith. She could so very easily love Parker . . . but what if he didn't love her back? What if she wasn't enough for him? With Brandt dead, Parker didn't need her anymore.

"Well, if that's true, we're all fucked." Isaac leaned back, brushed away her tears with his thumbs. "You're the strongest person I know. If you can't do this, can't put yourself out there . . . well, then, God help the rest of us."

She looked up at him through watery eyes. "I shot Brandt," she said, giving voice to the guilt that had been dogging her. "Killed him without a second thought."

"So?" Isaac said, looking at her as if she'd told him she'd crushed a roach beneath her heel.

"He was the only person who could have told us where Will is. What if . . ." She swallowed hard, fear and remorse and uncertainty riding her. "What if I killed the only person who could bring Will home?"

Isaac stared at her for a long time. Finally, when he'd studied every inch of her, considered every angle as he always did, he said, "Brandt was never going to leave that room alive, Georgia. You know that."

She thought she did. But what if . . . ?

"And that's not what's really bothering you."

It wasn't?

"You're worried that when push came to shove, when you had to choose, you chose Parker. Saved Parker." Isaac gripped her shoulders, holding her in place. "And, in so doing, left Will to die."

"Yes," she whispered, the word little more than a breath.

"If your places had been reversed, if Will had walked into that room, what would he have done?" he asked.

"Taken the shot." The answer hadn't required even a second's thought. Will would have done the right thing, saved the person who needed him then.

"It was never a choice, Georgia. It was instinct and training and the machinations of a greedy bastard who had no intention of backing down." Isaac stepped away. "You didn't choose Parker over Will, then. And despite whatever's rolling around in your brain, no one's asking you to choose now. You can care about them both. Loving Parker doesn't jeopardize your loyalty to Will."

"He might not feel the same way," she said, if only because she didn't really know what else was left. Isaac made it all look so simple.

"I'm standing here, aren't I?"

He was. Because Parker had sent him. For her.

"Why didn't he come himself?" she asked, voicing the last lingering doubt she had. How could she know this wasn't just misguided loyalty?

She'd saved Parker's life; it'd be natural for him to feel some sort of need to make sure she was okay.

"Because Parker knows that this has to be *your* choice." Isaac stepped away. "He has to trust that at the end of the day, you choose him."

Did she? Choose him? "Isn't this supposed to be easy?" she wondered aloud. Seemed like that was the party line. Love: when it's right, you know it. Simple. Uncomplicated.

"Would you want it if it was?"

She had always thought that crap sounded boring as hell. And nothing about Parker would ever be easy. Or boring. It wasn't who he was.

It wasn't who she was, either.

"Give it some thought," Isaac said, brushing a kiss against her cheek, then heading toward the door.

Georgia followed him, her thoughts and emotions a whirling dervish that made her dizzy.

"Georgia?"

"Yeah?"

"Parker wanted you to have that," he said, gesturing to the envelope he'd left on the counter, then ducking into the hall and leaving her with a decision to make.

She turned, surveyed the disaster that was her apartment, and smiled, thinking of the first time she'd met Parker.

Grabbing her mug, she picked up the package Parker had sent and made her way back to the living room.

Time to get on with her life.

Parker sat up, peeling his face from the glass surface of his desk, and groaned. Back in his loft and back to his old habits, he'd fallen asleep coding sometime earlier that morning, and he had the crick in his neck to prove it. Stretching, he popped his back and yawned. He didn't remember the desk being so damn uncomfortable. But then, he didn't remember being lonely in his apartment, either.

PITA rose and stretched, deliberating knocking off the color-coded pile of Skittles by Parker's elbow before jumping to the ground. Little bastard hadn't forgiven Parker for leaving him in the loft. Dead body aside, Parker couldn't understand why—there'd been plenty of food and water. Jumping to the kitchen counter, PITA chirped at Parker until he turned on the faucet and let the cat drink from the tap. Parker filled the bowl with kibble, then pulled a mug from the cabinet. He needed the restorative powers of caffeine before he tackled anything else this . . . morning? He glanced at his watch. Afternoon, apparently.

Whatever. It was nine in the morning somewhere.

A knock at the door tore Parker away from staring blankly at the variety of K-Cups littering his countertop. Dammit, he missed waking up with Georgia. A grunt here and a mumble there and a fresh cup of the French vanilla he preferred just magically appeared, ready to make everything all better.

Making his own coffee sucked.

Waking up alone sucked.

Life just sucked.

He pulled the door open, then stood there, stock-still and mystified. Georgia.

Had he wished her into being? Was he having a pre-coffee hallucination? He blinked. Then blinked again.

Still there.

"Can I come in?" she asked, a shy smile curling her mouth.

Parker nodded. Well, he thought he did. Whatever the case, it was enough, because Georgia stepped in close, tipped her head to look at him. She pulled something away from his cheek. She held it up for him.

Damn Post-its. They stuck to everything.

"Brought you a red-eye." She held up the coffee cup, the aroma of fresh-brewed intelligence infiltrating his nose and waking him up by gentle degrees. "Trade you for a conversation?"

"For coffee with an extra shot of espresso? You can have PITA," he said, plucking the coffee from her hand and stepping aside. The moment the first sip hit his tongue, he could hear all his bells and whistles, motors and gears churning to life. He took Georgia in, noting she had her hair down and wild against her cheeks. His fingers itched, so he clutched his cup tighter and thrust his free hand into his pocket. Dressed in jeans and a half-zip hoodie with an embroidered Marine Corps insignia on the chest, she looked . . . relaxed. Casual. Like she probably smelled of crisp winter and warm fabric softener.

Like the woman he wanted to spend the rest of his life waking up to. Stealing coffee from. Sharing candy with. Like his future and his heart and everything good he could ever hope to have.

Yeah, looking at her, wanting her, and not knowing if he'd ever actually be allowed to have her was about the worst kick to the balls he'd ever experienced.

"I had this all planned out in my head," she mumbled, stroking PITA when he came over to investigate. As she scratched the back of his head, he purred, then rubbed his body up and against hers.

Traitor.

"I'm sorry. I guess that's the first thing I should say."

She was sorry? For what? Believing in him? Saving his life?

"For leaving. For taking the easy way out." She shoved a hand through her curls.

It trembled, something he'd never seen before. Georgia had always been his rock. Steady. Confident. In charge. Even in vulnerability, she knew who she was. He ached that he'd brought this out in her. That he'd made her unsure. Ached, and yet hoped with every fiber of his being it meant she'd forgiven him. Meant she'd stay.

She rubbed her hand over her face, and Parker's coffee fully hit his bloodstream.

She wasn't wearing her brother's watch.

Parker dropped the coffee on the counter and grabbed her wrist. "Didn't you get it?" he asked, rubbing the madly beating pulse beneath his thumb. "I went back to the pawnshop. Had it delivered to your house." His voice cracked when she turned her wrist, settling her palm against his. "I know how much that watch means to you."

"I got it," she whispered.

"But you aren't wearing it. I . . . Why aren't you wearing it?" Had he somehow tainted that, too? Taken a precious memory of her brother and destroyed it?

"I—" She shook her head on a sigh, then reached into the pocket of her fleece, pulled out the Rolex that Parker had retrieved, then had cleaned, serviced, and returned to her. "I thought maybe it was time to stop wearing it."

"What?" He couldn't fathom it. In the short time he'd known her, he'd watched her reach for that little bit of family legacy time and time again. Why would she give it up?

"It's gotten pretty heavy," she said, and even functioning on half a cup of coffee, Parker knew she didn't mean it literally. "So many memories. Good. Bad. Awful. Wearing it was like a constant physical reminder. Much as it means to me, much as it's a part of me, it doesn't make me happy." She stared up at him, her expression naked and honest. "But you do."

Oh thank fuck.

He grabbed her by the waistband, pulling her flush against him, and stole her startled laugh for himself. Threading one hand into the hair at the nape of her neck, he let the other one slide in a smooth, steady slip down her back and over her ass, until he could curl his fingers to brush against her core. When she gasped, he took advantage, plunging his tongue in counterpoint to the steady back-and-forth drag of his fingers.

Finally, dizzy with the lack of oxygen and tired of the clothes separating them, Parker pulled back.

Georgia stood there, her eyes wide, her mouth red from the scrape of two-day stubble. He ran a hand down the length of her arm, cupped the hand that still held the watch.

"It isn't really mine," she said. Red tinged the tips of her ears. "My mother gave it to my father for their ten-year anniversary. I used to sit on his lap and twirl the bezel. Used to listen to my mom accuse my dad of loving it more than he loved her. Used to listen to my brother proclaim how it would be his one day—that drove me nuts."

"Yeah?" Parker asked, content to let her talk so long as she let him touch and explore. He stroked the curl by her face. Touched the freckle by her cheek. Cupped her hips in his palms. It would take a lifetime, but he'd map every inch of her, again and again, until even when he was old, deaf, and blind, he'd still intimately recall every inch of the woman who held his heart.

"It's part of me—but I got so wrapped up in the weight of it, in carrying it with me, that I let myself forget all the good memories it was supposed to represent. I don't want to do that anymore."

"If you don't want to wear it, I can lock this up. Keep it safe for you." He took a steadying breath. Parker knew they had to talk about it, that there could be no moving forward until they did. "I can keep it until we bring Will home." He waited for a flinch, for the sadness and worry and fear she carried to scroll across her face. "I don't care what it takes, Georgia. I'm going to fix this. We're going to find him." He'd already started, had spent days scouring files and servers and plugging data into his program. Already, a plan was coming together.

"You can't promise me that, Parker." She reached for him, placing a steady palm over his chest, his heart thumping out an excited greeting. "I won't ask you to make a promise we both know you might not be able to keep. You'll do everything you can; I know you will." She grasped his hand, turned his wrist so she could flick open the strap of his Swatch.

Removing it, she set it on the counter, then slid the Rolex over his fingers and clasped it into place. "I'm not in this alone anymore." With what looked like a great deal of effort, she lifted her chin and met his gaze, her expression naked and vulnerable, her fear easily visible. "Right?"

"Right," Parker said, staring down at his wrist and the watch that rested against his skin. She was right; it *was* heavy. A promise between them, a reminder that neither of them was alone, that they had each other, no matter what.

"I had it resized . . ."

He twisted the bezel, listening to the *click-click-click* as it turned. It was a noise he could get used to.

He glanced up, caught the uncertain expression on her face, and blurted the only thing that came to mind, the only thing that mattered. "I love you."

From the moment he'd seen her, Georgia had been beautiful. Strong. Sexy. An interesting package he wanted to unwrap and explore. She'd been sexy as hell running the tactical simulation. Beautiful and soft as she'd let him dress her wound. Fierce and sexy and playful and a myriad of other things when they'd gone to bed.

None of it compared to the radiance, the warmth, the breathtaking splendor that transformed every inch of her when he said those three words.

"I love you," he repeated, dropping his head to hers, just to be closer to the sun. "I love you."

If he spent the rest of his life in the pursuit, he'd never find happiness like this.

Two seconds later, as she always did, Georgia proved him wrong.

"I love you, too."

EPILOGUE

Ethan strode into the conference room, his shoulder tight but finally free from the sling he'd been forced to endure. His strength was returning in stages, though not fast enough for his liking. Still, his range of motion was back; he was regaining his accuracy on the firing range and compensating well with his left hand in the meantime. He was ready to get back to work.

Thank God. He trusted his team, had handpicked them for Somerton Security, after all, but being sidelined, letting other people handle things, run things, take point . . . It drove him nuts. Time to restore order to his universe.

"Good morning," he said, watching in satisfaction as everyone in the room quieted down and took their seats. "We've got a lot to cover," he said, moving to the head of the table. "First, we've got a couple of new people joining our team in part-time support capacities. Isaac Flores is our new in-house attorney and will be acting as our government liaison."

Judging from everyone's expressions, it seemed they'd all already met. Thankfully, Georgia looked at ease with the decision. She'd sworn she would be, that Isaac was the right man for the job, but Ethan had still wondered if it would present a problem. Judging by the way Parker dropped his chin on her shoulder and stole a handful of Reese's Pieces from Georgia's pile, he'd worried for nothing. They were solid—made each other happy and strong even as they drove each other crazy.

"And Henry Walsh is on loan from the Justice Department. As he was part of an active investigation into the CWU and has been thoroughly briefed, he's agreed to stay on and assist us with cleaning up the mess Charles Brandt left behind." Ethan sat back in his chair and resisted the urge to rotate his shoulder. "I'm sorry to say that there's a lot to do."

"I thought Somerton Security was in the business of private security," Ortiz said, twirling a pen between his fingers.

"We are," Ethan replied, relaxing into his chair. There'd been a time when he'd thought that was all Somerton Security would be—a business and exit strategy, there and waiting for the day he finally retired from active duty. "And as far as the public is concerned, we'll continue to grow our client list and provide a range of private security offerings—any of you are more than welcome to continue to work solely in that capacity."

"Why do I get the feeling you're about to offer us a much more interesting option?" Liam asked, scratching at the red stubble lining his jaw.

"Because thanks to Isaac's legal maneuvering and a newly struck deal with the Justice Department, Somerton Security has exclusive control over Parker's program. For all official intents and purposes, the government has washed its hands of it." Not the easiest sell in the world, though Isaac had managed to convince the right people that fighting Parker over the intellectual property rights—not to mention control—opened the door to serious liabilities. Between the very public hit at FedExField, a raid on a government attorney's town house, and a government-sanctioned hit on a high-value and very visible public contractor, the DoD had relinquished all control in exchange for iron-clad confidentiality agreements and a handshake deal that rendered Somerton Security an unofficial government contractor. Ethan couldn't have hoped for better.

"Everyone in this room has operational knowledge of the program and the events of the last several weeks," Ethan continued. "I hope you'll all consent to being part of a special division tasked exclusively with managing all program-based operations going forward."

"So nothing's changed?" Liam said. "We continue to operate as we have."

"Everything's changed," Parker said, sitting up straight and leaning toward the center of the table. "Brandt's actions, the money we traced back to him—it was the tip of the iceberg."

Parker glanced to Ethan, then back to the rest of the room. The confidence was a change Ethan hadn't been entirely prepared for, but one he was glad to see all the same. It had been a long time coming, and, though he'd never admit it, Georgia had been right. He hadn't done enough to foster it.

"We know of at least two dozen times Brandt used the program for personal gain. But there are at least as many predictive reports we can't trace back to buyers—or to Brandt."

"You're saying there's another player," Liam said.

"I'm saying it's a possibility," Parker explained, even as Georgia laced her fingers in his. Parker breathed, his nerves visibly rushing out of him. "It could be years before there's enough information out there, enough data to track, to figure out exactly how far this goes and who stands to benefit the most."

"Where do we even start?" Ortiz asked.

"Here," Parker said, his voice strong and firm as he pulled up a presentation. "Six months ago Charles Brandt authorized a raid on a cartel compound in South America. Both William Bennett and Ian Porter were reported killed in action." Parker paused, and Georgia squeezed his hand. "Several months after the raid, someone sent in a tip, first to Brandt, and when he never made contact, eventually to the Justice Department."

"Proof of life?" Henry asked, color draining from his face. "Did the cartel actually confirm Bennett survived?"

Ethan looked at Georgia as he said, "When rumor reached me that Will may not have died as we'd been told, I couldn't ignore it."

Georgia nodded once. They'd talked about it, and Ethan had put all his cards on the table. Explained why he hadn't wanted to tell her, to get her hopes up, until he had concrete evidence. In truth, he'd never really believed the rumor could be true. That one of his men, one of his friends, could have been left behind, forgotten. Not under his watch. But it had happened, and Ethan was determined to set that right. No matter what the cost.

"Is he still alive?" Ortiz asked.

"There's compelling evidence that as of six weeks ago, Will was still alive. But tensions within the cartel are escalating—their infrastructure is crumbling, and factions are fighting for power. It's making confirmation difficult."

"But . . . ?" Ortiz asked.

Ethan let a slow, predatory smile curl his lips. It'd been a helluva long time since he'd operated undercover, but come hell or high water, he intended to find Will. If he took down one of the largest human trafficking operations on the planet in the process, then so be it. "But Parker is going to use his program to find a way into the cartel, and a way to bring Will home."

"You're going undercover," Ortiz stated, his tone conveying just how insane he thought the idea was. "With one of the most violent cartels on the planet."

"Yes." And nothing and no one was going to stand in his way.

ACKNOWLEDGMENTS

Looking back over the course of writing this book, it's truly shocking to me just how many people lent me their enthusiasm, support, encouragement, and creativity. A thank-you seems terribly insufficient, but I'll do my best anyway.

Kelli Ireland, who has been there from the beginning of both my career and that one fifteen-minute train ride where I first conceived the idea that would become this book, thank you for your unwavering friendship and your steadfast conviction that I had a winner in Georgia and Parker. A bet is a bet: I owe you a steak. A big one.

Shana Lindsey, I don't think you realize the myriad ways your support and friendship has impacted my life and my writing. Your work ethic is something to both admire and envy and will be the reason you find your way to success. No one will be cheering louder than me when that day comes.

John Carey, the best accountabilibuddy a girl could ask for, thanks for reading so many of the early rounds, early pages, and sitting there and staring me down when I just didn't want to. And of course, thanks to your cat, who charmed my editor and found this book a home.

Elaine Spencer, agent extraordinaire, a thousand thank-yous for believing in both me and this book from the very beginning, and more, for your unwavering confidence that we would see this book to life—even when I had trouble keeping the faith. Hope is not a plan, but I'm forever grateful you keep it in your arsenal anyway.

Alison and Joel and the entire Montlake team, I don't think you know how incredibly thrilled I was to land among your enthusiasm and talent—I could not have hoped for a better home for this series.

And finally, a very special thank-you to Rachel Goodman, the jellyfish to my sea urchin. You get me, and for that, thank you seems woefully inadequate . . . so next round is on me.

ABOUT THE AUTHOR

Elizabeth Dyer likes her heroines smart and snarky, and her heroes strong and sexy. An attorney and recent coffee devotee, Elizabeth spends the majority of her time tucked into a corner table at Starbucks or pinned beneath her (overly affectionate) bullmastiff. When she isn't working or wrestling the dog, you can usually find Elizabeth writing the types of sexy, suspenseful books she most loves to read.

A born-and-bred Texan, Elizabeth resides in Dallas, where she indulges in Netflix marathons, Instagramming her dog, and brunch. *Definitely* brunch. Adorably awkward, Elizabeth hates the phone as much as she loves all the social media things and hearing from her readers. Follow her on Twitter (@lizdyerwrites) or Instagram (@elizabethdyerwrites) or Facebook (@elizabethdyerauthor).

Made in the USA
Monee, IL
31 August 2019